2/18

Erin Kaye was born in Co Antrim in 1966 to a Polish-American father and an Anglo-Irish mother. One of five siblings, she was raised a Catholic yet educated at a Protestant grammar school. In the decade following university she pursued a successful career in finance, before re-inventing herself as a writer. She now lives with her husband and their two young children on the east coast of Scotland. Her debut novel was *Mothers and Daughters*.

CHOICES

When Sheila gave birth to Claire she was just sixteen years of age. Persuaded by her family to give the baby up for adoption, this choice would affect her life — and the lives of those she loved — forever. Two decades later, Sheila and her older sister Eileen face heartache. Eileen's cancer has returned and Sheila can no longer live with the decision she made all those years ago. She wants her daughter back. But life is never that straightforward and Sheila's desperate yearning threatens to shatter family relationships. With her entire family in crisis, Sheila takes reckless measures to heal the wounds of the past.

Books by Erin Kaye
Published by The House of Ulverscroft:

MOTHERS AND DAUGHTERS

ERIN KAYE

CHOICES

Complete and Unabridged

CHARNWOOD
Leicester

First published in Great Britain in 2004

First Charnwood Edition
published 2005

British Library CIP Data

Kaye, Erin, 1966 –
Choices.—Large print ed.—
Charnwood library series
1. Adoption—Fiction 2. Unmarried mothers—
Fiction 3. Mothers and daughters—Fiction
4. Domestic fiction 5. Large type books
I. Title
823.9′2 [F]

ISBN 1–84395–871–6

Published by
F. A. Thorpe (Publishing)
Anstey, Leicestershire
Set by Words & Graphics Ltd.
Anstey, Leicestershire
Printed and bound in Great Britain by
T. J. International Ltd., Padstow, Cornwall

This book is printed on acid-free paper

For my parents, Pat and Jim

1

The sound of slow footsteps on the gravel path made Sheila glance up, through the rain-soaked window. It was Eileen, familiar in her dowdy mac and flat loafers, her battered handbag clasped protectively to her side like an old woman. Then Sheila noticed something peculiar about her sister's bearing that made her freeze, her hands suddenly idle in the sud-filled sink. Eileen held her head uncharacteristically erect and stared straight ahead, as though her thoughts were far removed from the few feet of gravel in front of her.

Intuitively, Sheila knew that something was wrong. Her thoughts turned to Claire, the instinct to protect her own unblunted after all these years. Had something happened to her? An accident? She sought for an answer in her sister's inscrutable face.

Sheila dried her hands quickly. Her long red nails flashed amongst the folds of the towel, like unhealed wounds on the tips of her manicured fingers. She tucked a loose strand of hair behind her right ear and adjusted her black silk-knit jumper, preparing herself.

'Eileen, what's wrong?' she blurted out as soon as her sister stepped into the kitchen.

Eileen did not answer at once but unbuttoned her navy raincoat slowly, shook it gently and draped it on the back of a pine chair before

1

sitting down. Silvery droplets of rain spotted the kitchen floor.

'Is it Claire?' demanded Sheila, her voice suddenly shrill and anxious, 'Has something happened to Claire?'

Eileen shook her head. Sheila's sigh of relief was audible.

'Paddy then?'

'No,' said Eileen wearily. 'It's me, Sheila. It's me.' A wry smile darted across Eileen's face. 'It's me and that bloody cancer.'

'Oh,' said Sheila and she sat down abruptly in the chair opposite Eileen.

They sat silently for a few moments, the soft buzz of activity audible from other parts of the semi-detached house. Sheila prepared herself to be positive, upbeat even, as she waited for Eileen to speak. But she did not meet her eye. She already knew what she was going to say.

'You know the way I've been exhausted lately?' said Eileen.

Sheila nodded.

'Too tired some days even to get out of bed. And I've been losing weight — not that I couldn't do with losing a stone,' she glanced down, 'or two.'

Sheila forced a thin smile and shook her head gently.

Eileen sighed softly and continued. 'Well, Dr Crory thinks it . . . well, he thinks the cancer might have come back.'

Fearing she would burst into tears, Sheila sought to keep Eileen talking while she composed herself. 'Did he actually say that?'

2

she responded quickly.

'No, but as good as. He wants me to go for tests in Belfast as soon as possible. On Friday. He arranged it on the phone while I was in the surgery.'

'Friday!' repeated Sheila. 'But that's only three days away!'

Eileen nodded, and folded her lips in on each other until they both disappeared.

Sheila sought desperately for words of comfort.

'We don't know anything for sure yet, Eileen. And there's no point worrying until we do. He's probably just being thorough, sending you up there so promptly. He's a good doctor, very conscientious. For goodness sake, we don't even know if it is cancer, and even if it is . . . well, you beat it before and you'll beat it again!'

Eileen regarded her calmly, her brown eyes full of tears, and Sheila felt like the little sister she was.

'You know as well as I do,' said Eileen gently, 'that the cancer never really goes away. It's just in remission. We all knew this would happen one day. I just thought . . . I thought I'd have longer. Much longer than this . . . '

'You're so brave, Eileen,' said Sheila and she put her hands out and enveloped Eileen's in hers. Her sister's palms were rough in comparison to her own and the nails short and unpolished.

'I'm not brave, Sheila. I'm not brave at all. To tell you the truth, I'm terrified. I'm just trying very hard not to show it.'

3

The door to the kitchen burst open. It was Sheila's middle son, Martin.

'Hi, Auntie Eileen! I'm starving. Any chance of a sandwich, Mum?'

Eileen put her hands to her face and swiftly brushed away two tears that had crept out of the corners of her eyes.

'Can't you see we're talking?' snapped Sheila. 'Your tea will be ready soon. I don't want you spoiling it. Go on, out!' She glared at Martin and pointed at the door. 'I said, *out*. *Now*.'

'OK, OK,' said Martin indignantly as he backed out of the room. 'Keep your shirt on, Mum. I was only asking.'

The door closed again and Sheila turned her attention back to Eileen.

'Does Claire know?' she asked softly.

Eileen shook her head.

'And Paddy?'

'No. I'm going to pretend I'm just going for a routine check-up. There's no point worrying them until we know one way or the other.'

'OK,' said Sheila, 'I understand. Did the doctor say what these tests would involve?'

'They want to do a mammogram to see if there's anything there. And if they find a lump then they'll need to remove it for analysis.'

'A biopsy?'

'Just a tiny bit of breast tissue. Dr Crory said it would be done under local anaesthetic.'

'I see,' said Sheila, remembering the last time they'd been through this over four years ago.

She recalled the trauma of each hospital visit and the dreadful treatment Eileen had to endure.

4

She remembered the first time she'd seen the scar where they'd removed Eileen's breast. How hard she'd tried not to recoil in horror and how Eileen had seen through her. The strain of being optimistic and cheerful in the face of the statistics. And then the sheer and utter relief when Eileen got the all-clear.

And now they were going to have to go through it again. Except this time maybe there would be no all-clear at the end . . . Sheila gave herself a mental prod in the back. She wouldn't allow herself to entertain morose sentiments. She had to be strong for Eileen.

'Anyway,' said Eileen, interrupting her thoughts, 'I'm not the only one who should be seeing a doctor. Have you been to see about your periods yet?'

'That's hardly a priority at the moment. Not until we get you sorted out . . . '

'No, I've been thinking about it, Sheila. It might be a symptom of something serious. If I've got — had — cancer, well, they say it runs in families. You should get checked out. Just to be on the safe side.'

A wave of panic swept over Sheila. Could she have cancer nestling deep inside, in the very heart of her? She told herself not to be so silly. There could be any number of explanations for her erratic and often absent periods. She'd put it down to hormones. She'd been emotional and weepy these last few months and she knew from her training as a nurse that symptoms of illness were often psychosomatic. The mind was sometimes more powerful than the body.

'I'm not convinced it's anything serious, Eileen. But you're right. I'll go to the doctor next week.'

After Eileen had gone Sheila got on with the preparation of the meal. She set the table and tended the pots but her mind was elsewhere, racing ahead of events. What if the cancer had come back? What if Eileen couldn't fight it this time? She couldn't die without Claire knowing the truth. Eileen would have to tell her. But how would Claire react? Suddenly, after years of yearning for the truth to come out, Sheila wasn't sure she wanted it to. What if Claire rejected her and Jimmy?

The pot of potatoes boiled over, water hissing as it hit the gleaming hob.

'Shit,' said Sheila.

She lifted the lid off the pot and the hissing subsided.

She told herself to stop getting carried away. She had Eileen dead and buried and she was only going for a check-up! And how selfish, concentrating on her own interests when she should be focusing on Eileen. There would be plenty of time to cross the other bridges. When they came to them.

★　★　★

Jimmy Gallagher watched as Bridget Kelly shoved the council papers into her large canvas shopping bag. As well as being his long-time friend, Bridget was the only other Catholic, and therefore Jimmy's ally, on the twelve-strong

6

Ballyfergus council.

'Come on,' she said. 'I'll give you a lift home.'

Bridget was one of those fat women who carry their weight gracefully and, in spite of her girth, she glided effortlessly down the stairs and across the carpark. He followed her dumpy figure out of the council chambers reflecting with frustration on tonight's unproductive meeting, which had disintegrated, as usual, into sectarian bickering.

'There's so much we should be doing and all we ever seem to do is argue over politics,' said Jimmy. 'We never even got round to talking about Redhill.'

'Well, that's the nature of local government in this country, dear. Look, don't be so down. Sure didn't we get the dry bar for teenagers up and running? The summer school activities last year had the best-ever attendance figures. And we'll get Redhill redeveloped too.'

'I suppose you're right.'

They got in the car and drove off. Jimmy sighed and stared at the grainy grey night outside. Bridget was right, of course. He mustn't let it get to him but he was disappointed in himself — he'd allowed himself to be sucked into an undignified squabble.

The car pulled up in front of the semi-detached house where Jimmy lived with his wife and three sons. The lights were on downstairs.

'Give my love to Sheila and the kids,' said Bridget. 'They all right?'

'Aye, fine. Conor's starting to be a bit of a handful, though. Answering his mother back when I'm not there — that sort of thing.

7

'That's boys for you, Jimmy. Girls are more of a worry but boys are harder to handle. My Seamus was a terror once he got into his teens but the girls were no bother. He grew out of it, mind, and now he's settled down with that wee Rosemary Clunie, happy as the day is long. You can't ask for more than that, now can you?'

'No, indeed, you cannot. That's all I want for my boys, too. Just to be happily married, have kids. All the usual stuff. Though it would be nice if one of them became a millionaire and kept me in me old age!'

Bridget laughed heartily.

'Thanks for the lift, Bridget. Goodnight.'

Thinking of his family put a spring in Jimmy's step and almost erased the frustration of the last few hours.

'Are you there, love?' he called, stepping gratefully into the warmth and smell of home.

There was no reply but the sound of the TV in the front room told him that's where he'd find the boys. He popped his head round the door. Danny and Martin, the two youngest, were sitting on the floor in their pyjamas. Conor lounged on the sofa. All three were engrossed in wrestling on TV.

'Hello, boys,' said Jimmy.

Only Danny got up off the floor to greet him.

Martin said, 'Hello Dad,' and Conor grunted.

'Dad, Dad, come and watch the wrestling,' said Danny excitedly, and he pulled him into the middle of the room.

'Not tonight, son. Anyway, shouldn't you boys

8

be in bed?' he said sternly, and was greeted with a chorus of wails.

'Ach, no, Dad,' said Danny, stamping his foot childishly even though he was nearly ten years old, 'I want to watch the wrestling.'

'It'll be over in ten minutes,' interrupted Conor. 'Sure they can go up then.'

'Aye, all right,' said Jimmy, suppressing the smile that Danny's antics brought to his lips.

These boys would never know how much he loved them. Sometimes he longed to hold them in his arms like they were still babies but they hardly needed him now they were so grown up and independent. Only Danny would still come to him for a cuddle but he knew the days of that were numbered. Once he left primary school he'd want to leave all that childishness behind him.

Sheila was in the kitchen, reading the evening paper over a cup of coffee, blonde hair fallen over her face like a veil.

'You didn't fancy watching the wrestling then?' he asked.

She raised her head to reveal a pained expression on her face. Indicating the small black-and-white portable TV perched on the kitchen counter between the toaster and the sink she said, 'That's all I get to watch nowadays with four men in the house. They hog that TV morning, noon and night.'

'Maybe we shouldn't let them watch so much,' he said.

'Sure you can't stop them the age they're at, especially Conor.'

'Well, so long as they're not falling behind with their homework.'

Sheila bristled and Jimmy immediately regretted those words. He couldn't seem to get on the right side of her these days. She folded the paper sharply with a dry brittle crack.

'I take care of that,' she said and got up.

She rinsed her cup under the tap and placed it on the draining-board to dry. Then she turned and looked at him directly for the first time. Her emerald-green eyes were carefully made up as was the rest of her face, the brown eyebrows expertly shaped into two exquisite arches. He still thought her the most beautiful woman he'd ever met.

'How was the meeting tonight, then?' she asked.

'Oh, the usual. You know,' said Jimmy noncommittally.

She nodded silently, uninterested.

'Look,' she said brusquely, changing the subject, 'I've got something to tell you. It's about Eileen. Dr Crory wants her to go up to Belfast for a check-up on Friday. It sounds as though the cancer's come back.'

She told him about Eileen's tiredness, weight loss and the mammogram.

It sounded bad all right. Poor Eileen — what that girl had gone through! Jimmy shivered and glanced at Sheila. Thank God it hadn't happened to her — he couldn't bear it.

'The doctor must think it's serious to get her referred so quickly,' he said.

'That's what I thought,' said Sheila, gloomily.

10

'And I can't go with her either — I've got to work Friday.'

'Listen, love, I'm sorry,' said Jimmy and he put his arm out to comfort Sheila but she crouched down suddenly and opened the oven door.

'Sit down at the table and have your dinner before it's ruined,' she said briskly. 'I'd better go over and see Eileen now.'

As he obeyed a little stab of pain went through Jimmy's heart. Over the last few months Sheila had been avoiding intimacy with him — it was almost as though she couldn't bear him to touch her. And mentally she was shutting herself off from him as well. They used to be soul mates. And the frustrating thing was that he couldn't remember exactly when things had started to go wrong. Little by little the crack between them had widened until now it seemed like a chasm.

Sheila placed a plate in front of him and removed the metal foil covering it. White curls of steam escaped from a hearty stew.

'Anyway,' she went on, as he began to eat, 'we don't know for sure that it is cancer. It could be something else. So don't go saying anything to Paddy or Claire until we find out.'

Jimmy nodded his agreement.

Sheila put the metal foil in the bin, her cup in a cupboard and the oven gloves in a drawer. Then she wiped round the spotless sink with the dishcloth. After checking there was nothing else to be done she sat down opposite Jimmy.

'I thought you said you were going over to Eileen's,' he said, between mouthfuls.

11

'I am,' she answered, 'but I want to talk to you about Conor first.'

'Oh?'

'He came home again today with his shirt ripped and when I asked him how it'd happened he wouldn't tell me.'

'Sure that's just boys' horseplay.'

'No, it's more than that, I'm sure of it. He's been asking for extra money for school lunches and when I ask him what he's done with his allowance he won't tell me.'

'What do you thinking he's spending it on? Girly magazines?'

'I don't think he's spending it on anything. I think somebody's taking it off him.'

Jimmy stopped eating and looked quizzically at Sheila.

'What are you saying?' he asked.

'I think he's being bullied.'

Jimmy put his knife and fork down and considered this. True, Conor had always been a quiet, gentle child but Jimmy had worked hard to build up the boys' confidence. He spent time with them, teaching them the skills they'd need to survive in a cruel world. Was it possible his son was a victim? He found it hard to believe.

'Have you asked him about it?' asked Jimmy.

'I tried to but he won't talk to me.'

'And he's more likely to talk to you than me,' observed Jimmy, dryly.

'True, but it wouldn't do any harm to try,' said Sheila, lifting Jimmy's cleared plate.

'OK, I'll try. You go over to Eileen's and I'll

12

have a word with Conor. We'll see if we can't get to the bottom of this.'

* * *

Aiden O'Neill woke up shivering. The sheet was wrapped round his naked body several times and the blankets had somehow found their way onto the floor. He got out of bed gingerly and rearranged the bedcovers before getting back under them. He lay quite wide awake now, and waited for his body-heat to warm the bed.

He'd had another broken night's sleep but that was something Aiden had got used to over the years. That and the nightmares. They were rarely exactly the same, though they all induced the same terror and anxiety that overwhelmed him. Sometimes he'd wake up sobbing like a child and it was then he realised he was completely alone.

The best part of each day was that precious moment on wakening when his mind was a complete blank. He'd tried to prolong the experience but could not prevent himself from remembering. As soon as it was conscious, his brain would seek out the memories, faces, references by which it defined Aiden O'Neill, age thirty, bachelor and loner. The rest of the time Aiden spent consciously focusing on the here and now, avoiding the painful memories that haunted him and marred his experience of life.

He looked about the miserable little room and wondered what it would be like to wake up somewhere where you were safe and happy, with a woman you loved lying beside you. Somewhere that, when you realised who and where you were, you actually smiled and thought, 'Yeah, life is great. This is where I want to be.'

'Sod it,' said Aiden angrily, throwing back the heavy blankets and jumping out of bed.

He wasn't going to let a bout of depression drag him down. Not today. Today he was going to do something positive. He was due money from Social Services for the three weeks he'd been unemployed when he'd first come to Ballyfergus. The giro should have been through by now and he could do with the money.

He showered in the bathroom he shared with two other lodgers on the same floor, changed and put on fresh clothes. He forced himself to notice that, in spite of the cold, it was sunny outside — the first sign of spring. In his room he boiled up a pot of tea and ate the remains of a loaf of bread spread with marmalade. Then he was ready to face the world with a smile on his face if not in his heart.

The Social Security Office was an ugly grey block of a building built in the 1970s. Surrounded by high wire fencing and a security gate it looked as inviting as a police station.

Aiden gave his name to the receptionist and joined the subdued claimants in the waiting-room for the optimistically named 'Jobseekers' Allowance'. He found the wait quite pleasant — it was warm and dry and people-watching provided a diversion by which to pass the time. He studied the overweight, coughing, wheezing claimants and thought they were more like

14

patients in a doctor's waiting-room than a potential workforce actively seeking employment. Eventually his name was called.

The girl behind the counter, who looked like she was barely out of her teens, asked him to sit down. He sat and explained why he was there.

Competently, she punched his details into the keyboard on the desk in front of her and waited for the computer to respond. Up close she was pretty. Her eyes were greeny-blue, the colour of the sea on a cloudy day, and her shoulder-length brown hair looked freshly washed. Aiden had a sudden urge to lean over and smell it. 'Ms C O'Connor' said her name badge, giving little away. He wondered what her name was — Cathy, Catriona, Catherine, Cassandra? He laughed to himself — no she didn't look like a Cassandra. And she looked too young to be a 'Mrs'.

Ms O'Connor knitted her eyebrows into a frown and he could see the lines of computer text reflected in her dilated pupils.

'Hmm . . . ' she said and turned her gaze on him, 'there seems to be a bit of a problem, Mr O'Neill. Your details went on the system all right but I think because you came off the Jobseekers' Allowance after only three weeks somehow your payments got cancelled. I'll have to get someone from the payments office to look into it and phone you. When would be a good time?'

'Well, I'm working shifts now so I'm not sure . . . '

'Oh, where are you working?' she asked brightly.

Her interest and smile were genuine and

15

uncharacteristic of the breed, thought Aiden. As a Social Security employee she was supposed to be unfriendly and unhelpful — at least that had been Aiden's experience to date. Her directness and naivety were attractive qualities, he decided. No doubt in a few years they'd have that knocked out of her.

'I'm on the ferries,' he said. 'I'm a steward.'

'Do you have to do the night boats as well?'

'Somebody has to,' he replied.

'Right,' she said, and he was immediately sorry he'd been short. 'Well, I'm really sorry about this delay with your giro. We'll get it sorted as soon as we can. Now when did you say would be a good time to call?'

'I didn't,' he replied. 'Look, I'll leave you my landlady's number. I don't have a phone in my room. But you can leave a message there for me.'

'OK. Thank you, Mr O'Neill.'

He turned to go but couldn't resist asking her.

'Ms O'Connor,' he said, 'what does the 'C' on your badge stand for? Only I've been trying to guess.'

'Oh,' she said and she looked down at the badge above her left breast as though noticing it for the first time, 'it stands for Claire.' She blushed and looked around her. 'Though strictly speaking I'm not supposed to tell you. Security and all that.'

'Don't worry, your secret's safe with me, Claire,' he said and left.

'What're you doing telling him your name?' said Deirdre, across the table in the staffroom.

Claire watched her friend grimace before

16

taking a bite of brown sandwich filled with salad. The pause allowed Claire time to decide how to answer.

'Who?' she said, affecting indifference, as she concentrated on peeling an orange.

'Oh, don't come over all innocent with me. That O'Neill guy. I heard you,' said Deirdre triumphantly.

'He only asked,' replied Claire, somewhat defensively.

'And you've been mooning around all morning. Since you interviewed him in fact.'

'Don't be daft, Deirdre. He's just a client.'

'Right.'

'Jesus,' said Deirdre all of a sudden, 'I'm sick of these healthy sandwiches. Give me chicken mayo any day. Two months I've been on this stupid diet and I've hardly lost any weight!'

She got up and threw the remains of her lunch into the bin with a vengeance. She returned to the table, removed a Mars bar from her lunch box and, with a satisfied air, took a bite.

Claire stifled a giggle. 'What did you think of him?' she asked at last.

Deirdre answered immediately, between mouthfuls, as though she'd been anticipating the question. 'Not my type. A bit too skinny. But he did have nice eyes, all dark and broody like.' She paused and then, screwing up her face, added, 'But he's a bit old, isn't he?'

'He's thirty. That's only nine, no, eight years older than me seeing as it's my birthday soon.'

'You really do fancy him, don't you?' said Deirdre.

'I thought he was nice. That's all.'

'But he's unemployed.'

'No, he's not. He works on the ferries as a steward. He only came in to see about money he's due from before.'

Someone came into the room, effectively ending the conversation.

'Come on, we'd better get back. It's past one,' said Deirdre.

The rest of the day was uneventful and Claire was glad when the hands of the clock finally crawled round to five o'clock.

On the bus home, she sat by the window looking out as it chugged and spluttered through the town. The rhythm was soothing, almost hypnotic, and her thoughts wandered to Aiden O'Neill, just as they had done a hundred times that afternoon. She knew he wasn't from Ballyfergus but apart from that she knew very little about him. He'd made his claim for Jobseekers' Allowance six weeks ago so that was how long he must have been in town. She'd never seen him before, that was certain, for she wouldn't have forgotten him in a hurry.

She alighted at her stop and walked the short distance in the dusk to the house. She thought of her mum and wondered what she would make of Aiden. Not a lot probably — she'd think he wasn't good enough for her. Mum had these daft notions about Claire marrying above herself, to a doctor or a lawyer. God knows where she got her ideas from. Claire just wanted to be happy and in love and she couldn't think of a better reason for marrying than that.

Inside, Claire shouted a greeting up the hall before going up to her room where she changed into comfortable jeans and a top. Downstairs, her dad was sitting at the kitchen table reading the paper. He smiled and looked up when she came in.

'Hello, love,' he said, in his gentle voice. 'How was work?'

So she sat down and told him about her day, omitting any mention of Aiden O'Neill, while her mum Eileen served pork chops, apple sauce, potatoes and carrots.

After her dad said grace quickly, they began to eat.

'Are you going out tonight?' Claire asked her father.

'Aye, I was thinking about going to the Club for a jar or two,' he replied.

'Ugh, Dad! I'm going with Deirdre and Jacqui! Mum, tell him he can't go!'

He chuckled and they both looked at Eileen but she appeared not to be listening.

'Eileen, love, are you all right?' he said.

'What? Yes, I'm fine. What were you saying?'

'Tell Dad he can't go to the Social Club tonight. I'm going with my friends. There's a band playing. You'll hate it, Dad.'

'I'm sure your father won't cramp your style, will you, Paddy? Not unless you're man-hunting,' she said, sharing a conspiratorial smile with him.

'Oh, Mum!' exclaimed Claire in disgust and they all laughed.

Afterwards, Claire went upstairs and got

ready. She decided on flared jeans and a tight T-shirt with high heels, put on heavier make-up than she wore during the day and brushed her hair. A spot of lippy and she was ready to go.

Downstairs, her dad was watching the TV in the front room. She found Eileen in the kitchen, sitting perfectly still with her folded hands resting on the kitchen table. The dishes had been washed and left to dry on the draining-board and the rest of the kitchen was as tidy as usual, that is to say not tidy at all.

'Mum, are you all right?' asked Claire.

'Mmm, I'm fine, love. Just fine. Oh, let me see you. You look nice.'

'It's just that you seem a bit . . . ' Claire sought for the right word, 'a bit preoccupied. You're not worrying about that check-up tomorrow, are you? I thought you said it was just routine.'

'Worried? Me?' said her mum, too brightly. 'Don't be daft. Now you get along or you'll be late.'

Before Claire had the opportunity to quiz her further, Aunt Sheila came through the back door. Her face lit into a broad smile when she saw Claire.

'You look lovely,' she said admiringly. 'Off out?'

'Yes, and she's going to be late if she doesn't get a move on,' said Eileen, shooing Claire out into the hallway.

★　★　★

Eileen was relieved when she shut the door behind Claire. Sometimes the child was too perceptive for comfort. Illogically she found Sheila's appearance at that precise moment irritating. She couldn't put her finger on why.

Sheila was waiting for her in the kitchen.

'You haven't told them then?' she asked.

'Sshh,' said Eileen putting her forefinger to her lips and gently closing the door on the noise of the TV. 'No, I told you I wouldn't,' she said in her normal voice, once she was satisfied Paddy could not hear them, 'but I think Claire's guessed something's wrong. It's my fault. I've probably been acting strangely. To tell you the truth, I'm worried sick about tomorrow.'

'Oh, Eileen.'

'I've had a headache all day. I feel as though there's this terrible weight on my head making everything all foggy.'

'Have you taken anything for it? I've some painkillers in the house,' said Sheila, making a move for the back door.

'No, it's all right, I've got something here,' said Eileen, rummaging in the back of a cupboard. 'He usually keeps . . . ah, here we are,' she said, emerging with a half-bottle of Jameson's whiskey in her hand. 'Want some?'

Sheila shook her head in a way that conveyed her disapproval as her sister poured a generous measure into a tumbler.

'Cheers,' said Eileen and took a large swig, feeling reckless.

The taste was unfamiliar and vile and, when she swallowed, the fiery liquid burned her gullet.

21

Undeterred, she took another swig. It was only a means to an end, she told herself, and that end was to get some relief from the pain inside her head.

The noise of the TV stopped and they heard Paddy heave himself off the sofa. Guiltily, Eileen hid the bottle and glass in the cupboard.

'Didn't hear you come in,' he said to Sheila, entering the kitchen. 'Is Jimmy going down the Club later on?'

'I think so. He's out at some meeting about Redhill. I don't know what time he'll be back.'

'Redhill, that's that old estate out by Carrickdun, isn't it?' said Paddy.

'Yes, the council are thinking of opening it to the public, restoring the gardens and holiday cottages. They're talking about holding open-air concerts there in the summer.'

'That would be nice all right,' said Paddy. He looked at the clock on the wall and went on, 'Well, I think I'll head on down there myself. You don't mind, do you, love?'

'No, of course not,' said Eileen hurriedly. 'You go on and enjoy yourself. Me and Sheila are just going to have a cup of tea.'

Paddy moved towards Eileen and she held her breath while he kissed her on the lips. After he'd left she finished the remaining whisky in the glass she had hidden and poured herself another one.

Unable to contain herself any longer Sheila ventured, 'Eileen, I don't think that's helping matters.'

'What do you know about it?' snapped Eileen.

22

'You're not the one going for the mammogram. You're not the one facing the prospect of telling Paddy and Claire . . . '

Her voice trailed off as she covered her face with her hands. She'd hardly eaten at teatime and the whisky was taking effect quickly, releasing the emotions she'd pent up so effectively these last few days. She felt the light weight of Sheila's arm around her shoulders and she sobbed quietly for a few moments.

She looked up when she'd composed herself and went on, 'It's not me I'm worried for, Sheila. It's Paddy and Claire. I don't think Paddy would be able to cope without me. And what about Claire? Oh, God, I always thought I'd be there to see her married, have children. It's so unfair.'

'Steady on, Eileen,' said Sheila. 'We don't know anything for sure yet. And as for Claire, I'll always be there for her. And Paddy.'

'I have a bad feeling about tomorrow,' said Eileen, choosing to ignore the last remark. 'I just know they're going to find something.'

'Eileen,' said Sheila crossly, 'will you stop talking yourself into a hole. And give me that,' she said, snatching the glass out of Eileen's hand and throwing the contents down the sink. 'The last thing you need in the morning is a hangover.'

Eileen sighed heavily and ran her fingers through her hair. 'I feel so helpless. I just want it over and done with.'

'And it will be. Tomorrow,' said Sheila firmly. 'So there's no point torturing yourself about it now.'

23

She paused and they were both silent for some moments. Sheila looked at her reflection in the window, then at her nails and then directly at Eileen. She seemed to be summoning up the courage to speak.

'About Claire,' she said cautiously. 'I've been thinking about something for a while now. Don't you think . . . '

'Did I ever tell you the whole story about me and Paddy?' interrupted Eileen, emboldened by the whisky and uncomfortable with her sister's tone of voice and the direction of the conversation. Without waiting for a reply she got up and filled another glass, ignoring Sheila's protestations.

'Come on through to the lounge,' she said.

Sheila followed her.

'I got this job as a temporary clerk in MacMaster's,' said Eileen, settling down on the green velour sofa. 'You'll remember them, that haulage firm on the Shore Road that went bust a couple of years ago.'

Sheila nodded. She sat down in the armchair and pulled her legs up under her, curled up like a cat.

'That's where you met Paddy,' she said.

'I wouldn't have looked at him, you know, only he was so different from the other lorry drivers. He never swore or read dirty magazines, not in front of me anyway, and he took the time to talk to me. You know, asked me what I thought about things. To the rest of the men I was just a bit of skirt. I remember when he asked me out for the first time. He was hanging around waiting for the others to leave and I kept asking if he wanted something and he kept saying, 'No'.' Eileen laughed at the memory. 'And then, when there was just the two of us left in the office and I was about to lock up, he blurts out, 'Will you go out with me?' And I was so shocked, it was so unexpected, that I just stood there like an idiot with the keys in my hand.'

'But you said 'Yes', didn't you?' said Sheila.

'Oh, aye, and you couldn't get us apart after that.'

Eileen paused, took another swig of whiskey and gasped before going on.

'It was his mother told him about me, you know, when she realised we were serious about each other. I don't think she meant any harm by it — she just didn't want Paddy to get hurt. She'd remembered from the papers at the time that the doctors said I wouldn't be able to have children when I grew up.'

Sheila uncurled her legs and sat upright, listening attentively.

'So you know what Paddy did? He never said a word to me, he didn't. He went up to the *Ballyfergus Times* office and asked to go through their archives and read about it for himself. And I don't think to this day he would have raised it, if I hadn't.'

'How did you tell him?' asked Sheila.

'He'd asked me to marry him and I knew I had to tell him then. You couldn't keep a thing like that a secret in a marriage. We were out for a walk on the promenade and I'd been summoning up the courage all week to tell him. I didn't know how he'd react, you see. We'd never talked about children.

'Anyway, we stopped and sat down on a bench and I said that I had something to tell him. And he never said a word. He just nodded and stared straight ahead. So I told him everything I could remember and everything I'd been told about it afterwards, and how I couldn't have children because the knife had damaged my insides so badly. And all the time he just sat there listening and never said a word.'

'And then? How did he react? What did he say?' gasped Sheila, her hand over her mouth.

'I could tell he was trying to contain himself for he didn't say anything for a while. And when he did, at last, speak he said, 'I know'. And then he went on to tell me how he'd found out, and that he loved me and how it didn't matter to him so long as he had me. He said if he ever got hold of the bastard that did it he'd kill him with his bare hands, but he knew he was locked up somewhere for life, and you couldn't let hate like that destroy your life. And he said how proud he was of me, that I'd survived it. Do you know it's the most I've ever heard Paddy say all in one go. And he never mentioned it again after that. We were married that summer.'

'I didn't know that,' said Sheila. 'About Paddy, I mean.'

'No,' said Eileen, 'there's a lot of things we never told you. You were only sixteen when we got married and, well, Mum wanted to protect you. That's why she didn't tell you about me until . . . she had to.' Eileen looked at the floor and then went on. 'Do you remember how Mum was dead set against Paddy? She thought a lorry driver wasn't good enough for me and that he was too old. But he's done all right by me — he's been a good husband and a good father to Claire.' She looked up, catching Sheila's eye. 'But he depends on me. Completely. It's him I worry about most.'

Sheila nodded in agreement and asked, 'Have you told Mum about tomorrow?'

'No, but I should. I just can't face it tonight. Would you do it for me?'

★   ★   ★

Sheila let herself into the house by the back door. All was in darkness and silent — Jimmy must still be at the Club. The kitchen was as she'd left it, spotlessly neat and tidy. She never could understand Eileen's sloppy ways round the house — it was as though she took no pride in her home. Not for the first time she'd had to resist the urge to give the place a good going-over.

She went upstairs and checked the sleeping boys, kissing each one gently on the cheek. Then she got ready for bed and reflected on what Eileen had told her. After all these years there were still secrets emerging, little details about her life that, as her sister, she should have known. But the six-year age gap between her and Eileen had ensured they would never be really close, as did the history between them.

Then she remembered her promise to Eileen to call her mum.

The phone was answered within two rings.

'What're you doing phoning me at this hour?' asked Moira Devlin irritably.

'Sure you don't go to bed 'til all hours. So, what's the problem?' said Sheila, thinking that her mother was getting very set in her ways. 'Look, never mind that now, Mum. I've something to tell you. It's not good news. Eileen has to go up to Belfast tomorrow, to the hospital. They want to check that the cancer's still in remission.'

'You mean it's come back!'

'No, we don't know that yet, Mum. That's why she has to have the mammogram,' said Sheila cheerfully, not sure if she could face another emotionally wrought conversation this evening. 'Eileen would have told you herself except she's a bit knackered and she's gone to bed. I don't think she wanted to talk about it any more.'

'I see. How're Claire and Paddy taking the news?'

'They don't know. Eileen didn't want to tell them just yet. You know what Paddy's like — he'd be worried sick.'

'Well, thank God Eileen has Claire anyway,' said Moira. 'That girl is so dear to her. It'll give her a reason to fight this thing.'

Sheila bristled. Why did her mum feel the need to remind her how precious Claire was to Eileen? Wasn't she precious to Sheila too?

'*If* the cancer's come back, Mum. The mammogram in itself won't tell us that. It'll only

28

show if there's a lump.'

'And if they find one?'

'They'll have to take it out to see whether it's benign or not.'

'Oh, my God,' said Moira.

'Let's not worry until we have something to worry about, eh?' said Sheila gently, sensing her mother's rising panic.

'It's not good though, is it, Sheila? I mean, with her having cancer before and all.'

'I know, Mum. But we just have to wait and see and try to remain positive. Look, I've got to work on Friday. Can you go with her to the hospital?'

'If she wants me to.'

'She will.'

When Sheila came off the phone she brushed her teeth and went to the toilet. Her period should have come months ago. She thought about her conversation with Eileen earlier in the week — it was time she made that appointment to see the doctor.

2

Moira Devlin put the receiver down carefully, and returned to the sitting-room where she'd been working on a book of crosswords and puzzles. They kept the old grey cells working, at least that was the theory, but more than that it passed the time. For the boys and Claire were nearly grown now and they didn't have so much of a need of a granny round the place. Marbles, the cat, cross at being disturbed, jumped onto the sofa beside her and curled into a tight ball.

She picked up the book and returned to where she'd left off, but found she could not settle. The news about Eileen weighed heavily on her mind for she sensed that this time there would be no reprieve.

She remembered the last loved one she'd lost — Kieran, her husband of forty-three years. That was nearly ten years ago, when she'd been left a widow at the age of sixty. His death of a heart attack was doubly cruel, in that he had been relatively young and it was unexpected. She never had the time to say the things she should have said over the years. At the time she'd believed a sudden death the worst thing but now, after everything she'd been through with Eileen and her fight against cancer, she wasn't so sure.

It was inconceivable that she would lose a daughter. Moira believed in the natural order of things and, by rights, she should die first. She would gladly have taken Eileen's place if she could. Her life was lived, Eileen's only halfway through. Still, she tried to reassure herself, they didn't know anything for sure yet. She was imagining the worst possible scenario when Eileen might be perfectly OK.

Moira looked at the clock on the mantelpiece. Twelve-thirty. Time to get ready for bed, she supposed, though why she bothered following any sort of routine she didn't know. There was no one else to please and she hardly slept these days, often lying awake 'til the early hours. And after the phone call from Sheila, she'd not sleep much tonight.

The bedroom was cold but Moira didn't mind — it was healthy to sleep in a cool room as her robust health testified. She put on a long flannel nightgown and got into bed. She lay there motionless for a while and waited for sleep to come but found herself replaying the telephone conversation with Sheila. She rolled over and tried to think pleasant thoughts; she pictured her girls when they were children but unhappy memories started to crowd in on that image so she thought of her grandchildren instead. But all sorts of mixed-up thoughts crowded into her head.

She remembered that she needed a new can of air-freshener for the bathroom and a loaf of bread. Was bingo on tomorrow night or the night after? She remembered the day Kieran took her to Portrush, before they were married, and they'd eaten ice cream sitting on the sea wall. Had she unplugged the TV? When did she

31

last change the sheets?

Frustrated, she got out of bed, pulled on her dressing-gown and wandered round the small flat. Why was it that your brain became most active at the time when you should be asleep?

She went into her tidy little kitchen, made tea, swallowed two herbal sleeping tablets and took her cup into the sitting-room. It was two-thirty, the very dead of night. All the pub and partygoers had long since made it home and it was too early for milk floats and paper deliveries. No one in their right mind would be up and about at this time, except insomniacs like her, and burglars. She shivered slightly, pulled back the net curtain and peered out into the street. It was completely deserted and not a single light was on in any of the surrounding houses.

She knew better than to switch the television on at this time for it was just rubbish — old repeats and B movies. Stuff that sucked your brain out. She switched on one bar of the electric fire, sat down beside it on the sofa and supped her tea.

This was the time too when memories were at their most vivid for Moira. It was a sort of twilight time when her brain was tired and she sometimes had difficulty distinguishing the past from the present. She rested her head on the tartan travelling rug she kept over the back of the sofa. Her legs were warm as toast.

Dear God, she prayed, please don't take my Eileen. Take me instead. Then she remembered that it wasn't her place to question the will of God. She must accept. If you can't do that then, dear God, make it quick and painless. I don't think we could bear to see her suffer. Oh, it's so cruel, so hard to bear. And what about poor Paddy? Sure the man can't even butter his own toast. He'd be lost without her. Oh God, hasn't the girl suffered enough? What has she done to deserve this on top of everything else? And how will wee Claire cope?

The memory of Claire's birth came suddenly to mind, the images as clear as if it were yesterday. Moira remembered the smell and weightlessness of the tiny body as she held her first grandchild in her arms, the little face red and swollen from her struggle into this world. And she saw her daughter lying exhausted in the bed, as pale and wan as a ghost. She looked so vulnerable and so young. It made her heart ache to think of it. No, she mustn't think of that now. It was all in the past and what was done was done for the best. 'Hasn't it all worked out in the end?' she asked herself and tried to ignore the nagging doubts that came in response.

Moira didn't remember dozing off, but when she woke up there was sunshine streaming through the window, the electric fire was still on and she had a crick in her neck.

★   ★   ★

Claire had been waiting in the foyer of the Club for nearly ten minutes when Deirdre and Jacqui finally turned up.

'I thought you said you'd be here at eight,' she said accusingly. 'It's nearly half past. I've been waiting here for ages.'

'I bet you weren't here for eight either,' said Deirdre in response. 'If we'd been on time, you'd have been late.'

'That's true,' said Claire, her good humour returning at Deirdre's twisted but accurate logic, 'but I was here before you and that's all that counts.'

'Oh, for goodness sake, you two,' said Jacqui, 'are you going to stand there all night arguing? Come on, I'm dying for a drink.'

They left their coats in the cloakroom and went into the ladies' toilets where they touched up make-up, applied hairspray and checked hair and clothes.

'God, that T-shirt looks fantastic on you,' said Deirdre admiring Jacqui's skin-tight black top with a silver starburst design on the front. She was tall and slim with a pert bust.

Claire looked at her own reflection and wished she was another half-a-foot taller. She wasn't fat but it was hard to look like a catwalk model when you were only five foot two in your stocking feet. That was why all her shoes had high heels. Then again, she thought, looking sideways at Deirdre's large reflection in the mirror, at least she had a good figure. Not that Deirdre's figure was an impediment to success with men — there were plenty of fellas mad after her. Claire noticed that Deirdre's low-cut top revealed an alarming amount of her ample bosom.

'I wonder if Mac'll be here tonight. He promised me a shot on his bike and he's never taken me out on it yet,' said Deirdre.

Mac was a biker with a reputation for being a bit wild.

'And you'd go on the back of a bike with him?' asked Jacqui.

'Oh, yeah — all that power and speed!'

'You're mad, so you are — you do know that, don't you, Deirdre?' said Claire. 'You could get killed. You'd be trusting him with your life.'

'Your hair'd get ruined under the helmet,' chipped in Jacqui.

'You two are complete wimps,' said Deirdre good-naturedly. 'You have to try things at least once in your life.'

'Well, that's one experience I can do without,' said Jacqui.

They entered the big function room which was full of chairs and tables, the bar lining one wall. Already all the regular drinkers were propped up against it, sitting or standing in their favourite spot. There was a fair crowd now and groups of people had started to take tables. The band were setting up on the small podium.

Claire crossed the dance floor to the bar self-consciously, for everyone scrutinised new arrivals before returning to their drink or conversation. Once she'd reached the safety of the bar she felt invisible again.

'Claire, look. That's him,' hissed Deirdre.

Claire looked into the crowd but couldn't see anyone of interest.

'Who?' said Jacqui, looking round conspicuously.

'This guy Claire's mad about. He came into

35

the office today and she was all over him.'

Instantly Claire felt her face turn red and a little flutter of excitement in her tummy.

'I am not mad about him,' hissed Claire, 'and keep your voice down, will you?'

'Where is he?' persisted Jacqui. 'Point him out.'

'That's him behind the bar,' said Deirdre.

'Ryan O'Malley?' said Jacqui, sounding incredulous.

'God, no. He must have gone out the back. Oh, there he is! The one with the dark hair carrying the crate of bottles.'

'Oh, I see. Who is he? *Do* you fancy him?' asked Jacqui, directing her questions at Claire.

'Sshh . . . ' said Claire. 'I thought he was nice, yes. But I hardly spoke to the guy. Deirdre's just winding me up.'

Deirdre, smiling, was obviously in one of her mischievous moods.

Aiden came over to take their drinks order and Claire thought she was going to die of embarrassment.

'What'll it be?' he said, and then, noticing Claire, surprise registered in his face. 'Hi, Claire. Didn't expect to see you here.'

Claire noticed the softness in his voice, a lyrical tone absent from the harsh Ballyfergus accent. His smile was warm and the sleeves of his white shirt were rolled up, revealing lithe, hairy forearms. His hair was ruffled sexily, like a movie star's.

'Hi, I'm Deirdre and this is Jacqui,' said Deirdre, and Claire introduced Aiden.

'You must be new here,' said Deirdre.

'I thought you said you worked as a steward on the ferry,' said Claire.

'Are you checking up on me?' said Aiden good-naturedly and Claire blushed again.

'It's the training,' interjected Deirdre. 'I work for the SS too. We can't help interrogating people.'

'I see,' said Aiden laughing and Claire noticed his straight, white teeth, 'I started here at the weekend. I still work on the ferries — this is just part-time.'

He got their drinks, Jacqui paid for them and he moved off.

'What'd you think of him then?' said Claire.

'I thought he was nice,' said Jacqui.

'Not my type,' said Deirdre. 'Too old, too hairy and too skinny.'

'Oh, shut up, you,' said Claire, pushing her playfully in the arm.

★   ★   ★

The Club was more crowded than a normal Thursday night — Jimmy had forgotten a band was playing. But he was pleased. It gave the place more atmosphere and he was in good form tonight. The meeting about Redhill had gone well — for once, everyone had set aside party politics to achieve something positive for the town. God knows, Ballyfergus could do with a few more public amenities.

Jimmy's mood darkened when he saw Paddy at his usual place at the bar and remembered about Eileen's hospital visit. He felt uncomfortable keeping this knowledge from Paddy but he'd promised Sheila he wouldn't say anything and he'd keep his word.

'Right you are, Paddy,' he said and squeezed in beside him at the bar.

'What're you having?' said Paddy. 'The usual?'

'Aye,' said Jimmy.

Paddy shouted over to the barman, 'Ryan, pair of Guinness here when you get a minute!'

The drinks arrived swiftly, for Paddy and Jimmy were well-known regulars. Jimmy sucked the black liquid through the white froth on the top of his pint and looked around. He took in all the faces he knew, nodding here and there.

'Quite a crowd tonight,' he observed.

He saw Claire and her friends talking to a group of lads at the end of the bar. They appeared not to have noticed either him or Paddy. Claire had on a short pink T-shirt that showed her bare midriff and dark blue flared jeans. Jimmy remembered, with a touch of nostalgia, when they were in fashion the first time round. He'd look a bit silly in them now, he thought, looking down at his small but perfectly formed paunch.

He sighed and looked back at the vibrant, youthful group. Claire's hair was up in a loose clip with strands sticking out casually at the back, although he guessed she'd spent hours perfecting it, and she wore a pair of strappy high heels. That'll be because she thinks she's too short, Jimmy chuckled to himself. She's a wee smasher, he thought with pride. If he was one of those lads he'd be dying to go out with her.

'There's our Claire over there,' he said.

'Aye,' said Paddy, taking a sup of the stout.

'Didn't she see you?' said Jimmy.

'Aye,' said Paddy, with a wry smile, 'she did. But she's pretending not to in case I show her up.'

Jimmy smiled and said, 'The boys aren't far off that stage either.' He paused and thought. 'In fact, I think Conor's already there — I get the feeling he thinks I'm a bit of an embarrassment.'

'Happens us all,' said Paddy. 'We were the same once.'

'Aye, that's true enough.'

'How'd the meeting go then?' asked Paddy.

'Good,' said Jimmy. 'It's a slow process, mind. But it's going to be fantastic, Paddy. A real boost to the area. We were looking at the architect's plans tonight for the visitors' centre and the café. He brought along these wee models so you could see exactly what it was going to look like. I feel as though I'm doing something really worthwhile.'

Jimmy noticed a dark-haired stranger behind the bar.

'Who's that?' he asked Paddy.

'The new lad? His name's Aiden something.'

'He's not from round here, is he?'

'Nope.'

'Wonder what's brought him to Ballyfergus,' said Jimmy.

Paddy shrugged.

'Did you see the match tonight, Jimmy?' asked John Pettigrew, coming up to stand beside him, and the conversation turned to football and hurling results.

With the help of a few more pints of the black stuff, the evening passed very pleasantly indeed.

★   ★   ★

Deirdre had dragged Jacqui over to talk to Mac. The band had packed up and Claire had almost given up hope of speaking to Aiden when she heard his voice in her ear. She must try to remain cool, calm and collected if she was to impress him.

'Thought I wasn't going to get a chance to speak to you on your own,' said Aiden.

'I thought you weren't going to speak to me at all,' said Claire, 'and me going out of my way to help you this afternoon.'

'And I thought you were just doing your job,' said Aiden, the corners of his mouth turned up in a half-smile, and Claire was sure he was laughing at her.

'Stop teasing me, will you?' she blurted out and then wished she hadn't for it sounded so childish.

'I'm sorry,' he said, suddenly serious and he placed the tips of his fingers on her elbow for a few brief seconds.

Claire's skin felt hot where he touched her.

'I wasn't teasing you,' he went on. 'It was just a bit of banter.' He looked at the bar, deep with dirty glasses. 'It's just been so busy in here all night and there's only the two of us behind the

40

bar. I didn't realise people in Ballyfergus could drink so much.'

'So where did you learn to be a barman?'

'Oh, here and there,' he said evasively.

'Oh, God,' said Claire, cringing with embarrassment, as two drunken figures approached.

'What is it?'

'It's my dad and Uncle Jimmy. Look at the pair of them, would you!'

'They're a bit worse for wear.'

'A bit worse for wear! They're pished, the two of them. My mum'll kill him.'

'Which one's your dad then?'

'Guess.'

'It's the one on the right, with the light hair — you're the spit of him.'

'Do you think so?' said Claire thoughtfully, trying to regard the familiar faces objectively, as would a stranger.

'Am I right?'

'No, that's Uncle Jimmy.'

'Hello, love,' said Paddy coming up and leaning heavily on Claire's shoulder. 'Aren't you going to introduce me and Jimmy to your boyfriend here?'

'He's not my boyfriend, Dad,' hissed Claire, thinking she could happily throttle him there and then.

'Give me your hand, son,' said Paddy, pumping Aiden's in his own, and speaking with uncharacteristic boldness brought on by drink, 'I'm Claire's dad, Paddy. And this here's my brother-in-law, Jimmy.'

'Glad to meet you,' said Uncle Jimmy and,

after a pause, screwing up his eyes, he stated, 'You're not from round these parts.'

'No,' said Aiden.

'Where then?' said Uncle Jimmy a little too directly.

'Newry.'

'What's brought you to Ballyfergus?'

'Work. On the ferries and here.'

'Come on, you two, will you stop interrogating the poor fella,' said Claire, sensing Aiden's uneasiness.

'We're just being friendly, taking an interest. Now mind you take good care of our wee Claire here,' said Uncle Jimmy. He put his arm around Claire's shoulders and squeezed so hard it hurt.

'Uncle Jimmy, please!' said Claire.

'Oh, I've every intention of doing that,' said Aiden calmly and he winked at Claire.

After they'd left Claire apologised for them.

'There's no need. Sure they didn't mean any harm,' said Aiden, good-naturedly.

'I sensed you didn't like Uncle Jimmy asking you questions.'

'I don't like talking about myself, that's all,' said Aiden and Claire decided that was an admirable quality.

Someone shouted over at Aiden. It was Ryan, the other barman.

'Are you going to stand there all night gassing? There's work to be done!'

'All right,' replied Aiden and then, turning to Claire, 'Look, I'd better go. I'll come and see you tomorrow at your work.'

And true to his word, he came into the office the very next day and asked Claire out.

★ ★ ★

'Right, that's it,' said Sheila, still in her nurse's uniform, 'I've had enough of this. I want you to tell me what's going on, Conor.'

His face was partially obscured by a bag of frozen peas.

'I told you, Mum,' he mumbled, 'there's nothing going on.'

Sheila snatched the bag of peas out of Conor's hand, revealing a swollen left cheek and eye. The skin around the eye socket was already turning purple.

'I want you to tell me who did this.'

'Just some kids, Mum. We were horsing around,' he said unconvincingly.

'And one of them just accidentally gave you a black eye. Is that it?'

'Something like that,' said Conor in a defeatist tone.

'What's going on?' said Jimmy, coming into the kitchen with his coat still on. 'What's all the shouting about?'

Conor hung his head.

'Show your father,' commanded Sheila, by now livid with rage. 'Go on. Lift your head. That's it. What do you think of that then?'

'Ouch, son, that looks like a bad one. What happened, pal?'

Conor shrank from his father's touch and got out of the chair.

43

'And where do you think you're going?' asked Sheila.

'Upstairs, to get changed,' came the sullen reply.

Sheila was about to get stuck into him again when Jimmy interrupted. 'It's all right, Sheila. You go on, son. We'll talk about this later.'

After Conor had left the room, he said, 'There's no point taking it out on the lad, Sheila. It's not his fault.'

'I know that. It's just — it makes me so angry seeing his face all cut up like that. And he won't tell me what's going on.'

Jimmy sighed heavily. 'I tried to talk to him the other night too but he wouldn't tell me anything. He said he was tired and wanted to go to bed. I think that's a first ever.'

'Well, I've had enough of it,' said Sheila determinedly, and she threw the bag of peas into the sink. 'It's time you and I went to see the school.'

'Mmm,' said Jimmy, 'I think you're right. We're not making any headway on our own, are we?'

'I'll make an appointment to see the headmaster next week. If I phone just now I should catch the secretary.'

She picked up the phone, dialled and an arrangement was made for Tuesday morning.

'Can you manage that, Jimmy?'

'I'll just make sure I can. I'll swap shifts if needs be.'

'As if we didn't have enough to worry about,' said Sheila looking anxiously at the clock. 'I

44

thought Eileen would've been in by now to tell me how she got on up in Belfast. Look, do you think you could hold the fort here while I go over and see her?'

'Aye, you go on.'

'There's shepherd's pie in the oven. It'll be ready in twenty minutes. If I'm not back you just need to do some peas. Might as well use those up,' she said wryly, indicating the discarded pack in the sink.

Without taking off her work clothes, Sheila walked the short distance to her sister's back door, knocked and went straight in.

She found Eileen and her mum sitting on the sofa in the sitting-room with their coats still on. Moira's face was strained.

'You're back! Why didn't you come and tell me?'

'We're only through the door,' said Moira.

'Well, love,' said Sheila to Eileen, 'how'd you get on?'

'They found a lump,' said Moira.

Sheila sat down on the sofa opposite them. 'Where? How big?'

Eileen looked up and answered, 'It's sort of here on the right side of the breast. It's not much bigger than a hazelnut but you could see it clearly.'

'And did they think it was . . . anything to worry about?'

'The consultant wasn't giving anything away,' said Moira. 'He said he wouldn't know until they'd examined it.'

'I suppose not,' said Sheila, and then,

addressing Eileen, 'Are you going to tell Claire and Paddy?'

'She'll have to tell them, now,' said her mother, authoritatively. 'They'll have to know about the biopsy.'

'I don't want to tell them, Mum. Not until we know whether it's come back or not.'

'But you can't not tell your own husband and daughter! They're going to have to know sometime. Besides, won't Paddy see the wound?'

'There won't be a wound as such, Mum. Don't you remember the last time? It was done under a local anaesthetic and it left little more than a pinprick and a bruise.'

'I don't understand you,' said Moira, shaking her head.

'Let her do what she wants, Mum. It's up to her,' said Sheila and then, changing tack, asked, 'When do they want to do the biopsy?'

'Thursday of next week. The consultant fitted me in as soon as he could.'

With that, Moira got up and said she had to go. The cat would need to be fed and she was worried about him cooped up all day in the house. She looked absolutely wrung out and Sheila sensed she could take no more today.

'You'll be all right now, love, won't you?' said Moira and Eileen gave a weary nod.

After their mother left there was nothing to say. They sat in silence until Sheila said, 'Conor came home today with a black eye.'

'Oh,' said Eileen mildly. 'What happened?'

'Well, that's the thing. He won't tell Jimmy or me.'

'Maybe he's embarrassed that he can't fight his own corner. He's never been a very physical boy.'

'Hmm. I think there's more to it than that.'

They heard the front door open and Claire's voice yelled, 'I'm home!'

'I don't want to tell her,' said Eileen, firmly.

'We're in here,' Sheila shouted and then more quietly, to Eileen, she said, 'OK, but try to cheer up.'

'What're you doing sitting in your coat, Mum?' asked Claire when she came into the room.

'I just caught Eileen coming in the door,' said Sheila, hastily. 'She hasn't had a chance to take it off.'

'God, I forgot. It was your check-up today, Mum!' said Claire, suddenly anxious. 'How did it go? Is everything all right?'

'Fine. Everything's fine, love.'

'Are you sure?' said Claire, looking dubious. 'The cancer's in remission, right?'

'It was just a routine check, love. Everything's fine.'

Sheila, sensing Eileen might be about to break down, said brightly, 'Of course it is. Your mum's just tired. It's a long day trekking all the way up to Belfast and back. Why don't you come and chat to me while I make a cup of tea for everyone?'

She steered Claire out of the room and into the kitchen.

'Mum's OK, isn't she?' asked Claire.

'Of course, why wouldn't she be?'

'Well, last night Dad was steaming. Normally she'd tear strips off him but this time she didn't say a word. It was almost like she didn't notice.'

'Maybe she's getting more tolerant in her old age,' joked Sheila. 'Anyway, tell me about this fella you met last night. Aiden, was it?'

'God, news travels fast round here,' said Claire.

'Jimmy told me.'

'He didn't half embarrass me last night, Auntie Sheila. He interrogated Aiden to within an inch of his life and Dad called him 'my boyfriend' in front of him.'

Sheila smiled at the heinous crimes outlined, savouring the fact that Claire was confiding in her.

'So is he?'

'Is he what?'

'Your boyfriend?'

'You're as bad as them, do you know that?' said Claire but her expression was good-humoured. She filled the kettle at the sink and added, 'He is now.'

'What do you mean?'

'He came into the office today and asked me out. He's taking me for a drink tomorrow night.'

'Oh, Claire, that's exciting. Do you really like him?'

'Yes, I do, more than I've ever liked anyone.'

Sheila felt her heart skip a beat, remembering the passion and excitement of young love. And she felt fiercely protective of Claire, for love made you vulnerable. If this Aiden, whoever he was, broke her heart, she'd kill him.

'I'd like to meet him,' said Sheila. 'I get the feeling he's going to be around for a while.'

'We'll see,' said Claire, affecting nonchalance.

★   ★   ★

On Saturday, inspired by an improvement in the weather, which he took to signal the first sign of spring, Jimmy decided to clear out the attic. It was time to get rid of the old toys, games and equipment that the boys had long outgrown, something Jimmy had been meaning to do for months.

Sheila's response was enthusiastic as he knew it would be — her penchant for organisation extended to all corners of the house.

Each item Jimmy unearthed brought back a rush of nostalgia — Conor's first bike, the kite they used to take up to the Sallagh Braes on windy days, jigsaw puzzles they'd spent hours making on cold winter nights. He found himself putting aside this and that, for memories' sake, until there was a sizeable pile in the corner. Making the decision to throw things out was painful — he realised now that was why he'd put off the job for so long. He told himself he'd have to be more ruthless.

Inside a large cardboard box he found photograph albums. He opened one, sat down on the plywood flooring beneath a bare light bulb and leafed through the pages. The album was full of pictures of the boys when they were young — playing in the garden, at the seaside, at Granny Devlin's, in front of the Christmas tree.

Underneath each photo was a date and description. '*Portrush. May Day Bank Holiday 1991,*' said one. Taken nearly a decade before, a chubby baby, Danny, wriggled in his mother's arms. And beside her, on either side, stood Conor and Martin, shivering in the fresh sea breeze. Sheila didn't look a day older now than she did then, he thought, smiling to himself.

He replaced the album, pulled out another one, and examined it curiously. It was small and fat and made of white faux leather. Inside were a series of photos of a blue-eyed baby, taken over a period of approximately a year. The pictures recorded all the milestones in the little girl's first year — her first mouthful of food, sitting up, crawling, her first tooth, her first steps. He'd never seen these pictures before. Each page was decorated with hearts and bunnies and ducks, all drawn in a child's hand. And his heart ached when he realised that Sheila had painstakingly compiled the album.

'How are you getting on up there?' called Sheila. 'There's a cup of tea ready, if you want it.'

Jimmy started and cracked his skull on a low beam. The album fell to the floor, sending up a little cloud of dust. He cleared his throat.

'I'll be down in a minute,' he shouted, hoarsely.

Guiltily, he picked up the album, dusted it off and returned it to the bottom of the cardboard box. He felt like he'd been caught prying into a part of Sheila's past that she'd obviously intended to be kept private.

He peered under the eaves and spied the wheels of a pram sticking out from under a sheet.

'At least that's something we definitely won't be needing,' he said and crawled his way over to it, careful not to hit his head on the rafters.

The navy-blue pram with its big wheels was still in good condition, if a little worn, but it was old-fashioned compared to the bright buggies you saw out and about now. Still, someone might be glad of it. There was a raincover, mattress, sheets and bedding to go with it, all carefully wrapped in brown paper and labelled in Sheila's handwriting.

He shifted the lot over to the hatch, climbed down the ladder and manoeuvred the pram through the small aperture. He put everything on the landing floor, along with the other things he'd persuaded himself to throw out.

'Here's your tea,' said Sheila, coming up the stairs.

'Thanks, love,' he said, taking the cup gratefully. 'It's thirsty work.'

Sheila stopped on the landing and stared at the pram. Her face fell.

'You're not getting rid of that,' she said.

'Sure we won't be needing it. By the time Claire'll be having babies she won't want this old thing. We might as well sell it.'

'I don't want to get rid of it.'

'I understand, love. I felt the same sorting through their toys. Each one brings back so many memories, doesn't it? Still,' he added brightly, 'we can't keep everything, can we?'

'No,' she replied, more forcefully this time, '*you* don't understand.' She faltered and then went on, her voice softer and more hesitant, 'I thought perhaps we might have another baby.'

'But you're thirty-eight going on thirty-nine, love! What're you thinking of babies for, when our family's nearly grown?'

'You know I always wanted a girl.'

Jimmy thought of the album in the attic. 'But don't you think you're getting on a bit, Sheila?' he said tenderly. 'I mean we both are. Our days of having babies are over.'

'No, they're not, not necessarily,' said Sheila defiantly. 'Lots of people have babies at my age. You read about celebrities all the time, having babies in their late thirties and early forties.'

'But what if it was another boy?' said Jimmy, reasonably.

'Why can't I have what I want for once?' said Sheila and she fled downstairs in tears.

And Jimmy was left standing there on the landing weighed down with sorrow, unable to go and comfort her. Quietly, he put the pram back in the attic.

★   ★   ★

Sheila fidgeted in the doctor's waiting-room and hoped she didn't meet any more people she knew. That was the problem living in a small town like Ballyfergus.

She'd already told a white lie to Joanne, the receptionist, about her visit. Then Maureen O'Farrell, that nosy friend of her mother's, came and sat down beside her. She told Sheila all about her angina and swollen ankles before asking Sheila why she was visiting the doctor.

Maureen was the type of woman who could, within minutes, convince you she was your bosom buddy. But Sheila was wise to her. Maureen had a big mouth and a small life and she'd nothing better to do than concern herself with other people's business. If you told Maureen anything, half the town knew about it by the end of the day.

'Routine,' she repeated, narrowing her eyes at Sheila. 'I see.' She sniffed and looked around her, seriously displeased that there was to be no disclosure this morning from her friend's daughter. 'And how about that boy of yours — Conor, is it? I hear he's been in a bit of bother at school.'

'Who told you that?' said Sheila, a little too sharply, and Maureen sensed she'd hit a raw nerve.

'Why, your mother of course,' she replied, soothingly, and waited for Sheila to speak.

Maureen was an expert in the use of silence, a technique guaranteed to break down even the most reluctant confidant. Most people were uncomfortable with long silences and felt the need to fill them. And if you talked long enough, Maureen usually got you to spill the beans.

'You know boys,' said Sheila, tight-lipped, and she picked up a magazine and pretended to read.

'And how's Eileen keeping these days?' interrupted Maureen after a while, undeterred by Sheila's brush-off.

Sheila bristled. 'She's fine, thank you.'

'Only that was a terrible business with the cancer, wasn't it? Losing her breast like that, poor thing. Still it's all over now, isn't it?'

'Mmm . . . ' mumbled Sheila non-committally.

Had this woman a sixth sense or what? When Maureen's name was called, Sheila breathed a sigh of relief and put down the copy of *Good Housekeeping*. It would be a long time before she'd be subscribing to that magazine with its features on comfortable clothes for the fuller figure and adverts for sensible shoes.

Maureen would probably complain to her mother that Sheila had been rude but she didn't care. She'd much more important things to worry about than a silly old bag like Maureen. Suddenly she felt anxious about her appointment. Dr Crory's surgery always ran late, because he talked too much, and she wished he'd hurry up.

A toddler pushed a trolley full of building blocks around the waiting-room. She collided with Sheila's legs and some of the blocks fell on the floor.

'Careful, Lauren!' called her mother.

'She's all right,' reassured Sheila and she bent down and spoke gently to the child. 'Shall we put these back in the trolley?'

Lauren's big brown eyes scrutinised Sheila suspiciously before she eventually said, 'Yessh.'

Sheila picked up the blocks and handed them, one by one, to the little girl who placed each one slowly and carefully in the trolley. Then she stood up and resumed her place behind the handle.

'Say 'Thank you',' called her mother.

'Ank oo,' repeated the child and she smiled at Sheila, the way only a child can. A smile of pure, unadulterated joy.

Sheila felt a tightening in her throat and looked away.

When her name was, at last, called she left the waiting-room quickly. The doctor, a tall man about her age with receding hair and thick glasses, welcomed her at the door of his surgery.

She described her symptoms to him — irregular periods, sometimes nothing for a few months and then two within six weeks, and excessive bleeding.

'How long has this been going on?'

'At least six months, maybe more.'

'And when did you say your last period was?'

'Nearly sixteen weeks ago.'

He scribbled something down in Sheila's notes. 'And have you noticed anything else?'

'Like what, doctor?'

'Oh, anything out of the ordinary. Any change in mood perhaps? Or excessive sweating or dizziness?'

'I have been a bit moody lately, more so than usual when I think about it. But sweating and dizziness? No, I don't think so.'

'Hmm,' he said and rubbed his chin.

He put his pen down, leaned back in the chair and joined the tips of his fingers together so forming an arch with his hands. He leaned his elbows on the chair-arms and rocked gently back and forth, ruminating. At last he spoke.

'And what do you think might be wrong, Sheila?'

This was one of Dr Crory's favourite questions, a sort of game he played with Sheila who, with her training as a nurse, was often able to diagnose quite accurately both her own ailments and those of her family. But this afternoon Sheila was in no mood for games.

'Look, Dr Crory, I don't mean to be rude but I'm really worried about this. And I don't know what's wrong. So, if you don't mind, could you please just tell me?'

If he was offended it didn't show. He leaned forward in his chair and picked up the pen. 'Do you know when your mother went through the menopause?'

'The menopause? In her late forties, I think. Yes, I'm sure of it. Why . . . surely you don't think that's what's wrong with me?'

'I don't know, Sheila, but it's one possibility.'

She stared at him, shocked. 'And what are the others?'

'Well, at the moment, there aren't any. That's why I'd like to do some tests.' He went on, talking to himself more than Sheila, as he flicked through her notes, 'If your mother had an early menopause, it would certainly be more likely. It tends to run in families. But you could just be unlucky.'

'So it could be something else?' asked Sheila hopefully.

'There's nothing else that springs to mind. I think we'd better rule out this possibility first.'

Sheila swallowed and fought to remain her composure. The menopause! Middle-aged woman went through the menopause, not someone young like her. Menopausal women wore sensible shoes and night cream and read *Good Housekeeping*. Dr Crory was wrong of course but quite determined. She'd just have to go along with him — the tests would prove him wrong. Though God knows what the cause of her problems really was. Best not to think about it now. Rule out this ludicrous proposition first and take it from there. One step at a time.

'So what's involved then?' she asked.

'We just need some blood to start with.'

'What are you looking for?'

'The level of FSH, that's follicle-stimulating hormone, in your blood. It rises significantly during the menopause, an indication of ovarian failure.'

'And after that?'

'If the diagnosis is positive we'll need to do a few more tests and then discuss treatment. But let's not jump the gun. We'll see what these results come back with.'

'Right,' said Sheila glumly.

'Look, try not to worry about it, Sheila,' he said kindly. 'If the test is positive there's a lot we can do to alleviate the symptoms. And don't forget it's a natural function of your body, not an illness. You're fit and healthy so I don't foresee too many problems.'

She looked at him blankly. If he was right, she would never be able to have another baby. She would be old before her time.

'I'll just give Nurse a call and arrange to get the blood test done now,' he said, businesslike.

He picked up the phone and spoke into it. Sheila looked round the room and everything seemed so sharp and clear that she was certain she would never forget a single detail about this interview.

'See Nurse on your way out, would you? And come back and see me in a week,' said Dr Crory.

★ ★ ★

Not much had changed from his schooldays, thought Jimmy, as he and Sheila sat on uncomfortable plastic chairs outside the headmaster's office. In an attempt to make it feel like a proper waiting-area, a small table with a vase of flowers had been placed between the two chairs. But to Jimmy it felt just like the old days when he'd spent many an afternoon in exactly the same place.

The school had been built in the late sixties so it was relatively new when he'd been a pupil there. But it had been shoddily built, like so many structures of the era, and was now showing serious signs of wear and tear. Just along the corridor from where they sat an aluminium bucket attempted to catch drops of water leaking from above. The ceiling tiles were stained with brown rings, evidence of previous water damage.

'Brings back the memories, doesn't it?' he said, 'Sitting here like the old days waiting to see 'Belter' Brennan.'

'What?' said Sheila distractedly.

He repeated what he'd said and then remembered that Sheila's schooldays here might be something she'd rather forget.

'It might do for you,' she replied. 'I was never called to see him, thank God. I had the nuns to worry about and some of them were right bitches. Do you remember Sister Bernadette?'

'Aye, she was ferocious,' said Jimmy, half-smiling.

'It wasn't funny then, I can tell you. She used to haul us out of our chairs by the hair.'

'I know. I saw her do it. They wouldn't get away with that nowadays.'

'Some things have changed for the better,' said Sheila, 'but it's gone from one extreme to the other. They can't so much as shout at a kid now without violating some EU law. I don't know how the teachers keep control.'

'That's what those lads who've been roughing up our Conor need — a good hiding. That'd sort them out.'

'I feel the same,' said Sheila. 'You got the belt every week and it never did you any harm, did it?'

'No,' said Jimmy thoughtfully, 'I don't suppose it did. But it didn't do me any good either.'

'What do you mean?'

'Well, it never made me apply myself any better to my schoolwork. I sometimes wish I'd made more of an effort to get exams. I never found the work hard, you know, but there just didn't seem to be any point.'

'You were in with a bad crowd, Jimmy.'

'I might have done better than a train

conductor if I'd had a few qualifications under my belt.'

'Jimmy, don't say that. You've done very well. Look at the work you do on the council. I'm proud of you.'

'You are?' he said, turning to look at her, his spirits suddenly uplifted.

'Yes, of course I am,' she said, but her smile was slightly strained and he wondered what it was she was keeping from him.

The door to the headmaster's study opened and Mr Bunratty came out to greet them. A skinny man in his late fifties, he wore navy corduroy trousers and a checked jacket that had seen better days. He ushered them into his office.

He sat down behind the modern veneered desk and Sheila and Jimmy took the seats opposite him. His secretary came in with three cups of coffee. Once they'd all finished fiddling around with the little sachets of UHT milk and sugar, and the plastic sticks that served as spoons, Mr Bunratty sat back and crossed his hands on his lap.

'So, what can I do for you?' he said.

'It's about Conor,' said Sheila and she looked at Jimmy for encouragement to go on.

He noticed that Mr Bunratty's expression had become more serious at the mention of Conor's name. But the headmaster said nothing and waited for Sheila to speak again.

'Go on, love,' urged Jimmy, watching the headmaster's face intently as he took a sip of coffee.

Sheila spoke about the missing money and the ripped clothes and how Conor feigned illness to stay off school.

'And then last week . . . ' she said and turned to Jimmy.

'He came home from school with a black eye,' said Jimmy, finishing the sentence for her, 'and Sheila and I think he's being bullied.'

Mr Bunratty had listened attentively and now he rubbed his chin and looked fleetingly out the window before his eyes came to rest steadily on them.

'I know,' he said, quietly.

'You know!' Sheila almost shouted. 'You know our son's being bullied and you've done nothing. Why didn't you contact us? Why did you wait for us to come to you?'

'Calm down a minute, Sheila,' said Jimmy. 'Will you let the man speak?'

With a sense of increasing dread he waited for the headmaster to talk. What could explain his failure to involve them? Had Conor done something? What the hell was going on?

'First of all, we don't know who's doing the bullying. We think it's a crowd rather than just one or two individuals. And they're careful not to touch him on the school premises, which makes it very difficult for us to know what's going on, or to get involved. Conor's form teacher came to see me because he was concerned about the change in Conor's behaviour. He'd become withdrawn and reticent. But I'm afraid there's not a lot we can do. Conor refuses to talk about it to any of the staff.'

61

'But why didn't you tell us? And why are they picking on Conor?' demanded Sheila.

Mr Bunratty cleared his throat and Jimmy was sure he blushed.

'Well, that's the thing. We hoped it might blow over. You see . . . what happened was . . . well, Conor has a crush on another boy in his form. He sent him a love-note and the rest of them got hold of it and they've had it in for him ever since. It started off with name calling — you can imagine what — and then progressed to physical attacks. I didn't want to have to tell you this,' he went on, his discomfort evident, and the next sentence tumbled out rapidly, 'but there was talk of him exposing himself to another boy in the toilets. Now that's just hearsay,' he added hastily, 'and it might be purely vindictive gossip.'

Jimmy stared at him in complete astonishment. Was the man mad?

After a pause, Sheila said, 'What do you mean 'a love-note'?'

'Precisely that. Apparently he said he was in love with this boy.'

Sheila was staring at the headmaster with her face screwed up in a frown as if trying very hard to understand what she'd just been told.

'You mean he's . . . are you saying he's gay?' said Sheila shaking her head in disbelief.

'Fourteen is a very difficult age for boys,' replied the headmaster evenly. 'Their bodies are full of raging hormones and they're often very confused about their sexuality. I'm sure this is only a stage he's going through. It's just unfortunate that it's become public knowledge.'

Jimmy felt shame engulf him like a wave. His son was a poofter, a queer, a homo. Exposing himself in a toilet. Jimmy felt physically sick. He couldn't bear to listen to Bunratty making excuses for Conor. Trying to make them feel better. It must be the talk of the whole school, staff and pupils alike. And they'd been the last to find out!

' . . . we'll continue to do everything we can,' Bunratty was saying and Jimmy stood up abruptly.

'I think we'll go now,' he said.

'Yes, I quite understand,' said Mr Bunratty, clearly relieved to be rid of them. 'You'll need time to think this over.'

Wordlessly, Sheila followed Jimmy out of the room.

At the door Mr Bunratty said, 'Do try to talk to Conor, Mrs Gallagher. He's going to need a lot of support until this difficult time passes.'

He extended his hand to Jimmy.

'Thank you,' said Jimmy through clenched teeth as he shook the offered limb lifelessly.

On the way past the secretary's office Jimmy's face burned with shame. They left the building, walked the short distance to the car and got in. Jimmy put the keys in the ignition and sat back.

He'd never been so humiliated in all his life. How could his son, his own flesh and blood, be a homosexual? It was disgusting, revolting. Unnatural.

Neither of them spoke for some time. Sheila rested her elbow on the window ledge and gnawed the knuckles of her left hand.

'What are we going to do?' she asked eventually.

'We're the laughing-stock of the school, the whole town,' he blurted out. 'You know what Ballyfergus is like! We won't be the first to know about this, believe me.'

'Is that all you're worried about? What other people think. What about Conor? Can you imagine what he's going through right now?'

Jimmy ran his hand over his thinning hair and said more softly, 'I just can't believe it.'

'I can,' said Sheila thoughtfully.

'What do you mean?' he said, looking at her in amazement. 'You knew?'

'No. But I've always thought he was different. A bit feminine — gentle and sensitive. I thought he might do something creative or arty. But I never thought he might be gay. Never in my wildest dreams.'

'How can I face him?' groaned Jimmy.

'We're both going to have to. And there's no point getting angry with him, Jimmy. It's not his fault. Maybe Mr Bunratty's right — it might just be a stage he'll grow out of. Or something,' she said unconvincingly. 'It would be best if I tried to talk to him first. Do you think you could just act as if there's nothing wrong?'

Jimmy nodded glumly.

'The school gets out in five minutes,' said Sheila, looking at her watch. 'We'd better get a move on.'

Jimmy turned the key in the ignition, the engine started and they drove home in silence.

He pulled up outside the house and Sheila got out.

'Aren't you coming in?' she asked.

'I can't,' he said, gripping the steering wheel. 'I just can't, Sheila. I'm going to need some time to — to think.'

'Typical!' she said sharply. 'The boys are due home any minute and you're going to run off. Just like that.'

'I'm sorry, Sheila,' he said, humbly. 'I just can't handle this right now.'

'And I can?' she snapped.

It wasn't fair, he knew, to leave Sheila to cope with this on her own right now. But he really didn't trust himself to keep his temper. He felt sure that if Conor came through the door right now, he'd slap him as hard as he could across the face.

She sighed with resignation and said, 'OK. You might do more harm than good in that frame of mind anyway.'

He parked the car down at the promenade, away from where they lived and the school and the prying eyes of anyone who might know him. An old man walked by with a cocker spaniel on a lead. He wound down the car window and the sweet pungent odour of seaweed, the smell of Ballyfergus, wafted in.

He thought of Conor and how he would have to go home and face the lad. A gay son! It was something he'd never thought about, ever. Homosexuals were to be despised and pitied, a source of material for crude jokes, not something you had to face in your own home. Had he nurtured this in Conor? Had he in some way been a deficient father? Was he responsible? Maybe it was heredity. Did he have latent homosexual feelings he wasn't owning up to? He told himself not to be ridiculous.

But how could Conor do this to them? He'd never be able to hold his head up high in Ballyfergus again.

He drove to a pub at the docks where no one knew him well enough to disturb his solitude. He sat at the end of the bar and drank solidly for the rest of the afternoon.

★   ★   ★

Sheila prepared her things for the night shift. Despondently, she folded her white tunic and trousers, and put them in a bag along with flat white shoes, her cap and a navy cardigan. She wondered what the night on A&E duty would bring. Probably the usual domestic violence cases and drunks brought in by the police.

Poor Conor! What an awful time he must be going through. How she hoped it wasn't true! Not for her sake, or for Jimmy's, or because she cared what the rest of Ballyfergus thought. But for Conor's sake because he'd have such a hard life ahead of him. He couldn't stay in Ballyfergus if he wanted to live as a gay man, that was for sure. He'd have to move to a city where there was a gay community, and preferably one outside homophobic Northern Ireland. And even then, would he ever find someone to love him? And what about AIDS? She shuddered involuntarily.

Had she been too protective of him as a boy? Was that why this had happened? Don't be silly, she told herself. It just happens sometimes. She wished Jimmy could accept that. A fat lot of use he was in a crisis, she reflected. She sighed heavily, zipped up the bag and carried it downstairs.

She was totally mad, she reminded herself, thinking about having another baby — she should be more concerned with the way the existing ones were turning out.

When the boys came in she checked Conor's clothes and bag carefully for signs of abuse but there were none.

They ate their tea and, when they asked, Sheila said Jimmy was working an extra shift. She found herself furtively watching Conor, looking for some outward sign of his affliction. But he looked just the way he always did, and the younger boys showed no signs that anything was other than perfectly normal. Perhaps they didn't know their elder brother was suffering this persecution. Sheila resolved to speak to Conor on his own. It would have to be done sooner or later and there was no time like the present.

After the meal, she followed him upstairs to his room, took a deep breath and knocked gently on the bedroom door.

'Who is it?' he said.

'It's only Mum,' she replied, entering the room and closing the door behind her. She sat down beside him on the edge of the bed and asked, 'How was school today?'

'Just the usual,' he said.

Sheila looked about the room at the posters on the walls and wondered if any of the unfamiliar stars were gay icons. She felt her nerve leaving her. She steeled herself and went on.

'Conor,' she said carefully.

'Yes?'

His blue eyes were wide now, anticipating something serious. With his shock of straight blond hair, he reminded her of Jimmy at the same age.

'Your dad and I went to see the headmaster, Mr Bunratty, today.'

Conor sat motionless on the bed and stared at her.

'He told us what's been going on at school,' she said, 'and why.'

Conor's bottom lip quivered like it did when he was a toddler and about to cry. Then, 'Leave me alone! Leave me alone!' he screamed.

'It's OK, Conor. It's OK.'

He threw himself on the bed and buried his face in the pillow. He made no sound but his whole body shook and convulsed alarmingly.

Hesitantly, Sheila extended her hand and rubbed his back until, gradually, he relaxed.

'It's all right, Conor,' she said, soothingly, after some minutes had passed. 'There's nothing to be afraid of. I'm not cross. Look at me.'

Slowly, he lifted his head from the pillow and his eyes met hers, vulnerable and afraid. She longed to hug and kiss him but that would never do, not a boy of fourteen.

'I did something very silly, Mum. I thought he liked me, you see, so I sent him a note but it turned out he was only egging me on. And he showed it to everyone in the class and now they all hate me.'

'I know,' she replied.

'And now everyone's calling me a poof and a sheep-shagger. They take my dinner money and rip my clothes and stuff. And I don't know what to do about it.'

'You've got to fight back, Conor! Ignore what they say. Don't let the taunts get to you. Threaten to report them to the school and, if they don't stop, do it.'

'I can't do that, Mum!'

'What have you got to lose? You can't go on like this, can you?'

He sniffed.

'I reckon threatening them will be enough. Bullies are all cowards underneath.'

'You think so?' he said, doubtfully.

'Oh, I'm quite sure of it,' she said, as confidently as she could.

'I'm glad you know, Mum,' he said and then thought for a bit. 'What did Dad say?'

'Well, he . . . he needs a little bit of time to think about it.' She paused and then added, 'Conor?'

'Yes.'

'Have you always felt like this about boys? Or is it something more recent?'

'I've always known, Mum. Right from I was little. I've never fancied girls. I like them but I don't fancy them. Why?'

'I just wanted to know,' she said, and paused before going on. 'I need to ask you something else. Mr Bunratty mentioned a rumour going about that . . . that . . . you had exposed your . . . private parts in the toilets.'

He shook his head vigorously. 'It's not true!' he said with feeling. 'Justin O'Reilly made that up after the other thing happened.'

'That's OK, son. I believe you,' said Sheila, with relief, and then added, 'I want to give you a hug, Conor. Can I?'

He shifted across the bed and allowed her to embrace him, fully and without protestation, for the first time in years. She kissed the top of his head and rocked him gently in her arms. Far from alienating her, knowing he was gay induced the most protective feelings in her.

'I want you to know that I will always love you no matter what.'

'And Dad?'

'Your dad loves you too but he has a different way of showing it. It's going to take him a little time to take this in. So I want you to be patient with him. But believe me, no matter what he says or does, don't ever doubt that he loves you. More than you will ever know.'

But in spite of her calm exterior and though she meant the words she said, inside Sheila felt a terrible sense of failure. Bad things come in threes, she reminded herself — first Eileen's cancer scare, then her own health problems and now this. Surely that was the end of their troubles for now?

3

'We've only just met,' argued Aiden, across the table in the Chinese restaurant. 'It's very early days.'

'I know that,' replied Claire. 'I'm not trying to rush you into anything but we've been out three times and Mum hasn't met you. She's not going to eat you, you know. And Aunt Sheila wants to meet you too.'

Aiden groaned. 'It'll be your Granny and all next,' he said, feeling he was losing the battle.

'Well, she might be there too,' said Claire mischievously, and then added, more seriously, 'They're not singling you out for special attention, Aiden. It's just that living next door to each other we all know each other's business. It's always been like that. Everyone would think it odd if I didn't take you over and introduce you to the Gallaghers.'

He looked at her expectant face and wondered how he was going to get out of this. If he refused she'd think he wasn't keen on her. He realised that he'd fallen in love with her the day they met. He'd had girlfriends in the past but none had lasted and none were like Claire. It felt like they'd been together for weeks rather than days.

'What is it you're afraid of?' she asked cautiously, her eyebrows knitted into a frown.

'I'm not afraid of anything,' he lied. 'It's just . . . '

He looked anxiously around, at the dusty red fan on the wall and the exotic fish swimming languidly in the tank by the door, searching for a means of escape.

Claire had told him all about her close-knit family and he realised they'd be the type that wanted to involve you. He'd been a loner for so many years that the prospect filled him with dread. A loving family environment had been alien to him for nearly a quarter of a century and he wasn't sure he knew how to function as part of one, albeit on the fringes. His pulse began to race and his face became hot with panic.

But how could he tell Claire? She'd think he was a nutter. He'd scare her off. She lived a perfectly normal existence with family and friends an integral part of her life, as they should be. He was the oddball, the one on the outside, looking in. If he wanted to have a chance with her, he'd have to overcome these irrational fears. And yet it was only a matter of time before she'd start asking questions about his family and his past. Places he didn't want to go. That was why he'd never formed a lasting relationship with anyone before. People always wanted to know so much about you; they couldn't just accept you as they found you.

Claire was waiting for him to speak her face creased with concern.

'What is it?' she said in a low voice, 'Tell me. Are you . . . having second thoughts about us?'

'No, of course not,' he said, anxious to reassure her. He reached for her hand, small and vulnerable in his own. 'No, you're right, Claire,' he said with forced enthusiasm. 'I should meet your family. I'd like to.'

'Well, how about tomorrow night then? Why don't you come to the house for eight? Stay for a cup of tea, and we'll call over and see the Gallaghers. And then we can go out for a quick drink if you like.'

She had it all worked out — how could he let her down?

With difficulty he swallowed a mouthful of cold, bitter beer and said, 'That sounds great.'

The waiter cleared away their plates and they ordered dessert.

'So, is this your treat tonight?' she asked.

'Yes, I got a giro through from Social Services this morning.'

'I know,' she said, pleased with herself. 'I went to see the girls in the payment office and got Janet, she's in charge, to do it straight away.'

'Clever clogs,' he teased. 'Well, here's to us!' He raised his beer bottle and clinked her wineglass.

Afterwards, he took her back to his lodgings. He hoped she didn't think it too grotty. He'd cleaned up and left one bar of the electric fire on so at least the room was cosy.

There were no chairs so Claire perched on the edge of the bed while he boiled the kettle for coffee. Thankfully, he'd remembered to get fresh milk. Claire looked around her, curiously.

'What do you think of it?' he asked.

'It's OK,' she said, 'but don't you miss home?'

'This is home.'

'No, what I mean is, you know, living in a

house with other people, your family.'

He put a teaspoon of coffee granules in each mug and filled them with steaming water. He watched froth form on top of the black liquid as he thought of ways to distract her.

'Milk, no sugar?' he asked.

'That's right,' she said, smiling. 'You remembered.'

He handed her a mug and sat down close beside her, their thighs touching. She smelt of soap and Chinese food.

'But I suppose you're older than I am,' she pondered.

'Thanks,' he said, 'I needed to be reminded of that.'

'Oh, but I like older men,' she reassured him, and then went back to her original train of thought. 'But I can't live with my family forever, can I?' She was nursing the coffee cup in both hands. 'One day I'll have to get a place of my own too.'

'Have I told you that you're beautiful?' he said.

She lifted her head to meet his eye. 'No,' she whispered, 'tell me.'

He wrested the cup gently from her grasp and placed it on the floor beside his.

His heart pounded in his chest as he brushed her cheek, gently, with the back of his hand. Her skin was smooth and tight and flawless. Between her full and slightly parted lips he could see a flash of wet, white teeth. Almost immediately he got an erection. He wanted to consume her.

He leaned forward and their lips met,

74

awkwardly. She pulled away and smiled and then kissed him again, confidently. Their lips explored each other and soon they found a hungry rhythm. He circled her waist with his arm and pulled her body close. Her breath came in heavy sighs. He pushed her gently onto the bed, light-headed, intoxicated with her taste and touch and smell.

Finally their lips parted and he opened his eyes. She was watching him. Unexpectedly she kissed him on the forehead.

'I think you're beautiful too, you know,' she said.

'Men aren't beautiful,' he replied, laughing. 'They're handsome, or rugged or I don't know what. But not beautiful.'

'No,' she said very seriously, stroking his hair, 'you are beautiful.' She kissed his left temple and brushed her lips across his eyebrow. 'I love you,' she whispered in his ear and a ripple of alarm ran through Aiden's body.

'How can you say that?' he said, quietly. 'We've only just met.'

'It doesn't matter,' she said. 'I just know.'

In laying her emotions open to him she should have appeared weak and vulnerable. But there was an unnerving strength about her, a calm purposefulness as she stared unflinchingly into his eyes.

Aiden could not tell her that he loved her. Loving someone was such a terrible risk. He knew because the people he'd loved most in the world had left him. What if Claire did the same?

So he buried his face in her hair, so his eyes would not betray his thoughts, and said nothing.

★　★　★

Aiden put on his leather jacket and, reluctantly, stepped into the fresh, spring night. It was not quite dark yet and a full moon hung like a globe in the sky. But Aiden was too preoccupied to fully enjoy the pleasant walk to Ladas Parade. Why had he agreed to this, he thought, when every fibre in his body fought against it?

He came to the house where Claire lived, and stopped. The lights were on downstairs and in the house next door, where Claire said her aunt and uncle lived. Both houses were semi-detached but not connected to each other, the dividing fence between the properties removed. These were former council houses in a street where most people were now owner-occupiers — you could tell by the well-tended gardens and the replacement PVC window frames.

Aiden swallowed, approached the house on the right and rang the bell. He stepped back startled when the door was opened almost immediately by a slightly plump, middle-aged woman, conservatively dressed in dark trousers and a jumper.

'You must be Aiden,' she said, standing back so he could enter. 'Come on in out of the cold, son.'

He crossed the threshold and stood awkwardly in the hall with his hands wedged in the pockets of his jeans. Standing half a foot taller than Mrs

O'Connor he could see streaks of grey in her short brown hair.

'I'm Eileen, Claire's Mum,' she said.

At first he could see no resemblance to Claire but then, looking more closely, there were similarities in the nose and chin. He wondered with a pang of disappointment if Claire would end up looking like her mother.

'Come on in,' she continued, pleasantly. 'They're in the front room.'

He followed her into a comfortable sitting-room dominated by two green velour sofas and a TV. Claire beamed at him and Paddy got up and shook his hand.

'Nice to see you again, Aiden. I'm afraid I was a bit the worse for wear the last time we met,' he said sheepishly. 'I hope I didn't offend you.'

'No, not in the least. It was Claire who was mortified, not me.'

While Aiden and Claire debated good-naturedly whether this was true or not, Eileen went away to make tea. They made small talk while Paddy, who said little, looked on benignly.

Eileen came into the room with a tray of tea things. Aiden felt as though he was the subject of an initiation ceremony and wished it were over. Claire got up to pour the tea, her black trousers moulded to the round shape of her hips and thighs. He longed to touch her.

She handed him a cup of tea that wobbled uncertainly on a thin china saucer and offered him a chocolate-covered biscuit. He placed it on the saucer where the chocolate instantly melted and stuck to the cup.

'So,' said Eileen, when everyone had their tea and was seated again, 'Claire says you're a steward on the ferries.'

'That's right.'

'Sealink?'

'Yes.'

'As well as working two nights a week in the Club,' said Claire, proudly.

'Yes, your dad told me,' said Eileen. She glanced at Aiden. 'It must keep you busy,' she said absent-mindedly. 'And your family's from Newry, is that right?'

'Yes.'

Mrs O'Connor nodded and took a sip of tea. She seemed preoccupied for she did not pursue the subject further as he'd expected she would.

'We're thinking of going down to Kelly's later on for a drink,' said Claire.

'I was thinking of going down there myself,' said Paddy.

'Dad!' protested Claire, glaring at him.

'He's only winding you up,' said Eileen, and Paddy chuckled.

Claire picked up a cushion and threw it at him, provoking only further laughter. Witnessing this little display of affection, Aiden felt a lump in his throat. He longed for the same sort of intimacy in his life.

Afterwards they went next door to the Gallaghers'. They followed the muffled sounds of the TV through the kitchen and into the sitting-room where Jimmy and his sons were watching football. Jimmy got up and shook Aiden's hand. Then he picked up the remote control and lowered the volume to cries of protest.

'Boys,' he said, 'this is Aiden. This is Martin here, and this is Danny and,' he added, without looking at the teenager in the corner of the room, 'Conor.'

The two younger ones said hello, Conor grunted and they all returned their gaze to the TV.

Jimmy peered at the buttons on the remote, put his forefinger over one and pointed it at the screen. 'Hold on a minute 'til I put this off.'

'No,' said Aiden hastily, 'not on my account. Sure they're enjoying it.'

Jimmy looked at the remote, shrugged and his hand fell to his side.

'Do you watch the football then?' he asked.

'When I can. I don't have a TV in my place.'

'Here,' said Jimmy, hospitably, pointing at his place on the blue leather sofa. 'Sit yourself down and watch this. Sheila'll be down in a minute.'

But before Aiden could take a seat, Sheila came into the room and introduced herself. Her handshake was firm and her smile warm. She looked so much younger than Claire's mum, and so like Claire, that he'd have put them down as sisters. She wore a tight-fitting T-shirt and pale blue jeans on her neat frame and her hair was streaked blonde. Her face was carefully made up but when he looked closely he could see evidence of ageing round her eyes and mouth. But all the same she was a very attractive woman, not that much older than himself.

'Are you not going to offer them a cup of tea?' she said to Jimmy.

'Sure they've only just come through the door,' said Jimmy, defending himself.

'No, it's OK, thanks,' said Claire. 'We had tea next door and we're just going out.'

'Looks like you're not going to get to watch the football after all,' said Jimmy, grinning.

Aiden sensed Sheila appraising him. Their eyes met momentarily and she gave him the briefest of smiles before averting her gaze.

Outside, Aiden breathed a sigh of relief.

'Bet you're glad that's over,' said Claire.

'Oh, it wasn't too bad,' said Aiden thinking about Claire's attractive aunt. 'I thought your house was worse.'

'What do you mean?' said Claire, a touch indignantly.

'It was more . . . well, formal. Your aunt and uncle's house seemed more relaxed.'

'That's funny, it's usually the other way round. But I know what you mean about tonight. Dad doesn't say much at the best of times but I thought Mum was a bit quiet.' After a pause she added, 'What did you think of Aunt Sheila?'

'She seemed very nice.'

'I thought she was staring at you,' said Claire. 'Was she?'

'She was probably sizing me up so she could compare notes with you later on.'

'Yes, she probably was,' said Claire, sounding relieved.

'Is there a big age gap between her and your mum?'

'No, only six years. But I know what you're getting at. Aunt Sheila's really young-looking. I'm always on at Mum to do something with her hair and clothes but she's not interested. She says she's happy the way she is.'

'That's the secret of life, isn't it?'

'What is?'

'Knowing what makes you happy,' he said, taking her hand.

★ ★ ★

It was five-thirty when Jimmy finished his shift and walked home through the mizzling rain. He could bear it no longer. Since the interview at the school, he'd hardly said a word to Conor. He couldn't bring himself to look his son in the eye and ask him about school or anything else. When he looked at Conor all he saw was Mr Bunratty pinned behind his desk, as mortified as he and Sheila had been, telling him that his son was a poof. In the nicest possible way, of course.

It wasn't the boy's fault, he kept telling himself, but it made no difference to the feelings of revulsion that welled up inside him. He ignored Conor and tried to carry on as if there was nothing wrong but the strain was killing him.

Jimmy reached the end of Ladas Parade and looked up the street to where he could see his house in the bend of the road. He remembered Eileen was to have her biopsy today and he shook his head sadly. Sometimes, if you thought too much about all the shit in the world, you began to doubt if there was a God at all.

As he got closer he noticed the car parked on the opposite side of the street. Sheila and Eileen were back and, in a few moments, he would have to face them all, with a smile on his face.

Abruptly Jimmy turned on his heel and retraced his steps quickly — he got to the end of the road, turned left and walked until he reached the chapel.

The heavy oak doors were unlocked and he glanced over his shoulder before slipping inside. In the vestibule he dipped his fingers in the icy holy water, disturbing the pinkish sediment settled in the bottom of the receptacle.

Inside, the chapel was deserted and the air smelt faintly of incense. Only the sound of his heels on the ancient stone floor disturbed the silence. He walked slowly up the aisle to the front of the church, genuflected in front of the altar and sat down wearily on a worn pew. On either side of the tabernacle, candles flickered soothingly behind ruby-coloured glass.

Jimmy slid onto his knees, and rested his head on his joined hands. He prayed for tolerance and understanding so that he could come to terms with his son's homosexuality. But he felt like a fraud. He didn't want to come to terms with it. He wanted Conor to be a perfectly normal boy again.

He heard a soft click and looked up. Father Brennan appeared through one of the side doors behind the altar. The old priest wore his everyday black suit and collar and had a piece of paper in his hand, which he placed on the lectern. Noticing Jimmy, he came down and sat in the pew behind him.

After a few minutes' silence he said, 'I'm just setting up for a wedding in the morning. It's John Pettigrew's son, Martin. He's marrying a wee girl from Glenarm, one of the Mulhollands.'

That's something he would never see, thought Jimmy bitterly — Conor getting married.

The priest was quiet again and then said, 'What brings you here at this time, Jimmy?'

Jimmy got up off his knees and sat on the wooden bench without turning round to face the priest.

'I've things on my mind.'

Another pause.

'Is it something you'd like to talk about?'

'No, I don't think there's anything anybody can do to help.'

'You might be surprised. A problem shared is a problem halved.'

Jimmy shrugged. He respected the clergy, not least for the sacrifice they made in remaining celibate, and he liked old Father Brennan. It wouldn't do any harm to tell him. He might even be able to put a different perspective on things.

'If you like we can go into a confessional,' offered the voice behind his ear.

'No, if it's all the same, I'll just tell you here,' replied Jimmy, looking round at the empty church. 'It's not a confession I want to make anyway.'

'What is it then?'

'It's . . . well . . . I don't know how to put it.'

The priest offered no help and waited for Jimmy to go on.

'We . . . our son Conor . . . well, it turns out he's gay.'

The priest considered this and then asked, 'And what makes you think that?'

Jimmy told him about the bullying at school and the interview with Mr Bunratty. He was relieved to unburden himself at last.

'And how do you feel about this?'

'I feel disgusted with Conor. I can't believe it. My son a poof! Sorry, Father, but it makes me sick to think of it.'

'And Sheila?'

Jimmy thought about this before he replied. 'She didn't seem all that surprised, not once the initial shock had worn off. And she doesn't seem as upset as I am.'

'Women are often more intuitive about these things,' said Father Brennan. 'You know, Seamus Bunratty is a very able headmaster. I'm sure he's right when he says it's probably something Conor will grow out of. He's only fourteen, after all.'

'But what if it isn't? Now when I look at him, I can see traits in him that I should have seen before. I should have noticed.'

'Like what?'

'He's kind of effeminate and slight and he's never taken to sports the way the other two have. And when I think about it, all his friends have been a bit like that too.'

'You'll have to learn to accept him the way he

is. If he is homosexual, there's nothing he can do to change that. But,' he said carefully, 'he can make choices about how he lives.'

'What do you mean?'

'It's a sin in the eyes of God to give in to homosexual desires. It might be helpful if you encouraged him to find a vocation that occupied him, kept him on the straight and narrow.'

'Like what?' said Jimmy, wondering where the conversation was going.

'Well, there's the priesthood. I hear Conor's a bright boy.'

Jimmy tensed and was glad that Father Brennan couldn't see his face. He thought of recent scandals in the church about homosexuals and paedophiles and he wanted to get up and run away. Father Brennan was suggesting his son become a priest just because he was queer!

Whilst Jimmy had a certain respect for the church, never in his wildest dreams would he have wished the priesthood on one of his sons. Never to know the warmth of human love, moved from one parish to the next like a nomad until you were too old to be of use any more. And then you ended your days, cared for by nuns, in a draughty home for retired priests in the West of Ireland.

Suddenly, Jimmy's anger towards Conor was redirected towards Father Brennan. The priesthood! Was that all Conor had to look forward to? It was bad enough that he'd never know what it was like to have a wife or family. He'd never live a normal life. If he was lucky he might find a partner somewhere, but he'd never be able to live openly as a queer in Ballyfergus, that's for sure.

'Have a think about it,' said Father Brennan and he pressed a bony hand on Jimmy's shoulder.

★ ★ ★

Maureen O'Farrell slipped out the side door of the Star of the Sea, just as quietly as she'd entered the chapel. Her rubber-soled shoes made no sound on the flagstones and she held her breath until she was safely outside.

Whoever would have thought! The Gallaghers' son was a homosexual! You read about these things in the papers, of course, but here! In Ballyfergus! And imagine sitting there, telling Father Brennan all about it, bold as brass. What was the world coming to, talking to a priest about filth like that?

Affronted, she shook her umbrella open vigorously and set off at a brisk pace. Bursting to tell someone, she thought briefly of calling at Mrs White's, then disregarded the idea. Her news would have much more impact if she saved it for tomorrow's coffee morning at the church hall.

She experienced a brief pang of conscience when she thought of her friend, Moira Devlin. But, if people would go blabbing in public, well, she could hardly be blamed for overhearing. After all, they could have gone into a confessional — that's what they were there for. If

86

you choose not to then, well, what did people expect?

★ ★ ★

Eileen lay in bed, relieved, at last, to have the house to herself. The strain of keeping up appearances had exhausted her but she wouldn't have to do that for much longer. She looked at the bedside clock. The appointment with the consultant was at two o'clock — just five hours until she'd know whether or not the cancer had returned.

Eileen tried to convince herself that the cancer had recurred so that she would be prepared when the bad news came. But hope would not be quelled and no matter how hard she tried she could not quite believe it. She tried to imagine breaking the news to Claire and Paddy but it was too painful to pursue these thoughts.

'Come on, Eileen,' she chided herself. 'This isn't helping.'

She got out of bed and went into the bathroom. She picked a towel off the floor where Claire had dropped it, and smiled. Her slatternly habits were rubbing off on that girl. Suddenly Eileen felt a longing to be near her daughter. She held the towel to her face and inhaled through her nose, the way she used to do with Claire's clothes when she was a baby. Foolishly, she expected to smell sweet baby skin but the towel was damp and smelled faintly of washing-powder.

'This won't do,' she said crossly and draped

the towel over the radiator to dry.

Eileen got in the shower and washed her body with Dove soap, avoiding the place where her left breast had once been. When she was finished she went through to the bedroom to dry herself. She caught a glimpse of her body in the mirror on the wall and stopped to look at her reflection.

She saw a plump woman, past her prime, with a terrible disfigurement instead of a breast. Eileen trembled with revulsion, not at her appearance for she'd come to see that as an acceptable price to pay for an extended life. But at the thought that a malignant disease was spreading, unseen and undetected, throughout her body. And there was nothing she could do to stop it.

She turned away from the mirror. She mustn't think like this — she must be strong. She paused momentarily to compose herself and then re-commenced the business of getting ready.

She found a clean bra in a drawer, inserted a prosthesis in a special pocket sewn into the left cup, and put it on. Then she put on the rest of her clothes, brushed her hair and went downstairs. She attempted to eat breakfast but managed only a cup of tea.

When the phone rang it made her jump. It was Sheila.

'I just wanted to check you were OK,' she said. 'I'm phoning you from work.'

'I'm fine,' said Eileen. 'No, I'm not. I'm afraid to find out.'

'I know,' said Sheila, her voice faint on the line. 'It's only natural.'

There was talking in the background and Sheila said, 'Hang on a minute.' When she came back on the line, she said, 'I'm really sorry, love, but I've got to go. I'll pick you up at half past twelve.'

'Right,' said Eileen. 'Bye, Sheila,' she added hastily but the line had gone dead.

She listened to the buzz for a few moments and then replaced the receiver. She wondered what on earth she was going to do for the next three hours. She walked aimlessly, from room to room, and all she could think about was sitting in front of Dr. Wright. She knew what the expression on his face would be when he broke the news to her, because she'd seen it before. She knew what he'd say and how he'd try to reassure her. She even guessed what he'd recommend — the removal of her remaining breast followed by more radiotherapy, or chemotherapy if the cancer had spread beyond the breast tissue . . .

She must do something to stop driving herself mad with these thoughts! She looked round the bedroom she'd shared all her married life with Paddy, at the unmatched bits of furniture and the clothes strewn on the unmade bed. A great anger welled up inside her at the unfairness of it and, violently, she tugged the duvet off the bed onto the floor.

Panting with exertion she removed the duvet cover, sheet and pillowcases, bundled the dirty linen into a ball and threw it down the stairs. Next, she did the same with Claire's bed. In the bathroom she changed all the towels and heaved the dirty ones over the banister.

Downstairs she scooped up an armful of towels. In her haste she stumbled over the remaining laundry on the floor, steadied herself against the wall and carried on through to the kitchen. She loaded the machine, poured washing-powder liberally into the drawer and slammed the door shut. The machine chugged into action.

She got the Hoover out and vigorously pushed the machine back and forth across the hall carpet. She started to sweat under the arms, stopped, stripped down to a cotton top and threw her jumper on the floor.

Exhausted she leaned against the wall and noticed the grubby marks on the glass-panelled door to the sitting-room. Leaving the Hoover where it was, she ran back to the kitchen, opened a cupboard and hauled bottles of bleach and toilet duck onto the floor.

'There it is,' she said triumphantly, grabbing a half-empty container of glass cleaner and a soiled cloth. Back in the hall she alternatively sprayed and rubbed the small squares of glass until they sparkled.

'Sheila would be proud of me,' she shouted above the noise of the Hoover and laughed out loud at the thought of her sister finding her so industriously employed.

⋆　⋆　⋆

Moira cut the Battenburg cake into four equal slices and arranged them on a plate alongside four Rich Tea biscuits and two of her own fruit scones. She put the kettle on and laid out cups and saucers and paper napkins for two on a tray.

How she wished she hadn't invited Maureen O'Farrell round for morning coffee! It had seemed like a good idea when she'd met her last week in the High Street. But that was before she knew Eileen would be getting the results of her biopsy today and now she could think of nothing else. Naturally, that made small-talk tiresome and even the prospect of some juicy titbit of gossip from Maureen couldn't raise Moira's spirits.

When the doorbell went she adopted her cheeriest smile but it didn't fool Maureen.

'Are you all right, Moira?' she asked, stepping over the threshold. 'You don't look at all well.'

'Me? I'm as fit as a fiddle,' said Moira firmly. 'Come on in and I'll put the kettle on.'

Maureen took off her coat and followed Moira into the kitchen. Moira made the coffee and carried it through to the sitting-room, listening absent-mindedly as Maureen rattled her way through a week's worth of gossip.

Then Maureen paused, set her cup and saucer down and folded her hands in her lap.

'Of course, I was sorry to hear about your Conor,' she said, her eyes wide like saucers.

'Conor?' repeated Moira.

Maureen blinked several times, feigning discomfort. 'It was the talk of the church on Friday morning. The talk of Ballyfergus if you're to believe the gossip.'

'What was?' asked Moira, hiding her irritation behind a smile.

Maureen put a hand over her mouth, her eyelids fluttering like butterfly wings. 'Well . . . I . . . ' she said in a show of embarrassment, 'I didn't want to be the one to tell you. Don't you know?'

'If I knew I wouldn't be asking,' said Moira dryly.

'Now it might just be a rumour. You know what people are like.'

Moira waited patiently, as she knew she must, while Maureen extracted maximum impact from her disclosure.

'Now I don't believe it myself,' said Maureen, reassuringly, 'and I said so to Annie Robertson but once a rumour like this takes hold it's hard to squash.'

'What sort of rumour?' asked Moira.

Barely disguising the glee in her voice, Maureen announced with a flourish, 'That your grandson, Conor Gallagher, is homosexual.'

'Don't be ridiculous,' said Moira, crossly.

'Now, Moira, don't take it out on me. I'm only telling you what I heard.'

'And where did such a ludicrous story start? Who told you?'

'Oh, I can't remember where it started,' said Maureen vaguely, 'but apparently he sent a love-note — '

'Oh, please!' said Moira holding up her hand. 'I really don't want to hear any more of this nonsense!'

Inside she was seething but, in spite of her

determination not to show her anger to Maureen, she felt her face flush. How dare people make up horrible stories about Conor! She knew he'd been having a bit of bother at school. Surely it wasn't related to these allegations? Did Sheila and Jimmy know something they hadn't told her?

'Like I say, love, don't blame me. I'm only the messenger.'

'I'm not blaming you, Maureen,' said Moira sweetly, as a wave of nausea threatened to overwhelm her. 'Look,' she went on, standing up abruptly, 'I don't mean to be rude but I've got to go out now.'

Maureen's beady eyes followed Moira's to the clock on the mantlepiece.

'Have you an appointment at the doctor's? You do look a bit peaky to me. If you like I'll walk down with you.' She eased herself out of the chair.

'No, I'm not going to the doctor's. There's nothing wrong with me.'

Maureen sat back in the chair and waited for Moira to go on.

'I'm going round to Eileen's as a matter of fact,' said Moira.

'Everything all right?'

'Yes. No,' said Moira and she put her hands up to her face.

'What is it, pet? What's wrong?' said Maureen.

Moira felt a terrible urge to unburden herself.

'It's Eileen,' she said. 'She gets the results of a biopsy today. Her and Sheila are going up to the Royal this afternoon.'

93

'Cancer?'

'We don't know but it looks very likely.'

'Oh, love, I'm so sorry. That's terrible news, so it is. How awful for you!'

A vague sense of unease disturbed Moira. She realised too late that she shouldn't have told Maureen.

'Now you mustn't go round telling people,' she said hastily. 'Eileen doesn't want anyone to know until we find out for sure, one way or the other.'

'Oh, yes, I quite understand. Don't you worry about that.'

'I'd better go now or I'll miss her,' said Moira.

'Of course, love,' said Maureen soothingly, and she was out the door before Moira had time to extract any more assurances of discretion.

★ ★ ★

Eileen was on her knees rubbing furiously at a stubborn mark on the glass when someone switched the Hoover off at the plug. She looked up to find her mother standing there with her coat on.

'Jesus, Mary and Joseph! Eileen, what's going on here? I came round to see how you were.'

Eileen looked at the laundry piled at the foot of the stairs, the Hoover abandoned in the hall, the open cupboard in the kitchen and the contents strewn on the floor.

She wiped her brow with the back of her hand and stood up.

'I'm cleaning,' she said, 'and changing the

94

beds and doing the laundry.'

'I can see that. But why today of all days?'

'Because I needed something to do,' said Eileen, suddenly overcome with fatigue.

She sagged against the doorjamb.

'Come on, love,' said her mother gently. 'Come and sit down.'

She led Eileen into the kitchen where she sank into a chair.

Under Moira's critical gaze, Eileen self-consciously patted her hair where it stood on end after ripping off her jumper, and looked down at her top. Sweat-stains spread out below the armpits. She felt weak and so very, very tired.

'What have you had to eat today?' said Moira.

'Nothing. Some tea.'

Moira tutted, took off her coat and hung it on the back door. 'You go on upstairs and clean yourself up. I'll make you a sandwich. It'll be ready in a minute.'

Suddenly Eileen was so very grateful her mum was there, taking charge, telling her what to do. She got up and nearly tripped over the things on the floor.

'That's all right love,' said Moira. 'I'll sort all that out for you.'

When she came downstairs again, after a few minutes, the Hoover was stacked neatly against the wall, the laundry and cleaning things had disappeared and lunch for both of them was on the table.

'I feel sick,' said Eileen.

'You must try and eat, Eileen,' said her mother, leading her gently to the table. 'You

95

need something in you.'

She held Eileen's hand in hers and they sat there, in silence, until the doorbell went. Eileen felt the pressure of the hand squeezing her own and she could see tears in her mother's eyes. She must get out quickly before one of them broke down.

At the door Moira gave her a brief, but fierce, embrace and said, 'Good luck, love.'

As they drove off she stood in the doorway and waved cheerfully with a smile pasted on her face, as though her daughters were setting off on a pleasant jaunt.

In the car, Sheila asked Eileen how she was.

'Do you mind if we talked about something else? I don't want to think about it.'

'No, of course not,' said Sheila and she glanced across at her sister, before pulling out onto the dual carriageway to Belfast.

She put the car into fifth gear, looked in the rear-view mirror and moved into the left-hand lane.

'What did you think of Claire's new boyfriend?' she asked, once they were progressing along at steady speed.

'Well, I'm not really that keen on him. He's too old for her and he's, well, he's only a ship steward and a barman. Apparently he's living in some sort of bedsit in Carson Street.'

Sheila snorted with laughter. 'God, Eileen, that's rich coming from you.'

'What do you mean?' said Eileen, indignantly.

'You're saying he's not good enough for her, is that right?'

'I think she could do better, that's all. And we don't know anything about his family.'

'You do realise that you sound exactly like Mum?'

'I do not.'

'Yes, you do. When you were going out with Paddy that's *exactly* what she said about him — too old and too poor.'

'That was different,' sniffed Eileen.

'Was it? Let me ask you this. What's more important? That she's happy or marries someone well off?' asked Sheila.

'I thought he was a bit shifty.'

'You're only saying that. He's perfectly all right. And Claire seems very keen on him.'

'I know,' said Eileen and sighed. 'I just want the best for her, that's all.'

'We all do,' said Sheila.

'I'd like to see her settled before, you know . . . '

They both fell silent. Sheila shifted in her seat and cleared her throat the way she did when she had something important to say. Eileen guessed correctly that it would be about Claire.

'On the subject of Claire,' said Sheila at last, 'don't you think it's time you told her?'

'About the cancer?'

'No. You know what I mean,' said Sheila, and Eileen knew perfectly well.

'No, I don't. And I don't want to talk about it. I can't believe you raised that today.'

'I'm sorry,' said Sheila hastily. 'You're right. I shouldn't have said anything.'

Another silence and then Sheila spoke again,

this time on a different subject. Painfully, she told Eileen all about Conor and the visit to the headmaster.

'God, you don't think he's really gay, do you? I never would have thought . . . How has Jimmy taken it?'

'Not well, as you can imagine. And to be honest I'm having difficulty coming to terms with it myself.'

So Conor Gallagher, her nephew, was gay. The poor lad! She'd better not tell Paddy. Whenever Graham Norton came on the TV, Paddy called him a queer and refused to watch even though she and Claire thought he was hilarious.

They merged with other lanes of traffic speeding into the city and Sheila peered at the overhead signposts. Eileen looked at the digital clock on the dashboard. An hour to go and they were already on the outskirts of Belfast city. The journey was going far too quickly.

'Are you speeding?' she asked.

'No, why?'

'Just wondered,' said Eileen and she glared at the passing warehouses and factories.

'We're making perfect time, Eileen.'

Tears pricked Eileen's eyes and the passing buildings and overpasses became a blur. How she wished they were driving anywhere in the world, rather than where they were going.

★ ★ ★

Moira watched the car drive off and her cheery smile evaporated instantly. She went inside and sat on the bottom stair and noticed that the skirting-board was thick with dust.

Eileen had not asked her to come with them and Moira had not offered. She told herself that Sheila was the best person to accompany Eileen to the hospital — she'd understand all the medical jargon and ask the right questions. And Sheila would know what to say if it was bad news — as a nurse she was used to dealing with these things.

When the girls were growing up Moira had always been strong for them. They'd rarely seen her cry and she remembered how her own mother had been a solid rock on which she'd leant. She knew that if the news was bad, she wouldn't be able to keep a stiff upper lip and she couldn't let Eileen see her breaking down.

Thinking of the ordeal her daughter was about to undergo, Moira allowed herself to cry quietly, rocking back and forth gently on the stair where she sat. Then, suddenly cross with herself, she brushed away the tears. Crying was no use to anyone — what Eileen needed was practical help, not sentimentality. She looked around the dusty hallway and thought that the least she could do was give the house a thorough going-over. It might not get another one for a very long time.

So Moira spent the rest of the day cleaning and polishing and ironing sheets and changing beds until she was worn out. But it provided a release for all her pent-up anxiety and when she'd finished she looked round with some satisfaction — the place was like a new pin.

Claire was just about to lock up when Maureen O'Farrell appeared in front of her desk. The waiting-room was deserted.

'How can I help you, Mrs O'Farrell?' she asked politely, wondering what on earth this old lady was doing in the Jobseekers' office.

'Oh, I just popped in for one of these forms,' she said waving a Jobseekers' Allowance application in her hand.

'For yourself?' said Claire, with unconcealed scepticism.

'Oh, no,' she said, stuffing the form into her handbag, 'it's for my son, Herby.'

'Doesn't he have a job at the Sports Centre?'

'Well, yes, he does for now. But you never know how long these temporary jobs are going to last, do you?'

'No, I suppose not,' agreed Claire, wondering if Mrs O'Farrell was going senile.

The old woman put her arm through the straps of her handbag and Claire looked pointedly at the wall clock.

'So,' said Mrs O'Farrell, 'how are you, love?'

'I'm great. Thanks for asking. Look, if you don't mind, it's after five and we were just about to — '

'Your granny told me about your mum. You're being ever so brave,' said Mrs O'Farrell. 'It must be terrible for you.'

100

Claire looked at her blankly.

'I had tea with Moira this morning. She told me that Eileen's gone up to Belfast to get the result of her biopsy.'

But Mum had gone shopping with Aunt Sheila. In Belfast. Claire felt tears welling up in her eyes. Surely this couldn't be true.

'Oh my God,' said Mrs O'Farrell, 'you don't know! When Moira said not to tell anyone, I thought she meant, well, you know, anyone outside the family.'

Claire pushed back her chair and stood up. She stared at Mrs O'Farrell, then turned and fled. In the staffroom she grabbed her coat and ran out of the building. Outside she looked for a bus but there was none in sight so she started to run home and soon had to stop to catch her breath. If Granny told Maureen O'Farrell all this, it must be true. But why hadn't Mum told her and Dad?

She put increased urgency into her pace. She must get home and see Mum. Maybe this was just some awful rumour that Maureen O'Farrell had started — Aunt Sheila was always saying she was a nosy old troublemaker. Claire told herself that Mum would be in the kitchen making tea and it would all turn out to be a pack of lies.

But when she got to 28 Ladas Parade, the kitchen was empty. The surfaces were clear, the floor washed and everything sparkled and shone. Something was amiss.

Claire leaned against the back door and it shut with a loud click. Her dad appeared in the doorway. The serenity of his expression told her he knew nothing about a hospital visit.

'Where's Mum?' asked Claire breathlessly.

'She's out shopping with Sheila. They're not back yet.'

'Where did they go?'

'Belfast, I think. Why?' he asked, a furrow appearing in his brow.

'They've not gone shopping,' she said flatly.

'What are you talking about, love? Come here and take the weight off your feet. You look done in.'

He pulled out a chair and indicated for her to sit down, but Claire remained standing.

'She's gone to the hospital, Dad. For the results of a biopsy.'

'A biopsy?' he repeated, his face crumpling in on itself as her words sank in. 'No, it can't be . . . '

He sat down heavily in the chair he'd pulled out for Claire and stared at her, his shoulders rounded like an old man. Compassion over-whelmed Claire.

'No, Dad,' she said, briskly, 'I don't believe it either. It was Maureen O'Farrell told me and you know what an old windbag she is.'

He nodded.

'You can't believe a word she says.'

He nodded again.

'Mum'll be home in no time and it'll all be sorted out.'

But he never answered. He just stared unseeing at the kitchen wall.

*   *   *

'Let's stop here,' said Eileen and Sheila pulled into the carpark without protest.

The shadow of Carrickfergus Castle loomed black and imposing over the dull grey waters of Strangford Lough.

'Do you remember how we used to love coming here as kids?' said Eileen.

'Yes,' said Sheila, in a voice that sounded small and tight.

'And your boys used to love running around pretending they were knights in battle.'

'They're a bit old for that now,' said Sheila, clearing her throat, 'or at least they think they're too old.'

Eileen looked out over the sea and felt a relative calmness descend on her. There was something comforting about being near the water, listening to the clicking of the pebbles. She thought that drowning wouldn't be such a bad death after all. She imagined it would be kind of peaceful, giving yourself up to the cold brine.

Eileen got out of the car and sat on a bench overlooking the shingle beach. The shoreline was exposed and a sharp wind tousled her hair. Her eyes stung from the crying she'd done and now they felt dry and itchy. She listened to the gentle lapping of the waves on the pebbles. Each one of them had been there a million years and would still be there long after she'd gone.

She felt her sister come up behind her.

'Eileen, we're going to have to go home,

sooner or later. It's nearly five o'clock. We can't sit here all day. Everyone will be worried.'

'I don't know if I can tell them, Sheila,' she said. 'It's different this time, you see. I won't be getting better.'

'Don't say that . . . '

'No, I know. I *feel* it.'

She looked out over the water and thought of the likely treatment she would have to undergo, so sensitively glossed over by the consultant. There would be further surgery and drugs accompanied by sickness and terrible pain and all of it would be a waste of time.

Eileen's faith had never been strong and now it all but evaporated. She found no comfort in the notions of purgatory and heaven and eternity. One day very soon her brain would just cease functioning and that would be it — her life extinguished in an instant. She would have no memory, no consciousness, just nothingness. And she would be alone.

Right now she believed only in the wrath of God. What had she done that was so terrible to deserve this fate? When she was little and the man had hurt her, she believed she'd done something naughty to deserve it. Of course she'd long since outgrown that notion but the suspicion that her misfortunes were some sort of retribution remained.

She'd always tried to live a decent, moral life. The only thing she'd ever done that she felt guilty about was taking Claire. Back then she'd thought her a gift from God, that it was meant to be. But now, looking back, maybe it was a test and she'd failed. So desperate was she for a baby of her own that she'd put her own desires before those of others, not thinking of the consequences . . .

'It's not fair,' she sobbed and put her hands over her face. 'What have I done to deserve this?'

'I know, love. I know,' whispered Sheila. 'But you can't just give up, Eileen. You've got to fight this thing. Come on. It's time to go home.'

They said little on the drive back to Ballyfergus, along winding country roads through familiar villages and hamlets. Each one brought back memories of days out or cycling excursions in the summer holidays and suddenly they all seemed so idyllic. Even the Glynn, with its red, white and blue-painted kerbstones and 'Red Hand of Ulster' flags tied to every lamppost, had a certain charm where once it had terrified her as she'd sped through on her bike as fast as her little legs could pedal.

'How do you want to do this?' asked Sheila when Ballyfergus came into view.

On reflection, thought Eileen, she should have told Paddy and Claire the truth about the hospital visits. At least they would have had some advance warning. Now the news, delivered to them completely out of the blue, would be all the more devastating.

'Do you want me to tell Mum? And Jimmy and the boys?' suggested Sheila.

'Yes,' said Eileen hoarsely and she swallowed, fighting to hold back more tears.

Sheila parked the car across the road from their houses. She looked at her watch.

'Claire and Paddy should be home by now,' she said and they both peered at the net curtain in Eileen's front window. 'Are you sure you don't want me to come in with you?'

'No, I'm quite sure,' said Eileen. 'This is something we're going to have to face alone, just the three of us.'

Sheila looked away and, almost imperceptibly, nodded her head. Without further discussion, they got out of the car and crossed the road.

Eileen opened the back door and stepped inside. Paddy sat at the kitchen table laid for tea with the evening paper in front of him but, oddly, he wasn't reading it but staring into space. Claire was at the cooker with her back to Eileen. The room was full of the smell of fried onions and pork chops.

Claire turned around and Eileen watched the colour drain from her face. Claire stopped what she was doing and walked over to Paddy. She stood behind him and put her hands on each of his shoulders, protectively. He seemed to awaken from the stupor he was in and he too turned and stared at her. Neither of them spoke.

'Where've you been, Mum?' asked Claire at length, her voice little more than a whisper, and Eileen could see her fingers digging into the flesh on Paddy's shoulders.

Eileen shook her head slowly and closed her eyes. The smell of the food made her nauseous and her legs felt weak. There was a silence in the room that seemed to last forever and everything that happened next was in slow motion.

'Eileen,' said Paddy's voice and she opened

her eyes. He was standing right in front of her. 'Eileen, tell us what's wrong.'

Eileen looked at Claire and then at Paddy, their faces frozen with tension.

'It's come back,' she said. 'The cancer's come back.'

And then she fainted.

★　★　★

When Eileen came round, Sheila was bending over her.

'She's all right,' said Sheila. 'She just fainted. Eileen, are you OK?'

'I'm fine.'

Sheila and Paddy helped Eileen to her feet and sat her down in a chair. The small kitchen was crowded now like it was on the rare occasions when Eileen and Paddy threw a party. As well as Sheila, Paddy, and Claire, Moira and Jimmy had joined them.

The pungent smell of burning filled the air.

'Oh, no,' cried Claire.

Gingerly, she pulled the smoking frying-pan off the heat and turned the gas off. Jimmy wrapped a tea towel round the pan handle and took it out the back door while Moira opened the window.

'Why don't we all go through to the front room?' said Moira. 'Eileen needs a bit of air.'

Everyone filed out until there was only Paddy left. He sat down beside Eileen and took her hand.

'Are you sure?' he asked.

'Quite sure, Paddy. Sheila and I went to see the consultant today. I'm sorry, love.'

'Isn't there anything he can do?'

'Oh, yes, plenty. He'll probably want to . . . ' she began and her voice tailed off. 'To take off the other breast,' she said quickly.

Paddy blinked and his Adam's apple bobbed up and down.

'And there'll be chemotherapy. Or radio-therapy . . . '

'Don't . . . ' he said and looked at the table. 'Why didn't you tell me?' he asked in a hurt voice and Eileen watched a single tear splash onto the table-top.

'I — I didn't want you and Claire to worry. I thought maybe everything would be all right.'

'Oh, Eileen . . . '

4

At ten o'clock the following Tuesday, Sheila found herself, once more, in the doctor's waiting-room. She rolled up her sleeve and examined the small, dirty-looking bruise in the crook of her elbow where the nurse had taken blood. Much as she tried to convince herself that the results of the blood tests would prove Dr Crory wrong, she felt incredibly anxious. Her stomach muscles knotted when a figure appeared in the doorway but it was only the district nurse looking for a stray patient. She smiled at Sheila and moved briskly on.

What had she got to be anxious about? thought Sheila. She thought of Eileen's scar and instinctively pressed her arm protectively against her own breasts. The consultant had described the cancer as aggressive. He wanted to remove tissue from under Eileen's arm to see if the cancer had spread to the lymph nodes. And, if it had, then chemo, and the horrific side-effects that accompanied it, would follow the removal of her breast. Sheila knew Eileen's chances were slim — they could hope for a few months — maybe a year or two, if she was very lucky.

Sheila fought the urge to dissolve into tears. The last few days, and especially Friday, had been so demanding that she simply felt drained. And this was only the start — she'd have to find a better way to cope over the next weeks and months.

She wondered where Eileen and Paddy were now. In a waiting-room, like herself? Or sitting in front of the consultant while he outlined the proposed treatment, as detached and professional as all his training and years of experience would allow.

So, when her name was called, Sheila's mind was elsewhere than on her own troubles. She gathered up her things and went along the corridor to Dr Crory's surgery. He greeted her with a grim smile.

'I'm sorry about Eileen,' he said, with genuine concern. 'It's bad luck.'

'Yes, it is,' said Sheila.

'Now,' he said, settling behind his desk, 'it's you we're here to talk about today.'

He opened the pink folder that contained Sheila's notes, and the blood drained from her face.

He removed a piece of paper from her file and said, 'This is the lab report.' He placed the paper in front of Sheila and pointed with his index finger. 'Look here,' he went on, 'This shows the level of FSH/LH reading.'

Sheila looked at the figures scrawled on the report. 'What do they mean?' she asked with trepidation.

'Well, according to these figures,' said Doctor Crory, 'you're definitely menopausal.'

Sheila looked out the window, through the narrow slats of the Venetian blinds. There was a tree outside, bathed in spring sunshine. It was in bud, ready to burst with new growth. She looked away quickly.

'Are you sure?' she said, not because she doubted the doctor's words, but simply because he was waiting for her to speak.

'I'm sure.'

'So you were right all along,' she said.

'I never really doubted it, Sheila. You're demonstrating the classic symptoms.'

If she was honest with herself, deep down she'd known that too. But on a conscious level she'd refused to acknowledge it. And, in spite of her medical training, she realised how little she knew about the menopause or its treatment. Perhaps it wasn't all bad news.

'Is it — is there anything we can do to reverse or delay it?' she asked.

'No, the treatment is really all about managing the symptoms. There's nothing you can do to turn the clock back.'

'Does this mean I can't get pregnant?'

'It's not impossible but, given the erratic nature and decreasing frequency of your periods, it's unlikely. I wouldn't recommend it either. The menopause is nature's way of telling you that your childbearing days are over. You've three healthy sons, Sheila. I'm afraid you're going to have to accept the fact that you're not going to have any more children.'

Anger welled up inside her. Who was he to tell her whether or not she could have another baby? She was sick of people telling her to be grateful for what she had. Why was it so wrong to want more?

'So what treatment do you recommend?' she asked, businesslike.

'Your slight build puts you at risk of developing osteoporosis, especially as you've started the menopause so young. So I'd like to book you in for a bone-density scan and arrange for you to see an endocrine specialist to get you on some HRT.'

Sheila stared at the doctor as panic swept through her. She saw herself as an old woman with brittle bones and a bent spine.

'HRT? Isn't that linked to breast cancer and blood clots?'

'There have been some studies suggesting a link, yes, but for most women it's the best option. Your sister's history of breast cancer will be taken into consideration. But I'm not an expert on this — we'll need to see what the specialist thinks, especially in view of your relatively young age.'

When Sheila came out of the surgery she was in a daze. Outside, the sunshine seemed unbearably bright and she couldn't bear the sound of children playing on the grass outside the health centre. All she wanted to do was scream. She hurried to the car, got in, and sat for some time staring at the grassy bank. The April sun beat in through the window, full of warmth and the promise of summer.

All this talk of osteoporosis and HRT terrified her — she felt as though she was losing control of her body. She'd always been fit and healthy. She'd taken care of herself. And now she was to be pumped full of drugs. It all

112

sounded so unnatural.

She thought of the bags of baby clothes in the attic and remembered the day Jimmy had tried to throw out the pram. Not that it mattered now. The idea of having another baby had grown slowly and was, before this news, by no means a fixed plan. But now that the chance was slipping away from Sheila, suddenly, it became the one thing in the world she desperately wanted.

The menopause signalled the end of her femininity — it was all downhill from here. She only had to look around her — Ballyfergus was full of menopausal middle-aged women willing to share their case histories with anyone who would listen. Was she to become one of their ranks? Angrily she thumped the steering wheel with her clenched fist and winced.

She massaged her hand where she'd hurt it and the tears came freely, lubricated by the pain she'd inflicted on herself. All she'd wanted was one more chance. Now she would never hold in her arms the baby girl that she'd seen so often in her dreams. Or smell and touch the soft flesh of a baby daughter's skin, so different from a boy. She'd had all that once and it had been taken away from her, so cruelly. She loved the boys, of course. Each one of them was precious. But a daughter was special. Your boys grew up and grew away. Mothers and daughters only got closer as the years went by.

She thought about the silly teenage girl she'd been over two decades ago and the memories of that time were clearer now than they'd been in years. Hatred began to well up inside her, the like of which she had never experienced. It was so strong and so bitter it almost made her retch and she was shocked.

'You fucking bastards! Mum and Eileen and you too, Jimmy!' she shouted. 'You had no right to take her! No right at all!'

She sobbed quietly for a while and then got out a tissue, blew her nose and wiped away her tears.

'What a stupid little idiot, you were then,' she said softly to herself. 'A stupid little fool.'

⋆ ⋆ ⋆

Kate Bush, Meat Loaf and Boney M dominated the charts in the summer of '78 and Sheila Gallagher knew the words to every single song. At the age of fifteen she had her whole life ahead of her and the world at her feet. For a start she was good-looking, everyone said so, and Jimmy Gallagher was her boyfriend. He was in the year above Sheila at St Pat's and everyone thought he was gorgeous. And so he was — tall, really blond hair which was very rare in Ballyfergus (everyone else's being varying shades of mousy brown or, in a few cases, red) and a nice face and teeth.

The only spoke in the wheel of Sheila's happiness was her family: Mum, Dad and Eileen. They all treated her like she was some sort of baby who needed protection from the world or else they thought she was an idiot. For they were never done telling her what to do and what not to do and Mum was *so* old-fashioned about boys and things. Sheila wasn't allowed out after eleven o'clock at night and Mum didn't even know she'd kissed Jimmy, never mind allowed him to grope her tits.

And Eileen was just as bad. You'd think with having a fiancé she'd be more with it, but her and Paddy were old before their time. They didn't go to discos or dances; they just mooned about making plans for their wedding in August. Sheila couldn't for the life of her see what Eileen saw in Paddy O'Connor. He was ancient for a start, much older than Eileen and he'd big hairy arms and he was fat. He was good to Eileen, though, and seemed to make her happy and Mum said there were more important things in a man than looks. Whatever that meant.

Sheila looked at her reflection in the mirror and decided, hideous though the pale-green bridesmaid dress was, no one could look any better in it than she did. It had long tight-fitting sleeves with ruffles of white lace at the cuffs, a high scooped neckline and a length of darker green ribbon tied empress-style just under the breast. She came out of the bedroom and went downstairs where Mum and Eileen were waiting in the front room.

They seemed satisfied with the dress, the result of many nights' hard work by both of them. Sheila knew she should be grateful that she was to be bridesmaid and she ought to make an effort, not least for Eileen's sake.

'It's just like the picture on the pattern,' she said, trying to show her gratitude. 'I wish I could sew like that.'

'You could if you could be bothered,' said her

mum sharply. 'You spend too much time running around, chasing boys. You've no time for anything else.'

Sheila stuck out her tongue behind her mum's back and Eileen shot her a warning look.

'It's a little loose round the waist,' said Moira, pulling at the excess fabric, 'but we'll leave any further alterations 'til a few weeks before the wedding.'

'Well,' said Eileen, 'at least that's one thing we can tick off the 'To Do' list.'

Sheila plonked herself down on the sofa.

'You'd better go and take the dress off, Sheila, before it gets spoiled,' said Moira, and then to Eileen, 'Yes, it's about time we issued the invitations. Has Paddy come up with a list for his side of the family?'

'Yes, I've got it here. There's not too many ... ' said Eileen rummaging in her handbag.

When Sheila came back into the room, Moira had an A4 pad on her knee and the list was nearly complete.

'How many are we asking then?' said Sheila.

'Hold on a minute 'til I add it up.' She mumbled figures to herself and then said, 'Sixty-three, including all of us.'

'Let's have a look then,' said Sheila, grabbing the pad from Mum.

She skimmed down the list looking for her own name (which was near the top) and Jimmy's (which wasn't there at all).

'Jimmy isn't on this list,' she said, indignantly.

Eileen looked at Moira and said, 'Mum

doesn't think he should be. He's not family.'

'But he's my boyfriend! Look, Paddy's sister's bringing her boyfriend.'

'Her fiancé, not boyfriend,' interjected Moira, 'and anyway she's a lot older than you. You have to think of the future, Sheila.'

'What's the future got to do with anything?'

'What if you finish with him? He'll be in the group photograph and you'll be reminded of him for the rest of your life. It might be embarrassing.'

'I'll not finish with him.'

'Well, he might finish with you.'

'No, he won't!'

'Don't be so silly, Sheila. The two of youse are still children,' said Moira dismissively, and Sheila felt her blood rise.

'If Jimmy doesn't go then I'm not going either!' she cried, jumping up and throwing the list on the floor.

'You can't not go to your own sister's wedding,' scolded Moira. 'You're the brides-maid.'

'I can and I will! Not go, I mean,' said Sheila, crossing her arms in a gesture of defiance. 'You don't like him, do you?' she said to Moira, her voice full of accusation. 'That's what this is all about, isn't it?'

'I don't dislike Jimmy and that's got nothing to do with this anyway. This is about what's right. And it's not the done thing to have teenage boyfriends at weddings.'

Mother and daughter glared at each other, neither willing to lose face.

'Look,' said Eileen calmly, 'I don't mind if Jimmy comes, Mum. If Sheila really wants him there it's all right by me.'

'It's not right,' said Moira in a clipped voice.

'It's my wedding and one more's not going to make any difference, is it?'

Moira remained unmoved, still glaring at Sheila.

'Look,' said Eileen, sounding exasperated, 'why don't we invite him to the evening do? I'm inviting the crowd from McMaster's and, Mum, you want to invite some of the neighbours, don't you? So why can't Sheila invite Jimmy and some of her friends if she likes as well?'

And so the compromise was made and Jimmy came to the wedding and perhaps if he hadn't things might have turned out differently for everyone concerned.

★ ★ ★

The date of Eileen's wedding would be embedded in Sheila's memory forever: Saturday 2nd September 1978. The morning held promise of a fine warm, late summer day that was to last until nightfall. Perfect for photographs in the grounds of the chapel.

Eileen, who was plainer than her little sister, was nevertheless radiant in her simple white wedding dress. She wore a short veil held in place over her brown hair by a fake pearl tiara and both she and Sheila carried bouquets of white carnations.

When Eileen was ready to leave the house,

Sheila asked her, 'How do you feel?'

Eileen thought carefully before she answered.

'I feel lucky,' she said, 'incredibly lucky,' and Sheila thought it an odd thing to say on the morning of your wedding.

'Don't you feel madly in love?' she asked and Eileen looked at her and laughed.

'Well, yes,' she said, 'but there are other things that are important too. Like companionship and . . . ' she thought for a moment before finishing the sentence, 'kindness. Yes, kindness.'

'But you are happy, aren't you?' said Sheila feeling a little confounded by her sister's equanimity and apparent lack of passion.

'Oh, yes, happier than I've ever been in my life,' she replied and Sheila found that answer eminently more satisfying than talk of kindness and companionship.

Sheila went ahead in the first car with Moira, and Eileen followed with Kieran. And even Sheila couldn't help being caught up in the excitement when she stepped out into the sunlight to be greeted by a small group of neighbours who'd turned out to see them off. She and Moira were greeted with a wave of 'Ahh's!'.

'Like your outfit,' said someone.

'Sheila, you look lovely!' called someone else.

'And Moira, you look gorgeous,' said another.

Inside the black Mercedes the smell of the cream leather was powerful and the seats deep and luxurious. Sheila ran her hands along the veneered door panel.

'Do you think you'd become used to this

luxury if you lived like this all the time?' she asked. 'Like royalty or millionaires?'

'You do come off with some funny notions, Sheila,' said Moira good-humouredly. 'How would I know, love?'

The ceremony went off without a hitch and Paddy didn't look too bad once he was cleaned up in a shirt and tie. Outside the chapel they all had their photos taken and then everyone made their way to the Marine Hotel for the reception. In the end there were more like seventy people squeezed into the smaller of the hotel's two function rooms.

The meal and the speeches seemed to last far too long and Sheila, seated at the top table, became restless. She thought of Jimmy and a ripple of excitement ran through her. She wondered what he would think of her in this dress. For all her reservations about it, it did make her feel very grown-up and sophisticated.

There was a lull around teatime, when some elderly guests left and the rest sat in the bar, drinking steadily, while they waited for the evening entertainment to begin. Suddenly tired, Sheila sat down at a table in the bar. Paddy came and joined her. He loosened his tie and undid his top button.

'All the photos taken then?' asked Sheila.

'Aye,' he replied. 'They're doing some more of Eileen but they don't need me any more.'

He peered past Sheila at the bar and licked his lips.

'Fancy a drink?' he said.

'Half pint of cider and blackcurrant,' said

Sheila, chancing her arm, but he went and got it without comment.

'Cheers,' he said when he brought the drinks back to the table, and he took a long slow drink of Guinness.

She tasted the cider, which was cool and sweet, and drank gratefully.

'Smashing,' said Paddy and he licked his lips.

'You look grand,' he said, his round face beaming with happiness, 'and you did Eileen proud today.'

'Thanks, Paddy,' said Sheila, colouring.

She regarded the big, soft-hearted stranger thoughtfully. He was one of the family now — he'd be there at the table every Sunday and at Christmas and Easter. It seemed kind of odd that there'd be another person to include when before there was only the four of them. Sheila wondered if she'd have to give him birthday and Christmas presents. Would they have a baby straight away? The prospect of becoming an aunt and pushing a pretty baby round in a pram was very appealing.

'I suppose you're my brother, now,' she said.

Paddy laughed heartily. 'Well, I don't know about that. I'm nearly old enough to be your father.'

Sheila blushed because that was exactly what she thought. She finished the rest of her drink and Paddy bought her another. Eileen came in and joined them briefly and then said she had to go and check on the catering arrangements for the evening guests. Moira and Kieran came in next and Kieran bought a round of drinks.

'What are you drinking, my girl?' said Moira suspiciously, peering into the empty glass.

'Blackcurrant juice,' lied Sheila and Paddy winked at her.

'She can have something stronger than that, surely, on her sister's wedding day?' said Kieran. Moira tutted and he said, 'It'll not do her any harm, Moira.'

He came back with a Bacardi and coke for Sheila.

'Put all that coke in, love,' he said, 'or you might find it a bit strong.'

Sheila obeyed and found the coke successfully masked the taste of the alcohol. By the time she went upstairs to get freshened up, she felt giddy and, looking in the mirror, her face was flushed pink.

'How much have you had to drink?' said Eileen.

'Paddy bought me a couple and then Dad.'

'Well, don't have any more, love, or you'll make yourself sick. And you've a long night ahead of you. It's not even seven o'clock yet.'

Sheila lay down on the soft bed and watched Eileen reapply lipstick and spray herself with perfume. Eileen's going-away outfit hung from the back of the door in a clear plastic sheath.

'Is this where you and Paddy are staying tonight?' she asked.

'You know better than to ask that,' said Eileen. 'It's a secret.'

'Have you slept with him?' asked Sheila, thinking that no matter how nice a person Paddy was she couldn't imagine anyone wanting to get into bed with him.

'It's none of your business! Now get off that bed, before you crease it. This room's ours for the night, whether we use it or not. Someone might need to stay over if they have too much to drink.'

Sheila got up and went to the toilet and when she came out Eileen was gone. She brushed her hair, wiped the smeared mascara from under her eyes, put on lipstick and used Eileen's compact to blot the grease on her nose, cheeks and chin.

Jimmy arrived with three of Sheila's school-friends just after eight o'clock and by nine the party was well underway. Everyone from McMaster's had come and the lorry drivers stood around with their wives drinking pints and looking uncomfortable in their shirts and ties. Most of the neighbours had turned out as well and Mum and Dad moved among them, happy and proud.

Sheila and Jimmy managed to sneak glasses of fizzy wine off the waiter which were being handed out to toast the bride and groom. Then everyone tucked into the supper but Sheila didn't feel like eating anything.

The DJ put on 'Night Fever' by the Bee Gees and people started to dance. Excitedly, Sheila dragged Jimmy up onto the dance floor. They boogied away, imitating John Travolta's dance moves, and Sheila roared with laughter.

'You're pissed,' said Jimmy.

'No, I'm not,' said Sheila indignantly but she knew it was true.

The dancing was making her hot and tired.

'Come on,' she said. 'Let's go outside.'

Jimmy took her by the hand and they wove their way through the tables surrounding the dance floor. Sheila saw Eileen watching her with a pained expression on her face. Sheila smiled broadly and waved at her with her free hand. She didn't notice the chair until she nearly fell over it and just managed to stay on her feet with Jimmy's assistance.

Outside the night had drawn in and the cold air felt good against Sheila's skin. They stood in the shadows just to the left of the hotel entrance and watched the twinkling lights of Ballyfergus below them. Sheila shivered and Jimmy put his arm around her shoulder. The weight of it pressed down on her and her skin tingled under his touch.

'What do you think of my dress?' she asked, raising her face to look at his in the gloom.

'It's not the dress I'm interested in,' he replied in a hoarse voice.

He inclined his head slightly and she allowed him to kiss her on the lips. They snogged for several minutes and Jimmy put his hands on her buttocks and pulled her body hard against his. She could feel his erection against her stomach and was thrilled by the sense of power it gave her. Jimmy ran his hands over her back and, more gingerly, he cupped her breasts in his hands. Sheila moaned with pleasure.

A car pulled up in front of the hotel and Sheila pulled away sharply.

'Not here,' she hissed. 'Someone might see us.'

Jimmy put his hands in his pockets and kicked

at the gravel with the toe of his shoe. Someone came out of the hotel, got in the car and it drove off.

'Where then?' he said.

'We can go up to the room later on. Once Eileen and Paddy have left,' said Sheila.

'Aren't they staying in it?' said Jimmy.

'No, they're going somewhere else. Come on. We'd better go inside. They'll be leaving soon.'

Mum met Sheila in the foyer.

'There you are!' she cried, eyeing Jimmy with undisguised mistrust. 'Eileen's about to go up and get ready. Go on. You're supposed to help her.'

Sheila scurried after Eileen who had already started to ascend the stairs. Inside the room, Sheila helped her take off her wedding dress, tiara and veil and draped them over a chair. Then Sheila sat on the bed and watched Eileen put on her going-away outfit — a flowery dress and navy jacket.

'Where *are* you going tonight, Eileen?' she asked again.

'Well, I suppose I can tell you now,' said Eileen, flushed with excitement. 'We're only going to Portrush but we're staying in a nice hotel. Paddy has to be back at work on Monday.'

'I'm sorry you can't have a proper honeymoon,' said Sheila.

'I don't mind a bit,' said Eileen cheerfully. 'We'll have a great time and I'd rather spend the money on getting things for the house than waste it on some foreign holiday.'

'I'm glad you're so happy, Eileen,' said Sheila.

'So am I,' said Eileen and she put her arms round Sheila and kissed her on the head.

'Now you look after yourself, love. I won't be around to fight your corner for you so you'll just have to get along with Mum and Dad.'

'It's not like I won't see you, is it?' said Sheila.

'No, of course not, we're only moving to Ladas Parade. But things'll be different once I've a house of my own.'

Eileen picked up her handbag and looked around the room.

'That's it then,' she said. 'Can you make sure the dress and shoes get home safely?'

Sheila nodded and got up suddenly from the bed.

'I'll miss you,' she said.

'I'll miss you too, little one,' said Eileen softly.

'If you have a baby girl, will you call her after me?' said Sheila.

Eileen, who had her back to Sheila, lifted her head almost imperceptibly, said nothing, opened the door and was gone. Sheila noticed the room-key lying on the bed, picked it up and put it in her pocket. Then she too left the room and closed the door gently behind her.

After everyone had seen Eileen and Paddy off, they returned to the disco where the DJ put on old dance tunes. On the table, at the place where Eileen had been sitting, were several untouched Bacardi and cokes. Sheila lifted a glass, and took a big gulp.

'Ugh!'

'What's the matter?' said Jimmy.

'This must be a double. It tastes horrible.'

'Here, put some more coke in it. Is that better?'

'Mmm. Don't you want some?'

'Nah. I shared a half bottle of vodka with Joe Reynolds before we got here.'

Sheila looked for Mum and Dad. They were floating round the dance floor like Ginger Rogers and Fred Astaire.

'Did you get the key to the room then?' said a voice in Sheila's ear and a ripple of excitement ran through her.

She turned and smiled at Jimmy.

'It's in my pocket.'

'Come on then. Let's go up before they notice us missing.'

Giggling, Sheila followed Jimmy out into the foyer. They checked that no hotel staff were about and then bounded up the stairs, laughing.

'This way,' panted Sheila when they got to the top of the stairs and she led the way along a carpeted corridor to Room 39.

'Wow,' cried Jimmy, bouncing on the bed. 'Is there a mini-bar?'

'Don't be daft. You only get mini-bars in five-star hotels.'

Jimmy found the remote control and switched on the TV. He channel-hopped for a few minutes, then grunted and chucked the remote on the floor. He lay back on the bed and put his hands behind his head.

'So, am I going to see what's underneath that dress, or what?'

'Oh, I need a pee,' said Sheila. 'I've been holding it in all night.'

When she came back into the bedroom it was in darkness.

'What's going on in here?' she said.

'Leave the bathroom door open,' said Jimmy's voice. 'It'll let just enough light in. Come here.'

Sheila walked over to the side of the double bed. Jimmy's long figure was reclined gracefully on it.

'Let's get under the covers and pretend,' he said.

'Pretend what?'

'That we're married.'

'You're daft, so you are.'

'You know I love you, don't you?'

'I love you too.'

Jimmy sat up on the bed and undid the zip on her dress. It fell to the floor. She took off her bra and got into the bed with her knickers on. He also removed his outer garments and joined her in the bed. They lay down together and Jimmy rolled over on his side.

'We shouldn't be doing this,' said Sheila. 'Someone might catch us.'

'We've got the key. So stop worrying.'

He leaned over and kissed her on the cheek. She turned her face to him and arched her back.

'Kiss me,' she said and he did.

She loved the feeling of his strong arm around her waist and the hardness of his chest against her soft breasts. He rolled on top of her and she ran her hands over the broad stretch of his back. He was beautiful, truly beautiful. Then his breath deepened and came in short gasps. His penis, rubbing at her pubic bone, was hard and insistent.

He squeezed her nipple between his finger and the pleasure was exquisite. She felt moistness between her legs and moved them slightly apart so that the tip of his cock was rubbing against her. She felt his hand go down and ease her knickers aside — they were little more than a triangle and two bits of string — and she did not stop him. She had a terrible longing that must be satisfied. She pushed her hips against him and moaned softly. And suddenly, ever so gently, he slipped inside her.

They both stopped moving and stared at each other in the half-light.

'We shouldn't be doing this,' she gasped.

'I know . . . I know,' murmured Jimmy and then his lips were on hers again and their bodies were grinding against each other in perfect unison.

'Don't move,' gasped Sheila, when Jimmy finally stopped. 'I can feel something running out of me. There, grab that box of tissues.'

She placed a handful of tissues under her bottom and felt Jimmy's flaccid penis withdraw. Silently she got up onto her knees and let the liquid run out of her. Clutching the tissues to her she went to the bathroom. When she came back, Jimmy was sitting naked on the edge of the bed.

'I'm sorry, Sheila,' he said. 'I don't know what came over me . . . us.'

She knelt on the floor beside him. 'I'm not sorry. I'm not sorry we did it. I just hope . . . everything's all right.'

'It'll be all right. I'm sure it will,' said Jimmy.

'You don't get pregnant just doing it the once.'

'Don't you?' said Sheila, as a terrible fear settled on her.

They heard someone coming along the corridor and held their breath until a shadow passed by under the door and the footsteps receded.

'I suppose we'd better get out of here, before someone comes looking for us,' said Jimmy.

They freshened up, dressed hurriedly and remade the bed as perfectly as they could. Sheila put Eileen's shoes, stockings, and headdress in a small bag, hung the wedding dress on a hanger and placed the plastic cover over it. She looked round the room carefully to make sure nothing else was amiss. When she looked at the bed she got a sick feeling in her stomach.

Downstairs the slow songs had started and a few couples were mooching round the floor to 'Three times a Lady' by the Commodores.

Inexplicably the lyrics brought tears to Sheila's eyes.

'Where've you been?' said Moira. 'I was just coming up to look for you.'

'I was packing Eileen's things away. Jimmy helped me. They just need to be lifted out of the room.'

'I see. Well, I think it's time we were all making tracks,' said Moira. 'It's been a long day. Do you need a lift, Jimmy?'

'No, thanks, Mrs Devlin. If it's all the same with you, I'll walk. Night, Sheila.'

When he looked at her his expression was one of remorse and she felt so sorry for him that she just wanted to run up and hug him.

'Night,' she said instead and he walked out of the function room.

Sheila couldn't remember when her period was due exactly but the next few weeks were a nightmare. She thought about the possibility of pregnancy every second of every day. By the time two weeks had passed she could bear it no longer. She would have to do a pregnancy test. But where on earth was she going to get the money for one? She'd seen them in the chemist's and they cost a fortune. Then she thought of Eileen.

She went round there straight after school and asked her for a fiver. Eileen was up a set of stepladders hanging curtains.

'Can't you ask Mum?' said Eileen, 'We're not exactly swimming in money here.'

'No, I can't.'

'What do you want it for, anyway?' said Eileen, checking the drape of the curtain she'd just hung.

'I can't tell you,' said Sheila.

Eileen came down the steps and stood in front of her. She studied Sheila thoughtfully for a few seconds and then said, 'Well, if it's that important . . . OK.'

Sheila breathed a sigh of relief. Eileen went over to her handbag, took out her purse and handed Sheila a crisp five-pound note.

'Just don't be making a habit of it,' she said, before releasing the note into Sheila's desperate grip.

There was no way she could go to O'Grady's,

where Mr O'Grady and his wife had known her since she was a little girl, so she went to MacFarlane's, at the quieter end of the Main Street, instead. She got there, breathless, just before closing time. Standing there in her school uniform and knee-socks, Sheila felt obliged to explain why she was purchasing a pregnancy kit so she said it was for her sister. But the girl behind the counter seemed interested only in the clock on the wall. Blushing, Sheila stuffed the green and white paper bag in the front pocket of her schoolbag where it burnt a hole all the way home.

Once safely alone in her room, she opened the testing kit carefully, scrunched up the cellophane wrapping and put it into her schoolbag. She sat on the bed and read the instructions and found out that she'd have to wait until the morning to do the test. She read the instructions twice more and examined the white plastic stick that she had to pee on. She told herself that it wouldn't, just *couldn't*, be positive. She wasn't pregnant. She didn't feel pregnant and she was far too young to have a baby! And then she went to bed and had the worst night's sleep of her life.

At six thirty the next morning Sheila sat on the toilet and waited for the little windows on the testing stick to change colour. She closed her eyes and counted to sixty. When she opened them a faint pinkish hue was forming in one of the windows.

Her heart pounded in her chest. She squeezed her eyes closed tightly and prayed that it wouldn't go pink. She said she was sorry for what she'd done and she knew it was wrong and she wouldn't do it again. But when she opened her eyes the window was pink, the colour of bubblegum. Everything, even her breathing, seemed to stop at that moment as she stared at the little spot of colour, smaller than a button, and its meaning sank in. Then Sheila dropped the stick — it skidded across the bathroom floor and came to rest at the side of the bath. The little flash of colour glared at her, bright and incontestable.

She began to shake and put her arms around herself and rocked gently back and forth. The early morning sun shone through the frosted glass and bathed the turquoise bathroom in a gentle glow. She looked at the fresh towels folded neatly on the towel rail and Dad's razor in a cup on the windowsill. She had never felt so alone in all her life.

She bit the back of her knuckles and sobbed quietly.

'It can't be. It just can't be,' she whispered.

She heard sounds from the room next door and hurriedly put the plastic stick and instructions back inside the box. Then she slipped quietly into her own room, and got back into bed.

What was she to do? She couldn't tell Mum and Dad. Could she get rid of it? That would be the best thing. But how? She was under sixteen, no doctor would agree to an abortion. And if she went ahead and had it, everyone would be looking at her and pointing and calling her a whore. God, would they make her go to school?

She touched her flat stomach and wished she'd never been so stupid. She thought of Jimmy and decided he'd know what to do.

When the alarm went off Sheila got up and got ready for school as usual.

'You don't look well, love. You're very pale,' said Moira.

'Am I?'

'Is it the time of the month? Do you want to stay off school?'

'No, I'm fine, really. I want to go to school,' and Moira looked at her strangely for Sheila had never said that in her life before.

On the way she stopped by a litter bin, looked around to ensure no-one was about and dropped the used test and packaging in the bin. She waited for Jimmy at the school gates.

'What's wrong?' he said. 'You look terrible.'

'I need to talk to you,' she said as calmly as she could.

'There's the bell,' he said. 'We haven't time now. See you at break-time?'

She put her hand out and caught him by the forearm and gripped it tightly.

'No!' she shouted and some of the kids nearby turned to look.

He stared at her, uncomprehending, and then a look of terror crossed his face.

'You'd better come now,' she said and he followed her to the back of the Geography rooms where no one could see them and she told him the news.

'What will you do?' he asked and Sheila felt a stab of pain.

So she was on her own.

'I thought you might know what to do,' she said.

Jimmy swallowed and there were tears in his eyes when he spoke.

'Like what? What can we do? Oh, Sheila, I'm sorry. I never meant for this to happen. I didn't — I never thought you'd get pregnant. We only did it the once for God's sake.'

'I shouldn't have been so stupid,' said Sheila bitterly. 'After all you've got off scot-free.'

'Don't say that. It's not true.'

'Isn't it? I'm the one who's pregnant.'

Jimmy looked at his feet. 'Are you going to tell your mum and dad?'

'Jesus,' cried Sheila, 'how can I? They'll kill me.'

'Eileen then?'

'No.'

'What'll you do?'

'I don't know. I could get rid of it . . . '

'Do you mean an abortion? That's a sin.'

'And what we've done isn't?'

'Two wrongs don't make a right.'

'That's rich coming from you.'

'I'm only trying to help.'

'Well don't,' said Sheila and she turned and marched off.

Nearly five months later she still hadn't told anyone, apart from Jimmy, and he was sworn to secrecy. All hell would break loose when Mum and Dad found out, so what was the point of telling them before they had to know? Watching them going about their day-to-day business, happy in their ignorance, Sheila didn't have the heart to tell them. For she knew the terrible shame she was about to inflict on the family.

It was Eileen, finally, who noticed, perhaps because she didn't see Sheila every day and therefore saw what those closest to her overlooked.

Eileen was helping Sheila with the dishes in the kitchen — Moira and Kieran had gone through to watch the news.

'Have you put on weight?' said Eileen, regarding her critically.

Sheila had taken to wearing oversized jumpers and loose tracksuit bottoms all the time.

'Hmm. Maybe a little bit,' replied Sheila.

'I'd say more than a little bit, Sheila. You're getting fat, you know. Your face is rounder than I've ever seen it and look at your tummy!'

Eileen put her hand out and pushed playfully against the front of Sheila's top. She met a solid rock of flesh. Sheila looked up at her and Eileen stood very still.

Then she said, 'Let me see, Sheila.'

Obediently, Sheila lifted her top and exposed her rounded belly. Eileen put her hands to her mouth and stepped back two paces. Then she said, 'Sheila, you'd better sit down and tell me.'

Eileen sat and listened to the whole story, or as much detail as Sheila could bear to tell her, with a stony face. When Sheila had finished she stood up.

'We'd best get it over and done with, Sheila.'

'I can't tell them now!' cried Sheila.

'When then? You're five months pregnant and

they still don't know!'

Moira came into the room.

'Who's pregnant?' she said, as she tipped the remains of her tea into the sink.

Eileen and Sheila said nothing and Moira turned and looked at them. Slowly the smile slipped from her face and she looked questioningly from one to the other.

'I — I am,' said Sheila and she looked at the floor.

Moira turned and looked out the window. She stood like that for some minutes and then walked out of the room.

'You stay here,' said Eileen and she followed Moira.

Sheila heard raised voices, including Kieran's, in the other room and then Eileen came back.

'You'd better come through,' she said.

Moira and Kieran were sitting on the sofa, their faces ashen. Sheila sat down opposite them and Eileen told them everything that Sheila had told her. When she got to the bit about her and Jimmy having sex in the hotel room at the wedding Moira flinched and briefly shut her eyes.

When Eileen had finished Moira said, 'So, she's five months gone?'

And Eileen said, 'More or less.'

Everyone looked glumly at each other and then Kieran spoke.

'It's too late to get rid of it then?'

'Don't be talking like that!' said Moira, 'Yes, it's too late. But how could she have an abortion? We're Catholics.'

'So what are we going to do?' said Kieran.

Moira glared at Sheila and for the first time she saw real anger in her eyes.

'How could you do this to us, Sheila? How could you? I warned you about that Jimmy Gallagher. I swear if I could get my hands on him right now — '

'I'd wring his bloody neck!' added Dad.

Sheila was forbidden to see or speak to Jimmy Gallagher ever again, not that it mattered much for she'd seen little of him these last few months. The atmosphere in the house over the weekend was strained. On Saturday afternoon Moira went out and when she came back she spent two hours talking with Kieran in the front room. Neither of them spoke to Sheila at all. On Sunday, after they'd all been to Mass, Eileen and Paddy came round and, after a tense lunch, they had a family conference in the front room.

'It's all arranged,' said Moira. 'I spoke to Father Brennan and he's spoken to the Mother Superior at Portrock convent. Naturally your father will have to make a considerable donation to the sisters. It'll use up all our savings.'

Sheila struggled to follow the conversation. Portrock convent? What was she talking about?

'They're prepared to take her straight away and, after the confinement, the baby'll be adopted and she'll come home.'

'Adopted,' repeated Sheila and she stood up. 'No one said anything about the baby being adopted.'

Moira glared at her.

'Yes, adopted,' she said coldly. 'Did you think

138

you'd be bringing the little bastard back here? In front of all our friends and neighbours?'

'Now, Moira, there's no need for language like that,' said Kieran.

'I thought — I thought,' mumbled Sheila and then she finished the sentence in a rush, 'that you and Eileen would help bring it up.'

Moira snorted. 'Well, you thought wrong.'

'Don't be so hard on her,' said Eileen and turning to Sheila she went on, 'It's for the best, Sheila, really. We've all talked about it and you're far too young to keep a baby.'

'And this way no one will know,' said Moira. 'Or as few people as possible and in time their memories will fade.'

'That's all you care about, isn't it? What other people think!'

'No, it's not,' said Kieran. 'We've got your interests at heart, Sheila. Keeping this baby would ruin your life. You'd never get to become a nurse and what fella would want to take on another man's child?'

'I don't care about making a good catch,' said Sheila derisively.

'But you will, love,' said Dad, 'in time you will. You've made a mistake, a big one, and you've shamed this family.'

Sheila looked at the floor.

'This is the only way,' he added firmly.

'But what about school?' said Sheila.

'The nuns, God bless them,' said Mum, 'will school you until the baby comes. You can sit what 'O' levels you're able for and, if needs be, go back a year at school.'

139

'How would we explain that to people?' said Eileen.

'Well, the headmaster will have to know the truth, of course, but we'll tell everyone that she's got severe glandular fever and has gone away to recuperate.'

'Where to?' said Eileen.

'Aunt Netta's farm in Donegal.'

Listening to them talk, Sheila realised that she had no say in what would happen to her or the baby. She sat silently while arrangements were made to take her up to Portrock and for Moira to visit the headmaster. In a strange kind of way, Sheila was relieved that her secret was out in the open. She would no longer have to go to extraordinary lengths to conceal it or live daily in fear of being discovered.

★ ★ ★

Eileen helped Sheila pack her clothes and schoolbooks.

'Take everything you think you'll need,' said Eileen, 'for you'll not be coming back until after the baby's born. We'll bring up some maternity clothes and anything else you might need.'

'Will you come and see me?'

'Of course, I will, love, every weekend. I don't know about Mum though. Give her and Dad a bit of time — I'm sure they'll come round.'

'I'm sorry, Eileen,' said Sheila.

'I know, love,' said Eileen, 'I know. I just wish . . . well, we can't put the clock back, can we?'

And she put her arms around Sheila and held her very tight.

The nuns were very well organised, given that they'd only had a few days' notice of her arrival. She and Dad had a brief interview with the stern Mother Superior throughout which Dad was very quiet and looked at the floor. She told Sheila what was expected of her — participation in daily services, application to her studies and complete obedience and respect towards the nuns. She was encouraged to reflect on the gravity of her sin and ask the Lord for forgiveness. Then Dad left and Sheila was handed over to the care of Sister Imelda, a kindly middle-aged nun, who would be responsible for her during her stay.

Sheila was shown to a small room furnished only with a bed, table and chair and a big crucifix above the bed. There was no bathroom — she would have to share that with the nuns — and no mirror so Sheila was glad she'd had the foresight to pack one.

The very next day Sister Imelda took Sheila to the Health Centre in Coleraine where she was assigned a doctor, a health visitor and a social worker. It turned out that Sister Imelda was a former midwife, which explained why she'd been given the task of looking after Sheila. When the time came the baby would be born in Coleraine hospital.

Sheila settled into a boring, predictable routine of morning prayers, followed by tuition, lunch, more tuition, then supper, evening prayers and bed. She took her meals along with the nuns but felt they were all looking at her, especially once the bump was obvious, and asked if she could have them in her room instead. Sister Imelda readily complied. There was a TV in a small room, which she watched some nights. Other evenings Sister Imelda would come and talk to her and tell her all about her childhood growing up in the West of Ireland and how she'd been engaged when she was twenty-three but the fella had died and then she'd become a nun.

The only times she got out were to visit the Health Centre for her regular check-ups, and to take walks along the cliff path below the convent walls. Once or twice she stopped at the cliff edge and imagined throwing herself off onto the black rocks below. That would solve the problem for everyone, she thought, and how sorry they would be that they'd been so cruel to her! But she couldn't quite bring herself to do it and a gentle hand would guide her back onto the path. Eileen and Mum came every weekend and brought her chocolate and magazines and maternity clothes out of Dorothy Perkins in Belfast.

The two nuns assigned to school Sheila were unfamiliar with the syllabus and most of Sheila's time in the classroom was spent quietly studying on her own. During study one morning at the beginning of June, nearly two weeks after her due date, Sheila felt a dull ache in her lower back and by mid-morning she was having contractions. Sister Imelda took her to her room and packed a small bag for hospital. Then she went and phoned Moira who said she would come but she'd have to wait for Kieran to get home from work.

'There's no point going to the hospital until you're well under way,' cautioned Sister Imelda but by lunch-time Sheila was in so much pain that they bundled her into a car and took her anyway.

The baby was born at five o'clock that day. Sheila had never been so afraid in all her life or felt so weak. Her breasts ached and her bottom was sore and raw. They took the baby, a girl, from her and returned her, washed and wrapped in a pink shawl along with a bottle of milk. Sheila was sixteen years old.

Sheila was asleep when her mum and dad arrived and woke to find Sister Imelda gently shaking her shoulder. The baby was asleep in a crib beside the bed.

'It's your parents,' said the sister, quietly retreating from the room.

Moira went over to the crib and looked down at the sleeping child. Then she carefully lifted the little bundle and held the baby in her arms. Her expression was a mixture of joy and sadness and Sheila could've sworn she saw a tear run down her cheek. But then she couldn't be sure for her own tears blurred her vision.

Moira put the baby back in the crib.

'How are you, love?' she said.

'I'm all right, Mum,' said Sheila. 'I just feel a little weak. She's beautiful, isn't she?'

'Yes, love, she is.'

Moira paused and looked at Kieran, as though for moral support, before she went on, 'It's best if you don't get too — too attached to her. You know you've got to give her up, don't you?'

Sheila felt tears run down her cheeks and she couldn't stop them.

'But I can't just give her away. To strangers. People we don't know. I'll never see her again! Don't make me!'

'It doesn't have to be like that,' said Moira.

Sheila stopped crying. Had Mum and Dad changed their minds? Could she keep her after all?

Mum looked at Dad and he nodded encouragement for her to go on.

'We've all been talking over the last few weeks. And we think there's a way that you — '

'Could get to keep her?' said Sheila, finishing the sentence.

'No,' said Mum slowly, 'not exactly.'

'I don't understand.'

'Eileen and Paddy have offered to take the baby and raise her as their own.'

Sheila went to speak but Moira raised her hand to silence her.

'Hear me out,' she said. 'That way she stays in the family and you get to see her growing up.'

'But why would Eileen and Paddy want her? Won't they be having babies of their own?'

Mum sighed heavily. 'No, they won't, not ever. Eileen can't have children.'

'But how do you know that? She's not been married a year.'

'There's something you should know about your sister, Sheila. Something happened a very long time ago that means she can never have children.' Moira went and stood looking out of the window, her face half turned away from Sheila. She took some time to compose herself before going on. 'When she was five I sent her across the green to get a pint of milk . . . I'll never forgive myself for that.'

Moira paused and her face contorted with pain at the memory.

'There was this . . . man. Chucky he was called. We all knew he wasn't right in the head but no one ever thought he would harm anyone. Well, she met him on the green and he . . . he attacked her.'

She stopped but Sheila said nothing, too tired and too confused to say anything. Dad hung his head.

'He raped her, Sheila,' said Mum quietly, 'and he put a knife inside her and damaged her so much that she'll never be right. When she'd been gone fifteen minutes we started to panic and your dad went out looking for her . . . '

Mum stopped unable to go on.

Sheila lay quietly, unable to take in what she was hearing. How could such a terrible thing have been kept from her all these years? Suddenly a flood of memories crashed in, one on top of each other.

She was never allowed to go to the corner shop or walk home from school on her own until she was at secondary school. She rarely got to go to school discos and when she did Dad was always waiting for her outside the school gates, anxious and worried. They wouldn't let her do a paper-round when everyone else at school was. And it explained too why she was hardly ever allowed to go to friends' houses, Mum always insisting that they came to her house instead. Her whole childhood had been stifling and over-protective and now she understood why.

'This is the only chance for Eileen and Paddy to have a family of their own,' Moira said, composed and in control again. 'They've got their names down for adoption but Paddy's well over thirty and there's hardly any newborn babies come up. I've spoken to the social worker and she says there won't be a problem as long as you agree.' She paused and looked hard at Sheila. 'You know you can't keep the baby, Sheila. Giving her to Eileen and Paddy would be the most wonderful thing you could ever do. They'll love her so much and give her everything. You've your whole life ahead of you. You'll meet someone nice and get married and have more children. This is the only chance for Eileen.'

And when she thought about it, Sheila knew that she had no choice. She thought of her sister and big, kindly Paddy and she knew the baby couldn't ask for better parents. Tears ran down her face and went cold on her cheeks but she nodded. And then she turned her back to them and faced the wall.

Sheila stayed on at the convent for three more weeks to allow herself time to heal physically and mentally. For four days her breasts were like huge hard melons that burned and ached. They gave her tablets and soon the swelling went down and the pain stopped. There was no question of sitting exams as she was so weak and exhausted by her ordeal. Meanwhile Claire, as Eileen and Paddy called the baby, was taken home and introduced as their newly adopted daughter. Half of Ballyfergus must have guessed the truth but no one said a thing.

When Sheila finally came home she looked ill enough to give credence to the story about glandular fever. She spent a quiet summer at home and, when the school term started, she repeated the previous year. Eileen had her round at the house often, keen to involve her as much as possible with Claire. Even though Sheila found the visits painful they were the highlight of her day. She took photos of Claire with Dad's camera and took her for walks after school. But the day Claire opened her mouth and called Eileen 'Mama' Sheila stopped going round.

She concentrated on her schoolwork and joined the netball team and dreamt about becoming a nurse. Jimmy had left school and she rarely saw him round Ballyfergus. She was banned from seeing him anyway and she was glad, for though she missed him, she couldn't help feeling that he was to blame for what had happened. And so, very slowly, she rebuilt her life.

⋆   ⋆   ⋆

With relief Jimmy locked up the tiny, dank office he shared with five councillors and set off for the Club. Tonight's surgery for his constituents had been particularly taxing. A man complaining for the third time about noisy neighbours — an old lady worried about the fate of her cat after her death — and a belligerent mother demanding a pedestrian crossing outside the nursery school. The blood of her son would be on Jimmy's hands, she'd threatened, if he didn't get something done about it.

Jimmy's pace slowed as he thought of his eldest son. Ever since his talk with the priest the other night he'd been confused. Though his anger towards Conor had mellowed, he could still hardly speak to him. He'd tried to engage him in light-hearted banter but he knew his tone of voice was odd and unnatural-sounding. And Conor was embarrassed by his approaches, seeing Jimmy's interest for what it was — a clumsy attempt to bridge the huge gulf that existed between them.

In the packed carpark his heart sank when he saw Paddy's beaten-up white Fiat, parked close to the entrance. He steeled himself as he opened the door. Paddy, the poor bastard, hadn't taken the terrible news about Eileen at all well. Who would?

Inside Jimmy made his way to the bar through the comforting smell of beer and cigarette smoke. Paddy was at his usual spot, slumped on a bar stool.

Jimmy ordered a pint of Guinness for himself and Paddy and sat down. Aiden brought the drinks over and looked pointedly at Paddy before handing Jimmy his change. The wet glass glistened invitingly and a trickle of creamy froth crept slowly downwards onto the beermat. Jimmy's took a grateful drink of the black liquid through parched lips.

Paddy stared morosely at the optics behind the bar, no words yet exchanged between the two men.

'Had my weekly surgery tonight,' offered Jimmy.

Paddy responded with a low grunt, which Jimmy took it as a sign of encouragement.

'Guess what I did?' he said, laughing. 'You remember old Ma McKinley?'

'Aye, she used to run the newspaper shop.'

'That's the one. She's been in to see me, oh, five or six times about her will. What she thinks it's got to do with me, God only knows. But anyway, she's worried about what'll happen to her cat when she dies. I don't know what got into me but I agreed to take the bloody animal. Just to get rid of her! She's going to get it written into her will.'

'People think you're a soft touch, Jimmy,' said Paddy, not unkindly.

'I don't know how I'm going to break the news to Sheila. Do you think there's any chance the old bird'll outlive the cat?'

Paddy stared into his drink, his big hands resting helplessly on the bar. Almost overnight his rounded face had taken on a haggard appearance. Beads of sweat glistened on his forehead and the greying hair at his temples was matted and damp. Some minutes passed before he spoke.

'This thing with Eileen. I can't go through with it,' he said, his voice dull and flat.

Jimmy nodded gravely and blinked into his

pint. He tried to think of words to comfort Paddy but what could he say? Eileen's prognosis was bad.

'When they took her breast,' said Paddy, 'everyone said the worst was over. I thought then that it couldn't get any worse. That if we just got through it . . . '

His voice trailed off and he took a deep breath.

'I know it can't be easy, Paddy,' said Jimmy, 'but you've got to keep it together, man. For Eileen's sake. And Claire's.'

Then, to Jimmy's surprise, Paddy began to weep soundlessly, big tears cascading down his ruddy cheeks. People near them noticed and looked away. Embarrassed, Jimmy put his hand out towards Paddy's arm and then withdrew it, sharply, without touching him. His stomach was tied in knots and he cursed his incompetence. If Sheila was here she'd know just what to say and do.

'Here, I'll get you another drink,' said Jimmy, almost leaping from his seat, relieved to have a distraction from Paddy's anguish. 'It'll help steady your nerves,' he went on, catching Aiden's attention.

When he asked for two double whiskies, Aiden frowned, glanced at Paddy and raised his dark eyebrow questioningly.

'It's all right, mate,' said Jimmy, in an urgent whisper, 'just this one.'

Aiden complied and Jimmy slid the money over the counter.

'Keep the change,' he said.

They drained their glasses in one. Jimmy gasped and slammed the glass down on the counter.

'All right now?' he asked, but Paddy did not respond immediately.

When he did, he said, 'I think I'll call it a night.'

Awkwardly, he heaved himself off the bar stool, stumbled slightly, and steadied himself against the bar.

'You're not thinking of driving, are you?' said Jimmy.

Paddy patted him on the shoulder like you would a friendly dog.

'Paddy, tell me you'll not drive. You've had too much to drink.'

'Ach, give it a rest,' said Paddy. 'You're not my mother.'

After he'd gone, Jimmy thought that he'd never felt so useless and pathetic in all his life. Except when Sheila got pregnant with Claire. The shame of that memory still haunted him — he pushed it to the back of his mind.

He was the one, supposedly, who helped people. But when it came to someone he really cared about, like Paddy, he was next to hopeless. He wondered if Paddy would get home all right and then he remembered the white Fiat parked outside.

'He'd never be that stupid,' he said, his gaze drawn to the exit.

He pictured Paddy's dishevelled appearance, his huge frame shaking with sorrow. He heard his voice again.

'I can't go through with it.'

Jimmy stood up abruptly. Paddy was a man of few words, but Jimmy had never known him to say anything he didn't mean.

In seconds Jimmy was out the door and standing in the carpark. As he watched, black spots of rain filled in the rectangle of grey tarmac where the Fiat had been. Everything was very still and quiet, save for the muffled sound of laughter emanating from the Club.

In a panic, Jimmy looked around. He ran into the street — looked left, then right. He tried to guess which way Paddy might have gone. In the faint distance he heard a siren and strained to listen. His blood ran cold.

Instinctively, he knew where to go and his feet carried him there at running pace. He tore along empty streets and through the park, stumbling in the darkness, and, when he got within the grounds of the hospital, he could hardly breathe. He stopped, leant his hands on his thighs and fought for breath. A flurry of activity at the entrance to A&E caught his attention. An ambulance, lights flashing but silent now, was backed up to the door and two figures were unloading a stretcher.

Jimmy pushed his aching legs into action and half-ran, half-stumbled the last hundred yards to the building. Inside, a few people sat in the waiting-area but no one paid any attention to the wet, panting figure at the door. Everyone's attention was focused on the commotion going on behind one of the curtained cubicles. Nurses ran back and forth — someone shouted. A doctor ran down the corridor, his stethoscope swinging back and forth in time with his gait, and disappeared behind the curtain.

And then the sounds quietened and everyone's movements slowed, the sense of crisis over. Jimmy moved slowly forward. He knew Paddy was behind the screen, lying on the bed, but he had to see for himself.

'Excuse me,' shouted someone but Jimmy paid no attention.

He reached out with his hand and pulled the edge of the curtain back. A doctor was leaning over the bed shining a small bright light into Paddy's glassy left eye.

The doctor looked up at Jimmy irritably, and then a flicker of recognition crossed his face. It was Dr McCabe who often did the same night shift as Sheila.

'Wait!' shouted a female voice. 'You can't go in there,' and Jimmy felt a woman's grip on his upper arm.

The doctor glanced beyond Jimmy, to the person standing behind him, and nodded. The restraining hand let go.

Jimmy walked to the head of the bed and stared at Paddy. His face was unmarked — he looked like he was asleep.

'I'm sorry,' said the doctor.

Jimmy put his hand out and noticed that the sleeve of his jacket was soaking wet. Gingerly he touched Paddy's still-warm, limp hand. In all the years he'd known Paddy, Jimmy had rarely touched him. He closed his hand round Paddy's and shut his eyes.

153

'There were severe internal injuries,' said Dr McCabe.

'He didn't stand a chance. It was a head-on collision with a lorry. And I'm afraid it looks like he's been drinking.'

Jimmy inhaled the sterile scent of disinfectant. It reminded him of the smell of Sheila when she came home from a shift at the hospital. In the oppressive heat, he felt light-headed.

'Mr Gallagher, are you OK?' said the doctor, his voice full of concern. 'Nurse, can you get Mr Gallagher a glass of water, please.'

Gently, the nurse prised Paddy's hand out of Jimmy's grip. She guided him along the corridor, all the while speaking to him in a calm, soothing voice as though he was a distressed child.

'We'll need to contact Paddy's next of kin,' she said.

Jimmy thought of Eileen sitting at home with Sheila, contemplating the horrific surgery ahead of her. Abruptly, Jimmy shook himself free of the nurse's grasp and stepped two paces away from her.

'I'll tell her,' he said. 'She can't hear it from a stranger.'

And with that he walked out of the hospital and into the rain.

'Mr Gallagher! Mr Gallagher!' called the nurse and Jimmy broke into a run.

Out of earshot, he slowed to walking pace and threw back his head. The cold raindrops splattered on his face and he let out a sound, halfway between a scream and a sob.

He stood for a long time outside Eileen's front

gate. He knew that Sheila would be in there, like she was most nights, comforting her sister. Jimmy put his hand on the black iron gate and noticed that his arm was shaking. Suddenly he felt very cold. The gate slammed shut behind him as he walked across the wet grass. At the back door he heard raised voices from inside. Surprised, he stopped and listened.

'I can't believe you keep raising this,' said a voice he recognised as Eileen's.

'And I can't believe you won't even discuss it,' retorted Sheila.

'It's been twenty-one years! Why all of a sudden are you so determined that Claire should be told?' There was a pause and Eileen continued, more doggedly. 'And why can't you just let sleeping dogs lie? You're going to upset the whole apple-cart when we've got along just fine all these years.'

'Be realistic, Eileen. She's going to find out eventually. What about when she wants to apply for a driving licence? She's going to need her birth certificate then.'

'She hasn't done so yet.'

'Yes, but only because you and Paddy talked her out of it,' said Sheila sounding exasperated. 'You told her it would cost too much to put her on your insurance and she can't afford to buy a car of her own. And what about when she wants to get a passport? She was talking about saving up and going to Spain next summer with Deirdre and Jacqui.'

'What I don't understand, Sheila, is why you're so desperate to tell her if you think she's going to find out for herself soon anyway!'

'It could take months, maybe years. She needs to be told now.'

'Why?'

'Because I think it's the right thing to do. I don't think it's honest keeping the truth from her.'

'Sheila,' said Eileen firmly, 'in case you haven't noticed, we've all been living a lie. For twenty-one years. And anyway it's not as if you don't see her, with us living next door to you. She's happy here with us. Can't you see that?'

'I know she's happy,' said Sheila. 'I'm not denying that, but she's mine.'

'No, Sheila, she's not. You gave up your rights to her when you handed her over to Paddy and me.'

Jimmy opened the door and stepped into the kitchen. Eileen and Sheila were sitting, confrontational, on opposite sides of the table.

'Why, Jimmy! You're all wet,' said Sheila. As soon as she saw his expression, she stood up and added quickly, 'What's wrong?'

'Paddy's been in an accident.'

Eileen stood up then, the feet of her chair screeching on the lino.

'Is he hurt?' she said, her hand on her throat.

Jimmy paused, looked from one woman to the other, and decided there was only one way to break the news.

'He's dead, Eileen. Paddy's dead.'

★ ★ ★

156

The funeral was arranged for the following week. To Eileen her loss was incomprehensible and grief would not come. For she did not, could not, believe that her big, kindly husband was gone. With the help of Sheila and her mother, calmly and in control, she made all the arrangements and comforted Claire as best she could. Inside she felt all twisted and dry, like a wrung-out dishcloth.

As the events of the night of Paddy's death began to unfold, Eileen became convinced that Jimmy had had a pivotal role in his death. The suspicion became a belief and then, as she pieced together what had happened from various witnesses, the belief became a conviction. It was the first thing she thought about when she woke up and it gnawed at her all day. The anger stoked up inside her, eclipsing all thoughts of the cancer and the treatment she was about to face.

The night before the funeral, alone with her mother, she confided in her.

'I know the truth about Paddy's death.'

Moira cocked her head and listened while Eileen told her that Jimmy had bought Paddy drinks when it was obvious to anyone that he'd had enough.

'Jimmy got him drunk,' she said, bitterly, 'and then let him drive home. I hold him responsible. If he hadn't bought those drinks, if he'd taken the keys off Paddy, none of this would have happened.'

Moira eyes grew wide with alarm as Eileen spoke. She got up and came and sat on the sofa beside her daughter.

'What are you saying, Eileen?'

'What a blind man could see. That Jimmy's responsible for Paddy's death. Just as surely as if he'd been driving the lorry that hit his car.'

'Listen, my girl,' said Moira, in a hushed voice, 'I know you've got your crosses to bear. God knows, more than any woman should have in a lifetime. But you can't go round making ludicrous accusations like that.'

'But it's the truth! You only have to ask anyone who was there. Even Jimmy doesn't deny what happened.'

'There's a quare difference between buying a few rounds and being responsible for someone's death!' said Moira.

'Why are you taking his side?' said Eileen, hurt and confused.

'I'm not taking anyone's side,' said Moira gently and then, more firmly, 'Now listen to me, Eileen. You're in a state of shock and you're not thinking right.'

'Stop talking to me like I'm an idiot. I'm not in shock. I'm only seeing things the way they are. And I don't understand why you're covering up for Jimmy. He could be convicted for this, you know. That's it, isn't it? That's why you don't want to face the truth! You don't want to see your son-in-law go to prison.'

'Eileen,' said Mum, in a patient tone Eileen remembered from her childhood, 'Paddy is — was a grown man. He was big enough to make his own decisions about what he did or didn't drink and whether he got behind the wheel of a car. Your cancer coming back

158

devastated him. We all know that.'

Eileen withdrew her hand abruptly from Moira's gentle clasp. 'Are you saying he killed himself? Deliberately?' she asked, horrified.

If this was true, then Paddy's blood was on her hands.

'No, I'm not saying that. All I'm saying is we don't know why it happened. Maybe it was God's will.'

'You think Paddy killed himself because of me!' cried Eileen. 'Because I'm sick.'

'No, Eileen, no!' shouted Moira.

Eileen stared at her hands in horror. She must get them clean. She wiped them repeatedly on the front of her shirt.

'It's not true,' she cried. 'It's not true! It had nothing to do with me. It's Jimmy's fault. Not mine.'

And then Moira had her by the shoulders, shaking her and shouting in her face. 'Listen to me, Eileen! It's no one's fault. No one's! Do you hear me? It just happened. It's not your fault and it's not Jimmy's.'

Eileen collapsed on the sofa and sobbed. Moira was wrong, of course. It was Jimmy's fault. And she would never forgive him. *Never*.

'I'm going to phone Dr Crory now,' said Moira in a shaky voice. 'I think you need a little something to help you get through tomorrow. You wait right here. OK?'

Eileen nodded dumbly and Moira left the room. Dr Crory came round within the hour and left some tablets. He said they would help calm her down. Under her mother's watchful eye,

Eileen swallowed one with a glass of water and, when she was alone, flushed the rest of them down the toilet.

The next day, Eileen found it hard to concentrate on the funeral service for she couldn't keep her eyes off Jimmy. He was making a good show of grieving, she thought bitterly. What an actor! When it was him that put Paddy six foot under. At the graveside, she saw Jimmy shed tears and she felt like slapping him across the face. It was only respect for Paddy that stopped her doing it.

Back at the house, the downstairs rooms were full and the crowd spilled out into the back yard like it was a bloody garden party. Tumblers of brandy were pressed into her hand and she drank them gratefully for they dulled the ache inside her.

'Eileen, you're not supposed to be drinking,' said Moira, cornering her on the stairs. 'Give me that glass.'

'Will you stop nagging me?' said Eileen sharply, turning sideways so the glass was out of her mother's reach.

'But those tablets — they're tranquillisers. They don't mix with drink.'

So they were trying to sedate her. So that she would forget about Jimmy and the fact that he had killed her husband.

'I threw them away,' said Eileen, 'so you can stop worrying.'

In the front room, Jimmy leaned on the mantelpiece, conversing with Aiden. A brief smile passed across his face and something inside Eileen snapped. How dare he smirk like that when Paddy was dead and it was his fault!

She walked across the room and calmly threw the contents of her glass in his face. The room fell silent.

'Jesus! Eileen!' he shouted, jumping like a scalded cat. 'What did you do that for?'

'Don't you know?' she asked sarcastically.

And then she advanced on him until their faces were inches apart.

'You might have fooled the rest of them,' she hissed, 'but you haven't fooled me!'

Jimmy stared at her, pretending not to understand, and shook his head.

'What are you talking about, Eileen?'

'I'm talking about you getting Paddy drunk and letting him drive home. You killed him just as surely as if you'd stuck a knife in him.'

A collective gasp filled the room and then Eileen started to cry.

★　★　★

Aiden put his arm around Claire and led her, sobbing, upstairs to her room.

'Did you hear what Mum said to Uncle Jimmy?' she said, her voice rising to a shriek. 'Did you hear?'

'I heard,' he said and held her tight.

He wished with all his heart and soul that he could do the suffering for her. He knew the sorrow and the pain of loss so well but Claire wasn't equipped to deal with it. She'd had no experience of it, not the way he had.

'Sshh,' he said, 'sshh.'

'Is it true?' she said. 'Did Uncle Jimmy do the things Mum said? Is he responsible for Dad's death?'

Aiden smoothed stray hairs off Claire's forehead. Her pretty face was white with grief and her eyes black and sunken from lack of sleep.

'Your mum's very upset, Claire. The things she said, no, they're not true. Jimmy didn't force drink on your dad or make him drive the car. You have to understand that grief makes people believe the most terrible things. Even when they're not true.'

'So why's Mum saying it?'

'I think it's her way of coping.'

Claire pulled away and looked at him blankly, waiting for further explanation.

'When someone dies,' he said hesitantly, searching for the words to describe the indescribable, 'you look for someone, or something, to blame. It makes — it makes the loss easier to bear.'

A memory flashed into his head of a hot summer, days spent playing in the dusty street where they lived. He saw himself, a little boy in blue shorts and football boots, dribble the ball and tackle the other boys with a ferocious determination. When he grew up he was going to play for Man. United. A silver car came into the cul-de-sac with the sun behind it, pulled into the driveway and he ran to meet it. Daddy got out and swung him so high in the air he howled with delight. He could smell the bag of red-and-white striped 'Clove Rock' Dad always brought home in his pocket on a Friday night. He put one of the boiled sweets, that smelt so strongly of cinnamon and clove, in his mouth.

And later, from his bedroom window, the boy saw the car sitting in the driveway, and it seemed as though the headlights were eyes and the radiator grill a mouth, twisted into a menacing grin. The little boy shivered and ran from the window.

'How do you know?' said Claire.

Aiden swallowed and looked away. 'I just do,' he said. 'I just do.'

'I love you,' said Claire and Aiden held her in his arms and kissed the top of her head.

'Why don't you lie down and have a rest?' he suggested and he helped Claire stretch out on the bed and covered her with a throw.

Downstairs, the heat from the bodies packed into the small space was oppressive. Aiden passed a stony-faced but calm Eileen seated with Sheila and Mrs Devlin on either side, like grim sentries.

It was only when he got out, into the fresh air, that Aiden realised he was shaking. He wiped cold beads of sweat from his brow with the sleeve of his shirt.

'Don't lose it,' he whispered to himself. 'Don't lose it, Aiden.'

★ ★ ★

'What was all that about?' said Sheila to Moira when they'd managed to calm Eileen down.

163

They were standing in the hall at the bottom of the stairs. They'd left Eileen in the kitchen with Maureen O'Farrell while they circulated with trays of sandwiches and sausage rolls.

Moira looked over her shoulder into the front room and lowered her voice to a whisper. 'Your sister's got it into her head that Jimmy's responsible for Paddy's death. Yes, I know it's ridiculous, but you have to remember she's had a terrible shock. I think it's just her way of coping.'

'What? Blaming it on Jimmy makes her feel better?'

'Something like that. Look, don't be too hard on her, Sheila.'

'God, no, of course not,' said Sheila frowning. The sandwiches on the tray in her hand were starting to curl up at the edges. 'I just find it hard to believe. Blaming Jimmy of all people. Paddy was like a brother to him.'

Moira sniffed and paused to dab both her eyes with a scrunched-up hanky. 'Anyway,' she said briskly, changing the subject, 'what's this Eileen's been telling me about you? Banging on about wanting to tell Claire the truth. What's got into your head?'

'Nothing. I just think it's time Claire knew. She's twenty-one — old enough to handle the truth. She could find out by chance any day so why keep it from her any longer?'

'I suppose she will find out, one day, but she hasn't done so yet,' said Moira thoughtfully. 'But tell me this. What on earth would be gained by telling her now?'

'She'd know I was her mother for one thing,'

said Sheila defiantly, tears pricking her eyes.

'Sheila, it wouldn't change anything. It's too late,' said her mother, in a clipped tone, 'and you're treading on dangerous ground. Have you any idea the effect this would have on Claire? Jesus, she's only lost her dad and Eileen might not be far behind. Don't be so selfish.'

'If anyone's being selfish,' said Sheila, sniffing back tears, 'it's you. And Eileen.'

Moira recoiled in shock, and all the anger Sheila had been suppressing since her last visit to the doctor rose to the surface.

'You took her from me,' she hissed, 'the lot of you. You had it all arranged, signed and sealed and you never asked what I wanted. No one ever asked me.'

'Sheila,' said Moira, recovering her equanimity, 'you were barely sixteen. How could you have kept her? And you're damn lucky Eileen and Paddy were willing to take Claire — especially Paddy. Many's a man in his position wouldn't have agreed to it.'

'Oh Mum,' cried Sheila in exasperation, 'will you stop making Eileen and Paddy out to be saints! Claire was the answer to their prayers! Sure they were trying to adopt — they'd have taken any baby. And what could be more perfect than a blood relation? I bet they couldn't wait to get their hands on her, could they? Was it their idea? The adoption?'

'You should be down on your knees every day thanking God,' replied Moira, ignoring her last remarks, and then more sharply, 'Look — you gave her away and you'll just have to live with that fact. You can't change it now.'

'Yes, I can.'

Moira sighed, softening, and put her hand on Sheila's arm.

'We did it for the best,' she said, her voice earnest and pleading. 'You must believe that, Sheila. And it was the right thing to do. For everyone, including you.'

Sheila shook her head, unable to speak for the tightening in her throat, like someone was strangling her.

'And you *have* to learn to live with it,' said her mother firmly.

'But I can't,' said Sheila quietly, when she could speak at last.

'You must,' said Moira, insistently, and she locked her eyes with Sheila's. 'You must. Telling Claire won't make one iota of difference to the past. And the past's what this is all about, isn't it?'

'But I don't want to!' cried Sheila and something inside her exploded. She lifted the metal tray in anger and threw it against the wall. Crustless triangles of bread and ham flew everywhere and bits of egg mayonnaise stuck to the wallpaper.

Through her tears, she saw Eileen standing in the hall with an expression on her face that told her she'd been there for some time. She turned and fled as people crowded out from the kitchen and the front room to see what the commotion was all about.

'That's it,' shouted Moira Devlin in a voice as authoritative as she could muster. 'I'm sorry but

I'm going to have to ask you all to leave now. Everyone's very upset and it's been a long day.'

She opened the front door and, urgently, ushered everyone outside.

★　★　★

Moira shuffled slowly into her living-room. She sat down on the sofa, wearily took off her shoes and lay down. Tonight she really felt her age — she was absolutely done in.

She reflected on the day's events and decided that it had been one of the worst days of her life. Possibly worse even than the day of Kieran's funeral. She recalled what Eileen had done to Jimmy and shivered in horror. But no wonder Eileen was struggling to keep her sanity — she'd just buried her husband and she had cancer.

Moira closed her eyes and rubbed them with the heels of her hands until they became wet with tears. She allowed herself to cry for Eileen and asked God, yet again, why He was punishing her daughter. She'd had more than her fair share of sorrow and He just kept dishing it out! Angrily, Moira threw a cushion across the room — it bounced off the wall and landed soundlessly on the floor.

But, extreme though it was, Eileen's reaction to Paddy's death was understandable. Doctor Crory had assured Moira that her daughter's uncharacteristic behaviour was a normal response to extreme stress. She would need careful watching, he said, but it would pass.

And so it was Sheila who, this evening,

167

disturbed Moira's thoughts the most. After nearly twenty-two years, out-of-the-blue, she wanted to tell Claire that she, the woman the child regarded as an aunt, was her mother. She was like a loose cannon that could go off at any time. And once she blurted out the truth about Claire's parentage there'd be no going back. Things would never be the same again, not for any of them.

Of course they'd all known this day would come eventually but none of them had ever talked about how and when they would tell Claire. The years had just drifted by, and now it seemed like there was never a right moment. Moira realised, on reflection, that they had made a mistake — they should have told her when she'd turned eighteen. But one thing was for sure, now was not the time with her father still warm in his grave and her mother diagnosed with cancer.

Moira thought about the joy Claire had brought to Eileen and Paddy and the love they'd lavished on her and told herself she'd made the right decision. Sheila had gone on to qualify as a nurse and, when she and Jimmy married, it was as mature adults and because they wanted to, not because they had to. When Sheila and Jimmy started a family, Moira was sure the ghosts of the past had finally been laid to rest.

But during the two pregnancies that followed Conor, Sheila talked about having a girl and Moira prayed every night that her wish would be granted. But each time she had a boy and, though she did her best to hide it, Moira knew that Sheila was disappointed.

But there was another reason why Moira was so disturbed by Sheila's outburst. For over twenty years Moira had ignored the nagging doubt that what she'd done all those years ago had been morally wrong. That she'd had no right to make the decision for Sheila, minor though she was. Of course Kieran and Eileen and Paddy, to a lesser extent, had all been party to that decision. But she, like many Irish mothers, now and then, had been the lynchpin that held the family together. They all looked to her for guidance and for strength. And she did not fail them. In the end, it was she who'd persuaded them all to come round to her point of view.

She thought of the priest and the convent sisters and how they'd all assured her she was doing the right thing. No decent Catholic family could be expected to keep the child, they'd said. It would be best for Sheila, best for everyone, if Eileen and Paddy adopted the baby. And Moira had cursed the voice inside her head that whispered 'No,' and she'd gone ahead and done it anyway. And she'd not had a good night's sleep since.

And now she saw all around her, or so it seemed, Catholic families helping their teenage daughters bring up bastard children and she felt ashamed. Ashamed that she hadn't had the courage to do the same, ashamed that she'd cared too much what other people thought. She couldn't bear the whispers and the innuendo and people laughing behind her back. Things were different twenty years ago, grant you, but that wasn't enough to wash away the guilt.

And now, after all this time, she saw that the neat and tidy solution she'd devised had exacted a high price. Moira pictured Sheila's angry, tear-stained face and realised that her daughter had carried her burden of sorrow for over twenty years. Those same years when Moira marvelled at how well things had turned out for everyone concerned and congratulated herself on her cleverness. And now it broke her heart to think of the terrible pain she'd caused.

It seemed to Moira that Sheila had reached a turning point in her life where she could no longer carry on the way things were. Sheila wanted her daughter back and she believed that telling Claire the truth would achieve a mother-daughter intimacy. Moira, on the other hand, feared the very opposite. She worried that Claire might be so hurt, and feel so rejected, that she would never forgive Sheila and Jimmy. Moira believed that both her daughters, for very different reasons, were perilously close to having breakdowns. And she wasn't sure that she could do anything to help them.

★ ★ ★

Jimmy took off the black tie and threw it on the bed. A waft of brandy rose from his shirt — he unbuttoned it quickly and threw it into the laundry basket. He lifted the suit jacket off the bed and held it to his nose.

'That suit'll have to be cleaned,' he said. 'It stinks of brandy. And the tie.'

Sheila who, bent over, was removing her tights on the other side of the bed, stopped what she was doing and looked up at him.

'She didn't mean it, you know,' she said.

'Didn't she?' said Jimmy, and he folded up the soiled jacket thoughtfully and cradled it in his arms

'She's just very upset and she had too much to drink. She's not thinking straight. It'll all blow over. You'll see.'

Jimmy sat down heavily on the edge of the bed and stared at the floor. Sheila hadn't been there when Eileen said what she did. She didn't smell the brandy on her breath or see the hatred in her eyes.

'That's easy for you to say, Sheila,' he said. 'You're not the one she's accusing of murdering her husband.'

Sheila sighed and said, 'I know. I'm sorry.'

All day he'd pondered the events of that night and what he could have done to prevent Paddy's death. Faced with his brother-in-law's raw grief, Jimmy knew his response had been inadequate. He'd been embarrassed by the public display of suffering — instead of encouraging him to talk, he'd plied the big man with drink to shut him up.

He should have taken Paddy home. He should have taken the car keys off him. He *was* responsible for Paddy's death, just like Eileen said.

'Come to bed, Jimmy. It's been a hell of a day and we've both got an early start,' said Sheila.

Jimmy got under the covers, naked, and stared

at the ceiling. He felt like a child who's done something wrong and just wants someone to tell him it's all right. How he wished Sheila would hug him and reassure him that he wasn't to blame! Tears crept out of the corner of his eyes, ran down his temples and spread damply onto the pillow beneath.

When he rolled over, Sheila's face was turned to the wall and the gentle rise and fall of her shoulders told him that she was asleep. Or pretending to be. He switched off the bedside light, shut his eyes and waited for the welcome oblivion of sleep.

His slumber was fitful and disturbed. He drifted in and out of semi-consciousness and vivid dreams. In one, Eileen came towards him, just as she had done at the funeral reception, holding a glass between her hands. But, when she got up close, the glass turned into a knife. She raised it above her head. Jimmy put his hands up to protect himself — Eileen thrust the knife downwards.

'No!' he shouted and woke up.

He sat bolt upright. Frantically he looked around and then relaxed, realising where he was. In the dim morning light he could see that the covers on Sheila's side of the bed were thrown back and she was gone. He touched the sheet where she had lain and it was damp with sweat.

As his eyes adjusted to the faint light he saw a pale figure on the chair in the corner of the room. The window beside her was flung wide open — he could feel the cool breeze on his face.

'What's wrong?' he said. 'What are you doing over there?'

'Cooling off.'

'Did I wake you?' he said.

'No.'

Jimmy switched on the light and they both squinted in the brightness. Sheila's blonde hair was damp and matted to her head. Jimmy crawled onto his knees, blinked and looked again. Her face and neck were flushed red and he could see tiny jewels of sweat on her forehead.

'Are you ill?' he said.

'No, I'm fine.'

Jimmy got off the bed, went over and touched her forehead with the back of his hand. She recoiled slightly.

'Sheila, you're covered in sweat,' he persisted, 'and you've got a temperature. Do you want me to call a doctor?'

'No. Stop fussing.'

'Sheila, there is something wrong. This isn't normal.'

She snorted derisively. 'I don't need you to tell me it's abnormal.'

'Whatever do you mean?' he asked, confused.

Sheila put her hands between her knees.

'I'm . . . going through the change of life. The menopause,' she said, addressing her hands rather than Jimmy.

'But isn't that what happens to middle-aged women?'

'Usually,' she said, and then added bitterly, 'but, hey, some of us get lucky and it happens early.'

173

Jimmy tried to work out the implications of this news. All he could recall was his father blaming his mother's mood-swings and bad temper on the menopause. And his mum used to talk about 'night sweats'. Is that what Sheila had just experienced?

'I've been to see the doctor and had all the tests. It's confirmed,' said Sheila, as though in response to a question.

Jimmy got down on the floor and lifted one of her limp hands into his.

'Oh, love, I'm sorry,' he said. 'Why didn't you tell me?'

Sheila snatched her hand away and looked out the window. Grey daylight filtered through the venetian blinds, illuminating her tight, angry face.

'I just have,' she said.

'Why are you taking this out on me?'

'I'm not taking anything out on you.'

'Yes, you are. You're pushing me away and treating me like dirt.'

'What difference does it make whether I'm going through the menopause or not? You don't want any more children. You said as much.'

'Is that what it means? That you can't have children?' said Jimmy.

'Your ovaries pack in. Of course you can't have children. That's why I want to tell Claire.'

'Tell her what? I don't follow.'

'I . . . we won't be having another daughter. And she's the only one I've got. I want her back.'

Jimmy stood up, suddenly aware of his nakedness, and shivered. 'You can't have her

174

back, as you put it, Sheila. For a start she's a grown woman.'

'She has a right to know who her real parents are.'

'It's her right to find out perhaps, but not yours to tell.'

'I wasn't planning on telling her myself. I think Eileen should.'

'Jesus, Sheila, the child's only lost her father. And Eileen's still got to undergo that surgery and treatment. Apart from anything else, don't you think your timing leaves a little to be desired?'

'Now's the best time. If we . . . if she loses Eileen then at least she would know she has us to fall back on.'

'She'll have us anyway. She knows that. You don't have to go round raking up the past for her to know she can rely on us.'

'What are you afraid of, Jimmy? What she might think of you after she finds out you gave her away?'

'Hold on a minute, Sheila! It was your family's decision. I didn't exactly get much of a look in, did I?' He paused and then added, 'I'm cold, I'm going back to bed.'

But Sheila grabbed his arm and held it fiercely. 'You should have helped me keep her,' she hissed. 'You let them take her away.'

'For fuck's sake,' he said, shaking off her grip, 'I was only a child, like you. What could I have done?'

'You could have tried.'

'I did. I came round to talk to your parents,

but your da chased me off. He said that if he saw me within a hundred yards of the house again he'd call the police.'

Jimmy walked round to his side of the bed and got in. He pulled the covers round his shoulders.

'I don't need this, Sheila,' he said but she made no reply.

★ ★ ★

The time between the accident and the funeral had been a blur, one nightmare day merging into the next. Claire had hardly eaten or slept or done anything else apart from cry. It was the first thing she did in the morning when she woke and she sobbed herself to sleep at night.

After Paddy was buried, she went back to work and, in the weeks that followed, tried to carry on as normal. But her perspective had changed — suddenly the world seemed a more serious place. She read the Deaths column in the local paper where before she'd skimmed over the tributes, poems and messages of loss and grief. When the news came on TV she listened to all the awful things that happened in the world and wondered if there was a God. Before Dad died she never really believed that Mum might die too. But now she knew better — nothing was guaranteed.

'You look shattered, love,' said Aiden when he met her outside work one night.

'I feel shattered. In fact I feel absolutely exhausted.'

'Do you still want to go for a drink?'

'Oh, I don't know. I feel like all I want to do is curl up and go to sleep.'

He kissed her gently on the forehead.

'Let's make it a quick one then. I want to talk to you about something'

'What?' she said, aware of the dullness in her tone, but lacking the will to rouse herself to anything more animated.

'Wait 'til we get to the pub,' he replied, linking arms with her and marching down the road as if he couldn't wait to get there. 'You're going to be thrilled.'

Claire doubted it but she kept her thoughts to herself, not wanting to quench Aiden's happiness with the overwhelming apathy that haunted her these days.

In the pub they got their drinks and sat down. Unable to contain himself any longer Aiden blurted out, 'Claire, how do you fancy us going away together for a few days?' A big pleased-with-himself grin spread across his face.

'Where to?' she said cautiously.

'Paris.'

Images of the Eiffel Tower, romantic candlelit meals and boat rides on the Seine came to mind. For the first time in weeks Claire's heart skipped a tiny beat.

'I'm sorry I can't afford to pay for everything for both of us,' continued Aiden, 'but if you could cover your flight, I'd pay for the rest. It wouldn't be anything fancy now — I can only afford a two-star hotel. What do you think?'

'Aiden, I'd love to go! And the accommodation doesn't matter, does it? We'd be out all the time sightseeing. Oh, but I can't leave Mum. I don't want to leave her on her own. Not when she's got her treatment coming up.'

'Claire, you're with your mum every day. And it'd only be for a few days. I'm sure your Aunt Sheila would keep an eye on her.'

'Mmm . . . ' said Claire thoughtfully, wondering if she was being selfish in entertaining the idea.

'Look, Claire,' said Aiden, 'you need a break. Look at you. Your face lit up when I suggested it and that's the first genuine smile I've had from you in weeks. It'd give you something to look forward to and help get you through this terrible time.'

'I suppose you're right. When were you thinking of?'

'At the end of the summer. That'd give us both time to save up.'

'OK then,' said Claire and she allowed herself a big grin. 'That'll give me plenty of time to get a passport.'

Later that night, Claire sat in the front room pretending to read a magazine. She was trying to work out how to broach the subject of her and Aiden going on holiday together to Eileen. Eileen was reading a book, or pretending to, for, when Claire looked up, she would find her staring at the wall.

'Mum,' said Claire, at last, 'do you know where my birth certificate is?'

Slowly, Eileen allowed the book to drop into her lap, put a piece of paper between the pages and closed it.

'What do you want it for?' she asked evenly.

'I need to apply for a passport. Aiden's asked me to go away with him for a few days.'

'Oh. Where to?'

She told her mother about their plans to visit Paris.

'And where will you stay?'

'In a hotel. Aiden's got it all planned.'

'In separate rooms?'

'Oh, Mum don't be so old-fashioned. Of course not. What would be the point of paying for two rooms?'

'I'm not happy about that, Claire. I don't approve of you two sharing a room.'

'I'm twenty-one, Mum. I can do what I like.'

Eileen tapped her fingers urgently on the brightly coloured book-cover. She took her time before speaking again.

'I don't think it's a good idea, Claire,' she said, measuring out her words carefully. 'You're not even engaged, never mind married. There's many a girl's got herself into trouble that way.'

'I'm not a girl, Mum. And I know what I'm doing.'

'Your father wouldn't have approved either, you know.'

'Oh, Mum, that's not fair — bringing Dad into this,' said Claire as the tears welled up.

Eileen shrugged. 'I'm only telling the truth.'

There was an uncomfortable silence between them which Claire broke by asking, 'So where is it?'

'What?'

'My birth certificate, of course,' said Claire,

thinking that her mum was being deliberately dense.

'I don't know where it is. It's — it's lost.'

'How can you lose a birth certificate? Isn't it in the box under the stairs with all the other papers?' asked Claire, getting off the sofa.

'Sit down,' said Eileen sharply, and then her voice softened. 'I don't want you going through that box. Raking up memories. There's photos of Paddy in there . . . '

'Oh, I'm sorry. I didn't mean to upset you, Mum,' said Claire quickly, ashamed of her thoughtlessness.

'It's all right, love. Can you just leave it be for now, please?'

Claire bit her lip and nodded. 'I'll make us a cup of tea,' she said and got up and left the room before she broke down.

'Mum?' she said, when she came back with the tea, 'don't you think it's time you spoke to Uncle Jimmy? You haven't said a word to him since the funeral.' She sat down with her tea and waited for her mother's reaction.

'I've nothing to say to him,' she said flatly.

'But, Mum,' pleaded Claire, 'you still don't think that he was responsible for Dad's death, do you? It was an accident.'

'Was it?'

'That's what the coroner said, Mum. You can't go round accusing Uncle Jimmy of causing Dad's death.'

'Why are you standing up for him?' asked Eileen, suspiciously.

'I'm not. I'm just trying to make you see

reason. The things you said, well, they're simply not true.'

'How do you know? Were you there?'

'No, and neither were you.'

'I still think Jimmy could have done something to stop Paddy driving the car.'

'Maybe. But that doesn't mean he's responsible for Dad getting killed.'

'I don't want to talk about it any more,' said her mum, picking up the book again.

'OK,' said Claire, satisfied that the subject had at least been aired.

She looked at the clock and stood up.

'I'm away to my bed. If I'm taking Friday off I'd better look sharp at work this week,' she said and was about to lean over and kiss her mother when she spoke.

'There's no need,' she said quietly.

Claire cocked her head as though she hadn't heard clearly. Because of Paddy's death Mum's original appointment for the mastectomy had been postponed. But a date for the surgery had now been set and the appointment on Friday was to go through all the pre-op tests and paperwork.

'Why, don't you want me to go with you?'

'I'm not going. I've decided.'

'But the operation's scheduled for next week. The hospital have bent over backwards to accommodate us. We really can't go mucking them about like this, Mum.'

Eileen put down her book deliberately and fixed Claire with a determined stare.

'I've decided that I'm not going to have the

operation,' she said.

'But Mum! You can't do that. The operation's your only chance. If you don't have the surgery — '

'Calm down a minute, love.' Eileen patted the seat beside her. 'Come and sit here.'

Claire obeyed and Eileen took her hands and rubbed them gently between her own. She seemed quite calm, serene even, and when she spoke, very sure of herself. 'I've given this a lot of thought, Claire. Even before Paddy died I was half-thinking it.'

'You can't do this. You're going to die!'

'I'm going to die anyway, love. We all are — it's just a question of time. The cancer's spread, and even if they take off the other breast I'm going to have to undergo chemotherapy. I've looked at the statistics, Claire, and my chances are next to nil with the type of cancer I've got. All we're doing with the treatment is buying time. And without Paddy . . . '

'But with treatment you could live for years and years!'

'No, love. All I'd gain would be a few extra weeks, or months at best. The surgery's bad enough but the sickness with the chemo . . . I'd rather just stay at home and let nature take its course.'

'How can you do this to me? You don't love me!' cried Claire, wild with fear.

'I love you more than you will ever know, my darling.'

She stroked Claire's hair slowly, concentrating on the movement of her hand, as though seeing it for the first time.

'And I'm sorry that your dad got killed and I'm sorry that I've got cancer. But we can't change those things. I see you with Aiden and I know he makes you happy.'

'I thought you didn't like him.'

'I never said that. I know that he'll take care of you. And Granny and Sheila and Jimmy love you very much. You'll always be surrounded by people who love you.'

Claire threw her arms round her mother's neck.

'Please don't do this, Mum!'

'It's my choice and you have to respect that, Claire. And we'll have the loveliest time, I promise you. No trekking up and down to Belfast and no horrible stays in hospital. We'll make the best of the time I have left.'

She pulled away from Claire and took her face in her hands. And Claire could see from the expression in her eyes that Eileen had made up her mind.

'I need you to support me in this,' she said and Claire nodded through her tears.

★ ★ ★

'It's what she wants to do, Granny,' said Claire, sitting at the tiny table in her grandmother's kitchen.

Moira slid a plate laden with home-made flapjacks across the table.

'Take one, love,' she said. 'You're all skin and bone. You need feeding up.'

183

'I'm not hungry,' replied Claire, pushing the plate away.

'I don't know what your mother's thinking of,' said Moira. 'What does she know about medicine and the treatment of cancer?'

'She's done a bit of reading. And she went on the Internet at the library and looked up stuff there too.'

Moira sighed heavily. She looked very old and weary. Claire got up and gave her a hug from behind.

'I'm all right, love,' she sniffed, 'really I am. It's you I worry about. I'm so sorry, love.'

'So am I,' said Claire and she felt hot tears coursing down her cheeks.

Moira settled her back in the chair, got out a box of tissues and poured her a cup of tea. When Claire had composed herself she remembered the conversation she'd had with her mother about her birth certificate. The very next day, when Eileen was out, Claire had looked through the box under the stairs where they kept all their important bits and pieces. She'd found yellowing copies of her mum and dad's birth certificates but not her own.

In fact, when she thought about it, it was surprising that she hadn't seen it before now. The only time she recalled needing it was when she'd applied for her job. She was only sixteen then and Mum had helped her to fill out the application form. When the job offer came she was asked to forward, among other things, her exam certificates, birth certificate and national insurance number. The birth certificate couldn't be found and Claire was going away for a week's holiday to stay with Deirdre at her aunt's in Bangor, County Down. So Mum said she'd find it and send it off. Before she went Mum got her to sign application forms for a bank account too — she said she would need one for her wages to go into — and Mum opened that for her while she was away. Funny, she couldn't recall seeing the certificates being returned by her employer either. But Mum said they'd come back and she'd filed them away in the box under the stairs.

'How do you go about getting a copy of your birth certificate?' she asked.

Granny paused momentarily. 'Why? Who's wanting one?' she said, broke off a piece of flapjack and put it in her mouth.

'I am. Mine's lost apparently.'

Moira chewed thoughtfully, swallowed and asked, 'What do you want it for?'

'Nothing,' lied Claire, avoiding eye contact with Moira, while she poured milk into her cup and stirred. If Mum wasn't happy about her going on holiday with Aiden, Claire could only imagine the dressing-down she'd get from her grandmother. 'I just wanted to see Dad's name on it. I thought it would be nice to have it, that's all.'

'I see,' said Moira, taking another piece of flapjack.

'You know, when I asked Mum where my birth certificate was, she seemed really upset and asked me to drop the subject,' said Claire, pausing to take a sip of tea. 'I thought it was very strange.'

Moira chewed slowly, swallowed and, choosing each word with particular care, said, 'Your mum's still very upset by Paddy's death, Claire.' She paused to stare out the window, and added, 'And the last thing she needs to worry about just now is a silly little bit of paper that won't tell you anything you don't already know.'

'Granny,' said Claire slowly, setting her teacup down carefully on the saucer, 'is there any reason why Mum wouldn't want me to see my birth certificate?'

'Of course not.'

'Granny?'

'Yes?'

'Where was I born?'

'In the hospital down the road. Sure you know that. Why are you asking me?'

'Were they married when I was born?' said Claire.

'Of course!' said Moira. 'What makes you ask such a thing?'

'It's just I was trying to think of reasons why Mum wouldn't want me to see my birth certificate.'

'I told you. You're reading far too much into what your mum said, child,' said Moira and she got up and started washing the tea dishes, noisily, in the sink.

But Claire couldn't help wondering why, if this was true, everyone was getting so upset about it.

5

'What do you think, then?' asked Claire, turning this way and that to view her neat figure in the mirror.

In Eileen's opinion today's fashions were just awful. How she longed to see Claire in a tailored suit, cut to show off her slim figure, or something glamorous and sophisticated. Instead, she wore a tight-fitting cropped T-shirt with a logo across the front, which Eileen thought would've been better suited to the beach, and a pair of oversized combat-style trousers. Her outfit was finished off with a pair of trainers with two-inch white platform soles. Inside, Eileen groaned.

'You look lovely,' she said. 'Is that a new top?'

'Yeah, do you like it?'

'Mmm . . . ' was all Eileen could muster but it seemed to satisfy Claire.

'We're only going to the Indian,' explained Claire, as though she could read Eileen's thoughts, 'so I didn't want to get too dressed up.'

'It's just the two of you, then?' said Eileen.

'Yep.'

'I still think you should have had a birthday party. You don't see as much of your friends as you used to, Claire.'

'It wouldn't have felt right so soon after Dad's death.'

A little stab of pain shot through Eileen's heart and she wished she could forget that Paddy was dead. If she could just pretend, even for a few minutes, that things were the way they used to be, then she would feel happy again.

'Yes, perhaps not, but you could have asked a few of your friends to the Indian as well. I don't like to see you cutting yourself off from your friends.'

'I'm not 'cutting myself off', as you put it, Mum. I just don't have time to see everybody as often as I used to.'

Eileen thought she wasn't making a very good job of this. What she really wanted to say was that when she was gone, Claire would need the support of all her friends, not just Aiden. Claire went into the front room and threw herself on the sofa in front of the TV. Eileen followed her.

'The only person you see these days is Aiden,' she persisted.

'What's wrong with that? I am going out with him, after all.'

'He might . . . he could let you down. And if you've dropped all your old friends . . . well, you can't expect them to pick you up just like that.'

'Aiden won't let me down. He loves me.'

But you're only a child, screamed a voice inside Eileen's head. She silenced it and bit her lip. The exchange with Claire was beginning to sound familiar, like the ones Mum used to have with the headstrong Sheila.

'What time will you be back, then?' she asked.

'Does it matter, Mum?'

'No, not really . . . only the last time you went out with Aiden you didn't get home 'til after three. What were you doing up to that time?'

'I told you. We were at a flat belonging to a friend of his. We listened to music and had some beers.'

The way Claire avoided eye contact made Eileen mistrust her. A shiver of fear ran through Eileen.

'You're not going further with Aiden than you should, are you?' she asked.

'Oh, Mum, sometimes I think you're living in the Dark Ages,' said Claire and she laughed. The hint of derision in her voice irritated Eileen.

'You're just like Sheila,' she snapped before she could stop herself.

Claire's mouth fell open slightly in surprise and she searched Eileen's face for an explanation.

'What do you mean by that?' she said quietly.

'Oh, nothing,' said Eileen, hastily, wishing she could retract what she'd just said. 'You just reminded me there of what she was like when she was young. Headstrong. And she wouldn't listen to her mother either.'

'Well, it never did Aunt Sheila any harm,' said Claire and Eileen had to bite her lip again. 'I know you're just concerned for me, Mum,' Claire continued, in a more tender voice, 'and I'm not going to do anything silly. With Aiden or anyone else. So you don't need to worry.' She paused and looked at the floor. 'I feel bad now, about arranging to go out tonight.'

'No. Go! You must go out. You can't sit around this house for the rest of your life.'

'What about you, Mum? Will you be all right on your own?'

'Of course, I will. Sheila's coming over. God, the way you lot go on you'd think I wasn't safe in the house on my own.'

Claire returned her good-humoured smile and they were friends again. The doorbell went. It was Sheila.

'You're early,' said Eileen, not altogether welcoming. 'I thought you said eightish.'

'I did,' said Sheila, excitedly, and Eileen noticed that she held, in her hand, a small gift-wrapped parcel. 'Is Claire still here?'

Eileen nodded and before she'd time to say anymore, Sheila walked past her and disappeared into the front room. Eileen closed the door loudly and followed her sister.

Claire was weighing the parcel in her hand, turning it over. It was beautifully wrapped in metallic red paper and decorated with gold ribbon and a bow. Eileen guessed it had been gift-wrapped in a shop — that meant it must be something valuable. Her heart sank.

'Thanks very much, Aunt Sheila,' said Claire. 'You didn't have to buy me anything, you know.'

With a hand gesture Shelia brushed aside Claire's words. 'Go on then, open it!' she said, barely able to conceal her excitement.

Eileen forced her features into a smile of encouragement, which felt like a grimace.

Carefully, Claire peeled back the shiny paper: inside was a square faux-leather black box. She glanced at the two women with an expression of childlike anticipation on her face. Then she opened the box and stared at the contents, dumbstruck.

'What is it?' said Eileen. 'Let me see, love.'

Inside the box was a heavy gold link-bracelet nested on a bed of blue satin. It was far too much, thought Eileen. She reflected with displeasure that it must have cost far more than the pretty little gold-plated watch she had given Claire.

'It's real gold,' said Sheila. 'Look there, on the clasp. That's the hallmark.'

'It must have cost a fortune!' said Claire.

'Well, we never got you anything really special for your twenty-first so we thought we'd make up for it this year. Here, let me help you put it on.'

She fastened the bracelet round Claire's right wrist.

'Look, Mum, isn't it gorgeous?' Claire enthused and Eileen was forced to concur.

'Yes, it's lovely,' she said flatly, but Claire did not seem to notice the diffidence in her voice.

'Oh, it's just fantastic!' said Claire, turning once more to Sheila. 'I can't thank you and Uncle Jimmy enough!'

And she threw her arms around Sheila and gave her a warm hug. Eileen watched them with a lump in her throat. Sheila's beaming face was towards her and she had her eyes closed. When she opened them she must have seen the fury embedded in Eileen's face for she quickly released Claire from her embrace.

'Well, love,' she said, 'Happy Birthday and health to wear your new bracelet.'

Aiden called for Claire shortly afterwards and they went out almost immediately. From the window Sheila and Eileen watched them disappear from view.

'You're not cross with me for buying that bracelet, are you?' said Sheila.

'It was a bit over the top. What were you thinking of, buying her something like that? I can't believe Jimmy went along with it.'

Sheila wrinkled her nose and looked away.

'He doesn't know, does he?' said Eileen.

'I haven't told him yet. But it's my money and I can do what I like with it. You can't stop me buying her presents on her birthday, for God's sake!'

'I never said you couldn't — ' began Eileen but Sheila interrupted.

'I thought it would cheer her up a bit. After losing Paddy.'

Eileen told herself she was over-sensitive and overreacting. Sheila had the right to buy Claire whatever she wanted for her birthday and Eileen should be grateful.

'It was a lovely thought,' she said softly. 'Thank you.'

Eileen wandered through to the kitchen and put the kettle on but, for herself, she got out a bottle of whiskey.

'Oh, Eileen, don't tell me you're at that again,' said Sheila.

Tonight Sheila was helping Eileen sort out Paddy's clothes and personal belongings, deciding what to throw out and what to give to Oxfam. And Eileen was dreading it.

'Look,' said Sheila, resting her hand gently on Eileen's shoulder, 'if you don't want to do it tonight, we don't have to. It'll keep 'til another time.'

'No, it's all right. I want to. What I mean is, I want it over and done with. And I'd rather do it when Claire's not here.'

'OK then. But that whiskey's not going to do you any good.'

'It won't do me any harm, either,' said Eileen wryly, 'not at this stage.'

'Come here and sit down,' said Sheila.

She led Eileen to a chair and sat down beside her. She took a deep breath before she spoke.

'Are you sure, absolutely sure, you've made the right decision about the cancer treatment?'

Eileen nodded and Sheila continued in a wavering voice.

'I'll support you in whatever you decide, you know that. But it's not too late to change your mind. I could be on the phone to Dr Crory first thing in the morning.'

Eileen put her hand over Sheila's, and gently shook her head.

Sheila swallowed and asked, 'How long did the doctor think you had?'

'If I don't have treatment, six months maybe. He couldn't say for sure.'

'But with treatment you could have years. Right? It might even cure you.'

'That isn't going to happen, Sheila.'

Sheila looked glumly out of the window and said nothing.

'I'm not afraid of dying, you know,' said Eileen. 'Whether I have the treatment or not, I've got this death sentence hanging over me and I know there's no way I can escape it. In a way the waiting is worse than the thought of it actually happening. When it does, I won't really be aware of very much. I imagine I'll be pretty spaced out by then, on morphine or whatever.'

'Oh, stop it,' shouted Sheila and she jumped up. 'What about Claire? What about me? Don't we matter? All you're thinking about is yourself!'

'I suppose I am, right now. It's not that I haven't thought about Claire. I know it's going to be awful for her but she's going to have to face it sooner or later. I just can't face the treatment, Sheila. You of all people must understand that. You've nursed people who've been dying from cancer. The treatment's not going to cure me. It's going to make me very sick and I just can't see the point. Claire has Aiden and I think he really loves her. I think she'll be all right. I'm tired, Sheila, and I just want to be with Paddy. Is that too much to ask?'

Tears streamed down Sheila's face, spoiling her make-up. Ignoring them, she got up, poured a large whiskey and put it down in front of Eileen. Then she leaned forward and kissed her gently on the top of the head. 'All right, love,' she said in a whisper. 'If that's what you want, then that's the way it'll be.'

A great wave of relief swept over Eileen and for a moment she felt almost elated. She'd been fighting everyone for weeks now. They could not understand why someone would say no to the chance of extended life, no matter how gruesome the price demanded for those few extra months. They all thought she wasn't

194

thinking straight because of Paddy's death. Maybe they were right. But Eileen knew that this was how she wanted it to be.

'There's something I want to ask you, Sheila,' said Eileen.

'What is it?' she said, dabbing her eyes with a tissue.

'Will you come with me to Donegal?'

'Donegal?' repeated Sheila as though Eileen had uttered the name of somewhere strange and exotic. 'Where we used to go on holiday?'

'Yes,' said Eileen, 'and I'd like Mum and Claire to come too. Will you organise it?'

'Yes,' said Sheila earnestly. 'When do you want to go?'

'Soon, just as soon as you can manage it.'

Later, they sorted out all of Paddy's clothes. Not that he had much — three drawers full of socks, underpants, T-shirts and jumpers, and half a wardrobe full of shirts and trousers. He'd only possessed two suits (one of which was now with him in his coffin) and a couple of formal shirts and ties. The rest were casual shirts and jeans he wore both at work and at home. There was precious little worth saving for Oxfam.

The exercise was not as fraught as Eileen had expected. She felt emotionally detached from the process, as though the garments they sifted through belonged to some stranger. Part of her, she knew, had still not accepted the reality of Paddy's death.

'Don't you want to keep something of his?' said Sheila, when they'd decided what to do with everything.

'No, I don't think I do,' said Eileen, as she rolled back onto her heels and eased herself, stiffly, into a standing position.

'I think we've done enough for one night,' said Sheila, taking a large black bin-bag in each hand. 'Let's get this lot down the stairs. Jimmy can take them to the dump tomorrow.'

'I don't want Jimmy touching them.'

'Oh, for heaven's sake, Eileen! How long are you going to keep this up? Jimmy didn't do anything.'

'So everybody keeps telling me.'

'The way you're going on you'd think you were touched in the head. Only I know you're not. It's not Jimmy's fault that Paddy died, Eileen. You're just looking for someone to blame.'

'I am not,' said Eileen, and marched out of the room.

'You are so,' said Sheila, struggling behind her with both bin-bags.

When they got to the bottom of the stairs Eileen noticed Sheila was sweating and her face was bright red.

'Are you all right?' she asked. 'I didn't realise those bags were so heavy.'

'They're not. I'm just a bit hot. I need some air.'

Sheila pushed past Eileen on her way to the kitchen, opened the back door and sat down on the doorstep. A cool breeze wafted in.

'What's wrong?' said Eileen.

'I need to cool off.'

'Have you got a temperature? Are you sick?'

196

Sheila let out a long, slow sigh and said, 'Sort of.'

'What do you mean 'sort of'?'

'I suppose you might as well know,' said Sheila, resignedly. 'I've started the menopause.'

'The menopause! But that's not possible!' Eileen sat down beside her sister, thinking there must be some mistake. 'Who told you that? Sure you're not even forty yet.'

'The doctor.'

'Oh. How long have you known?'

'A couple of months.'

'Why didn't you say something before now?'

'Well, there was so much happening with the accident and everything . . . ' She paused and then went on, 'But that wasn't the real reason. I didn't believe it at first. It just seemed so, well, so ridiculous. And then I started getting night-sweats and I realised it really was happening to me.'

'Oh, Sheila, I'm sorry.'

'It's not the physical symptoms that bother me — the hot flushes and mood swings and all that. I mean it would have happened eventually anyway. I keep telling myself that all that's happened is it's started a decade, or two, early, that's all . . . '

Eileen found she was hardly listening. She was thinking that, in spite of her brave talk, she didn't want to die. She thought of Claire with a flash of fierce, protective love. How she hated God for what He'd done! She closed her eyes and tried to suppress the bitter anger that welled up inside her.

And then she focused on what Sheila was saying and suddenly her sister seemed so self-centred.

'It's having to face up to the fact that I can't have any more children,' said Sheila, close to tears. 'We — I would have liked to try for a girl, you know. I've been thinking about it for a while.'

And then it all fell into place. This was the reason Sheila had suddenly taken such an interest in Claire — insisting she should be told the truth and buying her expensive gifts. She'd found out she would never have any more children and now she thought she could have Claire back. Just like that! She saw the expensive bracelet for what it was — a bribe, to try and win Claire over. When Eileen thought of the life fate had allotted to her . . .

'Can't you see how lucky you are?' she said sharply. 'You've got a lovely family. You've still got your husband and you've all got your health. And all you can do is bang on about the one thing you haven't got!'

Sheila stood up and put her hand over her mouth. 'I'm sorry,' she said in a quiet voice. 'You're right, Eileen. I've been so thought-less . . . '

Then she turned sharply and walked away, round the corner of the house and out of sight. And Eileen made no move to follow her.

Later on, Eileen rummaged in the black bin-bags. She found Paddy's favourite pair of jeans, the ones she was always on at him to throw out. She put them to her nose and they smelt of oil and diesel. Then she took them upstairs, rolled them up, and hid them under her side of the bed.

★　★　★

By the time Sheila had walked to the church and back she'd managed to compose herself. Eileen was right, of course. How could she have been so thoughtless? Her grief over the loss of her fertility seemed — no, it was — self-indulgent. She reminded herself that she had a lot to be grateful for — three healthy sons, a husband who loved her, and a beautiful home. No, she'd been dealt a fair hand.

And yet she was obsessed with Claire, her desire for a baby girl fuelled, she now saw, by the sense of loss she felt over her daughter. She'd thought that having a baby would somehow fill the aching hole she felt inside her. But it would never be the same as having Claire back. And then she realised that what she really wanted was to recapture the past. She wanted to relive Claire's childhood, only this time as her mum. And that was, of course, impossible.

Resentment began to raise its head again and Sheila told herself she must try harder. She'd made a mistake, she'd paid for it and she'd just have to live with the consequences. And the pain.

By the time she got back to the house, it was late. Jimmy heard her come in the back door and came down the stairs.

'The boys in bed?' she asked, taking off her jacket.

'Yes, they went up at nine. I thought Conor would have been home by now, though,' said Jimmy, and Sheila followed his eyes to the clock on the wall. It said eleven twenty.

She jumped when the phone beside her rang and answered it quickly. It was Moira.

'Is something wrong?' asked Sheila, for although Moira went to bed late she had a rule about not phoning people after ten o'clock at night. Her mother ignored her question and said, 'What have you been saying to Claire?'

'Nothing. Why?'

'She was round here the other day asking about her birth certificate. And very persistent she was too. Did you put the idea into her head?'

'No, I did not and I haven't the faintest idea what you're talking about,' replied Sheila, watching Jimmy's back as he left the room. 'If she is asking about it, it's got nothing to do with me.'

'Hmm,' said Moira, not sounding in the least bit convinced. 'You know she can't see it. She'll find out everything!'

'She's going to have to some day.'

'I realise that, but now's not the time.'

'Well, when is going to be a good time? You can't keep it from her forever. She's going to find out sooner or later. When she gets married or wants to apply for a passport, she's going to need her birth certificate. And you can't stop her getting a copy.'

'Well, it's up to Eileen to tell her, not you, Sheila. If she mentions it again, I want you to put her off.'

Sheila was still arguing with her when the back door opened, very slowly, and someone stepped into the kitchen. It was Conor. Sheila stopped listening and stared.

'I've got to go, Mum,' she said quietly and hung up.

Conor looked down at the floor, avoiding eye contact with his mother. Sheila went over and laid her hand on his arm. He winced. At first she thought his face was smudged with dirt, but now she could see that it was bruised and smeared with blood seeping from a gash above his left eye. His bottom lip was swollen smooth and shiny and it protruded, contorting his handsome face into something grotesque. She guided him over to the table where he sat down with his hands between his knees. Quickly, Sheila hauled the first-aid box out from under the sink.

'Jimmy!' she called.

'What is it?' said an irritated voice from upstairs.

'You'd better come down here. Now,' she commanded and she heard the creak of floorboards overhead.

She wrung out a clean flannel and gently cleaned Conor's face.

'Jesus Christ, what the — ' said Jimmy as soon as he saw Conor. 'What the hell happened to you?'

Conor mumbled something, incoherent because of his swollen lip.

'Sssh. Now look up,' said Sheila to Conor and then to Jimmy, 'Leave him a minute 'til I see to this.'

201

'Does he need to go to hospital?'

Sheila examined the wound above Conor's eye and dabbed it with antiseptic. He winced. 'I don't think so,' she replied.

She found some butterfly plasters and put one over the cut. Then she looked in Conor's mouth and checked for loose teeth or cuts. There were none. She asked him if he'd gone unconscious at any point or if his ears were sore or his vision blurred. He said no.

'Let me see that arm,' she said and lifted it and pulled it this way and that.

Conor flinched.

'Does that hurt?' she asked.

'A bit,' said Conor.

'I don't think it's broken. Are you hurt anywhere else, love?'

He shook his head.

'Get him a brandy, please,' she said and Jimmy obeyed immediately.

Sheila coaxed Conor into taking a few mouthfuls of the potent liquid. It was only when she was satisfied that no serious harm had been done that Sheila knelt down in front of Conor and took his hands in hers.

'Who did this to you, son?' she asked.

'A crowd jumped me on the way home from the youth club.'

'Who were they?'

'I don't know. I didn't get a good look at them.'

'What happened, son?' said Sheila.

Conor looked at the floor.

'Tell me,' probed Sheila gently.

'They called me a poof. And a queer.'

Sheila sighed and hung her head, torn between conflicting emotions of fierce protectiveness and anger. She put her arms around Conor and hugged his thin frame.

'I'm so sorry, Conor,' she whispered in his ear. 'You do know I love you, don't you?' Turning to Jimmy she asked, 'Do you think we should call the police?'

'No!' he said abruptly. 'What can they do? Did you see the blokes who did it?'

Conor shook his head.

'But maybe we should report it, anyway,' said Sheila.

'And have our business spread all over Ballyfergus?'

Sheila saw a flicker of hurt in Conor's face and she stared coldly at Jimmy, her irritation growing by the second. He hadn't so much as touched Conor since he'd come through the door.

'Is that all you care about?' she said. 'People finding out about Conor?'

Jimmy glanced at Conor and looked away again, uncomfortably. 'No. I just don't see the point in involving the police, that's all.'

'Jimmy, I wish you would stop running away from this.' She put her arm round the shaken boy. 'Conor's different and you're just going to have to accept it. And as for worrying about the rest of Ballyfergus finding out our business, as you put it, I think it's safe to assume that they already know.'

Jimmy glared from wife to son, opened his mouth and closed it again. Conor trembled and

Sheila tightened her grip, protectively, round his shoulder. Then Jimmy walked out of the room and up the stairs.

Sheila felt the tension drain from Conor's thin shoulders.

'He's never going to come round,' he said, flatly.

'He's trying, Conor,' said Sheila. 'You're just going to have to give your dad a bit more time.'

And she hugged Conor to her breast like she used to when he was a little boy.

★　★　★

'I'm not much fun, am I?' said Claire.

Aiden shook his head.

'I don't expect you to be,' he said, 'not after what you've been through.'

The waiter came to clear away their plates and Claire turned her face to the wall, her eyes filling up again.

'I know this is going to sound like an odd thing to say, Claire, but you must try to find some good in everything that's happened. Otherwise it'll destroy you — eat you up.'

Claire covered her face with her hands and then dragged them slowly downwards, contorting her features. When she spoke she sounded angry.

'Jesus Christ, Aiden, what in the name of God can possibly be good about losing Dad and now Mum?'

'All I'm saying,' said Aiden choosing each

204

word carefully, feeling as though he was tiptoeing round broken glass, 'is that you've got to find some way of — of coping. Look at it this way — at least you're going to have some time with your mum. Knowing she's dying is a sort of gift. In a way.'

Claire looked at him, uncomprehending, and Aiden knew he wasn't making a lot of sense. He tried again.

'Paddy died so suddenly — you had no warning. I think that's worse than someone dying of a long-term illness. You never get the chance to say the things you wanted to. You carry them with you for the rest of your life.'

When he'd finished talking Claire sat back in her chair, nodding thoughtfully. 'But what about the suffering? Aunt Sheila says that towards the end she'll be very sick.'

'I don't know what that'll be like,' said Aiden, staring glumly into his drink. 'I can only imagine.'

'So,' said Claire slowly, 'when you talked about someone dying suddenly, you weren't imagining that? Did that happen to someone you knew? Someone you loved?'

Panicked, Aiden broke eye contact and shifted in his seat. It was better not to talk about these things — the past was best left alone. But, in trying to help Claire, he'd raised her curiosity.

'Yes,' he said simply and Claire waited for more. 'I — I lost both my parents when I was a child.'

Claire's greeny-blue eyes were moist and full of sympathy.

'I never knew,' she said softly. 'I'm so sorry, Aiden.'

'It was a long time ago, Claire. I was very young.'

'What happened? Who brought you up?'

Instinctively, Aiden became reticent. He'd said too much already. He folded his arms across his chest, raising his guard.

'I don't want to talk about it,' he said.

'I'm sorry. I didn't mean to pry,' said Claire in a hurt voice and then, changing tack, 'There's something I've been meaning to ask you. When's your birthday? I hope I haven't missed it.'

'It's ages away yet,' he said evasively.

Aiden didn't celebrate his own birthday although try as he might to forget it, the date was etched in his memory. He sought for a way of ending the conversation and felt her present, small and hard, digging into his thigh.

He pulled out a small parcel and bent envelope from the side trouser pocket of his combats. He tried to straighten the envelope and the crumpled bow, without success.

'I've brought you something,' he said, 'for your birthday.'

He realised, as he watched Claire peel off the gift-wrap, that his offering looked pathetic. If only Claire knew how hard it had been going into the newsagent's and picking that card. And the courage it had taken to go to the jeweller's and choose her present.

'Oh, they're lovely,' she gasped, lifting one of the tiny gold earrings out of the box and examining it closely.

Aiden felt little pleasure in the giving, only relief that Claire seemed pleased. He was glad it was over. Tomorrow things would be back to normal.

'It's not much,' he said, his eye drawn to the chunky gold bracelet on Claire's arm.

Claire reached over and put her fingers to his lips.

'No, it is and they're lovely. Thank you. Thank you very much.'

Outside, a cold mist blew in from the Irish Sea, over the harbour wall and up Main Street, shrouding everything in a ghostly white blanket. A foghorn sounded in the distance and Aiden shivered. He put his arm round Claire and pulled her close.

'Do you want to come back to the flat?' he whispered, addressing the top of her head.

'No, not tonight.'

'But it's only ten o'clock,' protested Aiden.

'I know, but I want to get back to Mum. I was thinking of what you said about this being a chance to spend time with her. There'll be plenty of time for us afterwards.'

Aiden didn't try to change her mind for deep down he was glad to have some time on his own. Though he loved Claire with all his being, celebrating her birthday had felt like a chore. He took Claire's hand and they walked back to Ladas Parade.

'Will you still go to Paris with me?' said Aiden.

'I don't know now. Until it's clear what's happening with Mum I don't think I can make any plans.'

'Well, why don't we leave booking it until the last minute? We can both arrange the time off work and you can get your passport and that way we're all set. But if it doesn't work out, there's no harm's done.'

'I suppose so.'

'We can always go another time. Though I still think it would do you good to get away for a little while.'

'I know. Paris sounds so romantic. I'd love to . . . ' she said, looking at the lighted window of the house. 'But we'll see.'

They kissed perfunctorily and parted.

Aiden dug his hands deep into his pockets and returned to his lodgings. In his room he found a half-empty bottle of vodka, poured himself a drink, and reflected on the evening. He'd found it stressful and disturbing — it had stirred up too many memories for comfort.

Why was it that the things you wanted most in the world to forget would never let you be? In his mind Aiden had tried to recreate a normal childhood for himself, and thought, for a time, that he could make himself believe that it were true. And he'd tried. Boy, had he tried. But you couldn't rewrite the past. He lay down on the bed and closed his eyes.

★ ★ ★

That night, when Daddy came to tuck him in, Aiden told him that he thought the car was scary.

'What do you mean, son?'

'It's got big eyes and a horrible grin. And it was looking at me.'

'It's an inanimate object, son,' said Daddy, laughing. 'It can't look at you and it can't hurt you.'

'What's an 'inamit' object, Daddy?'

'It means that the car's not alive. It doesn't have a mind or a heart. It's just a machine.'

Aiden thought about this for a while and then asked, 'So how come you have to look under it before you get in? Mum said you have to check in case you get hurt.'

Aiden saw a look in Daddy's eyes, which he thought at first was fear — but it couldn't be, for Daddy wasn't afraid of anything. And then the moment passed and Daddy smiled at him the same way he always did.

'Don't you worry about that, son,' he said, stroking Aiden's forehead gently, rhythmically with his big, rough hand. 'I'm just being careful, that's all. Just making sure that I keep us all safe.'

'Why? Why do you have to keep us safe?' mumbled Aiden, his eyes heavy with sleep.

But he did not hear Daddy's reply — he remembered only a soft whisper in his ear as he drifted off.

'I love you, son. I love you more than you will ever know.'

And Aiden was sure he went to sleep with a smile on his face because, when he woke in the morning, it was still there.

He lay in bed for a few seconds before he remembered what day it was. His birthday! He jumped out of bed and ran through to Mummy and Daddy's room. They were both still in bed, hidden under a mound of covers.

'Mummy! Daddy! Wake up! I'm six today!'

He took the corner of the duvet and pulled it slowly off the bed — the figures beneath it stirred.

Mummy sat up and smiled.

'Come here, my big birthday boy, and let me give you a kiss,' she said and hugged him so hard he could barely breathe.

He squirmed and wriggled to be free. Mummy kissed him again on the top of the head and let him go.

'Daddy! Wake up, Daddy!' he shouted and Daddy's face emerged from facedown on the pillow, bleary-eyed and sleepy.

'Happy birthday, son,' he said and ruffled Aiden's hair.

'Can I open my presents now? Can I?'

Without waiting for a reply, Aiden clapped his hands, leapt off the bed and ran downstairs.

'Wait for your daddy and me,' Mummy called after him.

In the front room a pile of parcels waited for Aiden on the sofa. He ran out of the room again and shouted, 'Hurry up! Hurry up!'

Back in the front room, he jumped on the armchair, bounced off it and landed on the floor, laughing.

Mummy and Daddy ran into the room in their dressing-gowns. Mummy had the camera in her hand and Daddy held the video.

'You sit there with your dad. That's right. I'll take a picture of the two of youse with the presents. There, that's lovely.'

'Here, Roisin, you go over there and I'll video,' said Daddy. 'Even better, I'll set it up here and we can all get in it.'

Daddy positioned the video camera on the top of the TV cabinet and squinted through the viewer.

'Can I open them now?' said Aiden.

'Just a second . . . if I just . . . there, I think that'll do. Now,' said Daddy rubbing his hands together, 'what have we got here?'

Mummy put her hand on Aiden's arm and looked directly into his eyes.

'These are from your dad and me. Happy birthday, son. We both love you very much,' she said and Aiden's insides felt all warm and squishy.

'Go on then,' said Daddy and Aiden ripped the paper off parcel after parcel, barely pausing to look at what was inside. All of his presents were brilliant but the best one was the policeman outfit, complete with helmet and truncheon. Now he could pretend to be at work, just like Daddy. He could tell the other boys off for playing football in the street and walking on the neighbours' grass. And they'd all have to do what he said or he would arrest them and send them to prison.

'Look at the time, John!' said Mum, when Aiden had finished opening everything. 'You'd better get your skates on. And you, my lad,' she said to Aiden, pretending to be stern, 'had better come and get your breakfast if we're going to get you to school on time.'

'But I want to play with my presents.'

'You can play with them later. Come on. Chop, chop!'

Mummy made Aiden go through to the kitchen and eat cornflakes and toast. Daddy came down the stairs dressed in jeans and a short-sleeved shirt — he always changed into his uniform when he got to work.

'That's me off, love,' he called.

Aiden got out of his chair.

'Thank you for my presents, Daddy,' he shouted, and ran up the hall.

Daddy caught him and scooped him up in his arms.

'Is my boy too big to give Daddy a kiss then,' he said and Aiden laughed and kissed Daddy on the lips.

'Let's have a three-way kiss!' said Mummy and she put out her arms and encircled them both. Then they kissed the way they always did, with their faces close together, cheek to cheek. Daddy kissed Aiden's cheek while he kissed Mummy's while she kissed Daddy's, so completing the circle.

'I'd better dash,' said Daddy and he set Aiden down lightly. 'I'll try and get home a bit early, son, so I can catch the end of the party.'

Daddy opened the door and walked to the car, which was parked at the end of their long narrow drive. It was a bright clear morning — the sun already beat hot on the car roofs and on the road, wavy ribbons of heat rising into the air. Aiden stood on the threshold, rocking back and forth on the balls of his feet.

When he got to the car, Daddy turned and waved.

'Bye, then,' he shouted, opened the back door and threw his coat on the seat.

Aiden squinted in the bright sunshine and felt his tummy curl up into a tight knot.

Something was wrong.

Daddy opened the driver's door of the car and got in. Through the front window Aiden saw him put on his seat belt and adjust the rear-view mirror. Then he saw him raise his left arm and look at his watch — it caught the sun and a flash of blinding light winked at Aiden.

And then he realised what was wrong. Daddy had forgotten to check under the car! He opened his mouth to cry out and felt Mummy's surprise as he lurched forward. But he was too late.

He heard the growl of the key in the ignition and, instantly, the whole world became a ball of bright, intense light. A hot blast knocked him and Mummy to the floor, winded.

Aiden sat up, momentarily blinded. He felt little stabs of pain all over his face and put his hand up. When he took it away again, he saw that it was covered in blood.

He looked where the car had been and there was the black outline of a vehicle, engulfed in a yellow and orange blaze. Then there was nothing but silence, save for the crackling and spitting of the flames, for a very long time.

★   ★   ★

Since last night when Conor came home beaten up, Jimmy had been telling himself that Sheila was wrong. His main concern was Conor's welfare, not what other people thought or said about the Gallagher family.

He felt he had, slowly, been making some headway. He made an effort to tune into discussions on homosexuality on TV and the radio and the idea that his son was 'one of them' was, reluctantly, taking hold.

But last night, Sheila had tried to rush him, forcing a confrontation in front of Conor. What did she expect him to do? Go all soppy and throw his arms round the lad? She knew that wasn't his style. She'd simply been scoring points. Trying to show what a broadminded, supporting mother she was while he, Jimmy Gallagher, could barely speak to his own son.

'How's Conor?' asked Claire, appearing unexpectedly in the room.

Before Jimmy had a chance to reply, Sheila said, 'Why don't you go and ask him yourself, love? He's upstairs.'

'Nah,' said Claire, shoving her hands into the front pockets of her jeans, 'I'll see him another time.'

'Well, it's lovely to see you, pet, but I've got to be at work for nine,' said Sheila, easing herself to her feet. 'You can walk me down the road a bit if you like.'

'That's OK,' said Claire. 'It was Uncle Jimmy I came to see.'

Sheila stopped dead in her tracks and looked quickly from Claire to Jimmy and back again.

'Right then,' she said, brusquely, 'I'll see you in the morning.'

Her voice was more controlled than her appearance. She was furious — it showed in the steely glint of her eyes and the way she held herself, stiff and erect. Without waiting for a reply, she went out and slammed the door behind her so hard that Jimmy thought it would shatter.

Jimmy peered out the window at the noisy group of teenagers skateboarding in the street.

'It's time Danny and Martin were in bed,' he said.

'Don't call them in just yet,' said Claire and paused. 'Thanks for the bracelet,' she continued, playing with the chunky gold chain on her arm.

Jimmy was astonished that it looked so, well, expensive. Sheila had said something about a little bracelet to cheer Claire up on her birthday, but this must have cost two hundred quid!

'You're welcome, love,' he said. 'Health to wear it.'

'I know why they beat Conor up,' said Claire. 'Mum told me.'

'I see.'

There was a pause during which Jimmy looked at his feet.

'It's kind of strange, isn't it?' said Claire, 'Conor being . . . well, being gay. I mean you read about it in magazines and see it on TV all the time but you never think it's going to happen to someone you actually know.'

'You can tell me that again,' said Jimmy.

215

'It's OK though. I mean it's cool. No one minds nowadays.'

'Don't they? Why are they beating up on him then?'

'They're just stupid kids. It'll be easier as he gets older.'

'It might for him. Not for me,' said Jimmy.

'Don't say that, Uncle Jimmy. It's not Conor's fault. He can't help it. It's just the way he is. It'll all work out in the end. You'll see.'

Changing the subject, Jimmy said, 'Anyway, how's your mum tonight?'

'She's doing all right. Tired.'

'Is she still blaming me?'

Claire nodded.

'But I managed to talk to her about it the other day and I think I got through to her. A little bit anyway. She listened to me for a while and then said she didn't want to talk about it any more. I took that as a good sign.'

'How so?'

'Well, she couldn't argue with me because everything I said made perfect sense and I think she knew that. She just doesn't want to admit it to herself.'

'I hope you're right,' said Jimmy. 'You know, you're very . . . what's the word? Insightful, that's it. Very insightful for your age, Claire.'

Claire reddened with pleasure and then her face became serious again.

'Do you like Aiden?' she asked, suddenly. 'Do you think he's a good person?'

'He's a great fella. Why do you ask?'

'Mum doesn't like him. The other night, she

216

was on at me about dropping my friends for him and that he might 'let me down'.'

'And have you? Dropped your friends, I mean?'

'No! Well, maybe I have a bit. I just don't have time for everybody these days. Not when I want to spend as much time as I can with Mum.' Claire put her hands over her face, overcome with emotion. 'I love Aiden and I want Mum to love him too. I don't want her to die and think I'm not going to be happy. And I know Aiden loves me. He really, really does.'

Jimmy sat down on the sofa beside Claire. Gingerly he put his arm on her shoulder and patted her upper arm. He realised that, not since she was a little girl, had he physically touched her, apart from a peck on the cheek at Christmas.

'Why? Why did Dad have to die?' Claire cried out, between sobs. 'And now Mum. I'm going to miss her so much. It's just not fair.' She put her arms across her stomach and rocked gently back and forth. Tears cascaded freely down her face.

Jimmy could not speak. His eyes stung but he could not cry. He pulled Claire to him and she lay in his arms, small and vulnerable like a little child, sobbing into his chest.

'Sshh . . . sshh. I know, I know,' was all he could manage to say.

He wished he could tell her everything was going to be all right. But it wasn't. Eileen was going to die.

A warm rush of love caught Jimmy by surprise

and he held her more tightly. This was his daughter! His own flesh and blood! He wanted to protect her and love her and keep her safe from harm and hurt, always. He kissed Claire on the crown of her head where her pale, vulnerable scalp showed through her brown hair. He closed his eyes and wished he could take the pain away. He would gladly suffer for her if it would make her suffering less.

The strength of his feelings threatened to overwhelm him. Was this how Sheila felt about Claire? Was this the joy and the sorrow she lived with every day? To love this fiercely and yet not be able to declare that love. To yearn to touch Claire and hold her and tell her that she was theirs.

He felt the heat of Claire against his chest and Jimmy's heart was heavy with grief, for Sheila, and for himself.

★　★　★

Sheila let the garden gate slam shut behind her and marched down the road, the tails of her open shirt flapping behind her in the warm evening breeze.

'Son of a bitch,' she muttered to herself, under her breath, 'that fucking son of a bitch!'

She could see what was happening all right. Never before had Claire come over especially to see Jimmy — before it had always been Sheila. Their cosy chats over cups of tea, discussing Claire's current boyfriends or nights out, had been one of the mainstays of Sheila's life. And now that special place in Claire's life was to be usurped by Jimmy.

No wonder he didn't want Claire to be told the truth. Why should he? Now Paddy was dead, Claire was coming to him, looking for a father figure. No wonder he was happy for things to stay the way they were. She could see where this was going. Slowly, Jimmy would take Paddy's place in Claire's life and then she would be the one left out in the cold.

She was within spitting-distance of the hospital when she realised she was out of breath and sweating. She slowed down and forced her shoulders to relax.

Claire was her daughter, for God's sake, and soon she would be an orphan. There would never be a better time to tell her the truth. Eileen must help Claire understand why giving her up had seemed like the right thing to do. Sheila was sure that, if Claire understood all the circumstances, she would forgive her for what she had done.

'You're looking very serious,' said a voice behind her and Sheila spun round.

John McCabe stood in front of his BMW, jangling the car keys in his hand.

'Oh,' said Sheila breaking into a genuine, but subdued, smile, 'I've a lot on my plate right now. You know how it is.'

'Yes,' he said thoughtfully, 'I remember the night your brother-in-law came in.' The doctor shook his head and went on, 'He had the most severe internal injuries I've ever seen. I'll never forget the look on your husband's face . . . It must have been a terrible shock for the whole family. How's your sister?'

'You won't know, of course . . . Eileen's got cancer. Well, she had it before, years ago and had one breast removed. Anyway this time, it's everywhere and she has refused further treatment.'

'God, Sheila, I'm sorry. I'd no idea. If there's anything I can do . . . '

'Thank you, but no. There's nothing anyone can do now but wait. She's made her mind up and that's it. In a way I think she wants to die, to be with Paddy. She said as much to me.'

'Hasn't she got a daughter?'

'Yes — Claire. She's twenty-two now.'

'It'll be hard on her.'

'Oh, John, it's hard on all of us,' said Sheila and burst into tears.

She felt a strong, able arm around her, guiding her gently round the side of the concrete building, out of sight of the A&E Department and the carpark. Sheila felt a hand between her shoulder-blades, patting her comfortingly and then rubbing in a slow, circular motion. She pulled away and looked up into his face, which was full of compassion. You couldn't call John McCabe good-looking, but he did have strong animal magnetism.

'You know, I'm very . . . fond of you, Sheila,' he said. 'I hate to see you upset.'

For a moment Sheila felt like she was in an episode of a hospital drama on TV. All she had to do was pull away now, she told herself, and no harm would be done. She and John could carry on as though nothing had happened, because nothing *had* happened.

But something held her there, motionless, staring into his face, and her legs began to shake with fear. She'd never been unfaithful to Jimmy, not in fifteen years of marriage. She'd never even kissed another man.

John McCabe leaned over. Very slowly, and very hesitantly he kissed her on the lips, and she did not stop him.

6

Driving to Donegal, Sheila worried about how the boys would cope while she was away. She told herself to let go and relax. This was supposed to be Eileen's time and she should be concentrating on her. They had four days and three nights ahead of them, just Sheila, Eileen, Claire and Moira, with no distractions to worry about. Sheila resolved to make it as happy a time as she could for her sister.

'What are you thinking about?' said Eileen.

'Oh, worrying about the boys and what he'll give them to eat. Stupid, I know.'

'They're not going to die,' said Mum from the back seat.

Sheila glanced at Eileen and they both smiled.

'I know they're not going to *die*,' said Sheila. 'I'd just like to know that they're getting something better than fish and chips every night.'

'You worry too much,' said Mum and they all fell silent.

'When will we get there?' asked Claire.

'About teatime,' replied Sheila.

They drove west from Ballyfergus through the market towns of Ballymena, Portglenone, and Maghera. They passed rich farming land in the valleys and miserable smallholdings on the Sperrin Mountains. To avoid going through Derry City, they'd cross the River Foyle and the

Border at Strabane and then drive north to the Innishowen peninsula and their destination, Buncrana.

'Look, there's the sign for Strabane,' said Eileen.

Strabane was a large market town full of old-fashioned hardware stores, fruit and vegetable shops and bakeries. They stopped for fuel and sandwiches and then pressed on to the border crossing. Sheila approached it with trepidation, but the checkpoint was deserted and they drove straight through without stopping.

Once into Eire there was a noticeable decline in the quality of the roads which slowed their progress but the scenery more than made up for the lost time. As they approached Buncrana the sun came through the clouds for the first time that day and shone like a beacon on the grey waters of Lough Swilly.

'I couldn't get us into a nice B&B in the town itself,' said Sheila, 'so we're staying in one half a mile or so out of town. Here, we take this turning.'

Sheila turned sharply left and they all rolled to the right.

'Careful!' the passengers shouted in unison.

'Sorry,' said Sheila. In spite of her preoccupations she was excited. 'I picked this one because she's only got two rooms and we'll more or less have the place to ourselves,' she told the others, 'and she does an evening meal as well.'

The half-mile turned out to be more like three and the B&B, when they found it, was one of those ubiquitous and completely isolated, white bungalows you see built all over Donegal with European money. It was set back from the road on a slight rise, up a modest gravel drive. At the end of the drive, near the roadside, was a sign saying 'Castlereagh B&B'.

Inside and out all was pristine and new. The owners, a Mr and Mrs Connelly, came from Belfast. Bert had taken early retirement from his job with the Electricity Board and, with their children all grown up, he and his wife Sue had decided to make a fresh start. They got a grant to help with the building costs and opened for business two years ago. Having come all the way from Ballyfergus Sheila had been expecting Southern Irish accents, even a bit of Gaelic. She couldn't help but feel a little disappointed even though the Connellys were warm and welcoming.

Bert took them outside and pointed to a dirt track worn into the grass across an empty green field.

'Follow that path for a quarter of a mile or so,' he said. 'It'll take you to a — well, you'll see for yourself when you get there. Sue says dinner'll be ready in an hour or so. That should give you plenty of time to get there and back.'

Full of curiosity, they followed his instructions and, once they came over the brow of the hill, Sheila let out a little of gasp of astonishment. There lay below them the most magical sight — a small curved bay, completely deserted save for the wreck of an old sailing boat, washed up in a storm. The golden sand took on a reddish tinge in the evening sun and a cool North Atlantic breeze brought the smell of the sea into their hair and nostrils.

Suddenly Claire let out a yelp and ran down the sandy dunes onto the beach. Her brown hair flew out behind her like a mane and the three remaining women, standing on the path, looked at each other and grinned. Then they all followed her example and ran, laughing, onto the sands.

'Does this remind you of our holidays, Sheila?' said Eileen, breathlessly.

'I don't remember anywhere as beautiful as this,' she replied, drinking in the scene around her.

'Me neither,' said Eileen, staring at the horizon, her cheekbones prominent in her once plump face.

Involuntarily, Sheila shivered and looked away.

When they got back to the guesthouse, dusk was drawing in. A trickle of grey smoke came from the chimney and the earthy smell of burning peat, the smell of Donegal, hung in the air.

Inside they were treated to a homely meal of broth and wheaten bread, steak and chips and treacle pudding for dessert. True comfort food. Later they sat in the small guest lounge playing cards and then went to bed, exhausted.

The next day, after a huge cooked Irish breakfast consisting of black pudding, bacon, eggs, fried potato, soda bread and lashings of tea, they discussed what to do.

'Don't feel you have to clear out every day,

you know,' said their hostess. 'If you just want to stay round here that's fine by me. I enjoy the company.'

Moira and Claire decided to go into Buncrana, the town where Moira's father and therefore Claire's great-grandfather had been born and raised. Claire had never been before and was keen to explore it. Bert was going into town and said he'd give them a lift.

No sooner had they gone than Eileen announced she was tired and went back to bed for a nap. Sheila sat alone in the lounge and looked out the window at the gentle rolling hills, aware that this was the first time in years she had sat quite still with nothing to do.

She wasn't aware how long she'd been sitting when Sue came in with a cup of tea and stood at the doorway and watched her drink it.

'I thought you could do with that,' she said.

Sheila smiled.

'She's not well, then, your sister,' said Sue and Sheila looked up in surprise into two clear, grey eyes.

'No,' she replied, 'she has cancer.'

Sue nodded knowingly and looked out across the hills.

'Well then,' she said, coming over and touching Sheila lightly on the shoulder, 'we'll make her stay here as special as we can. I'll take her in a cup of tea now.'

And without waiting for a reply she was gone. Which was just as well, for that simple act of kindness nearly reduced Sheila to tears.

When Eileen finally got up, it was early

afternoon. They put on coats, for rain threatened, and headed for the beach.

They walked the length of the bay and back and then sat down together on a patch of coarse grass. The wind was blowing offshore today and, in the shelter of the sand dunes, it was strangely calm. Eileen pulled her legs up and hugged her knees. She stared at the lapping waves for a long time without speaking. Sheila was just about to suggest that they head back when her sister spoke.

'Sheila,' she said, 'I never thanked you properly.'

'For this?' asked Sheila, indicating the scenery with a broad sweep of her hand.

'No, for Claire.'

Sheila's heart skipped a beat.

'I never thanked you for what you did. For what you gave me and Paddy. And I'll be grateful to you for eternity, wherever I am,' she said, without removing her gaze from the ocean. 'But I want to apologise, too. You see, I told myself that Paddy and I were doing you a favour — taking this little baby off your hands when it was obvious to anyone that you couldn't look after her. I told myself that it would give you a chance to make something of your life. I believed, God forgive me, that we could give Claire a better home and more love than you could. I thought she was the answer to my prayers. Literally. For months I'd been making novenas every night, praying that a baby would come up for adoption soon.

'But I realise now that I wasn't being honest

227

with myself. When I saw Claire I wanted her so badly I thought I would die. I didn't for one second consider things from your point of view. I didn't care how you felt. And I'm truly sorry. For if I had done, I never would have taken her. I'm sure I could have talked Mum into helping you, if I'd tried.'

'Don't say that, not now. I can't bear to think what might have been,' said Sheila hoarsely and she paused. She'd waited twenty-one years to hear those words and yet, deep down, she knew that it was wrong to let Eileen shoulder all this guilt. 'Maybe your motives weren't entirely selfless, Eileen, but you shouldn't be so hard on yourself. There's another way of looking at it. If you hadn't adopted her she'd have been taken away and I never would have seen her again. That would have been unbearable.'

Eileen put a hand on Sheila's knee. 'No, you don't understand me, Sheila. It's important to me that you hear me out, painful though it is. I'm sorry, Sheila, I really am. Deep down I suppose I knew it wasn't right and that's why I've felt so guilty all these years. That's why I haven't told Claire the truth. Because the truth doesn't reflect well on me. I was the one who was selfish. And I didn't realise how much I'd hurt you, until I heard you in the hall talking to Mum, the day Paddy was buried.'

Eileen took Sheila's hand in her frail one and looked directly at her. When she spoke again her eyes burned with passion.

'I swear to you that I will tell Claire the truth before . . . before I die. But you must do something for me.'

'What?' said Sheila, alarmed by her sister's intensity.

'Please say you forgive me for what I did. And mean it.'

Sheila looked long and hard into her sister's eyes and knew that she must tell the truth. The hard core of bitterness in her heart softened.

'I forgive you,' she said softly.

★   ★   ★

Eileen sat on a wooden bench in the garden and waited for grandmother and granddaughter to walk up to the house.

Proudly, she watched Claire's animated face as she conversed with Moira and marvelled at the lovely young woman she'd grown into. She wondered how much of that she could take credit for and how much was in Claire's genes. Sometimes, she saw Sheila's mannerisms and personality traits so strongly in Claire that she doubted if upbringing had anything at all to do with it.

'Look, Mum, I bought you a present,' said Claire, rummaging in her pocket She pulled out a big bag of home-made fudge. 'Well, it's for all of us really. I thought we could have it after our tea.'

'That's nice,' said Eileen and then, turning to Moira, 'What did you think then, Mum. Has Buncrana changed much?'

'No, not really. A lot of the shops are different, of course, but it's much the same. The beach is as long and as white as I remember it.'

'There's loads to see,' said Claire. 'I picked up this leaflet at the tourist office,' and she opened the pamphlet in her hand and began to read.

'Perhaps you'd like to go in tomorrow and see for yourself?' suggested Sheila to Eileen.

'We could take a drive along the coast to Malin Head or Carndonagh,' said Claire.

'Or Inch Island, if you like,' added Moira.

Eileen surveyed the peaceful, rolling country-side around her and thought of the secret sandy bay, accessible only by the path across the fields. The grey overcast sky from earlier in the day had dispersed and sunshine peeked from between fluffy white balls of cotton-wool cloud. She thought of kindly Sue and Bert Connelly, busy inside, preparing a meal for them. She felt safe here, cocooned in their own private little world.

'I'm not sure I want to go anywhere,' she said quietly. 'I like it here.'

They all fell silent and looked at each other. There was no traffic on the road, and the only sounds were the sounds of nature — the breeze rustling through the long grass on the other side of the low stone wall — the sound of birds going about their business and the flapping of clean sheets on the washing-line.

'OK, love,' said Moira, gently, 'if that's what you want.'

Over dinner Eileen listened while Claire and Moira talked about the things they'd seen in Buncrana and they all reminisced about the holidays they'd had in Donegal. Afterwards, Moira produced a bottle of Baileys — they drank it in the lounge and ate the fudge, so sweet it made your teeth jump.

Too tired to join the others for a stroll after dinner, Eileen retired to the room she shared with Claire. She put on her pyjamas and got into one of the single beds.

She recalled the conversation she'd had with Sheila and wondered if that was why she felt so calm and at peace. Or maybe it was just the effect of this place, of being somewhere so serene and beautiful.

Eileen had resolved to do three things before she died. The first was to apologise to Sheila, which she'd done today. The second was to tell Claire the truth.

But when she tried to imagine herself doing so, she couldn't come up with a way to start. No matter how carefully she couched it, it was going to come as an awful shock. Claire would be hurt and angry at the very least. And some of that anger would be directed towards Eileen.

But Claire was strong, like Sheila. She would be able to handle it, Eileen knew that. But whether she would forgive Eileen and the rest of them was a different matter altogether.

When Claire crept in to the room, Eileen was still awake.

'Are you glad we came here?' whispered Claire, in the dark.

'Yes, it's — it's wonderful and it's just what I wanted.'

'I'm glad you're happy. I'm going to miss you, Mum,' she said and Eileen opened her eyes.

In the darkness she couldn't tell whether

Claire was crying or not, all she saw was the dark outline of a figure sitting on the other bed. Eileen reached out and found Claire's hand.

'I love you,' she said, 'and your father loved you. I don't ever want you to forget that. No one in the world could have loved you more than we did. And every day we gave thanks to God for you and the joy you brought into our lives.'

'I know, Mum,' said Claire, between quiet gasps for air, like she was suppressing sobs.

'It's important to me that you know. That there's never any doubt in your mind. No child was ever loved as much as you.'

'I know that, Mum,' she said simply. 'Now you try and get some rest.'

As Eileen drifted off to sleep, she felt the nearest thing to happiness since Paddy's death. She should have slept wonderfully but she tossed and turned all night, drifting in and out of light sleep, during which she had vivid and disturbing dreams.

She woke with a start and struggled for a few seconds to remember where she was. Then she grappled with the travel alarm-clock, found the button for the light and checked the time. It was two-twenty. In the other bed Claire slept soundly, the steady rhythm of her breath audible in the silence.

Eileen lay back on the pillow and listened to her own rapid, shallow breaths. The unnamed fear she'd dreamed about was still with her — lying in the small bed she felt very alone and very frightened.

She closed her eyes and tried to think pleasant

thoughts — she conjured up all her favourite memories of Claire as she was growing up, and the happiest days they'd spent with Paddy, together as a family.

She slept again and dreamt she was pregnant and gave birth to Claire in Coleraine hospital. And then a nun came in, dressed in a black habit, swaddled the baby in a shawl and said, 'I'm taking her away now.'

'No!' screamed Eileen and she tried to get out of the bed but she couldn't move.

The nun stopped at the doorway and regarded Eileen severely. 'She was never yours to keep. You always knew that.'

'Where are you taking her?' she cried.

'Somewhere where you'll never see her again.'

And Eileen began to sob uncontrollably.

Someone switched the light on and Eileen blinked. Sheila was in the room, leaning over the bed.

'Eileen, wake up,' she said, urgently. 'It's only a dream. Wake up, now.'

'It was Claire,' said Eileen, 'and I had her in Coleraine. But they said she wasn't mine and I had to give her back.'

'It was only a dream, Eileen, only a dream,' said Sheila in a reassuring voice, like she was talking to a child.

'A nun came and took her away. Is it because of something I did? I never understood, Sheila. Why me? Why did it happen to me?'

'Sshh now . . . ' said Sheila, leaning in close to Eileen, 'Claire's here, Eileen. Look, she's here behind me.'

Claire stepped forward into Eileen's field of vision and forced a thin smile.

'I couldn't wake you up, Mum,' she said. 'You were crying in your sleep.'

'Was I?' said Eileen, coming to properly.

'You had a bad dream, that's all,' said Sheila. 'Here, take this,' and she offered Eileen a pill and a glass of water, which she took without protest.

Then she lay back on the pillow and looked at the ceiling.

'I feel so afraid,' she said. 'I'm afraid of dying. And I think I'm even more afraid of suffering.' She rolled onto her side, pulled her knees up and buried her face in her hands.

'Come here, love,' said a voice from the past, a mother's voice, sure and strong.

She felt those arms around her, and smelt her mother's smell. Moira pulled her to her breast and held her in her arms, the way she used to when Eileen was a little girl.

★ ★ ★

Driving back in the car Claire reflected on their stay in Donegal and concluded that it had had a sort of magical effect on them all. Everyone seemed more peaceful, less tense, happier. Even Mum. Maybe that was the effect holidays had on you, for Claire felt it too.

The Connellys had been so nice to them and, when they'd left, urged them to come back again soon. But they all knew they would never be able to go back to the guesthouse and the secret

234

beach again. There would be too many memories of Mum.

Claire forced back tears as she watched the fertile, green hills of East Antrim roll by. They were nearly home.

Mum's nightmare preyed on Claire's mind. Why did she have a dream about Claire being taken off her? She said a nun had come in and taken the baby away. Claire knew that nuns, in the past if not now, ran homes for unmarried mothers. With a chill in her heart she asked herself if it was possible that she had been born illegitimate?

Then she told herself that it was only a nightmare and that Mum was taking lots of medication that might cause her to have strange dreams. It was perfectly natural for someone facing death to have disturbing thoughts. And she wouldn't have paid too much heed to Mum's ramblings but for one thing — she was sure that Aunt Sheila had been trying to hush Mum up. She'd bent over, using her body as a shield, as though trying to prevent Claire from hearing Mum.

Claire thought back to the reaction she'd got from both Mum and Granny when she'd asked about her birth certificate. Both of them had behaved very peculiarly indeed as though it was extraordinary that she should wish to see it rather than a commonplace occurrence. Moira had said that her parents were married when she was born. But had she been lying? Another possibility came to mind causing Claire to close her eyes with horror. Perhaps they had been married but Paddy was not her father. And if Paddy wasn't her father, who was?

Claire head was swimming from the possibilities and she pressed her forehead against the cool glass of the passenger window to help her think more clearly. The chatter of the women in the car receded to a dull buzz as she struggled to think logically. There was another possibility — she could be adopted and yet she found that hard to imagine. She bore such a strong resemblance to the Devlin women that she must be Eileen's daughter, if not Paddy's. Then she tried to rationalise with herself once more. Was she reading too much into innocent, meaningless comments? Was she paranoid?

She thought back to their stay in Donegal and decided that she was not. She recalled walking into the room on more than one occasion and the conversation stopping dead. With blushing faces Mum and Aunt Sheila and Granny would clumsily turn the talk to the weather or something equally banal. Claire couldn't help but feel that they had been talking about her. Her family had always been pretty open and there was nothing, or so she'd thought, that the women wouldn't discuss in front of her. Unless of course there was something they didn't want her to find out.

These thoughts were still troubling Claire the next day when she went to work.

'What's eating you?' said Deirdre at tea break, when they were alone at a table in the corner of the staffroom. 'Nothing,' said Claire glumly.

'Did you have a nice time in Donegal?'

'Yeah, it was really great. I think it was what Mum needed. It seemed to make her, well, happier. She seemed more at peace when we got back.'

'I'm glad. It must be awful for her, for all of you.'

'It's funny, but you do start to get used to it, Deirdre. I mean, used to the idea that Mum's going to die. Although it's always there, you can't be miserable all the time.'

'Life has to go on?'

'Something like that.'

'So what's bothering you, then?'

'I . . . well, this is going to sound really . . . no, I can't! It sounds so stupid.'

'Try me,' said Deirdre with a serious expression.

'Well, I think there's something they're not telling me.'

'Who?'

'Well, all of them really — Mum, Aunt Sheila, Granny.'

'I don't follow.'

'Well, it all started when I asked Mum where my birth certificate was so that I could apply for a passport. She went all funny about it. And then she said that it was lost.'

'What's strange about that? She doesn't want you going on holiday with Aiden. Of course she's going to try and stop you.'

'It's not just that. When I thought about it, I've never actually seen my birth certificate.'

'How come? What about starting work? Or registering for exams?'

'The thing is Mum always sorted those things out for me. And now that I think about it, that's odd, isn't it? For a girl of twenty-one never to have seen her own birth certificate.'

Deirdre shrugged. 'Maybe'

'It wasn't just that. The next day I mentioned it to Granny and she acted weird as well. She said there was nothing on it I didn't already know.'

'So she tried to put you off seeing it too?'

'Well, no, she didn't exactly say that. But I could sense by the way she acted that she wasn't happy about me asking about it. And I can't think why she would react like that. You see I didn't tell her that I wanted to go on holiday with Aiden.'

'I see.'

'And then, well, this sounds bizarre. But when we were in Donegal Mum had a nightmare and she was shouting about me being taken away from her by a nun. Well, the nuns used to run homes for unmarried mothers, didn't they? And I just started putting two and two together.'

'Two and two don't always make four.'

'But don't you think that it's all a little strange?'

Deirdre raised her eyebrows and said, 'I dunno.' Then she looked with concern into Claire's face. 'If what you say is true, what is it you think they don't want you to find out?'

'Well, isn't it obvious?' said Claire, feeling her bottom lip begin to tremble. 'There's lots of reasons but they're all too awful to contemplate.'

She paused then and put her hands over her face.

Deirdre touched her gently on the arm and whispered, 'It's all right. You're OK.'

'I could be illegitimate,' went on Claire, blinking hard to hold back tears, 'And Mum and Dad could have got married later, I suppose, after I was born. I could be Dad's daughter or I might not be. I could be adopted, though I look too much like a Devlin to make me think that's likely. But you never know.'

Deirdre nodded gravely and they both sat in silence for a few moments absorbing the implications of Claire's last remarks.

'Well,' said Claire purposefully, 'there's only one way to find out. I'm going to have to get a copy of my birth certificate. Am I right in thinking that I can't get one in Ballyfergus?'

'No, not after all this time. You'd have to go up to Belfast to the Registrar of Births, Deaths and Marriages. But Claire, are you sure you know what you're doing?'

'What do you mean?'

'Are you sure you can handle whatever it is you're going to find out?'

'Are you saying I shouldn't get a copy?'

'No, all I'm saying is that you should think through all the possibilities very carefully beforehand. You might find out something that could hurt you. Just go carefully.'

Deirdre's words of caution only fired Claire up with more determination. Later, when the office was quiet, she phoned the Register of Births, Deaths and Marriages in Belfast. She found out everything they needed to know to enable her to get a copy of her birth certificate: her date of birth, surname, parents' names, mother's maiden name, and place of birth. She wrote everything down carefully on a piece of paper.

'It'll be sent out first-class post,' said the voice on the line.

'Oh, no, I don't want it to come in the post.'

'Well, you'll have to come in yourself then, in person. There's an extra charge for that.'

Claire wrote down the directions to the office in Belfast and the opening hours. Then she folded the piece of paper carefully and put it in her handbag.

Aiden was waiting for her outside work.

'What are you doing here?' she said.

'I missed you. I thought I'd come and walk you home.'

They fell in together and she told him about her conversation with Deirdre and the phone call to the Registrar of Births, Deaths and Marriages.

'You've made up your mind to go and see it then. Well, if you're sure it's what you want to do . . .'

'Oh, God, not you as well!' said Claire, irritably, and she stopped walking and glared angrily at him.

'What d'you mean?' said Aiden in a hurt tone.

'Do you know something I don't? Because Mum and Granny and even Deirdre are trying to stop me from doing this.'

'I'm not trying to stop you, Claire,' said Aiden, taking her arm gently and continuing to walk, 'but I am worried. I can see you're upset already and you haven't even found anything out yet. That's if there's anything to find out. It's all speculation, as far as I can see. I just don't want to see you get hurt.'

'Well, it's gone too far now for me to drop it. I just have to see for myself and that'll be the end of it.'

'Will it though? Are you sure you can cope with what you find out?'

'I won't know for sure until the time comes,' said Claire and she sighed, 'but I've thought through all the options — I've thought of little else since I came back from Donegal. I know it won't be easy, but I'm pretty confident that I'll be all right, once I've had time to get used to the truth, whatever it is.'

'Of course, your suspicions might be completely wrong.'

'Oh, God, I hope so, Aiden.'

'Just promise me one thing?'

'What?'

'That you won't go rushing up there just yet. Take a little more time to get used to the possibilities before you do.'

★　★　★

In the weeks that followed their return from Donegal Eileen's condition deteriorated rapidly. A body scan revealed that the cancer had spread to her liver and kidneys. She became very weak and confined to bed.

One night, when Jimmy was alone in the house with the boys, Claire came rushing in.

241

'Where's Auntie Sheila?' she cried.

'At work. She's on night shift,' he replied, startled. 'What's wrong, Claire?'

'It's Mum. She's in a terrible state with the pain and I don't know what to do. You've got to go and get Sheila.'

'If she's that bad we'd better get the doctor,' he said, reaching for the phone on the wall.

'No!' cried Claire. Her eyes were wide with alarm and she had beads of sweat on her upper lip. 'She doesn't want the doctor. She's afraid they'll try and put her in the hospital. And she doesn't want that. She wants to be at home.'

'But Sheila's at work — ' began Jimmy.

'Will you just go and get her!' Claire shouted, her voice bordering on a scream. '*Please!*' Then she lowered her voice and added, panting with emotion, 'She'll know what to do.'

'OK then,' said Jimmy, relenting, 'I'll phone her.'

'There isn't time. She'll need a lift, anyway.'

He couldn't argue with Claire's logic. Without another word, he got his coat from the hall, and grabbed the car keys.

'You go on over to the house,' he said. 'The boys will be all right here with Conor. I'll just let him know what's happening.'

Jimmy drove quickly but carefully to the hospital, mindful that the last thing they needed was another accident. He'd thought it was time Eileen had proper paid nursing care but Sheila and Claire wouldn't hear of it. Sheila spent most of her time, when not at work, looking after Eileen, and Claire took over in the evenings. This only proved that it was getting too much for them.

In the hospital carpark he was about to get out of the car when something caught his eye — a flash of white at the side of the grey building. As he watched his eyes became accustomed to the gloom, and he saw two figures in the half-shadow. It was a man and a woman, both dressed in hospital whites, and they were locked in an embrace. The taller of the two, the man, had his back to Jimmy and as he released the woman, a petite blonde, from his arms, Jimmy saw them quite clearly. The man was Dr John McCabe and the woman Sheila. Jimmy blinked for he could not, at first, believe what he was seeing.

Sheila said something — Dr McCabe threw back his head and laughed. Then he pulled Sheila to him once more and kissed her fiercely, almost lifting her off her feet. Anger welled up inside Jimmy, more at the thought of that shared laughter than the physical intimacy. He couldn't remember when he and Sheila had last shared a joke. Suddenly the pair parted — Sheila put a hand on her hair, then smoothed the front of her tunic with both palms.

Dr McCabe walked towards the corner of the hospital building, glancing furtively from left to right. Sheila hung back, allowing him to gain twenty or so yards on her before following, so giving him time to enter the hospital well before she reached the door. When he reached the bright lights that illuminated the entrance to A&E, the doctor threw back his shoulders and

243

marched confidently through the automatic doors that opened as though at his command.

So she was having an affair. That was the cause of her mood-swings and bad temper. That was the reason she'd become so distant with him. Menopause, my arse!

Jimmy got out of the car which was only a stone's throw from Sheila. Her gaze fell on him and, slowly, her face fell. She did not say anything. She just stood there looking at him, guiltily at first and then her expression changed to one of defiance. She marched purposefully towards him.

'So,' she said, 'now you know.'

Jimmy was so angry he could barely speak. He could not, dared not deal with this now, for he knew he was very close to smashing her face in with his fist. He swallowed and looked away.

'Get in the car,' he said.

'I will not.'

'I said get in the car,' he shouted, and then said more quietly, 'Your sister needs you.'

'Oh,' said Sheila, losing her composure. 'What's wrong?'

Jimmy ignored her question.

'I'd better get my bag . . . '

'You're not going back in there,' he growled. 'Eileen's taken a bad turn and she needs you. Now.'

'I can't just leave my post like that! I'll lose my job. I'll have to clear it with Sister Watson. Wait here.'

She sprinted into the building while Jimmy sat in the car and gripped the steering wheel until has hands ached.

Within minutes Sheila appeared in the doorway to the hospital, ran towards the car and climbed quickly into the passenger seat. She threw her bag in the footwell and slammed the door. Without waiting for her to put on her seat belt, Jimmy put his foot on the accelerator and drove off. She stared pointedly out of the passenger window as they drove home in silence. Jimmy was glad for he did not want her to see the effect this revelation had on him. He still had some pride left.

After all the years they'd been together and everything they'd gone through, Jimmy couldn't believe it. Or he wouldn't have believed it if he hadn't seen it with his own eyes. That bastard, pawing his wife like she was a dog. Which she was. A bitch on heat. He glanced over at Sheila and his heart pounded in his breast with rage.

He imagined what else they'd done together and visualised Dr McCabe's hands on the most intimate parts of Sheila's body. He blinked several times and concentrated on the driving — pushed his left foot to the floor, changed gear, released the clutch, accelerated. She'd made a bloody fool out of him and he'd be damned if he was going to sit there and take it!

They got to the house — he slammed the brakes on and the car lurched to a halt. Sheila glared at him accusingly and, without a word, got out of the car and went straight in to her sister's house. When she was out of sight Jimmy put his hands over his face.

How long had it been going on? Was she in

love with him? Had she slept with him? Of course she has, you fool, he told himself, she's a grown woman. With a chip on her shoulder. If she'd set out to hurt him then she'd succeeded. In spectacular fashion.

Did this mean Sheila would want a separation, or worse, a divorce? He thought with dread of her leaving him. But how could he let her stay after what she'd done? He should kick her out. What kind of man would tolerate this? Only a wimp.

He hated her but he loved her too. Why had she done this to him? Was this her way of getting back at him about Claire? His heart felt like it would burst with grief.

And then he began to cry, brief whimpers at first, like an injured animal, and then, as sorrow overwhelmed him, great breathless sobs. It was the first time Jimmy had cried in over thirty years.

He looked through his blurred vision at the house they'd shared for fifteen years. At the white PVC windows Sheila had wanted so much and he'd spent a whole summer installing. At the window-box he'd made in the garden shed and the white picket fence that Sheila thought so pretty. Did she hate the house and everything in it? Did she cook and clean and keep the garden, not out of love but out of a sense of duty? Because she was trapped?

He'd worked his fingers to the bone renovating every inch of that house just to please Sheila. Just to make her happy. And this was how she'd repaid him. He thumped the steering wheel with his fist.

He sighed and put a hand to his face and roughly wiped away the tears that remained on his cheeks. So this was what it had come to? Sixteen years of marriage and all the years before that too. Right from when they first laid eyes on each other.

When they'd got married he'd worried that the history between them would be too much to overcome, that it would come back to haunt them and he was right. Sheila had never forgiven him for what had happened to Claire. She blamed him along with everyone else.

Inside the house, Jimmy found the remains of a bottle of whiskey in the sideboard and downed it in one. Then he climbed the stairs, wearily, to the landing where a light shone under Conor's door. Jimmy decided to ignore it — right now Conor's bedtime was the very least of his concerns. He thought of how foolishly he'd behaved over the whole business with Conor. Now he really had something to worry about.

The next morning when he woke up the space in the bed beside him was empty and the pillow uncreased. Jimmy's head was thumping. He could hear the TV blaring downstairs, signifying that the boys were up and watching cartoons. Gingerly, he put on his work uniform.

When he came downstairs Conor was sitting at the breakfast table. 'Where's Mum?' he said.

'I don't know.'

'Did she go back to work after seeing Aunt Eileen?'

'I said I don't know.'

'Did you have a fight?'

Silence.

'It's just that she's usually home from work by now,' persisted Conor.

'Will you give it a rest? I don't know where she is,' said Jimmy.

The back door opened and Sheila came in, still dressed in her hospital uniform.

'You're late getting back, Mum,' said Conor.

'I didn't go back to work last night,' she replied, stiffly. 'I stayed over at your Aunt Eileen's.'

'Oh,' said Conor, looking from Jimmy to Sheila. 'How is she?'

'She's comfortable again. We got her sorted out and the doctor's coming round to see her first thing.'

'I'm going to work,' said Jimmy and he walked to the back door.

'Wait a minute,' said Sheila, putting her hand on his arm. 'We need to talk.'

He shook her hand off, violently. 'It's a bit late for talking, Sheila. I think we're past that now, don't you?'

'We need to decide what we're going to do,' she said, quietly.

'No, *you* need to decide what *you're* going to do, Sheila. I'm staying here with my kids. You can fuck away off and do what you like.'

Conor looked from one to the other with a shocked expression on his face.

'There's no need for language like that,' said Sheila, looking pointedly at Conor. 'Not in front of the children.'

248

'Don't you tell me what I can and can't say in my own house,' he shouted. 'If you choose to go screwing around with someone else then that's fine, Sheila. But don't think you can then waltz in here and . . . '

Conor stood up.

'Stop it! Stop it!' he shouted and ran from the room.

'Look what you've done now, you idiot!' screamed Sheila.

'Me? Look what *I've* done? You're the one that's pulling this family apart! Don't you dare try to put the blame on me. I swear to God I'll — '

'You'll what?' she said.

But he did not rise to the bait. He calmed himself and looked her squarely in the face.

'I swear to God,' he said in a lowered voice, 'that I'll make sure you don't get this house or the kids.'

He saw a flicker of fear in her eyes. She took one step back from him and swallowed. Then he walked out.

★   ★   ★

Jimmy couldn't concentrate on the job and rode the train to and from Belfast in a daze. There was so much to think about and clear thinking was impossible while the image of Sheila and Dr McCabe burned in his memory.

Every time he calmed himself enough to concentrate and think logically, a blinding fury would engulf him. In an empty carriage he

249

rammed his fist into the backrest of a seat repeatedly, until his knuckles reddened. And then he sat down, his anger spent, and nursed his aching fist.

At home Sheila was nowhere to be seen. A note in the kitchen told him that the boys had had their tea, his was in the microwave and she was over at Eileen's. He opened the microwave, took the plate out and tipped the meal in the bin. Then he went out and got himself fish and chips. After, he left the remains of the carryout and the opened bottle of ketchup on the kitchen table, confident that it would infuriate Sheila.

Bridget called for him at seven thirty.

'Are you all ready then for your big night?' she said, when he got in the car.

'What do you mean?' he replied, blankly.

About to pull away from the kerb, Bridget hesitated, her hands motionless on the steering wheel. 'Your presentation on the Dry Bar. I thought you were putting your paper to the Council tonight.'

'Oh that. I was. But I'm not now.'

'But it's on tonight's agenda. I thought you were really keen to get it up and running.'

Jimmy sighed. 'Right now I couldn't give a shit.'

'Jimmy! What's wrong? You look . . . you look ill. Has something happened?'

'Will you just drive, Bridget,' he said tersely, glancing at Eileen's front window, 'please.'

The car pulled away and drove slowly down the road. Martin and Danny, playing football in the street, waved at them. Bridget responded enthusiastically with one of her broad grins and a toot of the horn. Jimmy sat stony-faced and stared straight ahead.

Once they had left Ladas Parade behind, Bridget said, 'Will you just tell me what's eating you, Jimmy?'

'My whole fucking life is falling apart. That's what's eating me, Bridget.'

'Do you want to tell me what on earth is going on, Jimmy?'

He told her about Sheila and Conor and she listened without interrupting. And by the time he had finished they were in the carpark at the council buildings and already fifteen minutes late for the meeting.

'Look, maybe this isn't a good idea, Jimmy. Why don't I drop you back home? You and Sheila need to talk.'

'There's nothing to talk about. Our marriage is over.'

'You don't know that.'

'For Christ's sake, she's screwing another man, Bridget.'

'I know it's very hard, Jimmy. But, well, there must be a reason why this happened and you need to find out. And about Conor, you mustn't get angry with him, you know. If he is gay, he can't help it.'

Jimmy sighed and said, 'Right now, that's the least of my worries.'

'I'll take you home,' she said, firmly, and turned the key in the ignition.

Overcome with exhaustion, both physical and emotional, Jimmy silently acquiesced. Bridget dropped him at the end of Ladas Parade.

'Don't do anything you might regret, Jimmy,' was all she said, then patted him on the arm.

The street was deserted, all the kids called in to do their homework and get ready for bed. Walking up the road, Jimmy's legs felt like lead weights, every step requiring a great deal of effort.

Inside the house he heard Sheila's voice from upstairs — it cut through him like a knife. She came halfway down the stairs when she heard the door and addressed him, her face expressionless.

'Eileen has asked to see you,' she said in a deadpan voice.

Eileen hadn't spoken to him, nor had he been in her house, since the day of the funeral.

'What for?'

'I don't know.'

'I'll go over tomorrow.'

'No, you'd better go now. She's anxious to speak to you tonight.'

Jimmy thought of his old friend, Paddy, dead now for nearly four months, and nodded. He owed him this at the very least. If Eileen wanted to abuse him, then he would sit and take it. He was too tired to fight any more.

The deterioration in Eileen's condition, since he'd last seen her some weeks before, shocked Jimmy. He knew they'd got her a proper hospital bed and a hoist and that she was on a morphine drip. But he hadn't expected the room to smell like a hospital or to find Eileen lying in bed with her eyes shut, like a wizened old lady. She'd lost so much weight, he wouldn't have recognised her.

Moira got out of the chair in the corner when he came in and said, 'I'll leave you two alone.'

He crept over to the side of the bed and whispered, 'Hello, Eileen.'

Eileen opened her eyes and smiled. Perhaps she wasn't angry with him any more. Or else she didn't recognise him — Sheila had told him she was disorientated because of the drugs.

'Jimmy,' she said and patted the edge of the bed with her skeletal hand, 'come and sit here, beside me.'

Jimmy's heart ached with compassion. He didn't have the strength to cope with this right now. But he found the courage from somewhere, steeled himself and sat down.

'They tell me I don't have that much time left,' she said, 'and I know that I'm a little confused from time to time.'

He nodded and waited for her to go on. She licked her lips and continued with some effort.

'I have two things left to do before I die. One of them is to tell you that I'm sorry about what I said at the funeral.'

Jimmy's heart beat faster.

'I know that you weren't responsible for Paddy's death and I suppose I've always known. I just didn't want to admit it to myself. I was looking for someone to blame and you were an easy target. Do you forgive me?'

Jimmy felt a terrible weight lift from his shoulders.

'Of course I do, love,' he said gently. 'Thank you.'

She lay quietly for a few moments.

'Eileen, you said there were two things you had to do. What was the second?'

'Oh, that's to do with Claire and Sheila.'

At the mention of his wife's name, Jimmy let go of her hand and looked at the floor.

'Something's happened between you two, hasn't it?' she said. 'I could sense it last night from Sheila.'

'She's having an affair, Eileen.'

'Ah,' she said, nodding her head in understanding, 'she's only doing it to get back at you, you know.'

'You mean you knew about it?' he said, lifting his head sharply.

'No,' she replied slowly. 'What makes you think I did?'

'You don't seem very surprised.'

'Sheila's been a walking time bomb for years, Jimmy. Only none of us could see it. She's never got over losing Claire.'

Jimmy hung his head.

'And this thing with the menopause has put her over the edge. You have to understand that she's very angry, Jimmy.'

'So what should I do?'

'Maybe it's time we gave her what she wants.'

'We? I don't follow.'

'Claire, Jimmy. Claire. She wants Claire to be told the truth and that's the last thing I have to do before I go to Paddy. I've been putting it off because I'm afraid how Claire'll react. But, in my heart, I know that she has to be told and it has to be me that tells her.'

There were tears in her eyes when she spoke again.

'There's something else I want to say to you, Jimmy,' she said, and he squeezed her hand. 'I want to thank you for giving us your daughter. I know that you didn't get much say in it at the time but you never made life hard for us. You never complained. Even though it must have been hard for you, watching her grow up and calling someone else 'Dad'.'

Jimmy felt a lump form in his throat.

'Claire was the best thing that ever happened to me and Paddy and I want you to know that we thanked God every day for her. But it should have been you and Sheila we were thanking. And I was so happy I never thought how awful it must have been for you.'

Jimmy cleared his throat. 'She couldn't have had better parents than you and Paddy, Eileen. No one in the world could have done a better job of raising her.'

She smiled, closed her eyes and soon her breathing deepened and she was asleep.

Moira appeared behind Jimmy and placed a hand on his shoulder.

'She needs to rest now,' she said, and slowly Jimmy got to his feet.

⋆ ⋆ ⋆

Claire left the house at her usual time with every intention of going to work. Aunt Sheila insisted she keep her job even though she would gladly have packed it in to look after Mum. But it was a relief to get out of the house and have something else, other than Mum, to occupy her mind for a few hours.

At the security gate outside work, the photograph on her identity card caught her eye — a carefree seventeen-year-old, before Mum had cancer and Dad died. Abruptly she turned away from the security gate, shoved the card in her pocket and walked briskly down the road, hoping no one had spotted her. She went and sat by the river and listened to the faint chug-chug of the train in the distance.

She wondered what it would be like after Mum had gone. She didn't think she could face being alone in the house with all the memories. She'd have to make some sort of plan — maybe she and Aiden could find a place of their own and move in together? They loved each other, they were sleeping together. Why not?

Only this morning Mum had asked her if she was still planning on going to Paris with him.

'Not for the time being,' she'd replied, truthfully and Mum seemed relieved.

'That's good,' she said. 'You'll not be needing that passport then.'

'No, I suppose not,' said Claire but she omitted to mention that she had every intention of pursuing a copy of her birth certificate. Somehow she felt it better not to mention this to Mum. If there was something she would rather Claire didn't know what was the point of distressing her when she was so ill?

The screech of brakes told Claire that the train had arrived in Ballyfergus. Since she'd made up her mind to get a copy of her birth certificate she hadn't had the opportunity to get up to Belfast. Every day was taken up with work and looking after Mum and she hardly had time to take a shower let alone go off for the day. But it had never left her mind, not for an instant, and she was becoming increasingly frustrated by not being able to go to Belfast.

But why not go today? She knew Uncle Jimmy wouldn't be on the trains today. Aunt Sheila had said he had the 'flu or something and had called in sick. So she wouldn't have to explain herself to him on the train.

She hurried to the station, phoned the office from a payphone and said she was ill. Before she knew it, she was sitting in a carriage watching the grey waters of the Lough and the green countryside fly by.

Too late for early morning commuters, she watched the train fill up with pensioners and mothers with small children in tow, all heading for the shops in Belfast. The rhythm of the train, lurching gently in and out of the stations along the way, soothed her. God, she was tired. The warm sun shone through the window and Claire closed her eyes.

When she opened them the train was pulling into York Street Station and the carriage was a bustle of activity as everyone prepared to get off. Suddenly, Claire felt nervous. What did she really expect to see on her birth certificate? Mentally she flicked through the various scenarios she had pictured and tried to imagine how she would truly feel if any of them were true. But each possibility just made her feel sick to the stomach. She collected her bag and got off the train, trailing the other commuters slowly along the platform.

She could, of course, wait for the next train back to Ballyfergus and not pursue this any further. She could try to put all those daft notions out of her mind and forget about it. But of course she knew she could never be at peace until she'd seen her birth certificate for herself. Especially now that Mum was dying — that gave her quest an increased urgency. If there was something dubious about her background and parentage, then Claire felt that she should know now. And depending on what she found out, it might be something she'd want to discuss with Mum. At the very least she would be due an explanation. No, there was no going back now.

Outside, people climbed into taxis and others waited at the bus stop for the shuttle service. Claire hovered impatiently at the back of the queue. It was only a twenty-minute walk to the city centre — she decided not to wait. She needed to expend some of the nervous energy that was building up inside her.

She crossed the lanes of busy traffic and, once she'd reached the safety of the pavement on the other side, marched briskly down the road. The thundering traffic stirred up the dusty city grime and hurled it in her face, forcing her to squint. She passed run-down commercial buildings and boarded-up shops, the old Gallagher cigarette factory and Yorkgate shopping centre. Forced to slow her pace in the heat she came, at last, to the City Hall. She asked for directions to the Register of Births, Deaths and Marriages and someone directed her to Chichester Street.

It took her just two minutes to find Oxford House, a grey utilitarian building. She stared at the glass doors and the reception desk behind them and her heart pounded in her breast.

Should she go through with this? Don't be silly, she hadn't come all this way just to turn on her heel at the last minute and run away. Think logically, Claire, she told herself. What's the worst that could happen? That Mum and Dad weren't married when they had her. So what? Or that Dad wasn't her real Dad? It was possible of course but when she thought of Mum she just couldn't see her ever being unfaithful to Dad. Unless of course Claire was born before Dad came on the scene . . .

She tried to imagine how she would feel if a stranger turned out to be her father and convinced herself that it would be OK. She would always think of Dad as her real father. What were the other possibilities? That she was adopted. Again, it would be a shock, but she just couldn't believe it might be true. For one thing she had such a strong resemblance to Mum's side of the family. And Mum and Dad were the ones that brought her up, loved her, gave her everything. If she were adopted, then their love would be all the more precious, given freely as it was to a child not of their own flesh and blood. Would she want to know who her real parents were? Right now Claire couldn't answer that question. Any one of these possibilities would provide a very strong reason why Mum and Granny didn't want her to see her birth certificate. She felt pretty sure she could handle them all. She might be shaken but none of these revelations would turn her world upside down.

'Can I help you, love?' said a voice and Claire looked up.

It was the security man from inside the building, holding the door open with his foot.

'Is this the Register of Births, Deaths and Marriages?' she asked.

'That's what it says on the door, love,' he replied, good-naturedly.

He directed her to the ground floor where she approached the middle-aged clerk behind the desk confidently.

'I'd like a copy of my birth certificate, please,' she said.

'No problem, love,' he replied pushing a form across the worn counter. 'I just need you to fill this out. We need to know your date of birth, mother's maiden name, that sort of thing. Give me a shout if you need any help.'

He turned away and busied himself at a computer screen. Claire moved to a small table and chair in the corner and completed the form. It all seemed pretty straightforward, exactly what she'd expected.

She took the piece of paper back to the counter and handed it over. The clerk glanced at the form over the rim of his glasses.

'That looks OK,' he said. 'Now you know that

there's a £10 charge for same-day service? That's in addition to the standard £7 charge.'

'Yes, I know,' said Claire.

'We could post it out to you, love. Save yourself a tenner . . . '

'No, I'd like it today. Please.'

'Well, it shouldn't be more than half an hour,' he replied, glancing at the clock on the wall.

Claire sat down in one of the chairs lined against the wall and picked up a dog-eared copy of *Hello* magazine, months out of date. Still, anything to take her mind off the wait. She flicked through the pages as the minutes ticked by on the clock on the wall. Thirty-four minutes had passed when she heard her name called.

Her heart leaped. This was the moment of truth. She walked slowly towards the counter. She wouldn't look at the certificate straightaway, not until she was out in the corridor at least, and away from prying eyes.

'I'm sorry but we can't find these details on the system.'

Claire frowned and said, 'I don't understand.'

'We've input the information you gave us and we're not coming up with a match. Can I ask you to take another look at the form and check that it's accurate. Are all the spellings correct, for instance?'

Claire answered without looking at the piece of paper he pushed across the counter in her direction.

'Yes, it's right. I'm sure of it. There must be some mistake.'

'It's very unlikely,' he said softly. 'Are you

quite sure that the information you've given us is correct? It happens sometimes that, well, people get it wrong.'

He had a look on his face that said he'd seen it all before.

She stared at him and then blushed. He was suggesting in the nicest possible way that the information she *believed* to be correct might not be.

'I — I — ' she stammered and put her hand on the form lying between them, 'I'll have another look.'

She looked at the questions and her answers on the form and wondered which piece of information could be wrong. Her date of birth? Her real name? Her place of birth? Her father's name? How would she ever find out?

'There is another way,' said the clerk and Claire looked up at him.

'You can search the records for yourself. It costs six pounds an hour. Given as it's quiet I could show you how to use the computer and get you started.'

He led her into what looked like a reading room in a library except on each table was a computer screen. Only one other table was occupied — a bookish-looking girl about Claire's age was sitting in front of a monitor, surrounded by files and papers.

The clerk sat Claire down and showed her how to use the computer.

'We usually find that it's best to start with date of birth. That's the thing people are less likely to tamper with. That's if they've tampered with anything,' he added hastily.

Once he'd shown her how to interrogate the data by using various commands, he left her to trawl through the records. She input her date and place of birth and the computer came up with six entries. Excited, she opened the list and scrolled down the records. She recognised two of the entries from her year at school but there was no sign of her own name.

What now? She sat back in the chair and gnawed her knuckles. She thought of the night Mum had that terrible dream in Donegal. What was it Mum had dreamt? She said something about Claire not being hers to keep and she'd mentioned a place. Where was it? Coleraine! She said she'd had Claire in Coleraine.

Claire's fingertips worked speedily over the keyboard. She input her date of birth and this time, instead of Ballyfergus, she put Coleraine as her place of birth. The computer threw up fifteen entries. She scrolled down them. There was no Claire O'Connor listed, only a Claire Devlin.

Her fingers hovered over the keyboard and twice she formed her hands into fists and put them in her lap. It was no big deal if Mum and Dad hadn't been married when she was born. And if Dad wasn't her real dad, well, he was more of a dad to her than a name on a piece of paper could ever be. Whichever it was, she told herself, she could handle it.

So she took several deep breaths to calm herself, moved the cursor over her name on the screen, hit the 'Enter' button and sat back.

The computer whined for a few seconds, the

list of names disappeared and in its place came up the full details of her birth. She was born Claire Devlin, at Coleraine Hospital on Friday 18th May 1979. And when she looked at the name of her mother, Claire's heart stopped beating.

Sheila Bernadette Devlin, spinster.

Her father: James Francis Gallagher, unemployed.

She sat perfectly still and stared at the screen.

'You found what you were looking for, then?' said a voice in her ear.

'Yes,' she replied in a voice that was so faint it was barely audible.

7

Aiden came to slowly and squinted at the alarm-clock — it was late. He'd been dozing in a semi-conscious state since dawn, dreaming (or was it remembering?) about Dad. Little things, like the way he used to shave over the kitchen sink, peering into a tarnished chrome mirror. He remembered white scum floating in the water, black stubble clinging to the sides of the bowl. It amazed him how much he could recall, things that before he never even realised he knew.

Not that the dreams were all as benign. In the dead of night he would wake breathless and soaked in sweat from a nightmare in which he reached out to save Dad and someone held him back. And then he'd see Dad's charred body through the orange flames and he'd smell the pungent odour of burning flesh, a smell you never forgot.

These episodes had become more frequent of late and more vivid. Aiden even found himself remembering things when he was wide-awake. He could trace this back to the conversation he'd had with Claire in the Indian on the night of her birthday. Somehow, talking about his parents, albeit briefly, had released a whole armada of memories that bombarded him night and day. It was as though Claire had opened up channels in his mind which he could not switch off.

How he wished Mum was here to comfort him

and stroke his head and tell him it was all right. Mum.

Why did you do it?

Come on, man, he said to himself, get a grip. He got out of bed and went to the bathroom down the hall. He noticed that he shaved exactly the way Dad used to, right down to the bits he did first and the way he held his razor, like a pencil. He splashed his face with cold water, dried it and looked in the mirror. He had his father's dark colouring and the same curly black hair that Mum always envied.

I could have made things better, Mum. If you'd only given me a chance.

Back in his room, Aiden dressed and sat down on the bed. He couldn't go on like this, talking to himself and listening to voices inside his head. If only he could find some way to make it stop.

He had to get out of his room and focus on something else. Like Claire — he'd go there now, to her workplace. He could take her somewhere for lunch.

When he called at the Social Security Office they told him she was off sick.

'Since when?' he said, surprised.

The girl behind the counter recognised him as Claire's boyfriend.

'She phoned in sick this morning,' she told him. 'Said she had a tummy-bug.'

That's odd, he thought. She never said anything about being ill when he spoke to her on the phone last night. He retraced his steps along the High Street and called into a florist's shop where he bought a small bunch of pale pink roses. Then he walked to Ladas Parade. The sun blazed in the sky and everyone was wearing shorts and T-shirts. Exactly the same sort of weather the day Dad was killed. *Stop it, Aiden.*

He rang the doorbell and waited. He took a few steps back and peered at the upstairs windows — there was no sign of life. He rang again and shuffled uncomfortably on the doorstep, conscious of the wilting bunch of flowers in his hand.

Then he went next door and rang the Gallaghers' doorbell.

Sheila came to the door almost immediately. She was wearing a strappy top the same colour of green as her eyes and a pair of very skimpy shorts. Her skin was golden tan all over.

'Oh,' she said awkwardly and paused. 'What are you doing here?' She noticed the bouquet in his fist.

'I came to see Claire. And to give her these,' he said, trying not to stare at Sheila's shapely legs. 'I rang the bell next door but there was no reply.'

Sheila's eyebrows furrowed slightly in the middle. 'But she's at work, Aiden.'

'No, she's not. I just came from there and they said she was off sick.'

'That's strange — I was next door until just a few minutes ago and she definitely wasn't there. Why don't you come in for a second? And I'll pop back over and check.'

He followed her down the hall into a small, neat kitchen and she pointed at one of the four chairs round the cramped kitchen table.

267

'Have a seat, Aiden. I'll not be long.'

He obeyed and watched her as she stood on her tiptoes and stretched for a silver key hanging from a hook by the door. The muscles in her calves tightened, then relaxed, as she retrieved the key from the hook and opened the door. She left it ajar — the top of her head passed across the kitchen window and out of sight.

Aiden set the flowers on the table, suddenly feeling foolish, and looked about the room. There was a chopping-board and a knife lying on the kitchen counter and a pile of vegetables on the draining-board. Otherwise not a thing was out of place.

Barely a minute had passed before Sheila appeared in the doorway.

'Nope. She's not there,' she said, replacing the key and shutting the door behind her. 'Have you time for a cuppa? I was just making one.'

Aiden glanced round the immaculate kitchen and noticed no signs of tea-making. He really ought to go, he thought, but instead he said, 'Yes, that'd be lovely.'

He sat and watched her while she made the tea.

'So, what exactly did they say at her work?' said Sheila, once she'd milked the two mugs.

'Not much. Just that she phoned in first thing and said she had a tummy-bug.'

'That's odd,' said Sheila, pouring the tea, 'because she left the house as usual this morning.' She handed Aiden a cup of tea.

'Perhaps she's gone to the doctor's or the chemist's to get something,' said Aiden.

Sheila leaned against the counter, legs crossed, cradling a mug in her hands. 'Possibly, though I'm surprised she didn't mention it to me.'

With nothing more to say on the subject they both fell silent.

After a little while, Aiden asked, 'How's Mrs O'Connor?'

'OK — today anyway. She's getting weaker by the day, Aiden, but at least they've got the pain under control. She'll rest now for a couple of hours.'

She placed her mug in the kitchen sink. 'Look, do you mind if I get on with this soup? I like to get things done when she's asleep.'

He nodded his acquiescence. She took an apron out of a drawer, slipped it over her head, and tied the strings around her slim waist. Then she got out a huge pot, peeled and roughly chopped a couple of onions. She tossed a chunk of butter in the pan along with the onions and soon the kitchen was filled with their smell.

Aiden drank his tea, watching her. He remembered a kitchen like this once, full of homely smells and sunshine. He remembered photos like the ones stuck all over the fridge — pictures of happy, smiling faces. He saw Mum standing at the sink like Sheila was now, humming happily to herself as she went about her work.

How he wished he could go back to those days and make things stay that way always. Stop the passage of time, right at that perfect moment when Dad was dozing next door in the armchair and he and Mum were wrapped up together in their perfect little world in the kitchen.

How he envied people who lived a normal life, who had a mother to hold them and soothe them and tell them everything was just fine. He'd loved Mum so much. Did he love her more than she'd loved him? He must have done. *You didn't love me enough, Mum. If you had done you never would have left me in this world on my own.*

'What did you say?' said Sheila.

He looked at her blankly. She was standing with a pair of rubber gloves on, the vegetable peeler in one hand and a potato in the other.

'Nothing.'

'You did. You said what sounded like 'You didn't love me enough, Mum'.'

Aiden opened his mouth to speak but no words came out. He simply stared. Sheila laid down the things in her hands and took off the rubber gloves. She came over and stood beside him. Being so petite, like Claire, her chest was level with his face.

'What's wrong, Aiden?' she said.

Wordlessly, he held out his arms.

Hesitantly, she moved into his embrace, and allowed him to bury his face in her breast. She gently stroked the back of his head, just like his mum used to do when he was crying. Her breasts were small and rounded and he pressed his face against them, inhaling her scent, trying to remember if that's how Mum smelt.

'Tell me what's wrong,' she coaxed.

'I can't,' he said, struggling to bring himself under control. 'I can't.'

'Yes, you can,' she urged him. 'Tell me.'

He was sobbing quietly now, unable any longer to stem the flow of tears. He clung to her slight frame, clutching at her warmth and her compassion. When he'd calmed down sufficiently to speak he said, 'After Dad was blown up, Mum killed herself in the bath. With a knife. She slit her wrists. She left me. How could she do that? I was only seven.'

'Shh . . . ' she said soothing with her soft voice, 'it's OK. Shh . . . '

And then he felt Sheila's fingers running through his hair in a way Mum never used to do. Then her hands on his shoulders, kneading the muscles with her fingers. He felt the slight pressure of her lips on the crown of his head and then she rested her head on his.

In an instant he was highly aroused. He pulled away from her and looked at her face. Her expression was enigmatic, the lips slightly parted. Without removing his gaze from hers, he placed both hands firmly on her bottom and she swayed slightly as if buffeted by a wind. She closed her eyes.

'Sheila?' he said.

'Don't say anything. Don't spoil it.'

She pushed one of her legs between his thighs and rubbed her knee gently, provocatively, against his inside leg. He put a hand up the leg of her shorts, took a buttock in his hand and squeezed. Then he lifted her onto his lap and she wrapped her legs around him. Their pelvises were in contact now, and they kissed hard and passionately, his groin grinding into her.

271

Sheila breathed heavily and Aiden was alive with desire. He pressed his lips firmly against hers and thrust his tongue into her mouth. She moaned in response. He ran his lips down her neck and onto her bare shoulder, sinking his teeth into the soft skin. Sheila threw back her head and writhed.

'Where's Jimmy?' he gasped.

'Out. He won't be back for hours.'

'Are you sure?'

'Yes,' she said hoarsely.

'And the boys.'

'School.'

In one movement Aiden got to his feet with Sheila in his arms, and carried her upstairs.

'In there,' she said, pointing at a door.

He kicked it open with his foot and laid her on the double bed. She lay there, passively, while he stripped her and stood back to admire her naked body. It showed signs of child-bearing in that her stomach protruded slightly and her breasts sagged a little. But Aiden found her highly arousing.

Then, she rolled onto her front and, lying across the bed, beckoned for him to come close. He walked over to the edge of the bed and, in one quick, expert movement, she undid his fly and pulled out his cock. Taking it in her hand, she placed his rigid penis inside her mouth — it felt hot and her tongue teased the tip of his prick. Aiden closed his eyes. He thought he would faint with the sheer, exquisite pleasure of it. He opened his eyes and looked down at her bare buttocks, legs extended, her feet squirming with pleasure. He could bear it no longer.

'That's enough,' he almost shouted and pulled away. 'I know what you need.'

With that he pulled his jeans and underpants off and straddled her where she lay across the bed.

'Do it then,' she said.

He thrust himself inside her in one violent movement. They both gasped with the shock.

Then they had frantic, wild sex.

It was over in minutes. Aiden rolled off her, spent, and lay on his back, panting.

'Jesus Christ,' he said, 'what happened?'

'I don't know,' said Sheila, in a quiet voice.

Slowly the sexual exhilaration gave way to creeping embarrassment and then horror. What in the name of God had he been thinking of, sleeping with her? Claire's aunt, for Christ's sake! Suddenly, he felt the urge to get away from here, and Sheila, as quickly as possible.

He got off the bed and, too embarrassed to look Sheila in the face, found his clothes and put them on. She sat up on the bed and pulled a throw, modestly, around her naked body.

'This — I — Sheila, this was a mistake. I never planned this.'

'Me neither.'

'I think it's best if we pretend it never happened.'

'Yes, that's what to do. It never happened.'

Sheila sounded the way he felt. In shock.

'If Claire ever found out — ' he began.

'She won't. Not from me,' said Sheila.

He stood at the door with his hands in the

273

pockets of his jeans, anxious to be gone from the scene of the crime.

'This is going to sound hard to believe but I really want it to work between me and Claire. I love her, you see. I really love her.'

'So do I,' said Sheila. 'I'd die before I'd do anything to harm her.'

Aiden was surprised by the passion in her voice. Sheila sat on the bed in the same pose he'd seen Claire adopt after they made love. She cocked her head the same way and her bare shoulders sloped gently in just the same manner. The resemblance was striking.

'I think I know where Claire is,' he said suddenly. 'I just remembered. Last night she was talking about going up to Belfast to get a copy of her birth certificate. She's been meaning to do it for ages. I don't know for sure but my guess is that's where she's gone today.'

He watched while the colour drained from Sheila's face.

'I know,' he said, misreading the expression on her face. 'She could be back any minute. I'd better go.'

But Sheila remained motionless, just staring at him. She was making him nervous. Jimmy could come in any minute and find them.

'You'd better put some clothes on, Sheila. In case Jimmy comes back.'

Suddenly Sheila crawled to the end of the bed, still clutching the throw.

'Didn't you try to stop her?' she hissed.

He shook his head. 'Stop her? Why should I?'

'*You fool!*' she screamed so loudly that Aiden

took two paces backwards, 'Why didn't you stop her? Oh, my God! Oh, my God!'

She leapt off the bed, frantically gathered her clothes up and attempted to get dressed. But she was in such a panic she made little progress and ran round the room moaning and pulling at her hair.

Aiden watched her with growing apprehension. What in the name of God was wrong with her?

And then, slowly, the truth that his subconscious had registered, but suppressed, became a conscious thought.

'Oh, Jesus,' he said, 'let it not be true.'

Sheila stopped running round the room and stared at him.

'She's your daughter, isn't she?' he said.

'She wasn't supposed to find out like this,' cried Sheila, distraught, and close to tears. 'Eileen promised me she'd tell her. It wasn't supposed to happen like this.'

She fell to her knees, put her face in her hands and started to cry.

Aiden turned and walked from the room, down the stairs and out the front door. He kept going until he was far, far away from the house. He did not know how long he walked but eventually he came to open countryside and quiet country roads. He stopped and leaned on a gate — everything was still and peaceful but inside he was wretched.

He'd done it this time — he'd really fucked up in a big way. He'd never had such highly charged sex in his life but now all he felt was disgust with himself and with Sheila. She should have known better. So should he.

He'd slept with Claire's mother. And, if she ever found out, he knew there was no way she would forgive him. He gazed into the horizon and, slowly, an idea began to take shape in his mind. A plan that would ensure Claire was protected from ever finding out about this.

★ ★ ★

At first the only feeling Claire could register was numbness.

She moved her eyes slowly from the computer screen to the face of the clerk who stood over her.

'Do you want a copy of it then?' he said.

'No! No, thank you.'

She didn't want a copy of her birth certificate — she didn't ever want to see it again. Suddenly the heat in the room was oppressive. Abruptly, she stood up, grabbed her coat and bag and made for the door.

Outside a breeze roared up the city street like a tunnel, cooling her heated face. Sapped of energy, she made her way slowly to the City Hall and sat on a bench overlooking the gardens. Buses and cars, in a seemingly endless parade, circled the City Hall and life for everyone else went on as before.

But for Claire it was changed forever.

How could she go home and carry on as normal? Why had Aunt Sheila and Uncle Jimmy given her up? And why had Mum and Dad raised her? And why had they no children of their own?

She thought of Conor, Martin and Danny — not her cousins now, but brothers. Why did Sheila and Jimmy not want her when they kept the three boys? Did they not love her? How could they have given her away?

Her whole life had been built around this one great lie. It would have been more tolerable if she'd learned her parents were strangers. She would have despised them for giving her up but thanked God she'd been adopted by Eileen and Paddy.

But this! This was something too cruel and awful. All of them — Mum, Dad, Sheila, Jimmy, Granny and Granddad — had pretended, all these years. How could Aunt Sheila watch someone else bring up her own flesh and blood? How could she stand by and hear Claire call someone else 'Mum'. There was only one explanation — she was a heartless bitch. And all that sucking up to Claire — pretending to be her friend, buying that expensive bracelet — it was all to salve a guilty conscience.

What age was Aunt Sheila now? Thirty-eight? That meant that she would have been sixteen when Claire was born. Old enough to keep a child, love her, raise her as her own. The pregnancy would have been a mistake, of course. But surely Granny and Granddad would have helped?

Sheila had been too selfish to put the interests of a child before her own. She must have dumped Claire on Eileen and Paddy. It was made all the worse by the fact that Sheila and Jimmy went on to get married and have a family of their own. A family of which Claire should have been part. For though she loved Mum and Dad her childhood had, in some ways, been lonely. She remembered how she used to long for a brother or a sister.

She'd no gripe with Mum and Dad. She loved Mum so much — she would be lost without her. Knowing that Eileen wasn't her natural mother only intensified her feelings, for Claire knew that her mum had given her complete and unconditional love in spite of the fact that she was not her own.

A man in a suit sat down on the bench beside her and took his lunch out of a paper bag.

Realising she was hungry Claire got up and walked the short distance to Marks & Spencer's where she bought something to eat. Then she wandered aimlessly along the busy pavements, chewing on a sandwich, wondering what to do next. She didn't want to go home but she knew she had to, sooner or later — there was nothing for her here.

She wished she could talk to Aiden. She wanted to tell him the dreadful secret she'd uncovered, she wanted him to hold her and tell her that he loved her more than anything in the entire world. Even if her own mother didn't.

On the train home Claire stared out the window, unseeing. Her heart was cold and full of bitterness. If her real parents had kept her, she would have had two fit, healthy parents and three brothers, not a dead father and a mother on her deathbed. She knew this was a warped and twisted way of thinking but it wasn't fair that she was to lose the two people she'd come to love most.

Just when, she asked herself, did they plan to tell her? After Mum was dead and buried? Did they think she'd fall into their arms then, their long-lost daughter? Or were they waiting for the day when she would find out for herself? They must have known that was only a matter of time, in spite of Eileen's best efforts to hide the truth from her. Why didn't any of them have the guts to tell her to her face? Why did they let her find out in this cold, abrupt manner? But she knew the answer to this question already — if she'd done what Sheila and Jimmy had done, she'd be too ashamed to admit to it either.

By the time the train pulled into Ballyfergus, Claire was enraged and ready for a fight. The more she thought about it, the more it seemed they'd taken her for a fool. It was her life after all, her history — none of them had the right to keep the truth from her. In a place like Ballyfergus there were surely other people who knew too. And they probably looked on her with pity — the poor little bastard whose parents didn't want her.

Claire flung open the door of the carriage, marched out of the station and stormed up the road.

★ ★ ★

It took Sheila a great deal of effort to calm herself. But she had Eileen to take care of and her nursing instinct took over.

Her first priority was to get rid of all evidence of Aiden.

She dressed quickly, in jeans and a T-shirt — there was no time for a shower — brushed her hair, fixed her makeup and doused herself in perfume. It seemed like hours since she'd answered the front door but, according to her wristwatch, only forty-five minutes had passed. How could so much have happened in such a short space of time? If only she'd ignored the doorbell, if only she hadn't invited him in . . .

Sheila straightened the bedcovers and replaced the throw on the foot of the bed. Then she ran downstairs and went next door. Eileen was dozing peacefully. Sheila rushed back to her own house, bent the stems of the pink roses in half, and stuffed them in the bin. She covered them with vegetable peelings then washed, dried and put away the cups she and Aiden had used.

Satisfied she'd removed all traces of him from her home, she spread her hands on the kitchen counter and hung her head. Her heart was pounding with exertion and with fear.

This time she'd really gone too far. She'd jeopardised Claire's happiness and she would never forgive herself for that. Her lips were sealed, but what about Aiden? What if he was one of these people who just couldn't keep a secret? She knew she could. She'd had plenty of practice.

She loathed herself.

First it had been John McCabe. She'd only slept with him to get back at Jimmy — she wanted to hurt him as much as she hurt, day in and day out, year after year. John meant nothing to her but each time they were together was her sweet revenge.

Since their last heated exchange, she and Jimmy had operated a silent truce, both going about their business, stony-faced in each other's company. And at night, while they still shared the same bed, they never so much as touched. They kept up appearances for the sake of the boys, for Claire and because Eileen was dying.

When she told John that she couldn't see him any more, she'd been disappointed in his response. He accepted it with far too much composure and level-headedness. It would have had to come to an end sooner or later, he'd said — they both had spouses and children to consider. She couldn't help but feel that he'd been using her. But she'd no right to complain, for she'd been using him too.

But what had sex with Aiden meant?

It had been mindless, insane, base. She was disgusted with herself. One minute she was comforting him, the next . . . she couldn't quite remember what had happened. All she knew was he was suddenly kissing her and caressing her and she must have him.

Sheila put her hands over her face. What had she become? An adulteress, a whore, sleeping with any man that crossed her path. But not just any man, oh no, that would be too tame. She had to sleep with the man Claire loved, a man at least eight years her junior. And worse, she'd done it in the home she shared with Jimmy and her children. Whatever Jimmy had done, he didn't deserve that.

She realised that she still had a shred of love left for him, but something in her was bent on destruction, hurting those she loved the most.

Like Claire.

She could be home any minute armed with the knowledge that Sheila and Jimmy were her parents.

'Oh, God,' said Sheila, and she sank into a chair.

She knew how she would react if she was Claire. She would be angry. No, more than that, she would be enraged. If only Eileen had done what she said she would. Then all this might have been avoided.

But perhaps she was expecting the worst. Claire was a sensible girl. She'd have time to think things over on the way home. She'd do the sums and realise that Sheila was little more than a child herself when she fell pregnant.

Maybe this was the best way, after all. At least it would all be out in the open. And despite her apprehension and her shame, that part of Sheila that had been shut down for twenty-two years began to come alive again.

★　★　★

Claire's heart was pounding in her chest as she walked purposefully along Ladas Parade. She hadn't worked out what she was going to say to

282

Aunt Sheila and Uncle Jimmy, but she knew she couldn't carry on as though nothing had changed.

A crowd of boys were playing football in the street, Danny and Martin amongst them. Danny picked up the ball when he saw her coming and the boys all stared as she marched past them without acknowledging their presence.

She put her key in the front door, pushed it open and stepped inside. She met Aunt Sheila coming down the stairs with a tray in her hands. She looked harassed, her hair all awry and smudged mascara under her eyes.

'Hello, Claire,' she said, slowly, 'I was just giving your mum something to eat.'

Claire shut the door behind her and dropped her coat and bag in the hall.

She swallowed several times before she spoke. She looked at the woman who was her mother and hate rose within her.

'I went up to Belfast today,' she blurted out, 'to get a copy of my birth certificate.'

'I know,' said Sheila, in a soft, almost apologetic voice.

'How do you know?' snapped Claire, irritated that some of her fire had been stolen.

'Aiden called to see you. He thought you were off work sick. He guessed where you'd gone.'

'I saw my birth certificate, Sheila. On the computer.'

Sheila sighed. 'I'm sorry you found out this way, love. Your mum meant to tell you, she promised me she would. None of us wanted you to find out like this.'

283

'I bet you didn't,' said Claire bitterly. 'Let me ask you one thing.'

Sheila waited in silence, her head tilted back slightly, bracing herself.

'When did you intend to tell me, any of you? How long did you think you could keep it a secret? And I can't believe you gave your own baby away. How could you do such a thing?'

'Sshh . . . Claire, please,' pleaded Sheila. 'Keep your voice down. I wanted to tell you years ago but none of them would let me. I think Eileen was afraid you would stop loving her if you knew the truth.' She extended her hand and touched Claire's arm. Claire withdrew sharply.

'Don't you tell me what to do in my own house. You've no right,' she hissed. 'You gave your rights away twenty-two years ago. You didn't want me then, did you? And it's too late to try and buy me now. Here, you can have this back. I don't want it.'

She ripped the chunky gold bracelet off her wrist, nearly lacerating her skin in the process, and flung it at Sheila. It hit her full in the chest but she barely flinched. Sheila closed her eyes briefly before she spoke again.

'Claire, it wasn't like that. Please listen to me. Look, come next door where we can talk.'

'I don't have to do anything you tell me,' said Claire. 'You're not my mother.'

Claire dispatched the words like bullets and Sheila's slight frame trembled with each impact. But she retained her composure. But then, thought Claire, you would need to be pretty tough to give away your own baby, wouldn't you?

'You'll wake Eileen,' said Sheila calmly. 'You don't want her to find out like this, do you?'

Reluctantly, Claire followed Sheila next door and into the front room where Jimmy was watching TV. He acknowledged Claire and ignored Sheila.

'We have to talk,' said Sheila wearily, and Jimmy shot her a vicious glance. 'About Claire. She knows who we are.'

Jimmy's face suddenly drained of colour. He mumbled something incoherent and examined the toe of his shoe.

'You'd better sit down, Claire,' continued Sheila.

Claire sat down on the edge of an armchair, crossed her legs and folded her arms across her chest. Sheila joined Jimmy on the sofa opposite. This would be interesting. She was almost looking forward to hearing their pathetic excuses. Sheila glanced nervously at Jimmy and took a deep breath before she spoke.

'I was fifteen when I got pregnant and Jimmy was sixteen.'

Her gaze was fixed on the wall behind Claire's head as though addressing Claire directly would make the telling of her story impossible.

'It happened at Paddy and Eileen's wedding reception. Anyway, you were the result. I didn't tell your granny and granddad until I was five months gone. I didn't know what to do. It was Eileen who noticed in the end. She thought I'd put on a lot of weight and then she realised I was pregnant.'

Claire looked from one to the other. Sheila's

expression was earnest, already begging forgiveness, Jimmy's stunned. She couldn't believe that these two people were her mother and father. There was nothing wrong with her — she'd seen lots of photos of herself as a child. She was a beautiful baby. How could they have given her up? Why didn't they want to keep her?

Sheila faltered momentarily, then looked at Jimmy, unable it seemed to go on.

'Sheila's parents were less than happy about the pregnancy,' he said, continuing where Sheila had left off. 'They wanted her to give the baby up for adoption. Your granny said she wouldn't help Sheila keep you.'

'I don't believe you,' whispered Claire. Her granny loved her, always had done from the very first. She would never have wanted rid of her.

'Listen to me, Claire. What I'm telling you is true. They sent Sheila away to a convent in Portrock and she stayed there after you were born, until she was well enough to come home. They told everyone she had glandular fever and had gone to your Great-aunt Netta's farm in Donegal to recuperate.'

Pregnant girls being sent away for their confinement was like something from a nineteenth-century novel. But it explained a number of things — why she was born in Coleraine hospital and how they'd kept the pregnancy, and her birth, a secret.

'So what happened after I was born? How come Mum and Dad adopted me?'

Sheila lifted her head and she looked as

though she had been crying, although there were no tears to be seen.

'It was Mum's idea,' said Sheila, staring past Claire again. 'She said there was an alternative to giving you away to strangers. At first I thought she meant that I could keep you . . . but that wasn't what she had in mind. She said there was a way we could keep you in the family and I could see you growing up.' She paused and shifted her gaze onto Claire face. 'She said Eileen and Paddy wanted to adopt you. Eileen, you see, well, she couldn't have children.'

'Sheila,' interrupted Jimmy, his salutation a warning.

Claire looked from one to the other, her curiosity aroused. Sheila bit her lip and stared at the floor.

'Why couldn't Mum have children?'

'She just couldn't,' said Jimmy.

'And she knew that then? When she and Dad had been married, what, nine months? You hear of people trying for years and then getting pregnant and going on to have loads.'

'Not Eileen,' said Sheila.

Jimmy gave his head a little, almost imperceptible shake, a warning not to proceed.

But Sheila, ignoring his caution, went on, 'Eileen knew long before she got married that she wouldn't be able to have children — '

'Sheila! No!' said Jimmy, and he glared at her angrily. 'It's not your place to tell her that. She should hear it from Eileen, if at all.'

Suddenly, Sheila turned on Jimmy. 'I'm sick of this family and its secrets! I've had my fill of

287

them. It's time they all came out. How can she understand why I gave her up if she doesn't know about Eileen?'

'For fuck's sake,' said Jimmy angrily and he threw a folded paper on the sofa in disgust.

Sheila ignored him and directed her full attention at Claire.

'The reason we knew, we all knew, was that something happened to her when she was a little girl. It meant that she was infertile.'

'I'm a big girl,' interrupted Claire testily. 'Will you please stop speaking to me like I was a child or an idiot. Now tell me straight, what on earth are you talking about?'

Sheila pursed her lips and regarded Claire severely.

'Eileen was raped as a child. No — more than that. She was assaulted in a very vicious and brutal attack. She suffered severe internal injuries that affected her reproductive organs. The doctors said at the time that she'd never be able to have children. And they were right. Eileen and Paddy wanted children of their own but they could never have them.'

Almost sick with nausea, Claire pressed her hand on her mouth. Suddenly she realised she didn't know her mother. In the face of all the awful things that had happened to her she remained stoical, and at peace with the world. Even now, lying on her deathbed, she blamed no one and asked for nothing, only to be with Paddy.

'So you see,' said Aunt Sheila, gently, 'when Mum, your granny, suggested that I give you to Eileen and Paddy, well . . . it felt like I didn't have any choice.'

'I still don't see — '

'They said it was meant to be, that I had it within my power to make Eileen and Paddy's life complete. They were on a waiting list for a new baby but the authorities more or less told them their chances were next to zero because of Paddy's age. There were few babies coming up for adoption then — girls were starting to keep them where before they would have given them away. And Eileen so desperately wanted a child.'

'So you gave me to them? Just like that?' said Claire, still unwilling to let go of her anger.

'Not exactly. They had to go through the formal process of adoption, but, because Eileen was a blood relation it was arranged quickly and quietly. I never *gave* you to anyone, Claire. You were taken. I wanted to keep you. I begged Mum but she said no. You were the answer to Eileen and Paddy's prayers, she said.'

'But you didn't *have* to give me up. You could have got a flat or something. The State would have supported you.'

Jimmy, who'd remained quiet for the last few minutes, interrupted. 'That's an unrealistic view of things, Claire,' he said, harshly. 'Sheila was only sixteen. Can you remember what you were like at sixteen?'

Sheila shot him a slight but grateful smile.

'Well, I can tell you that you wouldn't have been equipped to bring up a baby on your own, any more than Sheila was,' said Jimmy.

'But what about you? Weren't you around? You

ended up getting married to each other, for Christ's sake!' retorted Claire.

'That was many years later. Sheila's family warned me off. I'd just left school and I didn't have a job. I'd no means to support myself, never mind Sheila and a baby.'

'Well,' said Claire, standing up, 'it sounds as though you've managed to convince yourselves that you've nothing to feel guilty about. But I have news for you — you haven't convinced me.'

'We're not proud of what we did, Claire,' said Sheila. 'God knows what both of us wouldn't give to turn the clock back. We were just kids. Silly, stupid kids. There's not a day goes by when I don't regret what happened.'

'Me neither,' said Jimmy solemnly.

'So that makes it all right then? You fuck up my life and say you're sorry and that's it, is it?'

'But your life's not fucked up,' said Jimmy. 'You're young and beautiful. You've got your whole life ahead of you and a man who loves you.'

'In case you haven't noticed, my dad's in the cemetery and Mum's not far behind him. If that's not fucked up, I don't know what is.'

'We're going to have to tell Eileen that you know,' said Sheila.

'Are we?' snapped Claire. 'If she wanted me to know she would have told me herself. And I for one am not going to upset her by dragging all this up now.'

'That's up to you. But Claire,' said Sheila, 'you must believe us.'

There was an air of quiet desperation about

her that Claire found unbearable. She avoided eye contact by focusing on the square of carpet beneath her feet.

'Do you believe what we've told you? I swear to God it's the truth.'

'Yes, I suppose so,' said Claire, sullenly.

'Do you forgive us?'

'You can't find out something as big as this and then just carry on as before,' said Claire, ignoring the question. 'Everything's changed for me. Everything.'

★ ★ ★

'I warned you,' said Sheila, 'I warned you all! And would you listen? Oh, no, you all knew better.'

'Look,' said Jimmy, 'we all knew she'd find out eventually. OK, maybe we, all of us, made a mistake in not telling her before she found out by herself. But the outcome's the same. Now she knows and that's what you wanted, wasn't it?'

'Yes, I wanted her to know, but not like this.'

'At the end of the day, what difference does it make how she found out? I don't know what you're getting so het up about, Sheila. I thought she took it pretty well, all things considered. She didn't seem overly upset, to me.'

'Not upset! She hates us, Jimmy. Didn't you hear her? She blames me for giving her away.'

'What did you expect, Sheila? She's right when she says her world has been turned upside down. How can she look at any of us in the same light again? Knowing that none of us are who

291

she thought we were.'

Sheila looked at Jimmy and a fresh horror occurred to her. Maybe Claire would never forgive her. Maybe, far from making them closer as Sheila had hoped, the truth would forever drive a wedge between them. That would be unthinkable, worse than the way things were before.

'I couldn't bear it if she hated me,' she said but when she turned round she was alone in the room.

The conversation with Claire had clarified one thing for Sheila. Now that Claire knew the truth there was no longer any need for Eileen to tell her. Sheila realised that it had been unfair of her to place such a heavy burden on her sister. And it was important that she removed that burden as soon as possible. Claire said that she would not tell her mother what she'd found out. So Sheila resolved to tell Eileen that she'd changed her mind and that she no longer wanted her to tell Claire the truth. She'd speak to her in the morning when Eileen was generally at her brightest, not now, at the end of the day when she was weary with the effort of staying alive.

When hunger brought the boys in from playing in the street she served them the soup she'd made earlier.

'Where's Conor?' she asked.

They shrugged their shoulders and got stuck in, hungrily, to the broth and slabs of bread spread thickly with butter. She watched them eat with dirty hands and grubby faces, too tired to insist they washed or minded their manners.

At six o'clock she cleared away the dishes, leaving a place setting for Conor. She wondered what Claire was thinking now and remembered how Aiden had touched her. Seized with a desire to erase all memory of him, she ran upstairs, stripped and got into a hot shower. She scrubbed every inch of her body until it was pink.

Later, when she'd dried her hair and put on some fresh clothes, Jimmy came into the room and said the first civil words to her in over a week.

'Sheila,' he said, 'do you know where Conor is?'

'No. Why?'

'Well, Martin and Danny haven't seen him since they left for school this morning.'

Sheila laid the hairbrush down on the dresser slowly and suppressed the little ripple of fear that went through her. She'd been so absorbed in herself she hadn't properly registered Conor's absence.

'I just assumed he was at a friend's house,' she said, defensively.

'Which one?'

'Well, I don't know, do I?'

'Did he say anything about having his tea out?'

She shook her head and Jimmy looked at his watch.

'It's eight thirty. Don't you think it's time we checked where he is?'

Sheila nodded and said, 'I'll phone round his friends.'

She phoned the Knoxes first, then the Quinns, then Moira and then anyone else she could think of. She was on the phone for over three-quarters of an hour — no one had seen him that day.

Sheila put the phone down and tried to quell the panic that was rising fast. She must remain calm, she told herself. She must think. She climbed the stairs to Conor's room and surveyed the neat bed, the clear desk by the window, books lined up against the wall. There was something not quite right . . . what was it? The room was too tidy, too neat. She flung open the wardrobe and quickly riffled through its contents.

'Well, what did they say?' said Jimmy's voice from behind her.

'Look,' she said, 'his rucksack's missing.'

While Jimmy peered into the wardrobe, Sheila turned her attention to the chest of drawers.

'Some of his jumpers are missing too. And socks and underpants.'

She took two steps backwards into the middle of the room and stared at the contents of the opened drawers. She briefly covered her mouth with her hands, then took them away.

'He's gone, Jimmy. He's run away.'

'I'm calling the police,' said Jimmy.

He turned abruptly and left the room.

Terrible memories of what had happened to her sister flashed through Sheila's mind. What if someone hurt Conor? Abducted him? And then she told herself not to overreact. He was almost fifteen, nearly an adult, whereas Eileen was a little girl at the time of the attack.

There would be a straightforward explanation for his disappearance. He'd probably gone to a

294

friend's house and would walk through the door any minute. But which friend? She'd contacted everyone she could think of and some. Had they overlooked someone? She racked her brains.

A feeling of sheer panic threatened to overwhelm her — she inhaled deep lungfuls of air. She touched the pillow where Conor would have laid his head only the night before. She put her face into it and smelt him, an adult smell of sweat and greasy hair, not what she'd expected.

Jimmy came back into the bedroom followed by Danny and Martin who stood at the door, their mud-stained faces alert to the unfolding drama.

'Well, what did they say?' said Sheila, jumping to her feet.

'They took all his details and they're sending someone round first thing in the morning. If he hasn't turned up by then. They've asked us to look out recent photographs just in case he doesn't.'

'The morning? But they should be round here now. Doing something!'

'I know,' he said, 'but they say a teenage boy going walkabout, as the policeman put it, is more common than you think. He says most of them turn up the next day.'

Sheila put her face in her hands and began to cry, out of fear, worry and sheer frustration. She felt Danny's arm around her.

'Don't cry, Mum,' he said. 'Please don't cry.'

Martin came over and patted her shoulder. 'It'll be all right, Mum,' he said.

Later, they all got ready for bed and left the

lights on downstairs and the front door unlocked in case Conor came home during the night. Despite their concern for their elder brother the boys were soon asleep, exhausted. Jimmy and Sheila sat on the sofa and looked at the recent photographs of Conor they'd managed to find.

'Do you remember where that was taken?' said Sheila, presenting him with a photo of Conor standing beside a Harley-Davidson.

'That weekend I took the boys up to see the Northwest 200.'

'Conor thought the bikes were fantastic. Look at that smile on his face.'

A wave of emotion caught her unexpectedly and she pressed the photo to her breast.

'Oh, my God, Jimmy, if anything happens, has happened, to him!'

'It won't, love,' he said firmly, using a term of endearment Sheila hadn't heard in a very long time. She rewarded him with a thin smile.

Sheila wondered where Conor was now. Walking the streets of Ballyfergus? Or further afield? Belfast maybe? Sleeping on a park bench? Prey to all sorts of perverts and drug-dealers and thugs. She forced herself to push these thoughts to the back of her mind.

'Do you think he's run away because of the bullying at school, or because we haven't been there for him?' she said.

'We don't know that he has run away,' said Jimmy. 'There could be any number of reasons . . . '

'But his rucksack's gone, Jimmy,' she said and paused. 'I think,' she continued, carefully, 'that he might have run away because of us. That day in the kitchen when we were shouting at each other he got up and ran out of the room. Do you remember?'

Jimmy nodded glumly.

'He asked us to stop fighting,' she went on, 'and we were so angry with each other that we just ignored him.

That and the thing about him being gay. Maybe he couldn't take any more at school and felt he couldn't count on us at home either.'

'I'm sorry for any part I might have played in chasing him away.'

'So am I, Jimmy. So am I.'

'I love him, you know,' said Jimmy, his voice cracking with emotion.

'I know,' said Sheila and, after a pause, she added, 'and when he comes home you'll tell him that.'

★   ★   ★

Jimmy must have nodded off at some point for, when he awoke, the early morning sun was streaming through the curtains. Sheila was fast asleep in the bed beside him — he could hear the steady rise and fall of her breathing. The clock said five thirty.

He peeled back the bedcovers and crept out onto the hall landing. Gingerly, he pushed open the door to Conor's room. His heart sank when he saw it was empty — everything just as they'd left it the night before.

Downstairs, he turned off the lights, pulled

297

back the curtains and opened the front door to bring in the milk. He stood on the doorstep and surveyed the street — not a soul was around. He shivered in the chill air and wondered where Conor had spent the night. He tried to imagine what it would be like sleeping rough. Even though it was summer he would've been frozen without a sleeping bag.

If any harm came to Conor, he would be to blame. It was his failure as a father that had driven Conor to this. His inability to come to terms with his son's sexuality. Instead of accepting Conor as he was, he had spent his time and energies wishing and praying that he would somehow snap out of it. And, of course, Conor would've felt a failure because that's what Jimmy thought he was.

But what did it matter now, what Conor was or what he did? He could be dead. He could make it to London and disappear forever. They might never see him again. He thought of all the parents he'd seen over the years, giving press conferences on TV when their child went missing, and their incomprehensible grief, impossible to witness.

He shut the door quietly and came back inside, shaking. In the kitchen he laid out the breakfast table and remembered what it was like holding Conor in his arms for the very first time. Each simple act of caring for him, changing nappies, feeding him, bathing him, was just sheer joy. He'd been excluded from Claire's birth, of course — he'd never even seen her until she was six months old when he met Eileen and Sheila pushing her pram in the park.

Sheila appeared in the doorway, haggard and pale. She sat down heavily on a chair.

'What time did the police say they'd be here?' she asked.

'Eight thirty.'

'I'll go and have a shower then,' said Sheila. 'It'll pass the time.'

When the boys came downstairs he gave them their breakfast and told them to get ready for school. They both protested.

'It won't do your mother any good, you two sitting round all day. It's better if we just stick to our normal routine as much as possible.'

'Are you going to work then?' said Danny.

'No, son, I'm not,' said Jimmy, uncomfortably aware of his hypocrisy.

'It's not fair. I wanted to see the policeman,' said Danny and Jimmy had to remind himself that he was only a child. Perhaps it was just as well that he didn't fully understand the implications of what was happening.

Martin and Danny were about to leave the house when their grandmother arrived, bristling with nervous energy.

The first thing she said was, 'You're not sending them to school on a day like this?'

'Why not?' said Jimmy.

'Jesus Christ, Conor's just gone missing! We don't know what's happened to him. He could have been abducted by some — pervert,' she said spitting out the last word with vehemence. 'What if he's still out there, preying on young boys?'

'For God's sake, Moira!' Jimmy shouted, then

dropped his voice and hissed in her ear, 'Will you keep your voice down in front of the boys? You'll frighten them. We're trying to act as normal as possible. I don't need you to tell me how serious this is. And besides we know Conor took a bag and some clothes. He hasn't been *taken*. He's run away.'

She shrunk back, chastened, and smiled thinly at the boys.

After they'd left she apologised, 'I'm sorry about that, Jimmy. I didn't think. I didn't mean to frighten them.'

'Forget it. We're all under a lot of stress.'

At last a police car pulled up outside the house. Brought up in a staunch nationalist household, Jimmy didn't have much time for the Royal Ulster Constabulary. But it was funny how your views changed when you needed them. He watched as two uniformed female officers got out and approached the house.

After the briefest of introductions they got down to business — they asked about the events of the previous day, the more senior of the officers doing the talking, the other scribbling furiously in her notebook.

'Now,' said the constable, her voice gentle, probing, 'this might be hard for you to answer. But I want you to think about it carefully.'

She looked pointedly at each of them in turn. Sheila and Moira leaned forward eagerly, anxious to help.

'Is there any reason you can think of why Conor would want to run away? Problems at school, perhaps? Or at home?'

Moira and Sheila looked at each other.

'Yes,' said Jimmy, firmly. 'He was being bullied at school. We went to see the headmaster about it.'

'I see. And do you know why was he being bullied?'

Conor's life was at stake here and Jimmy didn't care any more who knew he was gay.

'He's gay and they've been picking on him because of it.'

'Gay,' repeated the officer, as she shot a disbelieving glance at her colleague. 'A boy of fourteen, gay?'

'Yes, that's what I said. He sent a note, a sort of love-note, to another boy. That's how they found out about it. And,' he added, glancing at Sheila who was watching him open-mouthed, 'we've been having some marital problems.'

'Please go on, Mr Gallagher, if you don't mind.'

'There were some fights. Shouting matches rather, nothing more than that. But Conor witnessed them and was clearly upset. I think that might be part of the reason he ran away. That and the bullying.'

'And you, Mrs Gallagher, what do you think?'

'Conor was trying to come to terms with his own problems and we, well, we weren't there for him.'

'You mustn't blame yourselves,' said the officer, sympathetically, and then she moved on briskly. 'Now, does he have any contacts outside Ballyfergus?'

All three of them shook their heads.

'None, apart from family and we've contacted all of them already,' explained Sheila. 'Nobody's seen him.'

'Does he have any older male friends? Or a close relationship with a teacher perhaps, or a youth club leader, anything like that?'

Again they shook their heads glumly.

'You can't think of anyone he might have gone off with then?'

'Not as far as we know,' said Jimmy.

'OK.'

'So what happens now?' said Jimmy.

'We'll start by circulating his picture to all the police stations across the province and we'll contact the main points of exit — ports, border crossings — and ask security to keep a lookout for him. But my guess is that he's still here in Northern Ireland, probably not far from home. He'll get tired and hungry and chances are he'll come home of his own accord. It happens all the time. At this stage I think it would be best if we tried to keep it quiet. We don't want to frighten him. So don't talk to the papers. If they get wind of this, they'll be rapping on your door looking for a story. Especially as you're a local councillor.'

'And after that?'

'If he hasn't returned by this time tomorrow, we'll consider going public.'

'Do you mean TV?'

'Yes, and radio and the papers.'

The interview concluded, Jimmy showed the officers to the door.

'Try not to worry, Mr Gallagher,' said one of

302

the officers. 'The fact that he's gone of his own accord is actually a good sign. It means he wasn't abducted. I'm sure this will all be over very soon.' After they'd gone, Jimmy left Sheila with her mother in the front room, went upstairs and locked himself in the bathroom. He sat on the closed toilet seat, shut his eyes and prayed.

He asked God to protect Conor and keep him from harm. He promised to love his son so long as he got him back safely. He vowed to accept him unconditionally. If only God would give him a chance to prove that he meant every word.

He thought about Sheila and how his feelings towards her had softened because of this crisis. Where would they go from here? It was all over between her and this doctor. Had she done it just to hurt him? If that were true he didn't think he could ever find it in his heart to forgive her.

And yet she was the only woman he'd ever wanted. Right from the very beginning. Their love had been tested by the loss of Claire but they'd survived. Surely this sordid little affair wouldn't be the end of their marriage? A lifetime together, a family destroyed. All for the price of a roll in the hay.

Jimmy placed his head in his hands. How had it come to this? A missing son and an adulterous wife. Where did it all go wrong?

8

Claire came over mid-morning for news of Conor. She had on an old cardigan of Eileen's, belted round the waist, and wore no make-up. She'd had a rough night between listening out for Eileen, attending to her and worrying about Conor.

Poor little Conor, all mixed up in the head about his sexuality, was missing. She still thought of him protectively — the seven-year age gap between them meant that she'd always acted the role of 'big sister'. How ironic that she really was his sibling, she thought.

Uncle Jimmy, for that was how she still thought of him despite the fact that he was her biological father, told her what the police had said. He looked absolutely awful and, though she would never forgive him and Aunt Sheila, Claire couldn't help but feel sorry for him.

Aunt Sheila joined them looking even more wretched than Jimmy. Her face creased up suddenly, she sat down on the sofa and put a hand over her mouth. Jimmy was at her side in seconds.

'It's all right, love,' he said. 'Come on. Keep your chin up.'

The friction that Claire had witnessed previously between them now seemed to have disappeared. When Sheila was composed again, Jimmy addressed Claire.

'You don't have any idea where he might be, do you?'

She shook her head. 'Sorry.'

She wondered if they'd noticed that she'd stopped addressing them by name. She just couldn't bring herself to call them 'aunt' and 'uncle' any more. And besides, what was the alternative? Sheila and Jimmy? No, it was too chummy to stomach.

Later on, when Eileen was asleep, Moira made lunch and they all sat down at the kitchen table. No one spoke. Sheila stared at the food on her plate and Jimmy chewed absent-mindedly on a sandwich like it was a piece of shoe leather.

The phone call came when Moira was clearing up. Jimmy jumped out of his seat and grabbed the handset while the first ring was still reverberating round the kitchen.

'Hello,' he said with his face like stone.

He held the receiver to his ear with both hands, his face contorted with intense concentration.

'Yes,' he said, obviously in response to a question.

He listened intently for a few minutes. Claire glanced at Sheila and Granny — they were both tight with anxiety, like coiled springs. She returned her gaze to Jimmy. He closed his eyes briefly and Claire could see his entire body relax as a wave of relief washed over it.

Sheila stood up. Her arms were by her sides, rigidly straight, fists clenched.

'What?' she said. 'Who is it? Tell us.'

'He's OK, Sheila. He's safe. Shh . . . '

305

Jimmy put his finger to his lips and spoke into the handset. Claire felt the tension in the room dissipate.

'OK. Is he there now?' said Jimmy.

Claire could hear the faint buzz of the other person's reply.

'All right. Let me get a pen and I'll write that down.'

Simultaneously, Moira, Sheila and Claire scrambled for pen and paper. Sheila found them first and thrust a biro and Post-it pad into Jimmy's hand.

He held the phone under his chin and wrote something down.

'Can you repeat that, please, so there's no mistake?'

He listened again.

'And the phone number? We'll be there just as soon as we can, say an hour at the most. You won't let him go, will you? I mean, are you sure he'll wait for us?'

More buzzing over the phone.

'OK. We're just leaving. I'm sorry, what did you say your name was? Peter. Peter, I can't thank you enough,' he said into the receiver and Claire heard a faint click as the other person hung up.

Jimmy removed the receiver from his ear, stared at it for a few seconds and replaced it slowly on the holder. A chorus of questions went up from the three women. Claire noticed a bright red welt on the skin round his ear, where he'd pressed the handset against his flesh. Sheila snatched the yellow Post-it out of his hand.

'The Imrie Centre,' she read. 'In Belfast. Is that where he is?'

'Yes,' said Jimmy. 'He turned up there this morning. They've no idea where he spent the night. But he's fine. Peter, the guy on the phone, persuaded Conor to let him make that call. He says he's talked to Conor and he's ready to come home.'

'But what's The Imrie Centre?' said Claire.

'It's some kind of drop-in centre for gay men.'

'What's he doing there?' said Moira.

'They provide advice and counselling — I guess he got there what he wasn't getting at home,' said Jimmy, and he screwed his face up as though trying to stop himself from breaking down.

Sheila sat down at the table again and burst into tears. Jimmy retrieved the car keys from the fruit bowl on the table.

'I'll go and get him. The place is up near the University. Sheila, do you want to stay here?'

'No!' she shouted through her tears. 'I'm coming too.'

'Well, go on, the two of you, if you're going,' urged Moira. 'Me and Claire'll see to the boys and Eileen. Just take your time and drive carefully, for God's sake!'

They watched them drive off in the car, their faces strained and grey behind the windscreen, Sheila clutching the little piece of yellow paper in her hand like a talisman.

'Thank you, God,' said Moira, and she raised her eyes skywards. 'Thank you for keeping him safe.'

307

She put her arm round Claire and hugged her.

Tears pricked Claire's eyes. She was being silly, she told herself. Conor was safe and everything was going to be OK.

She became aware of her grandmother's arm around her and she pulled away. She remembered what Sheila and Jimmy had told her — Granny had been prepared to put her own granddaughter up for adoption. If Eileen and Paddy hadn't taken her, would Granny really have handed her over to complete strangers?

She watched the back of Granny's greying head as she followed her into the kitchen, and decided that she was capable of such an act. While she was loving with Claire and the boys, she was also stern and ruled by a strict moral code. An illegitimate baby would have had no place in Granny Devlin's home.

Moira said something.

'What?' said Claire.

'I said we'd better call the police and let them know the news.'

She picked up the phone and dialled. Claire wandered into the front room and looked at her reflection in the mirror over the mantelpiece. She could see it now, the strong resemblance to Aunt Sheila. And there was something about her eyes and the shape of her full lips that reminded her of Uncle Jimmy. Funny how the evidence had been literally right in front of her eyes and she'd failed to notice it.

'They want us to let them know as soon as Sheila and Jimmy get back,' said Moira, coming into the room. 'They're sending someone round to interview Conor. And they want to make enquiries at that Imrie Centre place to make sure no crime has been committed.'

Suddenly anger bubbled up inside Claire like a pot boiling over. She saw her granny for what she was — a hypocrite. Running to the church every week, on her knees praying morning and night, pretending she was holier than thou. But she'd engineered Claire's adoption and would have given her up to the authorities without a second thought.

'What's the matter, Claire? You look a bit flushed. Aren't you feeling well?'

'Would you have gone through with it then?' said Claire coldly.

'Gone through with what, love?' said Moira, enunciating each word slowly.

'Put me up for adoption. If Eileen and Paddy hadn't agreed to take me.'

Moira's physiology changed instantly, adding ten years to her appearance — her shoulders slumped and her face took on an expression of weary resignation. She shuffled over to the sofa and sat down.

'I suppose you had to find out eventually,' she sighed.

'No thanks to you. None of you were planning to tell me, were you?'

Moira shook her head, her fingers working at the frayed arm of the sofa. 'Eileen was going to tell you. She knew you'd find out sooner or later but she wanted you to hear it from her. She was just waiting for the right moment.'

'You never answered my question. Aunt Sheila

said that you forced her to give me up. You wanted to put me up for adoption and then Eileen and Paddy stepped in. Is that true?'

'Eileen and Paddy were desperate for a child.'

'I know they were and I know why. I understand why I might have seemed like the answer to their prayers. What I don't understand is you.'

Moira looked like a frightened rabbit, caught in a car's headlights. Claire felt no mercy.

'Answer my question,' she demanded.

'You have to understand that we had — we had — Sheila's best interests at heart, Claire,' stammered Moira. 'She was only a child, barely sixteen when you were born.'

'No, I don't understand. Explain it to me.'

'How could a child of that age bring up a baby?'

'With your help.'

'It wasn't as simple as that. She would never have finished school, let alone gone on to do nursing. And what decent man would take on another man's child?'

'But she married Jimmy, my father, for Christ's sake!'

'That happened years later. And how were we to know it? We couldn't see into the future. We had to deal with the situation at the time including thinking of your interests as well, Claire. Imagine what it would have been like growing up a bastard, without a father? You would have been teased mercilessly at school and looked down on by the whole community.'

'Oh I see,' said Claire sarcastically. 'You had my best interests at heart.'

'Yes, we did.'

'Will you stop using 'we'!' snapped Claire, 'It was *you*, wasn't it? You decided and everyone else just had to go along with it.'

'Look,' said Moira angrily, standing up to face Claire, 'I don't have to explain myself to you. I did what was best for everyone. You had a good home and parents who loved you more than most. It gave Sheila a chance to get her life back together. You would have been a millstone round her neck. Only she can't see that.'

The words cut through Claire like a knife. She ran from the room, ignoring Moira's pleas to wait. Inside her own house, she locked both front and back doors, sat at the bottom of the stairs and hugged her knees.

Moans from upstairs alerted her to Eileen — she wiped the tears off her face, climbed the stairs two at a time and went into the bedroom her mum had once shared with her dad.

'It's all right, Mum,' she said. 'I'm here.'

She put her hand on her mother's pale, almost translucent, brow, saw her bony fingers work the morphine pump and then relax.

'Is that better?' she said.

'Yes,' murmured Eileen. 'Can I have some water, please?'

Claire cradled her mum's head in her arms and held a glass to her lips. Eileen took several tiny sips of water then closed her eyes, exhausted with the effort. When she'd returned her mum's head to the pillow, Claire noticed a corner of

311

denim fabric peeking out from below the bed. She knelt down and pulled out a pair of old jeans. She recognised them as her dad's, the faint smell of oil and diesel making it seem for a moment as though he was there in the room with them.

'What is it, Claire?'

'Nothing,' replied Claire, pushing the jeans back under the bed where she'd found them.

'I love you, Mum,' she said, still kneeling by the bed, 'I'm so lucky to have you and to have had Dad. He was the best dad in the world and you're the best mum. And I want you to know that I'm grateful for you both.'

Eileen smiled and opened her eyes.

'And I love you too,' she said. 'My precious little girl.'

★ ★ ★

Jimmy drove like a madman. More than once Sheila was moved to cry out but she bit her tongue and said nothing. She wanted to get there just as quickly as he did. The initial sense of euphoria at hearing Conor was alive and well had been replaced by a growing apprehension. Where had he spent the night? Who were these people at the Imrie Centre? And how had Conor found his way to them?

They made good time. The rush hour had not yet started and soon they were making their way briskly through the city. Sheila got out a map, located the address they were looking for, and called out directions. They found themselves in a leafy street of run-down three-storey Victorian terraces given over to a mixture of office accommodation and flats. The narrow street was jampacked with cars and they just managed to find a parking space halfway along the street. They got out and looked for number twenty-five.

Outside the building they paused. A small unobtrusive plaque was attached to the wall beside three tarnished brass knobs. From the outside the house was unremarkable and, looking up, there were no bright lights or Venetian blinds to indicate an office on any of the floors.

They glanced at each other, climbed the steps to the open front door and read the plaque, which said, simply: '*The Imrie Centre — Second Floor.*'

Sheila peered into the wide vestibule — the original black-and-white tiled floor was obscured by years of grime and the engraved glass in the inner door was yellowed with neglect. In its day it would have been a magnificent house.

'The bell's not working,' said Jimmy. 'Shall we just go on up?'

They took the stairs to the second-floor landing and, after knocking and receiving no reply, went through a solid wooden door.

They found themselves in a room with plastic chairs arranged round the edges and a coffee table in the middle, covered in magazines. On the peeling wood-chip wallpaper hung posters about safe sex, Aids and HIV. It was like a waiting-room in a rather run-down doctor's surgery.

313

Sheila followed Jimmy into the middle of the room.

'Hello,' she called and then more loudly, 'hello!'

A thin, good-looking man of around thirty appeared through a door on the other side of the room from which they'd entered.

'No need to shout,' he half-laughed and smiled broadly at them.

He was tanned and wore a tight-fitting black T-shirt and baggy black jeans. Round his neck was a beaded choker and a tattoo peeked out from under the sleeve of his T-shirt. His dark hair was gelled into a series of spikes, like a hedgehog. He had a gold ring through one ear, several smaller ones through one of his eyebrows and a silver stud in his nose.

'You must be Conor's mum and dad,' he said in a somewhat effeminate way.

She felt Jimmy tense.

'I'm Peter, one of the voluntary counsellors here,' he continued. 'Come on over here and sit down.'

'Where's Conor?' said Sheila. 'Can't we see him?'

'All in good time, Mrs Gallagher, all in good time.'

He shooed them like schoolchildren into two chairs, pulled one up in front of them and sat down. Sheila watched him, fascinated. His hand-gestures and mannerisms were so overtly homosexual that, if she hadn't known better, she would have thought he was performing a burlesque.

314

'Now, as I explained to you on the phone, Mr Gallagher, Conor turned up here this morning around eleven o'clock. It took us a couple of hours, and several cups of coffee I can tell you, to get out of him where he was from and that he'd run away from home. The poor boy was most upset. He's confused about his sexuality that's for sure. And I believe he's been having a rough time at school.'

Sheila nodded.

'He also mentioned fights at home.'

'Yes,' said Sheila, looking at the floor, 'there's been that too.'

'I see. It's very difficult for someone like Conor growing up in a small town. He doesn't know anyone else in Ballyfergus who's gay and he feels very isolated and lonely. When he felt he couldn't communicate with his family, well, I think he just felt he couldn't cope any more.' He paused. 'Now have you given any thought to what you'll say to Conor when you see him?'

Sheila looked blankly at Jimmy. His eyes were red and watery and he looked incredibly tired.

'The reason I ask,' said Peter, 'is that his actions are a cry for help. He needs understanding, not punishment. And you might want to give some thought to ongoing support.'

'What do you mean?' said Jimmy.

'The Imrie Centre is for adults only but I'd be happy to give you my telephone number. Conor could talk to me any time, as a friend. Here, I'll give you my card and you can think about it.'

He produced a business-sized card from his back pocket with a flourish and pressed it into

Jimmy's hand. Jimmy stared at it for a few moments, then put it in his coat pocket.

'Now, if you're ready, I think Conor wants to go home. I'll go and get him.'

Peter patted the back of Sheila's hand, got up left the room. Jimmy stood up and paced the room.

'It'll not be long now,' said Sheila, the words barely out of her mouth before Conor appeared sheepishly in the doorway.

It felt like she hadn't seen him in weeks, rather than the few hours that he'd been missing. He looked different somehow — so grown up. She realised with a pang of sorrow that this event marked a turning point in Conor's life. He was no longer her boy, he was a young man. Soon, he wouldn't need her any more. Conor moved forward into the room, followed closely by Peter.

'Hello, son,' said Sheila.

'Hello, Mum.'

She walked over to him, took him in her arms and then, to her amazement, she felt another pair of arms around them and realised that Jimmy was hugging them both. She heard the heavy sighs of his breath in her ear.

'Conor,' he whispered, 'Conor. I thought we'd lost you, son.'

'It's OK, Dad,' replied Conor, in a voice that betrayed concern at this display of tenderness in his father. 'I'm all right. Really I am.'

They remained like that for some minutes, clenched in a tight embrace. When Sheila eventually pulled away she saw Peter watching them with his left arm folded across his waist, the elbow of his right resting on it. His eyes were full of tears and the knuckles on his right hand were pressed into his lips as though he was trying to stop himself from crying.

'Oh, don't mind me,' he said to Sheila, 'I'm a sentimental fool. I'd cry at anything, me.'

She gave him a smile that she hoped conveyed her gratitude for all that he'd done.

'I love you, Conor,' said Jimmy as he stared into his son's face.

Sheila could have sworn that, in spite of the flush of embarrassment that reddened Conor's cheeks, he grew two inches in height.

'Right,' said Jimmy clearing his throat and taking charge, 'let's get you home. Here, give me your bag.'

He swung the rucksack onto his shoulder, walked over to Peter and took his hand firmly in his own.

'If it hadn't been for you, Peter . . . well, I don't know what would have happened to Conor. I'm grateful to you for helping him. And us.'

On the way home Jimmy asked, 'How did you know to go to that place?'

'Because of this,' replied Conor, and he pulled a crumpled magazine page from his pocket. 'I saw this advert in a magazine I picked up in the doctor's surgery. I thought they could help me.'

'And did they?' said Jimmy.

'Yes. Peter understood everything,' he murmured and before long he was fast asleep, his head resting in Sheila's lap.

A police car was waiting for them when they

pulled up outside the house. The kids in the street pushed forward, anxious to see what the drama was all about, and Sheila saw net curtains twitch in the surrounding houses. This would give them plenty to gossip about until someone else's troubles, more recent or more scandalous, took over.

Sheila woke Conor up. He sat up sleepily and looked around. 'We're home, son. Come on, let's go inside. And remember, you've nothing to be ashamed of.'

They got out of the car, Sheila keeping her head held high as they proceeded up the path and into the house. The welcoming party in the front room consisted of two police officers, Moira, Martin and Danny. Moira threw her arms around Conor and hugged him.

'Thank God you're safe, Conor,' she sniffed. 'It's good to have you home.'

Martin and Danny seemed a bit bewildered by Conor's homecoming and more interested in the police officers than they were in their elder brother's safe return.

'Conor's home, boys,' said Sheila, stating the obvious. 'Say hello to your brother.'

'Hello, Conor,' they chorused but Danny's eyes remained firmly fixed on the handgun that peeked out from a holster on the male officer's belt.

'Hello, Conor,' said the female constable whom Sheila recognised from that morning.

That interview with the police seemed a distant memory. Had it really been only a few hours ago?

'We'd like to interview Conor now, Mrs Gallagher, if you don't mind,' said the constable, 'and, as he's a minor, we'd like you or Mr Gallagher to stay in the room.'

'You stay,' said Jimmy and he led the boys and Moira out, shutting the door behind them.

Sheila sat down beside Conor on the sofa. The female constable perched on the edge of the armchair, legs tucked in neatly below her, knees and feet together. Her dark green skirt came, unfashionably, just to the knee and her black tights disappeared into a hideous pair of flat, lace-up black shoes.

She asked Conor to describe exactly where he'd been and what he'd done since his disappearance. When he mentioned hitching a lift to Belfast, Sheila closed her eyes. When she imagined what could have happened! But he was safe now.

The story he told was uneventful — a day spent wandering round the city shops, eating at McDonald's and a miserable night sleeping rough in the bus station. Then, the next morning, a bus journey to Arbour Avenue and The Imrie Centre.

'What time did you get there?'

'I dunno. 'Bout ten or eleven.'

'And you didn't spend the night there?'

'No. I told you.'

'Can you tell me exactly what happened when you got there?'

'We just talked and Peter made me coffee and went out and got me a sandwich and a doughnut.'

'So what was this Peter like?'

'I dunno. OK, I suppose. He was nice to me.'

'In what way was he nice?'

And suddenly Sheila saw where the questioning was heading. She felt a sense of injustice on Peter's behalf. Just because he was gay he was being treated like an out-and-out pervert.

'You're barking up the wrong tree, here,' she said. 'It was Peter who persuaded Conor to come home and it was he who made the phone call.'

'Please, Mrs Gallagher,' said the officer in an irritated voice, 'if you'll just let me do the talking. You're here as an observer.'

Sheila felt a rush of anger at being told to shut up in her own house.

'Right,' she said, narrowing her eyes, 'be my guest.'

'So, did Peter touch you at all?' said the officer, addressing Conor once more.

'Touch me?'

'Yes. Did he, for example, give you a hug or anything.'

'No, nothing like that. He never touched me at all.'

'You're sure?'

'Yes.'

'Well,' said the constable, closing her black notebook, and glancing at her colleague, 'I think we're finished here. Apart from saying that running away like that was a very silly thing to do, Conor. You could have come to serious harm, not to mention the worry it caused your family. Now you won't do it again, will you?'

'No,' he mumbled and looked at the floor.

Sheila showed the police officers out into the hall.

'We're going up to see this Peter at The Imrie Centre now,' said the female.

'You don't seriously think he did anything, do you? You heard what Conor said.'

'You never know with these types,' said the male officer. 'We'll check him out, just to be on the safe side.'

Harass him, you mean, thought Sheila as she closed the door behind them and breathed a sigh of relief. Thank God it was over. She wouldn't wish the last twenty-four hours on anyone. If only she could erase that incident with Aiden . . . but she wouldn't think of it now.

'This calls for a celebration,' said Jimmy, coming into the hall. 'Come on, I'm taking the lot of you out for tea! I'm sure the last thing your mother wants to do is start cooking a meal.'

Sheila wanted to stay tucked up at home, away from prying eyes, but Martin and Danny were on their feet instantly.

'Pizza! Can we have pizza, Dad?' shouted Danny.

'Looks like it's the Italian, everyone,' said Jimmy smiling. 'That OK with you, Conor?'

'Great,' he said, 'I'm starving.'

Conor's safe return *was* something to celebrate, thought Sheila, and she determined not to be a damp squib.

'I'll just get freshened up,' she said, going upstairs.

Halfway up, she turned and called down to

Moira who was arranging her hair in the hall mirror.

'What about Claire? One of us'll have to stay with Eileen.'

'I don't think Claire'll want to go,' said Moira, crisply.

'Why not?'

'She just won't.'

'Did you two have a fight?'

'No, not exactly.'

'Words then?'

Moira said nothing.

'Come on, tell me,' said Sheila.

'I told you, nothing happened. Now just leave it, will you?'

'Keep your hair on,' said Sheila sarcastically, and then she added, 'I'm going to pop next door and check on Eileen before we go out.'

'Suit yourself,' came the sullen reply.

Next door, there was no sign of Claire downstairs and Sheila climbed the stairs calling, 'Claire, where are you?'

The door to her bedroom opened and Claire came out onto the landing in a dressing-gown, with a towel wrapped round her head. 'Oh, it's you,' she said, in a uninterested voice, 'I didn't hear you come in. I'm just out of the shower.'

'Conor's back.'

'I know. I saw the car.'

'Well, aren't you going to come over and see him?'

Claire put a hand to the towelling turban wrapped round her wet hair. 'Not tonight. I'm sure he's had enough fuss for one day. I'll speak to him tomorrow.'

'We're all about to go out for an Italian meal — to celebrate Conor's safe return. Will you be OK here?' asked Sheila, nodding in the direction of Eileen's room.

'Sure.'

'You haven't told her anything about Conor's disappearance, have you?'

Claire shook her head, 'I didn't see the point in upsetting her.'

'Good. You did the right thing. Is she awake now?'

'I've already seen to her if that's what you're here for,' said Claire testily.

'No, that's not why I'm here,' replied Sheila evenly. 'I just want to have a quick word.'

'I think she's asleep,' said Claire.

'We'll see,' said Sheila and she went into Eileen's bedroom and carefully shut the door behind her.

Eileen was asleep, her breath a soft rasp as her chest rose and fell. Sheila leaned over the bed and said, 'Eileen, it's me. Sheila.'

Eileen moaned softly.

'Eileen, wake up,' persisted Sheila and she put a hand on her sister's bony shoulder and rocked her gently.

Eileen opened her eyes, squinted, blinked several times and then said, as though she was cross that she'd been disturbed, 'What do you want?'

'Eileen, I've been thinking about things and I've decided that I don't want you to tell Claire the truth after all.'

'But why?' said Eileen and she paused to swallow and then went on, 'Why have you changed your mind?'

'I've been selfish in trying to force you to tell her when you didn't want to. And I've been doing a lot of thinking and I've realised that it's best if you don't do it.'

'But, Sheila,' said Eileen, her voice little more than a whisper, 'I thought it was what you wanted more than anything in the world.'

'It was at one time,' said Sheila and she stroked Eileen's forehead with the flat of her hand, 'but I realise now that it doesn't matter. Claire is your daughter and she always will be.'

'But I promised you — ' began Eileen and she winced with pain.

'Sshh, that doesn't matter now. You can forget all about it.'

Within ten minutes Eileen had fallen asleep again and Sheila crept quietly from the room. She was surprised to find Claire waiting for her on the landing, now fully dressed and with her hair roughly dried.

'How long is she going to go on like this?' asked Claire, peering over Sheila's shoulder as she pulled the door shut behind her. She pulled an old cardigan round her like she was cold.

'I don't really know,' said Sheila, truthfully, 'but I can't see her lasting more than a few more weeks.'

'I just can't bear to see her suffering like this. It's just awful,' said Claire, and she put a white knuckle up to her pale lips. 'I know this sounds really hard, but I wish she would just have a heart attack and die. Tonight.'

'I understand why you feel like that. The thought has crossed my mind too. But all we can do is help her as best we can and let nature take its course. When it's her time, God'll take her.'

'If there is a God why is He letting her suffer like this?'

And, in spite of her years of nursing experience with the dying, Sheila could not answer that question.

★ ★ ★

It was early evening when Aiden approached Claire's house with a grim determination. Since yesterday morning he'd thought about nothing but how he was going to face Claire. Over the last few weeks he'd thought he was losing touch with reality. It was funny how it took something like this to knock a bit of sense into you.

He could not risk losing Claire, that much was certain. He was also certain that she must never know the truth. Not only had he betrayed her but, by sleeping with her mother, he'd committed an unforgivable crime.

He must protect her from the truth and from Sheila for he couldn't trust her to keep her mouth shut. Look at the way she'd behaved when she found out Claire had gone to see her birth certificate — the woman was deranged, unbalanced. The best way to protect Claire was to take her as far away from here as possible. So far away that she would have little contact with Sheila and, hopefully, never see her again.

He opened the back door and let himself into the kitchen. He heard Claire's soft voice from upstairs and his heart ached with remorse. He listened to the silence, broken only by the dull sounds of movement and suffering from above. And then he heard Claire's footsteps padding down the stairs.

He steeled himself for their meeting. Would the guilt show in his face? Would she sense a change in him?

He needn't have worried. As soon as she saw him Claire threw her arms around his neck and wept. He savoured the feel of her in his arms and the sense of being needed.

'What is it, love? Is it your mum?'

'It's not just Mum. It's everything,' she sobbed. 'Conor ran away. Oh, Aiden, you don't know what's happened.'

'Calm down, love, and tell me. Take your time.'

'I saw my birth certificate and I can't believe it! Conor's back now so that's OK but it was just awful — and Mum's getting worse.'

'I don't know what you're talking about, Claire. Wait a minute. Here, sit down. There, that's better. Now tell me, slowly, one thing at a time.'

Claire sniffed and looked at him resentfully. 'Aiden, where have you been? I've been trying to get hold of you since last night! I phoned and phoned, last night and this morning and all afternoon.'

'I was working last night and I — I never got the messages.'

That was a lie, of course. He just couldn't speak to Claire, not after what he'd done.

'That bitch! Your landlady swore she'd get my messages to you.'

'Never mind about her. Tell me what's happened. Your mum's worse?'

'She's getting weaker all the time. Dr Crory's coming in every day now and I get the feeling, though he hasn't said anything, that he doesn't give her much longer.'

'I'm sorry, love,' said Aiden. 'What — what does your Aunt Sheila think?'

'I'm not really speaking to her at the moment,' replied Claire and Aiden felt relieved.

That was one good thing at least.

'Oh Aiden! I went up to Belfast, like I said I would. Do you remember?'

He nodded.

'I saw my birth certificate. And, oh my God — ' she put her hand over her mouth, 'you're never going to believe it!'

'What?'

'Sheila and Jimmy are my parents.'

'They are?' said Aiden, not entirely faking his surprise for Sheila had said nothing about Jimmy being Claire's father. 'But I don't understand. If they're your parents how come you were brought up by Eileen and Paddy?'

Claire pushed a strand of unwashed hair behind her ear and sighed heavily.

'It's a long story. Sheila was only fifteen when she got pregnant. It seems Granny decided I should be adopted and Eileen and Paddy, who couldn't have children of their own,

327

took me and raised me.'

'I see,' said Aiden.

'I just feel like an idiot. All these years they've lied to me. And I never suspected a thing.'

'They didn't really *lie* to you, Claire.'

'Avoided the truth then. Call it what you like, but in my book it's lying.'

'I'm sure they were trying to protect you.'

'Oh, they say they had my best interests at heart but I can't forgive them. Sheila and Jimmy for giving me up, and Granny for engineering the whole thing.'

'You've confronted them then?'

'Everyone but Mum,' she said, raising her eyes to the ceiling. 'I don't blame Mum or Dad for their part in it. They were only trying to help Sheila out and they gave me a great childhood. When I found out why Mum couldn't have children, I couldn't blame her for wanting Sheila's baby.'

'Why couldn't she have children?'

Claire told Aiden what she knew about the attack on Eileen and her resultant infertility.

'Jesus Christ,' he said when she'd finished, and fell silent, allowing the information to sink in.

Claire sat there staring at the floor.

'And what's all this about Conor running away?' asked Aiden eventually.

Claire looked up. 'Oh, he's back now. I just saw them all get in the car an hour or so ago. Didn't tell me where they were going though. I had a fight with Granny, you see, just before Sheila and Jimmy got back from Belfast with Conor.'

'Over your adoption?' said Aiden, wondering when Sheila would return. He wanted to avoid her at all costs — at least until he'd got the answer that he needed out of Claire.

'Yes. But I don't want to talk about that now. Anyway Sheila and Jimmy only noticed that Conor was missing last night. But it turns out he didn't go into school at all yesterday. He hitched a lift to Belfast instead.'

She filled him in on the details of Conor's disappearance and safe return.

'You've had a rough time, love — come here.' He pulled her to him and hugged her. He stroked her hair and buried his face in her neck. 'If you ever left me, Claire, I'd die, you know. I couldn't live without you.'

She pulled away and looked at him earnestly. 'I'll never leave you. You'd have to leave me first. You know I love you, Aiden.'

He looked her in the eye and spoke the words that for so long he'd been unable to say: 'I love you, too.'

'Oh, Aiden! I knew you did. I knew it. Oh, I love you so!' cried Claire and she threw her arms around him and kissed him repeatedly — on his lips, his nose, his eyes, his cheeks. It was like being attacked by a happy puppy.

'Claire! Claire!' said Aiden playfully, gently pulling her off and holding her hands in his. 'There's something I have to ask you. I'm serious now.'

She stopped laughing and looked directly at him. 'What?'

He took a deep breath. He didn't have the

right to ask her. He wasn't good enough. But he must have her.

'Will you marry me?' he said.

'Yes,' she said and her face lit up like a beacon. 'I love you and you're the only person I can trust, Aiden. The only person I love who hasn't lied to me.'

'Thank you,' mumbled Aiden, as he tried to shake off the feeling of unworthiness that threatened to reduce him to tears.

Her belief in him was complete. It's only one little lie, Aiden told himself. Just the one and it will never, ever happen again. Especially if he could get Claire to agree to his next proposal.

'I'm going to make you the happiest woman in the world,' he said. 'From this day on I swear I'll never lie or cheat or make you unhappy.'

'I know,' she said, 'and I'm going to make you happy too.'

'There's something else I want you to think about, Claire.'

'What's that?' she said eagerly, settling down to listen.

'You know the way I talked about going to the States?'

'Yes,' she replied, warily.

'And I told you I'd a cousin out there in Chicago?'

She nodded.

'Well, he's doing really well. He's started a building business and he wants to take me on.'

'You mean you want us to go to America?' said Claire, her brow furrowed.

'Not right now, obviously, with your mum and

everything. But as soon as practical, yes, I'd like us to go.'

'But I've hardly been out of Ballyfergus, never mind going halfway across the world. What about all my friends?'

'You'll make new friends. We both will. It'll be a fresh start for both of us. We'll have a wonderful life.'

'But I don't want a fresh start, Aiden. I like it here. I know I said I'd never forgive Sheila and Jimmy and Granny but, well, I can't imagine not having them near me. And the boys. Especially after Mum's gone. I thought maybe you and I could get a place of our own . . .'

'And we will. But this is a great opportunity, Claire. I'd not just be a labourer working for someone else — Kevin says he'll make me a partner. There's more work out there than he knows what to do with. We'd be so much better off.'

'You have a job, Aiden. In fact, you've got two jobs.'

'And what are they? A lackey on a boat and pulling pints behind a bar! I've no career prospects and how could I keep a family on wages like that?'

'I could work.'

'Wouldn't it be nice to have the choice not to?'

'I don't know, Aiden. How would we get in anyway? You need a 'green card', don't you?'

'We wouldn't bother with that. We'd just go as tourists on a return ticket and not come back. Everybody does it.'

'Then we'd be illegal immigrants.'

Aiden swallowed. He sensed she could be persuaded but he had to give her a compelling reason to say yes.

'Claire, listen to me. This is very, very important. I don't want to stay in this country. I have reasons . . . reasons I never told you about before.'

'What is it, Aiden?' she said, her eyes filling up with concern.

He had to get Claire to agree to go to the States. He had to get her as far away from Sheila as possible. He had only one chance to get it right.

He took a deep breath.

'There's something I have to tell you, before you make up your mind.'

★ ★ ★

There was no opportunity over the meal in the Italian restaurant to question Moira about her terse comments regarding Claire. Sheila could only presume that they'd had an argument of some sort. And she'd a fair idea what it would've been about.

She looked at Moira's inscrutable face and wondered what Claire had said to her. The girl was in fighting form and Sheila imagined that she would have given Moira a piece of her mind just as she'd done to her and Jimmy. Only Moira really did have a case to answer whereas she and Jimmy were innocent. She hoped they'd been able to convince Claire of that.

And if Claire had upset Moira, then, secretly

Sheila was pleased. Sheila narrowed her eyes and glared at her mother. She wondered what defence she had put up. Did she really believe, even to this day, that she'd done the right thing, as she kept insisting? Or deep down, did she feel responsible for the mess she'd made of everyone's life?

'Here's to Conor, everyone. We're glad to have you back, son,' said Jimmy and Sheila raised her glass in a toast.

She looked at her three beautiful sons and offered up a silent prayer for Conor's safe return. She sensed a change in Jimmy that she could trace back to the moment Conor went missing. The way he'd conducted himself with the overtly gay Peter had surprised her. Jimmy definitely had homophobic tendencies and yet he'd been humble and respectful towards the counsellor. Perhaps Conor's disappearance was the wake-up call Jimmy needed. For if he'd carried on the way he was going he'd surely have lost his son forever.

Sheila reflected on Jimmy's kindness to her throughout this short but intense crisis. She guessed he might just be able to find it in his heart to overlook her affair with Dr McCabe, but if he ever found out the extent of her betrayal she knew forgiveness would be impossible.

And she was surprised to find that she actually cared. Deep down she wanted Jimmy to forgive her — she wanted their relationship to work. It was ironic that she'd all but destroyed any love there was between them, before realising it.

They all squeezed into the car and dropped

Moira off at her flat before driving the short distance to Ladas Parade. The boys got out of the car and went inside. Jimmy took the key out of the ignition, stared at the road ahead and sighed.

'That was one hell of a day,' he said.

'Jimmy?'

'What?'

'I'm proud of the way you behaved today. I know it wasn't easy for you at the Imrie Centre, dealing with that gay man, Peter. And the way you handled Conor was brilliant.'

'Yeah, well. I think I finally realised that if Conor was running away from anything it was me.'

'I think I'm to blame too.'

'How come?'

'Well, we wouldn't have had those fights if I hadn't . . . done what I did.'

'Why did you have the affair, Sheila?'

Sheila knitted her brows and stared out the passenger window.

'I don't really know.'

'Was it to hurt me?'

She looked at him fearfully. His grey-blue eyes were fixed on hers, waiting for her answer. Should she lie and say it was because she was lonely, or unhappy, or craving attention? No, there'd been enough lies already.

'Yes,' she said.

He seemed satisfied by her answer. As though it was confirmation of something he already knew.

'That's what Eileen said.'

'She did?'

'Yes, she said that you were still hurting over Claire and that you blamed all of us for what happened. She said it was your way of getting back at me.'

'I suppose she's right,' confessed Sheila, ashamed to admit to a motivation that sounded so childish and petty. 'I'm sorry, Jimmy,' she said at length, 'for what I did and for hurting you.'

He nodded slowly.

'Do you think you can ever forgive me?' she asked.

'We'll see,' he said enigmatically.

And Sheila knew from his answer, and the flicker of hope that crossed his face, that he *would* forgive her. It was only a matter of time.

Inside the house Sheila was shocked to come face to face with Aiden and Claire.

She stared at Aiden, amazed and speechless at the brass neck on him. Standing there in her house, uninvited. Hadn't he got any decency at all? Couldn't he have avoided coming round until the memory of what they'd done had faded? She stood there glowering at him, as he shuffled his feet on her carpet and stared at the skirting-board.

Claire was gabbling away excitedly.

'Are you listening, Aunt Sheila?'

Sheila shifted her gaze away from Aiden and forced herself to concentrate on Claire.

'What, love?' she said, noticing that Claire's face was flushed and animated.

The coolness in Claire's voice had also gone. Did this mean Claire had forgiven her? Could they be friends again? And, in time, become the mother and daughter they should have been from the start? Inside, she ached with hope.

'I'm engaged to Aiden,' said Claire. 'We're going to get married. We couldn't wait to tell you.'

The warm glow Sheila felt inside disappeared to be replaced with a deadly chill. This man wasn't good enough for Claire. He'd betrayed her once and he'd do it again. She was sure of it. Claire, her beautiful daughter, was throwing herself away on a waster, a liar, and a cheat. He'd break Claire's heart and ruin her life. Sheila wanted to reach out and claw him to bloody shreds with her nails.

Jimmy stepped forward, as if in slow motion, and Sheila watched, as he pumped Aiden's hand and slapped him on the back. Momentarily Aiden caught her eye and, guiltily, looked away again. Then Jimmy embraced Claire and kissed her repeatedly on the cheeks.

'Aren't you pleased for us?' Claire asked her, when she'd untangled herself from Jimmy. 'You don't seem very happy?'

'I am,' she said. 'It's just . . . it's just . . . been a long day for all of us.'

'How thoughtless of me!' cried Claire. 'I forgot for a minute what you've been through.'

'No, love, it's OK,' said Jimmy reassuringly. 'Don't let our troubles spoil your moment. Anyway, Conor's home now and everything's fine again. Isn't it, Sheila?'

'Yes, everything's fine,' she repeated, mechanically.

There was nothing she could do to stop Claire from marrying Aiden. And the bastard knew it. He'd told Sheila he loved Claire. But he didn't love her enough — not nearly enough in Sheila's eyes.

'So when's the big day?' said Jimmy.

Aiden took Claire's hand, possessively, and she beamed at him.

'We've no plans as yet with Claire's mum being so ill. But we'd like to get married as soon as we can.'

'Your mum would love to see you married, Claire,' said Jimmy. 'It's one of her greatest wishes. I know it would make her very happy. Wouldn't it, Sheila?'

Sheila stared back at him, speechless. There was only one way to stop this — she would have to tell Claire that she'd slept with Aiden.

Then she looked at Jimmy's face glowing with happiness and pride and thought of her three sons who would be so excited at the prospect of Aiden joining the family. She thought of her sister, lying in the house next door, her life ebbing away. She knew that seeing Claire and Aiden married was the one thing that would allow Eileen to slip peacefully into the next world. And finally Sheila could hardly bear to look at Claire, naked with vulnerability and joy, staring adoringly into Aiden's face.

The happiness of so many people depended on Sheila. If she told the truth, Claire would be spared but the lives of everyone else would be ruined. Jimmy would never forgive her, their marriage would be over and the boys would grow up in a broken home. Eileen would die knowing Claire was wretched and alone. Claire would never speak to Sheila again. Everyone would hate and despise her.

And she decided she would never tell.

'It would make Mum happy, wouldn't it?' said Claire as the idea took hold. 'Why don't we get married as soon as we can, Aiden? While Mum's still aware of what's going on.'

'I think that's a great idea, Claire,' said Jimmy. 'How quickly can a wedding be organised, Sheila?'

'A few weeks,' she said, listening to her own voice as though it was someone else speaking. 'Probably sooner, given the circumstances, if we speak to the parish priest.'

'It doesn't need to be anything fancy,' said Claire.

'You'll have to be married in the chapel,' said Jimmy, 'but I'm sure Father Brennan would do a blessing in the house for Eileen.'

'Let's go and tell her now,' said Claire excitedly and she led Aiden out of the room by the hand.

Later, Sheila lay in bed and stared at the ceiling.

'That's great news about Claire and Aiden, isn't it?' said Jimmy.

'Yes, it is.'

'He's a decent lad, Aiden. And with him being that little bit older than Claire I think he'll be good for her. Especially when Eileen dies. She'll need someone to lean on.'

Dizzy with exhaustion, Sheila thought back

over the last forty-eight hours. Only a couple of days ago the thing that mattered most to Sheila was that Claire should be told who her real parents were. The burden of that secret had weighed her down for over two decades, eating away at her, night and day. The moment when the truth was revealed was something she'd looked forward to and dreamt about for years. It should have been a high point in her life. It should have signalled the end of oppression and lies.

But by sleeping with Aiden, she realised with despair, she'd replaced one lie with another. And this one she'd have to take with her to the grave.

'It's all right, love,' said Jimmy gently and Sheila realised she was crying.

'Come here,' he said, and took her into his arms. 'It's been a hell of a day. But he's safe now. And I think that, if we give him a bit more support, he'll be fine from now on. Don't you?'

Sheila turned her face to Jimmy's chest and wept and wished with all her heart that she could turn the clock back.

⋆　⋆　⋆

'The news about Claire and Aiden's exciting, isn't it? Though I do think she's a bit young. But still, he seems like a decent, hardworking lad. What are you wearing to the wedding, by the way?'

Sheila glanced round the coffee shop, only half-listening to her mother's chatter. 'I haven't given it any thought. There's only going to be a handful of us. I'm sure I have something in the wardrobe I can wear.'

'I was thinking of wearing a hat. You know that navy blue one with the white feather. She is my only granddaughter, after all. What do you think?'

In one week's time Claire was going to marry the man Sheila had slept with, and all Moira could talk about was hats.

'I don't know if that would be appropriate,' she said dryly.

'You don't seem very excited?'

'Well, it's going to be a very low-key event, isn't it?'

Moira scrutinised her face and Sheila busied herself with the fruit scone in front of her, spreading each half with soft yellow butter.

'I wish you'd tell me what's been going on between you and Jimmy,' said Moira.

'There's nothing going on,' replied Sheila, watching thick globs of jam drop from a spoon.

'Oh, don't give me that — you've been at each other's throats for weeks and now all of a sudden you're all lovey-dovey again.'

'We're not all lovey-dovey. We're just glad to have Conor back, that's all.'

'It's more than that though, isn't it?'

Sheila looked at her mother thoughtfully. 'I'll tell you if you tell me what you and Claire were fighting over the other night.'

'I don't want to talk about it,' said Moira, stiffening.

'Well then, neither do I.'

Moira sighed. She looked furtively round at

the empty tables surrounding them and then turned her attention back to Sheila.

'Oh, all right then. She basically accused me of . . . she couldn't understand why you gave her away. To Eileen and Paddy.'

'I know what she thinks of me and Jimmy. She told us. What does she think of you?'

'She blames me for not helping you to keep her. She seems to think I forced you to give her up.'

'Well, you did, didn't you?'

'It wasn't like that. I thought you understood . . . '

'You know fine well I wanted to keep her.'

'But you agreed to give her to Eileen and Paddy. You agreed it was for the best.'

'No, I did not. I never got a choice in the matter. You just want to believe that so you feel better.'

'Sheila, love, I wish you'd try to understand. I thought I was acting for the best. I really did.'

'And do you still think that?'

'I don't know any more.'

Sheila was stunned.

'I also said something to Claire that I shouldn't have,' said Moira, hesitantly.

'What?'

'I said that she would have been a millstone round your neck. She ran out in tears at that point. Anyway,' she went on, obviously keen to change the subject, 'what about you and Jimmy?'

'OK. I had an affair with a doctor at the hospital. It didn't mean anything but Jimmy found out.'

Sheila watched Moira's face closely to assess the impact of her disclosure. She was surprised to see an expression, not of disgust, as she'd expected, but merely dismay.

'I see,' said Moira, and she replaced her teacup carefully on the saucer. 'And how are things between you and Jimmy now?'

'We're taking it a day at a time.'

Mum nodded her head, thinking. 'And why did you do it?'

'I wanted to hurt him. I suppose I've never really forgiven him for not supporting me over Claire. He just disappeared off the face of the earth for months.'

'He was only a boy,' said Moira, 'and your father warned him off.'

'I know that. But I still wanted to hurt him.'

Moira regarded Sheila with a gaze of such intensity that she became uncomfortable and looked away.

'Sheila,' announced Moira, 'I'm sorry if what I did was wrong. I'm sorry that you've suffered because of my actions.'

Sheila felt her eyes fill up with tears. She'd waited half a lifetime to hear those words. Moira spoke on, her voice earnest and heavy with emotion.

'I wanted you to marry someone because you loved them, not because you had to. I didn't want your chances ruined by an unwanted pregnancy. I didn't want you to make the same mistake I made.'

'What mistake?' whispered Sheila.

Mum took a deep breath and went on.

'I was pregnant with Eileen when I got married. Your dad was the father, of course, but it meant we had to get married. I liked him well enough and he was a good husband — I've no complaint really. It's just that I never really thought I loved him. Not the way I should have.'

Sheila had never been so shocked in her life. Her mum, who never smoked or drank, went to Mass three times a week and ran a strict Catholic home!

'He wasn't the love of my life, you see. I was still looking for him when your Dad came on the scene. I'd been working in Patterson and Macdonald's, the solicitor's office, for nine years. All my friends were married and I knew people were beginning to talk about me as an old maid. Your dad had a decent job and he was good company. I'd just never thought I'd marry him, that's all.'

'I'm sorry, Mum. I never knew.'

'I made sure no one knew,' said Mum grimly. 'It would have been a big scandal in those days. I made my own bed and I had to lie in it, Sheila. And that's why I didn't want you to keep Claire. I wanted you to have a better crack at happiness than I did.'

'Is that why you were so strict with me when I was growing up?'

'Partly. And because of the attack on Eileen for which I still blame myself. But mainly because I didn't want you to get into any trouble. It backfired on me though. I realise now that I was too strict. As soon as you got the

chance, you rebelled. And look at the consequences. If I'd given you a more balanced
upbringing then none of this might have
happened.'

They fell silent then, lost in their own
thoughts.

'But there's something I don't understand,'
said Moira.

'What?'

'Why you're so, well, sad is the only word I
can use to describe it. If things are sorted out
between you and Jimmy and Conor's fine and
everything, why are you so down? Claire seems
to be thawing out a bit towards you and her
wedding to Aiden's something to look forward
to. I know we've all got to face Eileen's death,
God help us. But that's something we've known
about for months.'

Sheila shook her head and fought back tears.
'There are things I can never tell you, Mum.
Things I can never tell anyone.'

Mum patted the back of her hand gently and
whispered, 'It's all right, love. You don't have to.'

And Sheila thanked God that her mother had
the wisdom and experience not to press her
further. For she was very close to blurting out
her secret.

★ ★ ★

Father Brennan married them within a fortnight,
in the same chapel where Claire's mum and dad
had been married, and her granny and granddad
before them. Kneeling on the crimson carpet in

front of the altar, Claire made the same solemn vows they had made decades before her. She knew with conviction that this was her destiny — to be with Aiden, to care for him and love him, all the rest of her life.

She thought back to the moment when the last barrier between them had been broken down — the night Aiden told her the tragedy that was his childhood. Claire had been both engrossed and horrified. It made her love him even more, if that were possible, and she vowed to make the rest of his life as happy as she could.

She was ashamed of her self-absorption and self-pity — in comparison to what Aiden had endured her life was charmed. She'd grown up in a loving home, surrounded by people who cared for her. So what if Eileen and Paddy weren't her real mum and dad? They'd loved her as though they were. And as for Sheila and Jimmy, she'd no right to be their judge and jury. Who knows what she would have done if she'd fallen pregnant at fifteen. She could even understand how Granny thought she was doing the right thing at the time.

And once she knew the truth how could Claire refuse to go to America with Aiden? He'd suffered so much and his heart was set on it. It wasn't fair of her to refuse. He wanted a fresh start, in a new country, away from the memories. And who could blame him?

All of a sudden, the benign country Claire had grown up in seemed full of hidden menace. She'd heard of such atrocities but, marooned in the relative tranquillity of Ballyfergus, they might as well have happened on the other side of the world. Now, she could no longer ignore the hatred and the bigotry that was all around her.

When the ceremony was over she stared into Aiden's dark eyes and felt the flesh of his palm on hers and she'd never been so certain of anything in her life. They'd decided to keep their plan to emigrate a secret for the time being. Aiden said her mum would only worry about them, alone in a strange faraway country, so they agreed they wouldn't leave until she had passed away.

Claire had suggested Aiden move into Ladas Parade after they were married but he insisted on remaining at his flat. The doctor visited daily now and Aunt Sheila was there almost all the time. Aiden said he didn't want to get under everyone's feet, and Claire admired his thoughtfulness.

The mood of the small party, as they made their way back to Ladas Parade on foot, was subdued but joyful. Claire wore a cream suit bought for the occasion but with future events in mind. So though it lacked the dramatic excesses of a traditional wedding dress, it was beautiful in its simplicity and elegance. In her hand she carried a small posy of pale pink roses, her favourite flower.

Father Brennan came back to the house to perform a blessing. Sheila had washed Eileen's hair, dressed her in a pale pink bed-jacket and applied some blusher and lipstick for the photographs. Eileen sat propped up in bed by fluffy white pillows, wasted and drawn. She cried when they repeated their vows and smiled when Father Brennan performed the blessing.

Sheila sat by the bed, holding Eileen's hand, and dabbed the tears off her cheeks with a scrunched-up tissue. Sheila's face looked grim and tense with the effort, Claire supposed, of holding back tears. Claire took her lead from her. It wouldn't be fair on Mum to cry so she pasted a smile on her face, when inside her heart was breaking.

Aiden and Claire perched on the bed, either side of Eileen, and Jimmy took some photographs.

'You look beautiful, pet,' whispered Eileen. 'Really beautiful. My little darling. Look how you've grown into a woman.' She paused, summoned more energy and added, 'Paddy would have been so proud. I wish he could have seen you.'

'So do I, Mum. So do I,' said Claire softly.

And Claire picked up her mother's hand in her own and kissed it.

9

Eileen lay with her eyes closed and listened to the sounds around her — birds singing outside and a hum in the room, like a piece of machinery. The bedcovers weighed heavily across her chest, immobilising her.

She fought against the numbness that threatened to overwhelm her. She had one more thing to do before she gave into it. What was it now? She couldn't quite remember. She forced her brain to function.

Ah, yes, Claire. She had to tell Claire that she wasn't her real mother. Sheila had told her that it didn't matter any more, that she no longer wanted her to do it. But Eileen knew that Sheila was only saying that because she was dying. And Eileen had promised not only Sheila, but also herself. Sheila's reasons may have been suspect, but her instinct was right. Claire should learn the truth from the woman she believed to be her mother. Eileen had to do it — it was the one piece of unfinished business that had to be laid to rest. When it was done she could give into the terrible weariness. Her body cried out for sleep but she knew she must not give in. Not yet.

She knew her time was very limited now. When was it Claire had sat on the bed with Aiden? She remembered they'd got married and, involuntarily, her lips formed into a smile. Claire was married. She was safe. She didn't have to worry about her any more. Aiden would love her and cherish her and take care of her.

She heard noises at the door. Someone walked across the room. A hand touched her forehead lightly and then her left wrist, competent fingertips pressed firmly into her pulse point. Then her hand was laid back on the bed, gently, and soft fingers stroked the skin on the back of her hand.

'I can't believe how much Mum's gone downhill since last week,' said Claire's anxious voice from the direction of the door. 'It's happened so fast.'

'I know love,' said Sheila, her breath on Eileen's face.

Eileen tried to open her eyes but she seemed to have lost the power to control them. She tried to open her mouth but the muscles would not respond to the command from her brain.

Please God, don't let me be too late! Give me the strength to do this one last thing.

The pain began again and her fingers closed around the morphine pump. But she resisted the urge to apply pressure and released it from her grasp — the pain was good, it made her sharper, more alert.

'I noticed it straight after our wedding,' said Claire.

'Yes,' said Sheila, 'it's as though she kind of gave up.'

But she hadn't given up. Not yet. She must try harder. Please God, help me, this one last time, I beg you.

'I'm glad we got married. I think it made

349

Mum happy and put her mind to rest. She knows I'll be safe with Aiden.'

With superhuman effort Eileen forced her eyes open and, when Sheila's blurred image came into focus, saw the surprise on her face.

'She's awake!' cried Sheila. 'Eileen! Eileen, love. It's me, Sheila.'

'Claire,' said Eileen, surprised by the sound of her voice, faint and rusty. Unused. She saw Sheila gesturing wildly with her left hand.

Eileen heard the creak of footsteps as someone crossed the room. A figure leant over the bed and Claire's face came into view.

'Claire,' repeated Eileen, noticing that her lips were dry and cracked. She tried to moisten them but her mouth was dry.

'Yes, Mum, what is it?'

'Just you.'

Claire turned her head to the side and whispered, 'I think she wants to be alone with me.'

Eileen heard the shuffle of light footsteps across the floor, the whoosh of the door closing across the carpet and the quiet click of the latch. Claire lifted Eileen's hand and held it between her own.

'Yes, Mum, what is it?'

Eileen knew she didn't have the strength to say all the things she wanted to. It would have to be the bare and naked truth. And then Claire would have to find out all the reasons why for herself. It would break her heart, poor child. Eileen had never meant to keep it a secret for so long — it was just that the right moment had never presented itself. Time flew by so quickly.

And now there was no more time left. It was now or never.

'Claire,' she said and faltered.

She focused all her energies on summoning up the strength to speak.

'I'm not your real mother,' she said, her voice barely more than a whisper, 'Sheila is. And Jimmy . . . he's your Dad.'

There, it was done. At last. She closed her eyes, breathless with exhaustion.

Claire's hands gripped hers tightly. Her face was so close that Eileen could feel the heat from it.

'I know, Mum,' said Claire softly.

How was this possible? After all the agony Eileen had gone through in arriving at this moment.

'I found out by accident a month or so ago. I went to get a copy of my birth certificate and saw for myself. But I want you to know that it doesn't make the slightest bit of difference to me,' she went on, with fierceness and desperation in her voice. 'Or the way I feel about you. Or felt about Dad. I love you and I loved Dad. No one could have had better parents. I'm glad you brought me up and I'm glad I'm your daughter. I couldn't have asked for more. All I remember, all my life, is being loved so much.'

A wave of happiness, the purest form of joy Eileen had ever known, washed over her and suddenly the pain receded. Claire still loved her. It was all she wanted to hear.

Claire was still talking but Eileen couldn't

concentrate on the words now. She felt wet tears on her arm. She wished she could comfort Claire but she was so tired. She felt herself drifting further and further away from the small room where she'd spent the last weeks.

Claire's voice became more and more distant and eventually it stopped altogether. And then there was nothing but silence.

★　★　★

Eileen had slipped into unconsciousness for, when Sheila came back into the room, they couldn't rouse her.

Sheila stood on the other side of the bed and took her pulse.

'Her pulse is weak,' she told Claire. She looked at her watch. 'Dr Crory's due round in an hour. I don't think there's any point in getting him to come round sooner. What happened?'

'She spoke to me briefly,' replied Claire. 'It seemed to require a great deal of effort and then, when she finished, she shut her eyes. I was talking away to her and I just thought she'd fallen asleep.'

'What did she say?' said Sheila, adding hastily, 'I mean, if you want to tell me, that is.'

'She told me that you and Jimmy were my parents.'

Sheila sat down in the chair beside the bed.

'She kept her promise then.'

'What promise?'

'I asked her to tell you the truth and she agreed to do it before she died.'

'And you held her to that promise?' said Claire, the disbelief clear in her tone of voice.

'No, after you found out and said that you wouldn't be telling her, I told her I'd changed my mind. I said it didn't matter any more and she should leave things be. She never wanted to tell you. She thought that you might stop loving her and Paddy.'

'I'd never do that. They're my mum and dad,' said Claire loyally.

Sheila blinked and Claire realised how hurtful that must have sounded.

'Why did you want her to tell me?' she said, moving on quickly.

'Because I wanted you to know the truth. And I was sick of living a lie.'

'I can imagine. Lies are terrible things. They eat away at you and destroy you. That's why I'm so glad I've found Aiden. Everything between us is so honest and open. It's like I'm getting a fresh start after finding out I've been living a lie all my life.'

Sheila stared at her with her face screwed into a strange expression. Then she got up abruptly and walked over to the window. Claire stroked Eileen's cheek with the back of her finger. The skin was dry and thin, like paper.

'Do you think she'll wake up again?' she asked.

Sheila came over to the bed and stood behind Claire. She put a hand on each of Claire's shoulders and, before she spoke, Claire knew what she was going to say.

'I don't think so, love. I think it's time.'

＊　＊　＊

Aunt Sheila was right for Eileen was dead within the week and Claire felt nothing but relief and guilt. Relief that, for Mum, the terrible suffering was over and guilt that she should feel like this. Where were the feelings of grief and sorrow that she'd expected to overwhelm her following her mum's death? She felt only numb with tiredness.

As soon as the undertakers took away Eileen's body, the health authority, with unseemly haste, came and removed the invalid paraphernalia. With the bed, hoist, drip, and commode all gone, the bedroom returned to normal. Claire put on load after load of washing until all evidence of her mum's long illness was erased save for the smell of her, which seemed to linger in the air.

Between the three of them, Claire, Moira and Sheila made the arrangements for the funeral and a small reception to be held at the house. At night Claire slept well and soundly — her whole body seemed to ache with fatigue. During the day she felt so weary that it was an effort to do anything. She pottered round the house for the next few days, and rather ungraciously received visitors who called with cards and the traditional gift of home-made food for the funeral reception.

Granny or Aunt Sheila or someone else was nearly always with her as though they were afraid to leave her on her own. But, if anything, she was happier alone in the house, surrounded by Mum and Dad's things, the mundane and everyday items reminding her at every turn of the happy

354

times they'd spent there together.

Three days after she died, Mum was buried in the same grave as Dad, her coffin lowered in on top of his. As she walked away from the graveside Claire heard dull thuds as the sods of earth landed on the wooden coffin. Strangely, she found the sound comforting. Doctor Crory had been right about losing someone after a long illness — the feelings were very much more muted and reflective compared to the raw and open grief of sudden loss. And in her heart Claire knew that her mum was where she wanted to be — with Paddy.

Back at the house, Aiden stuck close by her side, a source of strength and support.

'Congratulations,' said Maureen O'Farrell, and it took Claire some anxious moments to realise what she was talking about.

Claire remembered the day Maureen had come into her workplace and told her about her mum's hospital appointment. The stupid woman couldn't keep her mouth shut about anything.

'My mother's just been buried,' said Claire coldly. 'This isn't a day for celebrating weddings.'

And she turned her back pointedly on the old woman.

After everyone had gone Aiden stayed with her and they made love in the single bed in Claire's room. Claire couldn't help but feel uncomfortable, as though Aiden was a lover she'd sneaked into her room and Dad would storm in at any minute and find them together. She had to remind herself that she was a married woman now, mistress of the house and everything in it.

Afterwards, in the early hours, she lay in his arms and stared at the night sky through the open curtains. She imagined Mum and Dad together again and happy, watching over her like guardian angels.

'Do you want me to go?' said Aiden.

'No, stay the night. In fact, why don't you move in now? Officially.'

'It wouldn't seem right, somehow, moving in so soon. And anyway, I thought it wouldn't be long before we went to the States. There's nothing to keep either of us here now.'

'When were you thinking of?'

'The end of the month.'

'That's only four weeks away, Aiden! What's the big rush?'

'Kevin phoned me last week. I didn't say anything before now because of the funeral. But he's desperate for me to go out there as soon as possible. He says he's going to have to take someone else on if I can't get out there by the end of August.'

'But what about the house and all Mum and Dad's things?'

'All you'd have to do is sort out personal things. The house can go on the market straightaway and you can get a house clearance firm to come in and clear the contents. Your aunt and uncle would handle it for you, you know they would.'

'But there's so much to sort out, Aiden. Why don't you go on ahead and I could come out later?'

'I don't want us to be apart.'

'You know a fair amount of money will be coming my way from the sale of the house. We're not destitute. We don't have to rush out there like we're penniless immigrants.'

'But I thought we'd agreed! It's not about money. It's about us having a fresh start. Together.'

'But what about work? I'm supposed to give them a month's notice.'

'Under the circumstances, I'm sure they'll understand.'

'Oh, Aiden, I don't know. Do we have to go so soon?'

'We've been through all this, Claire. You know I can't stay here.'

Claire sighed heavily.

'You're right. What is there to keep us here now? We might as well get on with it.'

★　★　★

It was late the next morning when Sheila came looking for Claire, having put off her visit for as long as she could. The poor girl would be exhausted physically and mentally after the funeral yesterday. And Sheila had more bad news for her, news she wanted to delay giving Claire as long as possible.

The back door was locked when she tried it but she could see a figure moving behind the frosted glass. She tapped the glass sharply with her knuckles. The door opened and she was horrified to see a half-naked Aiden standing in

357

front of her, wearing only boxer shorts. She stiffened and looked away.

'You'd better come in,' he said and moved away from the door.

'I didn't know you'd moved in,' she said acidly.

'He hasn't,' said Claire's voice from the hallway.

Claire came into the kitchen dressed in a white towelling robe and Sheila guessed she'd nothing on underneath it. Inside she seethed with anger. How she hated Aiden for what he'd done!

'He just stayed over last night,' continued Claire. 'Do you have a problem about that?'

'I was just surprised to see Aiden here, that's all,' said Sheila, evenly. 'Anyway, how are you this morning, love?'

'I'm OK. And you?'

'Not too bad, I suppose. Look, there's — '

'We've something to tell you,' said Claire, interrupting her.

Claire went over to Aiden and took his hand. Sheila watched them with a growing sense of dread as Aiden patted Claire's wrist and whispered something in her ear.

'I know this will come as a bit of a shock but me and Aiden have decided to move to the States.'

'The States,' repeated Sheila, stupidly, quite certain she'd misheard.

'Yes, Chicago. Aiden has a cousin out there who's got a building business and he's offered Aiden a partnership. It's a great opportunity. We're planning to leave in four weeks.'

Claire would never dream up a scheme like that on her own. Aiden was taking her away. Because of what they'd done together.

'But what about the house and everything? You can't just up and go like that.'

'We've been thinking about it for some time and I can arrange most of it before I go,' said Claire, 'And I thought, well, wondered if you and Uncle Jimmy would take care of things for me.'

Uncle Jimmy. So that was how she thought of them still. Nothing more than relatives.

'I suppose so,' Sheila said sullenly.

'Thanks, Aunt Sheila, I knew you wouldn't let me down,' said Claire and she threw her arms around Sheila and hugged her.

Oh, God, it was too cruel. She'd lost Eileen and now she was to lose Claire as well.

'But I don't understand,' she said. 'Why do you have to go to the States? Why can't you just stay here? You've got this house and everything. It's a great start for you. For both of you.'

'It's what Aiden, what *we*, want. A fresh start. Isn't it, Aiden?'

'Yes, that's right,' he said firmly.

'If it's the idea of staying in this house,' argued Sheila, 'you could move to that new development out near Redhill. The houses are supposed to be lovely. As nice as you'll find anywhere.'

'But we don't want to stay here in Ballyfergus or Northern Ireland for that matter,' replied Claire.

'Since when? I thought you liked it here.'

'I do. I just don't like the bigotry and politics

359

in this country,' said Claire vaguely. 'There's too much bad history.'

This was the first time Sheila had heard Claire express these sentiments. Aiden had filled her head with a load of nonsense.

'I'm sorry, Aunt Sheila,' said Claire, 'but we've made up our minds. Look, I'd better go upstairs and put some clothes on.'

'No, wait a minute,' said Sheila, almost shouting. 'I came over here to tell you something, Claire. And I'm afraid it's not good news.'

Claire's face went completely white and she sat down abruptly on a chair. Sheila immediately regretted her tactless introduction.

'It's OK. No one's died or anything like that. Deirdre's been involved in an accident. But she's OK. Just a few broken bones, that's all.'

'What happened?'

'She came off the back of a motorbike after she left the reception here yesterday.'

'It'll be that maniac,' said Claire. 'Do you remember me telling you about Mac, Aiden? She's been talking about going on the back of his bike for ages. Jacqui and I told her she was mad.'

'Yes, Mac, that's the name her mum mentioned,' continued Sheila. 'She phoned me last night because she couldn't find your number. I hope you don't mind, love, but I didn't come over and tell you straightaway because I thought you had enough on your plate yesterday. When I found out that Deirdre was OK I thought it could keep 'til this morning.'

'Where is she now?'

'She's still in hospital. She was knocked unconscious when she came off the bike so they're keeping her in for observation until tomorrow morning.'

'I'll go and see her this afternoon. What time's visiting?'

'Two thirty.'

'I'd better go and get ready,' said Claire absent-mindedly and left the room.

Sheila listened to her footsteps on the stairs and then the sound of the shower being switched on. She advanced on Aiden until their faces were inches apart.

'You bastard!' she hissed.

Aiden stared at her coldly.

'Why are you doing this?' she demanded.

'Doing what?'

'Don't play the innocent with me! This nonsense about America. Why are you taking her away from us?'

'I'm not taking her away.'

'Yes, you are. Is it because of what happened between us?'

Aiden returned her gaze, unflinching.

'There never was an 'us',' he said, coolly. 'Nothing happened between you and me.'

And Sheila was quite certain then that Aiden was determined to take Claire as far away from her as possible. She was losing Claire because of what she'd done. And there was nothing she could do to stop it.

★ ★ ★

On the way to the hospital Claire kept telling herself that Deirdre was OK. But she'd lost two people she loved in so short a space of time that she couldn't help but fear the worst.

She arrived early but a nurse, who recognised her as Sheila's niece, showed her to the ward.

When she saw Deirdre, Claire burst into tears. Her friend's face was swollen and purple with bruises and both eyes were bloodshot. Her left arm lay over the bedcovers encased in a fresh white plaster.

'I'm all right, Claire, really I am. It looks worse than it is or so the doctor and nurses keep telling me. Nothing that won't heal in time.'

'I'm sorry,' said Claire, dabbing at her eyes. 'I just didn't expect you to . . . I didn't know what to expect.'

'That bad, eh? No wonder they wouldn't let me have a mirror.'

'You don't look that bad. Really,' said Claire, smiling in spite of the tears. 'What happened?'

'Mac was showing off. He took the bike up the motorway and just got faster and faster. I'm sure he was trying to scare me. Well, we got to that bend where you turn off for the airport and he just lost it. I could feel him tensing up and the next thing I knew we were heading straight for the hedge.'

'Oh, God, it must have been awful. What about Mac? Is he hurt?'

'They had to operate on his shoulder but I think he's going to be OK. I remember flying through the air, sort of in slow motion, and the next thing I knew I woke up inside the

ambulance. I must have been knocked unconscious as soon as I hit the ground.'

'You're very lucky,' said Claire, admiring
Deirdre's matter-of-factness about the whole
incident. 'You could've been killed.'

'I know,' said Deirdre thoughtfully and
winced.

'God, you poor thing. You must be in a lot of
pain,' said Claire.

'They've given me strong painkillers but I
daresay I'll feel worse once they've worn off.
What are you doing here anyway? You should be
at home with Aiden.'

'Don't be daft. I had to come and see you as
soon as I found out.'

'You look pretty washed out, Claire.'

'I am. I've been absolutely exhausted since the
day Mum died. Everything's such an effort.'

'I thought you handled yesterday really well.'

'Thanks,' said Claire.

She sighed and looked around the faded
room. There were four beds, each one covered in
thin, washed-out green blankets, and only two
were occupied. The curtains were pulled round
the other patient's bed and there were no signs
of life behind it.

'Who's in that bed?' asked Claire.

'Some old dear from the geriatric ward. They
had to bring her down here because they've run
out of beds. She hasn't moved or said a word
since she came in.'

Claire leaned in towards her friend.

'I've something to tell you,' she said solemnly.
'You're not going to believe it.'

'Try me.'

Claire squirmed in the uncomfortable plastic chair, summoning up the courage to tell her friend the truth about who she was. 'Mum and Dad weren't my real parents,' she whispered at last. 'I found out shortly before Mum died.'

She explained to Deirdre how she'd found out, about the confrontations with Sheila and Jimmy and Granny and how she'd pieced together the story of her early life from what they'd told her.

Deirdre listened quietly all the while and Claire was aware of her friend's uncharacteristic reservation. Perhaps Deirdre was sedated for normally she would have interrupted with exclamations and questions.

When Claire had finished talking, Deirdre asked, 'Why are you telling me now?'

'Because, just before she died, Mum told me. Up 'til then I felt it was something I should keep to myself. For her sake.'

Deirdre plucked at the frayed blanket with the fingers of her right hand and nodded slowly.

'Deirdre,' said Claire, 'you don't seem very surprised.'

Deirdre's fingers became still and she looked Claire directly in the eye.

'I knew,' she said. 'I've always known. When I was very young, I overheard my mum talking about you to my dad.'

'Oh,' said Claire and she stood up suddenly, looked around her and sat back down in the seat again with a thud. 'You knew all these years and you never said!' she demanded angrily. 'Why didn't you say something?'

'What was there to say? At the time, you were just another girl in the class and it didn't seem important. And when I was old enough to realise what it meant, we were friends and I didn't want to hurt you. I never told a soul.'

'But how come your mum knew?'

'She was best friends with your Aunt Sheila. They went to school together. I remember her saying once that she was at your mum and dad's wedding reception.'

'That means the whole of Ballyfergus must know,' said Claire, feeling vulnerable and exposed.

'I don't know about that. I never heard Mum telling anyone else. Only Dad and she didn't know I was listening. I should have been in bed.'

'I can't believe you knew all these years. And you never said a thing.' Part of Claire was angry at her friend's deception, but she also knew that Deirdre had done the right thing. It wasn't her place to tell her.

'There was always a chance that it was just malicious gossip. You know what people in Ballyfergus are like. And I never thought it was important anyway. It never made any difference to the way I felt about you as a friend. I liked you for who you were, not who your parents were. You shouldn't let it upset you. You're your own person.'

'That's easy for you to say. You weren't born a bastard. You know who your parents are.'

'But what if they weren't my parents? Would it make any difference to how you felt about me?

Would I be a different person?'

'No,' said Claire, slowly, 'not at all.'

'And wouldn't you be saying to me exactly what I've just said to you?'

'Yes,' said Claire reluctantly, 'I suppose I would.' She pressed her hand gently round Deirdre's fingers. 'I've got some more news for you,' said Claire. 'I'm moving to Chicago with Aiden.'

This time she elicited a strong reaction from Deirdre. 'The States! When?'

'In a month.'

'But you can't,' said Deirdre. 'What'll me and Jacqui do without you? And why on earth would you want to go halfway across the world to a place you've never even seen before?'

Claire swallowed. 'Aiden wants to go. He reckons it's a great opportunity for both of us. And ever since I found out about Sheila and Jimmy being my parents, I can't treat them the same way I used to. Now that Mum and Dad are gone, there's nothing to keep me here. Apart from you, of course. But I have to make my life with Aiden.'

'Bugger!' said Deirdre crossly and then she said sincerely, 'I'll miss you, Claire.'

'I'll miss you too,' said Claire and she barely managed to get the words out for fighting back tears.

'Listen, when I get out of this place and I'm back on my feet,' said Deirdre, 'we'll have a big farewell party. What do you say?'

'Yes, I'd like that. Can I invite someone?'

'Sure. Who?'

'Mac.'

'Don't you dare,' said Deirdre and they both laughed.

'I'd better go now,' said Claire. 'I don't want your mum to see I've been crying. She is coming in to see you?'

'God, yes, her and half the extended family,' said Deirdre, rolling her eyes.

'I'd best be off then,' said Claire and she stood up. 'Just one thing though, Deirdre.'

'What?'

'Promise me you won't be going on any more motorbikes.'

★   ★   ★

Conor had to choose his subjects for 'O' level and, prior to the start of term, a parents' night was being held to discuss the options open to fourth years. Sheila and Jimmy were both going.

At mealtime, Conor was quiet and ate little.

'Are you all right?' asked Sheila.

'Yeah,' he said unconvincingly and pushed his plate away.

When Conor went up to his room to get ready, Jimmy followed him. He perched on the edge of Conor's bed with his hands joined loosely between his knees. Conor sat opposite him, awkwardly, on the chair he used for studying.

'You're not worried about tonight, are you?' asked Jimmy.

Conor shrugged.

'What?' said Jimmy.

'I'm afraid of some of the boys picking on me.'

367

'Well, don't be. I won't leave your side all night and if anybody touches you, they'll have me to answer to.'

Conor's stooped shoulders visibly straightened and he looked at Jimmy and smiled shyly.

'Bullies are cowards underneath it all, Conor. You've got to show them that you're not afraid of them.'

'That's easier said than done, Dad,' he replied.

'I know, son, but you can't let them get you down. Come on. We're going to be late.'

The evening began with an informal tour of the main teaching rooms. Wandering round, from room to room and along the corridors Jimmy was aware of sideways glances being cast in their direction and the sniggering of schoolboys when they passed. But he held his head up high, and silenced the sniggers with his fiercest stares.

In the Art Room, the teacher came over to them as soon as he saw Conor.

'You must be Mr and Mrs Gallagher. Please do come over here and sit down. I particularly wanted to speak to you tonight.'

Conor wandered off and joined a group of kids on the other side of the room. The teacher, a middle-aged man with strands of thin black hair plastered over his bald patch, introduced himself as Mr Campbell.

'Some of the work Conor has done this term is brilliant,' he said, surprising Jimmy with his enthusiasm, almost bordering on fervour. 'It shows ability way beyond his years — the result of a real innate talent. I truly think Conor has artistic genius in him and I'm very keen to discuss his future with you.'

Jimmy looked at Sheila. He knew Conor was fond of art and Sheila had told him often enough that he was good. But a 'genius'? Sheila looked equally surprised.

'Do you really think he's that good?' said Jimmy.

'Haven't you seen any of his work this year?' said the teacher.

'Well, er . . . ' said Jimmy embarrassed to admit he'd taken little interest. He'd always thought art was for sissies. But he didn't think like that any more.

'I have his folder here if you'd like to see it,' said Mr Campbell and, without waiting for a response, he got up and spread the contents on the table.

Many of the pictures were sketched in charcoal, some in pencil, and there were watercolours and a couple of acrylics too.

Jimmy picked up a charcoal drawing of a naked man and stared. Jimmy was no artist — he doubted if he'd ever held a paintbrush in his hands, even as a child. He'd always been too busy chasing footballs.

He knew nothing about art but as he looked at the image in his hand he understood what the teacher meant. In a few broad, confident strokes, Conor had captured the very essence of man — the strength and beauty of every muscle and sinew cried out from the page.

He picked up another, similar picture executed with the same panache.

'These are incredible,' said Sheila, holding a water-colour up to the light.

'What do you think, Dad?' said a hesitant voice behind him.

'I — I'm stunned. These are amazing. Who is this, Conor? Did someone pose for these?'

'No, I studied pictures in magazines and holiday brochures but mostly I see them inside my head.'

Jimmy looked up at Mr Campbell and he was smiling.

'They're good, aren't they? Very, very good. I've shown them to a few of my colleagues in the art world and they share my enthusiasm. Has Conor told you that he wants to go to art college?'

Jimmy glanced at Conor, who blushed.

'I didn't tell you, Dad,' he said haltingly, in a very quiet voice, 'because I didn't think you'd let me.'

Jimmy's initial hurt at Conor's failure to confide in him quickly gave way to the realisation that it was his own fault. In the past his reaction would have been precisely what Conor feared. He would have told him to get out there into the real world and start earning money. It would take time to show Conor that he had changed. He realised that he'd been so busy with his work on the council, so busy helping other people, that he'd neglected his own family. But all that was set to change.

'No, you're wrong, I'd be proud to have a son at art college,' he said. 'But Mr Campbell, I don't know if we could afford to send Conor.'

'We don't need to worry about that for a few years. But if he continues to develop as I hope, I'm pretty sure we can secure him a full scholarship. He has a very exciting future ahead of him. If you're agreeable, then I think Conor's main focus should be art and the rest of his subjects should be tailored round that. History might be a good idea, for example, because he'll study the history of art at college. And English literature too, as classics can be a great source of inspiration. Of course, Conor's form teacher will discuss all this with you in greater depth.'

It all seemed so far away in the future. Conor was only a boy and here they were discussing what he would study at college. Jimmy looked at Conor then and saw that he was completely focused on the teacher. His eyes shone with hunger and passion and he hung on every word Mr Campbell said, desperate for the dream laid out before him to come true.

They were the last to leave the Art Room.

In the corridor Jimmy turned to Conor and said, 'I'm really proud of you, son. I don't know where that talent comes from but you've got a special gift. And I'm going to do everything within my power to help you make the most of it.'

'Oh, Dad,' said Conor, and his eyes shone with pure joy, 'you don't know how happy I am. I'm going to art college. I can't believe it.'

Jimmy walked down the corridor towards the main assembly hall with his beautiful wife and his talented son on either side of him. And he thanked God for giving him the chance to put things right.

* * *

Sheila woke up at dawn and crept quietly into the bathroom. She pulled the pregnancy test from the pocket of her dressing-gown and sat down on the closed toilet seat to read the instructions. They hadn't changed much from the first time she'd used one.

The memory of that day, when she sat in her parent's bathroom and agonised over what to do, was suddenly very vivid. Today her stomach was churning just the same way and she felt the same giddy nausea. But the reason for her anxiety now was very different — then she'd have given anything not to be pregnant, today it was quite the opposite.

She did the test and waited and when she saw the result she put her hands over her face and cried.

By the time the rest of the household woke up Sheila had showered, put on make-up and more or less composed herself. She was in the kitchen making toast when her two youngest sons came in.

'Mum, can we stay to the end tonight?' asked Danny.

Claire and Aiden were setting off for the States in the morning and tonight was their farewell party at the Club. Deirdre had organised it, literally single-handed, for her left arm was still in plaster. She'd been signed off work for six weeks and insisted on organising it all herself. She said it would stop her going out of her mind with boredom and Sheila had been more than happy to let her for she'd been dreading this day for weeks.

But right now Sheila had something more pressing on her mind than Claire.

'We'll see. It might be late,' she said.

'But Claire's going to America, Mum,' argued Martin, 'and we won't see her again! Please let us stay to the end!'

'Don't say that, Martin,' said Sheila. 'Of course, you'll see her again, we all will. We can go there on holiday maybe. You'd like that, wouldn't you? And they'll come back and visit us.'

Sheila sounded more hopeful than she felt. They hadn't the money to go on holiday to Butlin's never mind the States but she wasn't going to admit that to the boys. And as for Claire and Aiden visiting Ballyfergus, she guessed Aiden had no intention of ever coming back.

'So can we stay to the end of the party then?' repeated Danny.

'We'll see what your father says.'

Jimmy came down and said of course the boys could stay to the bitter end and Sheila couldn't help but smile to herself. It was exactly what she knew he would say. There was something so very dependable about Jimmy. Would he be so dependable though when she told him the result of the pregnancy test?

'See you later, love,' said Jimmy and he kissed her and left for work.

His kiss lingered on her flesh, and made Sheila's cheek burn with shame.

No, she mustn't think like that. She must think of the future, not the past. How could he be hurt if he never knew the truth? All she had to do was keep it from him. And she was good at keeping secrets, she thought ruefully — after all, she'd had plenty of practice.

When the front door closed behind the kids, Sheila took a key out of her pocket, went next door and let herself in. The house was still and silent — Aiden was down at his flat packing up the last of his things and Claire had a hair appointment at nine o'clock in preparation for the big night.

Claire had made good progress with sorting out the house contents. Boxes lay on the floor everywhere, labelled either for charity, storage or shipment to the US. She's just like me, thought Sheila, the way everything's organised with military precision.

Upstairs the room Eileen had died in was empty. Sheila walked over to the window and looked out on the small gardens and backs of houses.

'What would you do, Eileen?' she asked. 'Can you blame me?'

But, of course, there was no answer, only the echo of her own voice in the empty room. But she was sure she felt Eileen's presence all around her and she stood there, by the window, and thought for a very long time.

At length the sound of the bin lorry at the front of the house disturbed her thoughts and she realised the time — Claire would be back soon. She left the house as quickly and quietly as she'd entered it. And when she closed the door behind her she knew what she would do.

Sheila got ready for the party with particular care. She wore a tight black skirt with high heels and a black sequinned sleeveless top. She painted black kohl round her eyes and put bright red lipstick on her lips.

'You look fantastic, Sheila,' said Jimmy when she came downstairs.

'You don't look too bad yourself,' she replied playfully.

Sure he had a bit of a middle-aged paunch but he was tall and could carry it. His hair might be thinning but he still had that winning smile. And that thoughtful, concentrated way of looking at you when you spoke, that made you feel as if you were the only person in the world at that moment. And it wasn't just Sheila's imagination — she'd seen the way other woman batted their eyelids and flirted with him. Her husband was still a good catch. And a good father.

The small function room was packed with friends and relatives of the emigrating couple. Deirdre's mum had baked a cake in the shape of a flag and decorated it with stars and stripes. Jimmy said a few words wishing Claire and Aiden good luck and saying how much they would be missed. Claire started to cry, Aiden put his arm around her and Sheila looked away.

'Are you all right, love?' said Moira. 'You look a bit peaky. I suppose you'll miss her terribly like the rest of us.'

Moira wiped a tear from the corner of her eye and then the music started and it was impossible to be gloomy to the strains of Abba's 'Waterloo'. Jimmy took her hand and led her onto the dance-floor.

Sheila looked around the room at all the people she'd known for years and wondered at how calm and collected she felt. She watched her three boys gyrating to the music and smiled. Claire's leaving did not affect her to the degree she'd expected. She was sad, of course, and she would never forgive that bastard, Aiden, but her focus was somewhere else now.

'Aunt Sheila,' said a voice and Sheila turned to see Claire, alone, by her side.

'It's a great party,' said Sheila. 'Deirdre's done you proud. Tell me I'm seeing things. But she's not over there with that madman who nearly killed her, is she?'

Claire followed Sheila's gaze to catch Deirdre locked in a passionate embrace with Mac. 'I'm afraid she is.'

'She's forgiven him then.'

'Looks like it. You know, I think they're actually very well suited. They seem to be crazy about each other.'

'She'll miss you.'

'Oh, I don't know about that. Deirdre's never stuck for friends,' said Claire and then she added, sadly, 'I think I'll miss her more.'

They were quiet then for a few moments, each lost in their own thoughts.

'Aunt Sheila,' said Claire, and she cleared her throat. 'I want you to know that I don't hold any grudge against you and Uncle Jimmy. I know I said some pretty hurtful things when I found out you were my real parents. But I was in shock. I'm sorry.'

'Thanks, Claire,' said Sheila. 'That means a lot to me.'

'Will you tell Uncle Jimmy for me? In case I don't get a chance to speak to him tonight.'

'Of course I will, love. Claire?'

'What?'

'Good luck in Chicago. I hope you and Aiden are happy there.'

Claire came over suddenly and put her arms around Sheila and hugged her. Sheila closed her eyes and inhaled. There was no trace of the little girl Sheila remembered, only the grown-up smells of perfume and make-up.

'Thanks for everything you did for Mum,' said Claire. 'I couldn't have done it without you.'

'You don't need to thank me. She was my sister, Claire, and I would have done it a hundred times over.' Sheila sniffed and added, 'You'd better go. Aiden's over there looking for you.'

She watched Claire walk over to Aiden and slip her hand into his. Maybe she was wrong about Aiden — she hoped so. She sought Jimmy out amongst the crowd on the dance floor. He saw her looking and in a few minutes he was at her side.

'Don't you want a drink?' he said.

'No, thanks.'

'Are you sure? I'm going up to the bar anyway.'

'No, Jimmy. I don't want a drink.'

'Are you all right?' he asked.

'Yes, Jimmy, I'm . . . I'm fine.'

'What is it?'

'Jimmy,' she said, 'I've something to tell you.'

His face went white and Sheila felt her legs about to give way under her.

'What here? Now?' he said, his face deadpan.

'Come away from the crowd. Over here. Let's sit down at this table.'

He acquiesced without comment, joined his hands loosely and rested them on the top of the table. He looked like a man who knew he was about to hear bad news.

'I'm sorry I haven't told you this before now,' said Sheila hesitantly, 'and I know my timing's bloody awful, deciding to tell you tonight. But I wasn't sure how to tell you. I didn't know how you'd take the news.'

'Just tell me, Sheila. Please,' said Jimmy, his stare cold and glassy.

'I'm pregnant.'

To her surprise Jimmy's face registered sheer and utter relief.

'That's wonderful!' he cried suddenly and half-rose out of the chair, 'I thought . . . never mind what I thought. It's fantastic news.'

And almost as quickly his face fell again and he sat down abruptly.

'What?' said Sheila, 'What are you thinking, Jimmy? Tell me.'

'I'm sorry, Sheila. But I have to ask you this.'

'What?'

'Is the baby . . . is it Dr McCabe's?'

'God, no!' cried Sheila with genuine indignation and then she remembered she'd nothing to be indignant about. Jimmy had more right than he realised to ask her such an awful question.

'No, no, it's not,' she said softly.

'You're quite sure?'

'Yes. I hadn't slept with him for weeks before you saw us together that night outside the hospital. I never saw him again after that and I had a period . . . '

'I don't need to know the details, Sheila. Just so long as you're sure.'

'I'm positive. It's not Dr McCabe's.'

He was making this so easy for her. The baby was Aiden's, about that she was quite sure. And she didn't even have to lie, not directly anyway, for Jimmy had not actually asked her if the baby was his own. He could never conceive a betrayal as depraved as the one Sheila had committed. He would never suspect that there had been a second lover, never mind his identity.

'Then,' said Jimmy, unable to conceal his excitement, 'why don't we tell everyone tonight?'

'No, I don't think so,' said Sheila hastily, catching a glimpse of Claire and Aiden on the dance floor together. 'It's Claire and Aiden's night. It wouldn't be right to take the limelight off them. And anyway, it's early days yet, Jimmy.'

'Yes, yes, you're right, of course. Oh Sheila, how do you feel?'

'Excited. Pleased.'

'It might be a girl.'

The thought hadn't occurred to Sheila. Even if it was a girl she knew her happiness would always be tainted by her guilty secret. Every time she looked at the child, no matter whether it was a boy or a girl, she would always be reminded of Aiden and the terrible thing she had done.

'It could be. Jimmy?'

'Yes?'

'What did you think I was going to tell you?'

He sighed and tears welled up in his eyes. 'I thought you were going to tell me you were leaving me.'

'But why? What made you think that?'

'After everything that's happened, Sheila, do you need to ask? And you've been acting strangely these last few days.'

'I suppose I was worried about telling you I was pregnant.'

'But why? Didn't you think I'd be pleased?'

Sheila shrugged. Thank God he never knew the half of it. And never would. 'I thought you'd think we were too old to be having another baby.'

'Old? No, not at all. You're as beautiful as the day I married you, Sheila. If anything, you've got better-looking with time. And in any case, you'll always be young and beautiful in my eyes.'

When Jimmy had gone to get her an orange juice, Moira came and sat down beside Sheila.

'What were you and Jimmy talking about? You looked very serious.'

'Oh, nothing.'

'Have you been crying, Sheila?'

'No, don't be silly, Mum.'

Moira said nothing but stared at Sheila, unconvinced.

'Look, Mum, there's nothing wrong,' said

Sheila, avoiding her mother's eyes. 'Everything's going to be all right. I promise.'

Moira placed her hand over Sheila's and patted it gently.

'I hope so, Sheila,' she said. 'I think this family's been through enough already, don't you?'

★ ★ ★

It was April in Chicago and Claire was glad the hard, cold winter was over. The winters here were real — snow and hard frost for weeks on end. And cold so cruel you'd die if you got locked out of your car or spent the night on the street. Not half-hearted, pretend winters like in Ireland where you rarely saw snow and if it did fall, it melted within days if not hours. The winters there had a softness, a gentleness about them that Claire missed.

But then so much of life in Chicago was fast and hard and brutal in a way. Not that she'd go back now — the business was doing well, Aiden was full of plans for the future and they were happy.

She'd just come in the door of the apartment she and Aiden were renting, when the phone rang.

'Uncle Jimmy! It's great to hear from you!'

'Sheila's had the baby, Claire.'

'She has? Tell me! Are they OK?'

'Yes, yes, they're both fine. It's a girl, Claire,' he said, his voice breaking with emotion. 'It's a girl. I can't believe it. After all these years. We never thought we'd have another child. Oh, Claire you don't know what this means to Sheila. To both of us. I've never seen Sheila so happy.'

And after he'd gone off the line, Claire picked up the phone again and started to dial Aiden's mobile number. But for some reason, she stopped. Something bothered her and always had, ever since the day she'd introduced Aiden to Sheila. She couldn't think what it might be. She'd thought at the time that Aiden fancied Sheila but that was absolutely ridiculous, wasn't it? She was ashamed for allowing such a stupid idea to even cross her mind.

She was just being silly, she told herself, but she replaced the phone in its cradle all the same. The news could keep.

She poured herself a glass of wine, sat down and wet her baby sister's head.

We do hope that you have enjoyed reading this large print book.

Did you know that all of our titles are available for purchase?

We publish a wide range of high quality large print books including:
Romances, Mysteries, Classics
General Fiction
Non Fiction and Westerns

Special interest titles available in large print are:
The Little Oxford Dictionary
Music Book
Song Book
Hymn Book
Service Book

Also available from us courtesy of Oxford University Press:
Young Readers' Dictionary
(large print edition)
Young Readers' Thesaurus
(large print edition)

For further information or a free brochure, please contact us at:
Ulverscroft Large Print Books Ltd.,
The Green, Bradgate Road, Anstey,
Leicester, LE7 7FU, England.
Tel: (00 44) 0116 236 4325
Fax: (00 44) 0116 234 0205

Other titles published by
The House of Ulverscroft:

MOTHERS AND DAUGHTERS

Erin Kaye

Catherine Meehan was born into a respectable working-class Roman Catholic family in Ballyfergus on the coast of Antrim. She is determined to flee the poverty, bigotry and antagonism that shaped her early years . . . Jayne Alexander is infused with the privileges that go with being part of a well-to-do Protestant family. Despite her self-assurance, she has a need for love and yearns for approval . . . From 1959 to 1984, the lives of the Meehan and Alexander families become inextricably linked, in moments of great passion and hatred, as deeply held loyalties are threatened.